Winter Wishes at Swallowtail Bay

KATIE GINGER

ONE PLACE. MANY STORIES

This novel is entirely a work of fiction. The names, characters
and incidents portrayed in it are the work of the author's
imagination. Any resemblance to actual persons, living or
dead, events or localities is entirely coincidental.

HQ
An imprint of HarperCollins*Publishers* Ltd
1 London Bridge Street
London SE1 9GF

HarperCollins *Publishers*
1st Floor, Watermarque Building, Ringsend Road
Dublin 4, Ireland

2
This edition published in Great Britain by
HQ, an imprint of HarperCollins*Publishers* Ltd 2020

Copyright © Katie Ginger 2020

Katie Ginger asserts the moral right to be
identified as the author of this work.
A catalogue record for this book is
available from the British Library.

ISBN: 978-0-00-838058-8

MIX
Paper from
responsible sources
FSC **FSC® C007454**
www.fsc.org

This book is produced from independently certified FSC™ paper
to ensure responsible forest management.

For more information visit: www.harpercollins.co.uk/green

Printed and bound in Great Britain by
CPI Group (UK) Ltd, Melksham, SN12 6TR

For Matt and Magda,
Welcome home!

Chapter 1

October

The assistant yanked the changing-room curtain back with such vigour, the shiny metal pole it hung from nearly flew off the wall. Out strode Cat, Nell's best friend, in an exquisite off-the-shoulder fairy-tale princess wedding dress. The ivory bodice clung tightly to Cat's petite frame and the enormous skirt puffed out in a series of cascading ruffles. In the warm orange lighting of the boutique Cat's skin took on a dewy glow.

Nell's hand flew to her chest, pressing on a heart that was over-flowing with love. 'Oh my gosh, Cat, you look incredible. Like an actual movie star at the Oscars. It's just beautiful. Isn't it beautiful, Brenda?'

'It's lovely, darling,' Cat's mum replied, ignoring Nell's over-enthusiasm and speaking directly to Cat. 'But please tell me you're going to dye your hair back to blonde before the wedding? It'll look much better in the photographs.'

Cat hitched the dress to walk to the pedestal, then stepped onto it, allowing the dress to fall from her fingers so she could see herself in the 360-degree, floor-to-ceiling mirrors. Within seconds, the assistant placed a pair of high-heeled shoes in front of her. Cat stepped into them and, brushing her fingers down the skirt, turned left and right, watching the fabric float around her. 'I hadn't really thought about my hair. I was going to keep it pink.'

With her mouth pursed in disapproval, Brenda's face contorted even further, and Nell stifled a giggle. The phrase 'a bulldog sucking a wasp' came to mind. Nell waited for her to ask about the eyebrow and nose piercing too. There was no way Cat was going to remove those for her wedding day. She'd worn them every day since they were done one drunken evening at university, and Nell was glad. Cat was pretty amazing as she was, there was no way she should be any different on her wedding day.

Brenda picked lint from her expensive tailored skirt. She wasn't the type of woman to dress in jeans and oversized thick woolly jumpers. She wore a matching lilac tweed skirt and jacket with a cream blouse underneath. Her blonde hair, heavily streaked with grey, was coiffured into a helmet that daren't move for fear of being attacked with even more hairspray. Not a strand was out of place and neither was her lipstick.

Since Kieran had proposed on Cat's birthday at the start of October, Brenda had been more than a little excited about her daughter's upcoming nuptials but was sometimes surprised at the choices Cat made about her big day. Nell wasn't. Cat had always been down to earth and had her own individual style. Secretly, Nell hoped she wouldn't change the hair colour she'd had for the last few years. Out of all the colours Cat had tried (orange had been particularly disastrous) pastel-pink suited her best.

The only bridal shop in Swallowtail Bay sat at the furthest end of town, in a small, cobbled side street full of boutique clothes shops. They were lucky to have every type of shop in the bay from delis to chocolatiers and homeware stores. There were art galleries, cafés and restaurants, and on top of this, the town was blessed with spectacular scenery from the rolling green fields on the edge of town, to the long, arcing coastline with a pebbly beach and promenade where you could walk and enjoy the seasons by the sea. Nell especially loved Christmas in Swallowtail Bay when the town became like somewhere from a movie; shop doors were decked with Christmas wreaths and all along the promenade strings of fairy lights glittered off the surface of the water. October was virtually Christmas as far as Nell was concerned, but she was resisting the urge to get out the Christmas tree just yet for fear of annoying what few guests she had booked in. Maybe after Halloween she could get it out and go nuts.

Normally, Nell would have walked through town, enjoying the sights and smells of Swallowtail Bay, but this morning with the wind ringing an autumnal tune and the rain coming down in heavy sheets, they'd driven as near as possible so as not to damage any of the gowns with sopping wet hair. When they'd arrived, they'd been stripped of their thick winter coats and glasses of prosecco were shoved in their hands. Well, in Nell and Cat's hands anyway. Brenda had preferred a cup of tea, which she'd been pleased to see was served in a white cup and saucer – no mugs in sight. Cat and Nell had then snuggled on a sofa while Cat described the types of dresses she wanted to try and the colours she liked. Brenda had also made her opinions known, but then, she couldn't help but do otherwise. After that, and with Cat and Nell giggling like schoolgirls at the fun of it all, the actual trying on had begun.

Nell couldn't wait until it was her turn to do something like this. She was more than a little excited at being Cat's maid of honour, and at hosting the wedding at Holly Lodge, her boutique hotel newly licensed for wedding ceremonies. She considered what type of dress she'd have. Something with a long train and the softest fabric. That was an impossibly long way off for her as there wasn't even a sniff of a new man in her life, but it would happen eventually. For now, the excitement of watching Cat was more than enough for her.

3

'What do you think of that dress, Cat?' she asked, but Nell already knew the answer. As beautiful as the dress was and as gorgeous as Cat looked in it, her eyes weren't sparkling.

She swished again. 'I'm not really sure—'

'But it's divine,' Brenda chimed in. 'You look like a princess.'

'I'm not sure I want to look like a princess, though. I don't know if it's really me. I always pictured myself in something a bit different. Something pretty but less … dramatic. Not your normal wedding dress attire.'

'Anyone would think you want a suit.'

'Now there's an idea,' said Nell, and she and Cat shared a mischievous flash of eyes. 'You could have a theme wedding! Vicars and tarts—'

'Harry Potter?' Cat suggested. 'You know how much I love Harry Potter.'

'Gangsters and molls?'

'Yes!' Cat replied enthusiastically.

'Girls!' Brenda screeched, then tried to cover it with an indulgent glance.

'Or,' Nell continued, enjoying the moment too much to let it go, 'as it's Christmas you could dress up like Mrs Santa and Kieran could be Mr Santa and we could all be little elves!'

'Great idea, Nell.'

'Don't be silly, darling,' Brenda chided, but the slight twitch at the edge of her eye showed them she was actually worried by this one.

'Only kidding, Mum, but I'm still not a hundred per cent sure about this dress.'

'What sort of thing would you like to try?' asked the sales assistant, earning a glower from Brenda. The poor girl looked slightly terrified. Luckily, Nell had grown immune to Brenda's evil-eye stare, having received so many of them over the years.

'I think I'd like something vintage. Not actual vintage, obviously, I don't think we can afford that—'

4

'Of course we can afford it.' Brenda's high tinkling laugh was directed at the assistant. 'But why pay an extortionate amount for second-hand when you can have something new and exquisite like this?'

'I love those long gowns from the 1930s with all the beading and sequins—'

'Sequins?' Brenda squawked. 'This isn't a Seventies disco, Catherine.'

'Or something shorter, like from the 1950s.'

'You can't wear a short wedding dress!'

'I know exactly what you mean.' The assistant nodded vigorously. 'And I know just what will suit you. We've got some gorgeous dresses that I can picture you in already.'

The assistant sped away to some racks at the front of the shop and Brenda followed swiftly behind. Nell and Cat watched them both go and as soon as they were out of earshot, Cat said, 'Help me out of this dress, will you? It's absolutely killing me. It's like being in a back brace.'

Nell followed her into the changing room and began to undo the dress. 'Won't the assistant tell me off for getting my grubby hands all over it?'

'It's either that or I faint.'

'Then I don't care if she tells me off.'

It took a minute to unfasten all the hooks and undo the corseting but then she was free. Cat relaxed and leaned against the changing-room wall in mismatching bra and knickers, sipping prosecco. Nell too enjoyed the feeling of the bubbles popping on her tongue and the insides of her cheeks.

'Did you like that dress?' Cat asked, completely at ease in nothing but her undercrackers. The heating was on in the bridal shop and with the glow of a mid-morning prosecco they were both perfectly comfortable.

'It was beautiful, but I could tell from your eyes you weren't blown away by it.'

'I just want to be comfortable on my wedding day. I want to look nice too and of course I want Kieran's jaw to drop when he sees me—'

'Which it will because he loves you and you're gorgeous.'

'But I want to *feel* nice as well. I don't see why I can't have both. I mean, getting married at Holly Lodge feels perfect. I think my wedding dress should feel the same, shouldn't it?'

'Definitely.' Nell pushed her long blonde hair back over her shoulder. 'I mean, I don't know anything about getting married, but that's how I'd want to feel.'

When Cat had heard the news that the hotel was now licensed to host weddings, she and Kieran had insisted on having their whole day there. Nell had been beyond grateful and had been clear it wouldn't bother her in the least if they decided to go somewhere else, especially as this would be her first one, but they were not to be dissuaded. The only hitch was, they'd set a date with terrifyingly short notice. Eight weeks from today to be exact. Just thinking about it made Nell's stomach tense with worry, and it was already a bit fluttery with the excitement of the day and the glass of prosecco they'd drunk while choosing the first few dresses.

Adding weddings to her business was a pretty natural step considering Nell loved all things romance to a slightly manic degree. She loved seeing people happy on one of the most important days of their lives and the prospect of being instrumental in making that happen had forced her business plans forward, even when life had become difficult. Since the opening of the Langdon Mansion Hotel, a giant plush, swanky place with a ballroom and lounge bar, business had, unfortunately, fallen off a cliff, but indulging her love of love, Nell had decided to branch out into weddings in an effort to diversify her earnings. Cat and Kieran were having a Christmas wedding and as far as Nell was concerned, there was nothing more romantic than that. Refusing to let her thoughts linger on her business's failing finances on such a joyous

6

occasion, Nell instead mentally replayed the moment in *27 Dresses* when Katherine Heigl tries on all the bridesmaids' dresses showing them to James Marsden. It was one of her favourite moments in the film.

'Earth to Nell. Earth to Nell, this is your friend Cat calling.'

'You should definitely have both,' she said quickly, picking up their conversation where she thought it had left off. She had a habit of wandering off into her own world. 'And it's your day, so you should have the dress you want. If you wanted an Eighties-style, giant, pink taffeta dress with a bow on the bum, huge puffy-out shoulders and a matching parasol, that's what you should have and sod everybody else.' Nell ran a hand over her heavy fringe making sure it wasn't sticking up. The wind had whipped her hair into a full-on Eighties rock god style on the way to Brenda's car, but nothing stopped her loving the colder weather. In summer, when the sea was calm and clear, the air carried a freshness and the scent of flowers. Now, the air was crisper and cleaner, and when the tide crashed onto the shore it filled your nose with a salty sting if you were brave enough to walk along the beach.

'Did you hear anything I just said, Nell?'

'Yes! I was listening. Anyway, that "this is your friend calling" was more like them doing the scores in Eurovision.'

'Yeah, I know.' Cat giggled and took another sip of her prosecco. 'Isn't Graham Norton just the best.'

'He certainly is. Let's have a toast to Graham Norton.' They clinked glasses and Nell savoured the taste as it swirled around her mouth. 'Just in case I misheard you, what did you say?'

'See, I knew you weren't listening.' Cat studied her friend for a moment. 'Were you imagining that bit in *27 Dresses* when she opens her closet and shows James what's-his-name – the cute one – all the dresses, then she tries them on.'

'No.' Nell's cheeks began to burn, and she turned her attention back to the bubbling prosecco in her hands.

7

'Yes, you were.'

'Wasn't.'

'Was too.'

Nell met her eye and it twinkled with the excitement of the day. 'Maybe a bit, but I couldn't help it. It just popped into my head.'

'You know that film off by heart and every other romcom ever made. Oh look, they're coming back. Mum's giving me the death stare for being in mismatched bra and pants. I bet she says something. Just wait.'

Brenda tottered after the assistant who had a number of exquisite dresses over her arm. From Nell's position, she could see a pale rose-pink, floor-length 1930s gown with beading on the top and a long skirt of some wafer-thin material that floated as she walked towards them. At the bottom of the pile, there was a gorgeous 1950s ivory tea dress made of a heavily laced white fabric, complete with petticoat. Judging by the way Cat's eyes brightened as she craned her neck to see, Nell had a feeling that was the one she would go for.

The sales assistant hung the dresses on the hooks around the wide dressing room. 'I've double checked, and these are all available within your tight timescale. Which one shall we try first?'

They were all beautiful and totally different to the fairy-tale gown Cat had just tried on, and to the plain fishtail halter-neck before that, and to the one before that Brenda had insisted on which had long sleeves and looked like it should come with a wimple. Unsurprisingly, it didn't suit Cat's petite frame in the least and she looked like she was off to play Maid Marian. But it hadn't been as bad as the other one Brenda had made her try on which was wider than the three of them put together and made Cat look like one of those old-fashioned fairy toilet roll covers.

'That one,' said Cat, pointing to the 1950s tea dress, gravitating towards it. 'It's gorgeous.' The soft, lacy fabric slid through her fingers. She was captivated and Nell felt her chest burn with excitement.

Nell shuffled out of the room to give Cat some privacy but couldn't help hearing Brenda whispering, 'I told you to wear matching underwear, Catherine. Surely you have some?'

Cat mouthed the words 'I told you so' at Nell as Brenda stepped out of the assistant's way and the curtain was closed in front of them. Nell had to bite her lip to stop the laughter escaping.

Moments later, Cat appeared in the dress and high heels the assistant had provided her with earlier. She skipped onto the platform and her face was aglow with joy. Just from the way she held herself, shoulders back and head held high, Nell could see this was the dress for her. She waited for Cat to speak.

'This is it. This is the one. I love it.' Her eyes were misting. 'It's perfect. Absolutely perfect!'

Nell felt tears sting her eyes and she and Cat looked at each other. 'You look so beautiful, Cat. And I love it with your pink hair. You look amazing. Oh, come here.' Nell ran forwards and Cat hopped off the pedestal to hug her best friend, both of them laughing and crying and fluttering their eyelashes to try and stop the tears from ruining their mascara.

'She does look beautiful, doesn't she?' said the assistant enjoying the moment as much as the two best friends. Nell backed away from Cat and retook her position in the centre of the room to look at the dress again, while Cat's gaze shifted to her mum.

Brenda's fingers were pressed to her lips, but it was impossible to decipher what her expression meant. 'It's very nice, Cat, but don't you think it's more the type of thing someone would wear to a registry office wedding?'

'So? What's wrong with a registry office wedding?' asked Cat. 'If that's what someone wants for their day, then they should have it and get hitched wearing whatever dress they want.'

'Yes, but it's not quite as …' She searched for the right word. 'Glamorous. Can't you try on that ruffled one again?'

9

'The last one?' Cat asked, her voice tightening a little.

'Yes. I mean if you insist on that 1950s one, we can just get you something like that from a normal shop. Those sorts of dresses are everywhere. But that beautiful gown you just tried on made you look so much taller—'

Nell saw her chance to step in. 'I think the massive heels were doing that more than the dress, Brenda.'

'Thank you, Nell. Have you told the assistant here that Holly Lodge is hosting weddings? They might be able to stock some business cards for you or something.'

'Oh yes, Nell's already been touch,' the assistant replied.

Nell resisted the urge to stick her tongue out at Brenda. 'The Love Heart Boutique are coming to the wedding fair I'm hosting, aren't you?'

The sales assistant nodded.

Somehow, Brenda managed to speak through her gritted teeth. 'Well, why don't you go and talk to them about it?'

'We can chat later, can't we?' Nell replied, eager to stay by Cat's side. As much as she wanted to promote her business, she could do that after she'd dealt with this. Right now, she was too worried about where this conversation was heading. She wanted to be there for Cat for moral support. While she didn't particularly love the idea of being on Brenda's bad side – no one *wanted* to be, but a lot of people ended up there without doing very much at all – Cat was her best friend and the most important thing was that she came away from today with the dress she adored for that all-important moment when she pledged her life and love to another human being.

'The thing is, Catherine,' Brenda continued. 'This is your wedding day, not just a party. You'll only get this opportunity once—'

'I know what you mean, Brenda, but isn't that exactly why Cat should wear the dress she wants?' Brenda's jaw tightened as if she was biting back her next sentence. Her evil eyes bored into Nell, but Nell stayed firm. 'I think Cat wants to be comfortable as well as look nice and this dress ticks all the boxes for Cat. Plus, she looks so elegant and drop-dead gorgeous, but still herself.'

Brenda ignored Nell again. 'As I was saying, Catherine, you'll only get this opportunity once. This is the one and only chance you'll get to look so beautiful.'

Nell's jaw nearly fell open and she could see the effect this thoughtless comment had on Cat. Her head suddenly dropped to study the hem of the skirt that she touched gently with her fingertips, caressing the fabric. Nell was just opening her mouth to defend Cat when Brenda continued. 'And as your father and I are paying for the dress, I'd just really like you to try it on one more time and give it a second chance. Please?'

There was a slight wheedling tone to Brenda's voice that grated, and Nell was just about to risk Brenda's absolute displeasure by speaking up again, when to her horror, Cat slumped and, with a quiet sigh, agreed. 'Okay, Mum.'

'I'll help her get changed,' said Nell, dashing into the changing room and pulling the curtain closed behind her. 'Are you okay?' she whispered. Cat's face had lost its glow. 'If you want that dress you should have it. Do you want me to tell your mum for you?'

'I'm not sure,' Cat replied. 'Maybe Mum's right. This is my big day and I could wear a dress like that to a party. Well, not that colour or that fancy—'

'So not actually that dress then.'

'No. But you know what I mean.'

'But your face. Cat, when you put that dress on, you really loved it. I could see it in your eyes. It was like it was made for you. Are you sure you want to try that other one on? Wouldn't it be easier to just tell your mum now that it's not what you want? She might get the hump, but she's got time to get over it.'

'I'm going to think about it for a bit. I don't have to buy a dress today. I know I haven't got much time, but I can sleep on it and ring them tomorrow.' Cat's voice became stronger as if she was convincing herself.

'Okay. If you're sure.' Not wanting to push her, or ruin a day that should be fun, Nell didn't argue – she was seeing Cat again tomorrow, along with Kieran and her other best friend, Tom, for a drink at the hotel. Instead, she held out Cat's glass for her and she downed the contents. 'Do you want another one?'

'Yes, please,' said Cat. 'I think I'm going to need it.'

Nell backed out of the changing room, a heavy feeling settling on her shoulders. The change she'd just seen in her friend was astounding. She'd always been one to stand up for herself and say it straight. Hopefully, it was just a case of Cat wanting to find the right words to explain to her mum what she wanted. But as Nell knew all too well, when money was involved, life suddenly got a lot more complicated.

Chapter 2

Nell delivered a tray of drinks to the table. A lager each for Kieran and Tom, a gin and tonic for Cat and a tea for her as she was on duty. The prosecco they'd consumed yesterday had hit her mid-afternoon and she'd had to have a nap before Zoe, who covered reception for her, had left. She didn't drink very much normally, and the bubbles had left her mind and body dulled this morning. With no guests to bother her, Nell had pottered around, ensuring the place was ready for any walk-ins and had then focused on the wedding brochure she was creating.

The day had passed slowly but now Nell and her friends were snuggled into the comfortable velvet armchairs in the lounge, the heat from the open fire burning fiercely in the large fireplace warmed the room. She pulled a thick, woollen blanket over her knees as the wind whipped around the building. Even though she was wearing her favourite enormous Seventies-style flared jeans and a big jumper, she was still a bit chilly.

Holly Lodge had been Nell's home since she was eight years old when her parents had opened the hotel. When they'd decided to move down to Devon and open a second hotel two years ago, Nell had jumped at the chance to take over and now lived in the basement flat of Holly Lodge, next to the kitchens.

Above her were four more floors; the ground floor, where they were now, was home to the dining room, and then each of the floors above had three bedrooms. Running the lodge was more than just a job to Nell: it was a way of life. Working every hour of every day was a passion, one that none of her previous boyfriends had understood. Though that passion had been tested over the last few months when everything had felt like an uphill struggle, she'd stayed focused and positive hoping the slump would pass.

A converted Victorian townhouse, Holly Lodge had the most perfect setting on the seafront. It was called Holly Lodge rather than Pebble House or something more seasidey because of the tall holly hedges that surrounded it. It could have been imposing, but the large iron gate was always pinned back, held by bright flower pots, and the sweet stone path that led to a ramp up to the front door was also lined with flowers – all of which combined to feel homely and welcoming.

Inside, she'd made the place her own since taking over. The walls were painted in heritage colours of sage-green and subtle shades of blue with a few lavenders here and there, but to add a more modern, luxurious feel, the Chesterfield sofas and wingback chairs in the lounge were mustard-coloured velvet or a bright teal covered in blankets and scatter cushions to make the guests more comfortable. Against the period features of grand fireplaces and decorative plaster mouldings this boldness worked, giving a luxurious and sumptuous feel. Where the large arced iron gate interrupted the hedge, Nell could see out to the beach where a high tide railed against the wind. It thrashed the sea, producing high white waves, and the gale shook the bright red berries nestled in the boxy hedge of prickly holly.

'So how was dress shopping yesterday?' asked Kieran as they sat by the wide sash window at the front of the house. The rain hadn't stopped since yesterday and the drops drummed on the pane, racing each other down.

'You can't ask that,' said Tom, taking a sip of his drink. 'The dress is secret, isn't it?'

Cat glanced at Nell before snuggling further into Kieran's side. Kieran grinned down at her and squeezed her tight. His tall, sturdy frame filled most of the sofa; he and tiny, petite Cat, made an odd but endearing couple. She reached her head up and he gave her a gentle kiss. They were so adorable together, a real case of true love. Like when Mark Darcy and Bridget Jones kissed at the end of *Bridget Jones's Diary*. God, Nell loved that film. She might have to watch it tonight. With the hotel empty and no need to get up for breakfast in the morning, it didn't matter if she was slightly late to bed. When she looked up, she was surprised to see Tom watching her, but he looked away when she caught him. Maybe he was hoping for a hint from her about the dress.

'I think I know which dress I'm going to go for,' Cat said.

'Which one?' asked Nell, hoping it was the vintage tea dress and not the princess gown Cat had described as like being in a back brace. 'It's not the one with a wimple, is it?'

'A wimple?' cried Kieran, looking alarmed.

'Shush!' Cat motioned for Nell to be quiet then jabbed a finger playfully into Kieran's ribs. 'I can't tell you now in front of him.'

Nell scratched her head and some of her hair caught in the large chunky ring she was wearing. 'Ow!' She unwrapped the hair and Tom leaned over to help. When she was free and he'd sat back down, she said, 'Okay, but you have to tell me before you leave tonight.'

'Whatever she wears she's going to look absolutely stunning,' Kieran said, earning himself another kiss.

Tom shook his head. 'Nice recovery. But can you two love birds cut it out? You can snog at home. How's the wedding fair coming along, Nell?'

As Nell turned and looked at him in the soft orange light from the fire, she couldn't believe he hadn't found The One yet like Kieran and Cat had. Tom was so warm and friendly and had grown into a really handsome man. His dark blond hair had been not exactly long, but definitely floppy, since they'd met at uni and though a lot of men would look weird with it now, it still suited Tom. Nell hoped it wouldn't be long till he found someone. She didn't like the thought of him being lonely or sad. He was too lovely for that. Nell knew that when she found The One it would be a moment she'd never forget. Love at first sight. Or at least a stirring in her heart like a thousand violins all playing to a crescendo; a choir of angels singing in her soul. She suddenly imagined a gorgeous man unexpectedly walking into her hotel needing a room and there it would be – the music, the feeling – the beginning of something special.

'Nell?' Tom asked again.

'What? Oh, yes the wedding fair—'

'She was in a daydream again,' said Cat, teasingly. 'What was it this time? An airport chase scene or fireside lovemaking?'

'Actually, I was thinking about my to-do list,' Nell lied, fiercely pulling herself back and focusing her mind on the enormous list that filled an entire sheet of A4 paper currently sitting on her bedside table. It wasn't that Nell wasn't interested in what Tom or other people had to say, it was simply that she couldn't stop her mind from dragging her off to somewhere else. She'd always been this way, imagining things, picturing them in her mind. Her mum had told her you made things happen by visualising them in your head first. She and her dad had done exactly that with their dreams to open Holly Lodge and it had worked for them. And it didn't do anyone any harm, did it?

'What's left to do?' asked Tom.

'I've got all the slots filled now, thanks to another caterer the assistant at The Love Heart Boutique told me about, and with just over a month to go, I think that's pretty good. For the brochure, it's just dressing the place and taking some photos, which I plan to do tomorrow.'

'That's brilliant.'

Tom had always been incredibly supportive of her ambition to run a boutique bed and breakfast and his support had only grown when times had become tougher with the opening of the Langdon Mansion Hotel. Both Cat and Tom had tried to get her to go and visit to scope out her competition, but Nell had refused. At first, she'd believed the opening of the hotel could only mean good things for her and Swallowtail Bay. For a big hotel chain to develop here it meant people wanted to visit and stay in the bay. They were becoming a tourist hotspot. Surely some of those people would want to stay somewhere smaller, maybe a bit chicer and more personal. Nell had truly believed they wouldn't be in competition, but that they'd support each other, recommending the other when their own place was full. As the year had passed and her bookings had dropped off, she'd told herself, while watching adverts for the posh hotel appear on TV, that if she believed in herself it would all be okay, the slump would pass. She'd thought that the chic, boutique feel and top-quality service she offered at Holly Lodge would be more than enough. Unfortunately, as her place remained resolutely empty, she'd been proved wrong. But on a positive note, it had given her the push to start the wedding business.

'I'm really excited about it,' Nell said, hoping they were still talking about the wedding fair. 'It's going to be just the thing to get me back on track. I don't expect I'll get any bookings on the day, but if I get some enquiries and can show people what we have to offer, I'm sure something good will come of it next wedding season.'

'We'll be here,' said Cat, sitting up to sip her drink, but threading her hand into Kieran's so they were still connected. 'We'll be telling everyone how fab you are.'

Nell hugged her tea close to her, enjoying the warmth of it beneath her fingertips. 'I'm sure that if I do weddings and combine them with the dinner idea Tom and I have been working on, next year is going to be better.'

'What dinner idea?' asked Cat.

'We've been talking about opening up the dining room of an evening as a restaurant. I'm just trying to work out what food I'd offer and how much to charge.' She looked over to the large dining room adjacent to the lounge.

The rooms were separated by bi-fold doors that she could push back so everything became open plan. The dining room was big enough to seat around fifty people on the different dark wood tables, but there were still lots of sums to do before she could say for certain it was a workable solution. She felt it was, but as a businesswoman she had to do the maths too. As much as she loved a daydream, she couldn't do that when it came to running the hotel. What she really needed right now were more room bookings. Swallowtail Bay always slowed down in the winter season and normally, what she made in the summer would carry her through this quieter time, but with bookings being down all year, she needed to come up with something else to bring people in.

'We really should go and see what the Langdon Mansion offer though,' said Tom, brushing a hand through his hair. He often did it without thinking. There were a few gentle lines appearing on his forehead and around his mouth where he smiled so much. 'I've been saying for ages you need to go and actually have a look around. We can get one of their wedding brochures too.'

'I've already got one of those. Brenda got me one as soon as I mentioned the idea. She thought it would give me some standards to work towards.'

'That's my mum,' Cat said with a sad shake of her head. 'Ever supportive.'

Though Cat was joking, Nell sensed something more from her tone of voice and a weight behind her words. She mustn't forget to ask her about the wedding dress before the night was out.

'You should definitely go,' said Kieran. 'It'll be good for you to see the space and what they offer. Pictures are fine, but there's no substitute for being there.'

'We could all go,' said Nell.

'Nah, you and Tom go. We've got wedding plans to discuss most nights.'

'That's true,' Cat agreed. 'We're going to get busier and busier as things count down. I cannot wait to become Mrs Kieran Gleeson – or you can take my surname.'

'I don't mind that.' Kieran's chest puffed out. 'I think Kieran Wilson sounds quite nice.'

Kieran and Cat shared another sweet kiss and Nell turned to Tom. He raised his eyebrows in a 'they're-at-it-again' expression.

'But,' said Cat, 'it is about time you went to the Langdon Mansion, Nell. You can't keep pretending it's all going to be all right in the end if you just cross your fingers and believe. You've taken some tentative steps, but you really need to get moving. You're like one of my newly pregnant ladies who're nervous of doing anything because of their babies.'

Cat was a midwife and an amazing one at that. Nothing seemed to faze her, and she knew just what to say to chivvy you along without sounding cross. At least she did most of the time. Tonight, she sounded a little stern with Nell. Was that what she'd been doing so far? If so, Cat was right, and it was definitely time to plough ahead with the dinner idea and check out her competition. 'Okay, then.'

'Great,' said Tom. 'I'll book us a table.'

The evening went on nicely with chatter and laughter and a few reminiscences of old times, and Nell enjoyed it, but she still hadn't had a chance to speak to Cat about the dress. At ten o'clock, when they were about to leave, it seemed desperate measures were called for and she grabbed Cat's arm, pulling her away from Kieran and Tom who were still chatting, having only made it to the front door. 'So, which dress is it? I've had to wait all evening to find out because you've been glued to Kieran's face.'

'Jealous much?' Cat teased.

'Completely but that's not the point. I need to know what dress you've chosen.'

Cat looked away, and dread pressed down on Nell. 'I thought I'd go for the ruffled one.'

'The princess gown that feels like a back brace?' Gripped by surprise and worry that Cat was letting her mum guide her too strongly over the wedding, Nell said, 'Are you sure that's what you want?'

'I thought about it and I think Mum's right that this is the most important day of my life and I should wear something that looks amazing. She said the tea dress looked like something I could wear to a party. And they are paying for it.'

'But that's no reason to—'

'It's fine, Nell. Honestly. I've made up my mind, okay? I don't need you pushing me about it.'

'Okay,' Nell replied, shrinking back. She didn't want to row with Cat over this or anything else for that matter. She wanted her wedding planning to be as fun as the big day. To Nell, that was even more important for brides-to-be because they often spent more time on the planning than they had on the day itself. Every aspect of the run-up should be fun. And it was Cat's choice at the end of the day. No matter what Nell thought about it, Cat had always made her own decisions and Nell would support her. Yet, it wasn't sitting well, and she didn't really know what to make of it.

With the conversation finished, she said goodbye to them all and with no guests in the hotel and none expected to arrive, locked the front door and made her way to her basement flat to watch *Bridget Jones's Diary* – or should it be *27 Dresses*? She hadn't had the chance to watch that last night and right now she just wanted to disappear into a world where it was certain that everything would work out in the end.

Chapter 3

November

Thursday afternoon, Tom arrived back from his lunch break to watch his apprentice, Janie, plonk a bunch of pale cream roses into the silver display bucket. The stems bounced off the bottom making a tinkling noise that set his teeth on edge. Pushing back his floppy, blond hair, he said, 'Janie, don't forget to treat the flowers gently. If you throw them around, you'll bruise the stems or the petals and then we won't be able to use them. Okay?'

Janie turned, looking like he'd just praised her to high heaven rather than told her off a bit. 'Okay, boss.'

Tom shrugged off his thick wool coat and hung it out the back. He wasn't very good at telling people off and really should have been firmer as it wasn't the first time Janie had done it, but then, she was such a sweet girl and so perpetually cheerful he didn't want to be the one to make her frown. She was still learning but was coming on well and showed a particular aptitude for the management side of things. She'd also proved incredibly responsible and given all of that, he didn't mind waiting till the next time she did it. He'd be just a little bit firmer then, using the tone of voice he kept for Nell when she'd fallen into her own little

21

dream world again, or become pessimistic about the hotel. It was a tone of voice he found himself using more and more as she was worried about failing her parents and running the lodge into the ground. All nonsense, of course, and he'd tell her so when they went for dinner that night. The Langdon Mansion Hotel had been so busy, this was the first reservation he could get. Just then, Janie placed a cup of tea in front of him, bringing his attention back.

'Thanks Janie. We've got a few orders to make up this afternoon. Do you want to do the birthday hatbox or the new baby basket?'

Janie blew on her tea to cool it. 'Is it for a boy or a girl?'

Tom checked his order book. 'Girl.'

'Then I'll do the baby basket. I love doing girlie ones. Did they say what colours they wanted?'

Tom checked again and as he did little dots appeared in front of his eyes. He tried to blink them away, but the stubborn swimmers refused to budge until he squeezed his eyes tightly shut and opened them slowly. 'Umm, I've written pinks and creams with splashes of yellow for a touch of joy.'

'That sounds nice.'

He waited for her to say something about the blinking incident, but she didn't seem to have noticed and was now choosing the basket and flowers that would hopefully make someone's day.

Standing side by side, they both took a moment to assess the array of blooms in front of them. The till counter ran across the back of the shop and along one wall was a workbench covered in tools, ribbons and trinkets that he and Janie shared between them. The other wall was stacked high with silver buckets all of which contained the most beautiful seasonal flowers and foliage. Bright yellow walls made it feel like the sun was shining, even on this cold, gloomy November day. Through the large front window onto the high street, the sky above was a plethora of shades of grey. Between the dark charcoal rain clouds, smaller, hopeful misty white ones were buffeted together, losing the battle against impending rain.

Even though it was only early November, Christmas orders were beginning to come in and Tom couldn't wait to get started. He was a big kid at Christmas and absolutely loved getting into the festive spirit, doing so as early as possible. Tom could just see himself and Janie dancing around in Christmas hats as the radio played out and they created gorgeous green wreaths, and winter-inspired bouquets with shiny red baubles. A new catalogue had arrived yesterday full of Christmas things he could decorate his bouquets with, and it was going to be a struggle not to order everything in it. The window display would be changed soon, losing the pumpkins, the warm orange roses and the all-important symbolic poppies, and gaining something festive. Something containing mistletoe and holly with ruby-red berries, and lots and lots of tinsel and giant Christmas baubles and … He could feel the excitement building and took a sip of his tea.

They settled into their normal working pattern of listening to the radio which was already starting to play Christmas songs in between the normal cheesy pop Janie loved. There were numerous cups of tea and a few moments where they assessed each other's arrangements and made some suggestions. Janie was developing a great eye and Tom was becoming ever prouder of her as she grew and developed under his tutelage.

Just before five, Kieran popped in. His job as a gardener meant he tended to finish with the daylight, and sure enough, the sky behind him was turning a muted dark blue. Somehow the rain had stayed away, the strong winds having blown the cloud cover over them and out to sea. Though his shaved head made him look a little bit like a thug, in reality, you couldn't meet a gentler soul, and he'd only shaved his head after going prematurely bald at 28. Without thinking, Tom ran a hand through his hair almost to check it was all still there.

'Whatcha.' Kieran pushed the door open and winked at Janie,

coming to rest on the counter behind which Tom was fiddling about and preparing for the following day. 'You coming to the pub, Tom?'

'Ah, no, sorry, mate. I'm meeting Nell at the Langdon Mansion for dinner. We're scoping out their menu.'

'Oh, yeah.' Kieran wiggled his eyebrows in an innuendo-laden manner. 'Your date.'

Feeling the heat rise on his cheeks, Tom turned to Janie. 'Do you want to finish for the day, Janie? There's nothing else to do and if you go now you can catch the early bus, can't you?'

Her eyes widened in hope. 'Are you sure?'

'Course I'm sure. You've worked your socks off today. Go on.'

'Thanks, boss.' Rushing out the back to grab her coat and rucksack, she said a hasty goodbye and made her way into the darkness.

Once she'd left, he turned back to Kieran. 'Will you please stop doing that in front of Janie? I don't need the whole world knowing how I feel about Nell.' A sudden wave of panic washed over him as cold as the winter sea. 'You haven't let slip to Cat, have you?'

Tom always worried that with them being engaged, Kieran might accidentally tell Cat that Tom had been in love with Nell for years. The four of them had been friends since they all met at university in the nearby city of Halebury and Kieran had guessed his secret quite early on. So far, he'd managed to keep his gob shut, but Tom did worry that might change with Kieran and Cat now getting married. Married couples shouldn't have secrets as far as Tom was concerned and he felt a twinge of guilt that he was placing Kieran in an awkward position. His fear of rejection and how uncomfortable things would be if Nell found out were forcing him to keep Kieran quiet.

'Don't worry, I haven't. Your secret's safe. The whole world doesn't know, only me. You don't have to tell the whole world though, you know. You could start with just telling Nell. It might be …' He shrugged. 'Helpful. That's why I engineered this date for you. Did you like the way I did it? All subtle, like.'

'I'll tell her when the time's right,' Tom replied even though he'd said it a million times to both Kieran and himself. 'It just never has been so far. Either I've been in a relationship, or she has. And I'm still not sure she could feel that way about me.'

The fact was, whenever Tom was with Nell he felt totally complete. That's why his previous relationships had failed. He'd go into each new one feeling like they could be The One, giving all he had, but after a while a feeling of emptiness, or something being not quite right crept in. Whatever happened, and no matter how long it took, his heart inevitably came back to yearning for Nell. For her funny, in-her-own-world-half-the-time brain, a smile that lit up his life and a laugh he could listen to from now until the end of time.

The closest he'd come to getting away from his feelings for Nell was his last girlfriend, Naomi. They'd been together for three years, breaking up a couple of years ago. She'd said that it was because they wanted different things, but Tom knew it was because she was waiting for a ring and he could never quite bring himself to ask her. Every time he passed a jeweller, he'd look in the window, but he'd only ever see himself proposing to Nell. Despite serious attempts, the picture had never included anybody else. There was no one else like her. She'd always been just a little bit different – a woman of contradictions, both dreamy and focused – a little more caring, and she had her own style. That was why she and Cat had bonded so well. Both of them were different to all the other girls at university.

'Anyway,' he warned Kieran, knowing thoughts of Nell had taken over again, 'stop doing weird things with your eyebrows in front of my staff. I know it's the only hair you have left on your face, but still.'

'Okay. Fair enough.' Kieran watched Tom bustling around behind the counter, beginning to cash up. 'You're finishing early, aren't you?'

'Yeah, I want to swing by the care home and see Grandad. I said I'd take him a bunch of flowers for Enid.'

'He's a devil, your old grandad. Is she a looker?'

'Enid?' Tom laughed. 'She's 89! And Grandad's blind as a bat anyway. She could look like Godzilla for all he knew. Actually, she's a very lovely old lady and she really makes him laugh. There's that saying, isn't there? Love is blind? It's the only reason Cat's agreed to marry you.'

'Oy!' Kieran clapped his hands together. 'Right, if you're not coming to the pub, I'll be off then. Cat's got a planning meeting with Nell and her mum right about now, so I'll be hearing all about it once she's home.'

'You love it really.'

'Yeah. I do. Whatever makes her happy.'

With Kieran gone, Tom cashed up the till and closed the shop, locking the door firmly behind him. After waiting for the alarm to beep and show it was set, he turned and took a moment so his eyes could adjust to the darkness. It seemed to be taking longer and longer to get used to the dim evening light and a horrible niggling worry was growing inside his mind. The cold wind whipped around him, freezing his cheeks and running down his spine. Protecting the bunch of flowers Grandad had asked for, Tom pulled his coat tighter across his chest, hopping about on the spot as eventually everything came back into focus and he was able to make his way to the van.

The florist's stood bang in the middle of Swallowtail Bay high street, next to a café and an artisan cheesemaker, and there was absolutely no parking nearby. He strolled down the cobbled streets enjoying the bright golden lights spilling from the shop windows. The town had quietened as the trading day drew to a close, and because it was winter.

Tourists flocked to the place in the summer bringing life and energy to the town. The high street would be full of visitors in backpacks, eating ice creams – but in winter, only the locals shopped, and a quietness settled on the high street from about mid-afternoon onwards.

Tom's fingers were rapidly turning pink from the cold and he hurried on. Through the windows, fellow shopkeepers tidied and cleaned, readying for the next day. A few had already installed Christmas window displays and tinsel glittered while paper stars and giant snowflakes twirled in mid-air. Some had strung fairy lights around the edges, framing their windows in sparkling lights, while others had strings of them hanging down from the ceiling like icicles. Tom thought about his again. Once Remembrance Day was over, he'd start on one too. His grandad had lived through the Second World War and had been evacuated down to Swallowtail Bay, so Tom always made sure his shop had a full poppy display in honour of those who'd served, but he couldn't wait to change his and any time inspiration struck he made a note on a piece of paper. Maybe tomorrow he'd sketch it out.

Overhead the council and business forum had already begun preparations for the town's displays, and holders for small Christmas trees had been attached to some of the buildings. They were new for this year and in between the strings of giant lights that criss-crossed between the buildings it would look beautiful. With a nose red from cold, Tom was at his van and happy to be in the warm, he sped to the nursing home.

After he'd parked up again, he stepped out into the night and his breath fogged on the air. The stars were spectacularly clear tonight, bright and shining overhead, and the lack of cloud meant a frosty morning tomorrow. Cherry Wood Nursing Home was a large white building in pretty landscaped gardens. A couple of benches positioned out front next to large bushes invited people to sit and enjoy a moment before they entered. From the large windows he could see the residents moving back and forth, staff helping with walking frames, and people sharing jokes. Grabbing the bunch of creamy white ranunculuses tied with a big purple ribbon from the passenger seat, he made his way up the gentle slope of the entrance ramp.

The wave of heat that hit him as he walked through the door nearly knocked him over. In fact, all five of his senses were assaulted. As well as being hot, the home had the brightest lights he'd ever seen and smelled heavily of talcum powder mixed with lavender. The television was on so loud it was deafening and with his eyes being a bit weird at the moment, the last thing he needed was a ringing in his ears too.

Before Grandad Nigel had come here, they'd looked at other care homes that were unbelievably quiet, more like libraries than places to live, but Cherry Wood was different. Noise, chatter, discussion and, most of all, laughter was actively encouraged. At this time of night, most of the residents were gathered in the large open-plan TV room watching the six o'clock news. Tom needed to hurry if he wanted to get changed before meeting Nell for dinner. After a quick glance at the numerous chairs all filled with older people, some more lively than others, he spied Grandad Nigel, with a blanket over his knees, next to Enid.

Enid, though aged, didn't look like Godzilla. She was small and a little hunched in her chair with a head of fine, wispy white hair, but there was a vibrancy and life to her voice and a cheeky laugh that carried across the room. Tom could see exactly why Grandad Nigel liked to sit with her. Hiding the flowers behind his back, Tom made his way over.

'Hello, Tom, love,' said Enid, as her eyes turned up to meet his.

With a flourish, he pulled the small bouquet from behind his back. 'I bought you some flowers, Enid, I hope you like them.'

'Cheeky bugger,' shouted Nigel, not quite realising how close Tom was. Only a short time ago he'd gone completely blind, but his eyesight had been failing for years. A smattering of wiry grey hair stubbled his chin and Tom made a mental note to get him a new electric razor for Christmas. His old one wasn't picking up everything and as it was the safest thing for him to use now, he needed a decent one. His grandad had always been proud of his appearance – of his tall, lithe frame that Tom himself had inherited – and Tom wanted him to continue feeling that way. 'Don't you listen to him, Enid. They're from me actually. Paid for with my own money. I told him to get them for you as he's a florist. After all, you don't keep a dog and bark yourself.'

Tom bent down and squeezed his grandad's shoulder. 'All right, old man, I'm only teasing. I think Enid knew they were from you really.'

Enid gave Nigel a loving smile and Tom wished with all his heart his grandad could see it. Her voice was loud and cheeky and didn't look like it belonged to her slim figure. 'I knew they were from you, you silly bugger.'

'If Tom was going to deliver flowers to anyone,' Nigel continued, 'it should be that lovely girl, Nell, he's friends with. He's like a lovesick pup when she's around but he won't do it. I don't know why. I'd be perfectly happy to have her as a granddaughter-in-law.'

'Only because she brings you treats,' Tom countered. 'And if you start this again, Grandad, I'm going, and I won't give you the massive bar of Dairy Milk I snuck in for you.'

Nigel's eyebrows raised quizzically. 'Hand it over, boy, before they see you.' Tom did as he was told and watched Nigel's tired old hands, shaking with age and exertion, unwrap it and break some off for Enid and then himself. It wasn't that he wasn't allowed chocolate. It was that the piggy old boy didn't want to share any with the other residents. Other than Enid, that was. 'Oh, lovely,' Nigel said, savouring the taste. The smell made Tom's own tummy rumble.

'Is there anything you need for tomorrow, Grandad? If not, I'll be off.'

'Got plans, have you?'

'Yes,' Tom said, repressing a sigh. He'd told his grandad several times already that he was having dinner with Nell tonight, but his memory wasn't what it used to be, and he didn't need teasing all over again.

'Get on with you then. And no, I don't need anything else, thank you, boy.'

Grandad had always called him *boy* which was quite funny really considering he was now a grown man of 35. Tom gave Nigel's shoulder another squeeze, bid Enid good night and made for the door. On his way, Tracey, the manager of the care home caught his attention with a wave.

'Hi Tom.' Tracey's permed curls bobbed about as she cheerfully manoeuvred her plump frame nearer to him. 'Are you still okay to help put up the Christmas decorations next week?'

'Yes, that's fine.' He was quite looking forward to it. The residents of the home would enjoy it and it would be nice to spend a whole Sunday with Grandad.

'We haven't got much so it shouldn't take long. And there's no budget to buy new ones for this year but we'll just have to manage. The residents do love a bit of festive fun.'

Tom glanced around at the plain cream walls of the care home. The boring magnolia paintwork was broken here and there with some drab, unspectacular paintings, but apart from that there really wasn't much life to the decor. Some Christmas decorations and greenery would really brighten the place up. 'We'll make the place look great; don't you worry. See you next week.'

As soon as Tom began the walk down the entrance ramp, he made an involuntary grab for the handrail. Once again, his eyes needed time to adjust to the light. His body wanted to move normally but the message sent from his eyes to his brain was that he wasn't quite ready to keep going. By the time he got to the van and had the headlights on, he'd reassured himself he was okay to drive, but maybe he'd walk to the Langdon Mansion Hotel anyway. He was probably just overtired and had strained his eyes at work. Yes, that's definitely what it was. It couldn't be anything else.

Chapter 4

'Those pants are literally the ugliest pair of undercrackers I have ever seen.' Nell stretched out the pair of bright white sculpting knickers in wonder. She could feel the tension in her biceps as she pulled the sides apart to the width of a human body. How anyone could fit themselves into these elasticated torture devices was beyond her, and her arms were on the verge of giving way with the effort. 'Proper Bridget Jones style. They look so painful, and considering you're shoving your giant hooves into three-inch diamante-encrusted heels, that's saying something.'

Cat giggled and sipped a gin and tonic, examining her feet which were undeniably wide for such a petite frame. 'Mum said I have to wear shapewear knickers on the day. They squeeze all the fat from my bra-line down into my ankles. Between those and the boned corset I'm going to need an external lung. Do you think anyone would notice if I hid an oxygen cylinder under my wedding dress?'

It was entirely possible Cat would strap the one she carried in her gigantic midwifery kit to her thigh. She did that sort of thing. Or at least, used to when they were at university together. But back then it had been more moving temporary traffic lights and stealing cones than adhering things to her person.

Nell looked over the top of the thick waistband. 'Seriously though, they don't look very romantic or remotely comfortable. How do you even get them on and off? You'll be sweating like a pig from the effort.'

Cat sighed and watched the ice cubes bob in her drink. 'I'm not allowed to be comfortable, apparently. It's my wedding day. I have to look nice. Comfort doesn't come into it.'

'Is that what you want?' Nell asked gently. Cat shrugged in response.

When she didn't answer, Nell was dragged into her imagination, running through a scene where she dressed on the morning of her own wedding. In front of an antique full-length mirror that she didn't currently have, in a giant house she didn't yet own, she slipped an enormous but beautiful and comfortable wedding dress over flattering silky underwear. Once dressed, she held out her hand like a princess in a Disney movie and admired the ring on her finger. Nothing flash, nothing fancy. Just a small, shining diamond set on a simple gold band. Perfect.

She longed to fall as madly in love as Cat. She didn't entirely mind being single, but it would be nice to meet that person destined for her sooner rather than later. All her previous relationships had been fairly short-term because once the mad, initial romance wore off, they'd fizzled out, unable to live up to her expectations. One day though, 'The One' would walk into her life.

A waving hand in her peripheral vision brought Nell out of her dream. Thankfully, she'd had a last-minute booking and had one lovely old couple staying in the hotel. 'Evening, Mrs Limstock,' Nell called. 'Is there anything I can get you?'

'No, we're fine, thank you, Nell. Having a lovely time.'

'I'm so pleased to hear it. But do let me know if you'd like anything at all. I can make you another drink or find you some nibbles if you're hungry.'

'No, no. Honestly dear, we're fine.'

Relaxing back into her chair, Nell picked up a cup of tea and took a sip. She was meeting Tom at the Langdon Mansion Hotel as soon as this planning meeting was done and would have a drink there. The lovely Zoe was covering reception for the night. 'What does Kieran say?' Though he was incredibly happy at the prospect of gorgeous, outrageous Cat becoming his wife, surely even he couldn't stand idle while Cat's mum railroaded her into having the wedding of *her* dreams, rather than Cat's.

Cat ran a hand through her long, pink hair. 'I haven't actually told him about it.'

'Why not?'

'I just didn't see the point. He's busy with work and when we talk about wedding stuff, I want it to be fun and nice. If I told him about Mum, he'd get cross, and I don't see the point in starting World War Three before we've actually made it down the aisle.'

This was exactly what Nell had expected. She didn't have time to disagree with her though, as the woman herself walked in. Brenda's coat rested over her left arm while in her right hand she waved a plastic folder – the dreaded wedding file. From the corner of Nell's eye, she caught Cat leaning forward.

'Before she can hear us, I've booked the caterer for tomorrow. Mum's got a thing so we can meet him on our own.'

Nell watched her normally crazy, vibrant friend shrink back into her chair. 'Hi, Brenda,' Nell said, standing for the obligatory air kiss.

'Hello, darling.' She pretended to kiss Nell's cheeks then turned her attention on Cat. 'Come on sweetheart, stand up and give me a kiss.' Reluctantly putting her gin glass down, Cat stood and did as she was told before flopping back down into the chair. 'So, where are we with the wedding plans? I've brought my file. Where's yours?'

Cat, who had by now picked up her glass again, took a big slurp and pointed at Nell: her walking, talking wedding file. Nell grinned while Brenda pinned her with a death stare. Unsure what else to do, she wiggled her fingers in a wave. It didn't go down well.

'Huh.' Brenda adjusted her shirt. 'It's a good job I'm here, isn't it? How you think this wedding is going to organise itself I've no idea. Especially as you've set such an impossibly short timescale.' Cat glanced at Nell in defeat. 'I hope you're going to make this place extra Christmassy, Nell. I know you love Christmas, but we want something really classy, don't we, Catherine?'

'Yes,' Nell began. 'Cat and I talked about it the other day and I've been making a list of supp—'

Brenda thrust out a hand to silence her and nearly hit Nell in the nose. 'I've timetabled that for later. Right now, I wanted to talk to you about the flowers, darling.'

Though thankful that Brenda had removed her hand (it smelled of floral hand cream), Nell shifted warily. Tom doing the flowers was a given. It always had been. And it was what Cat wanted. She'd said she didn't want anyone else touching her wedding bouquet and had been clear on that from the start, but Brenda had reservations. Both Nell and Cat had reassured her time and again that Tom, who really had a gift, was the man for the job. Casting a glance at Cat, Nell knew that as the fight seemed to have gone out of her at present, it fell to her to fight Tom's corner.

'Are you absolutely sure you want Tom to do the flowers?' Brenda began without even opening the folder. 'I know he's your friend but—' Cat opened her mouth and Brenda threw out a finger to silence her protests '—a male florist? Is he really going to be any good? Generally, men know nothing about flowers or how to arrange them. The last time I asked your dad to put some flowers in a vase it was a disaster. He didn't even—'

To Nell's amazement Cat interrupted. 'Tom's amazing, Mum. You loved your birthday flowers, didn't you?'

'Yes, but—'

'They were from Tom's.' Brenda's expression perfectly mirrored that of someone who'd misjudged a fart. 'He's great and I'm sticking with him. He knows what I want and, more importantly, he knows what I hate. It's fine.'

Seeing the matter was closed, Brenda flicked open the folder and began thumbing through pages, letting out a sigh that said, *Fine, but if it all goes wrong, I told you so*. Nell and Cat both enjoyed the small victory.

A furry grey face and a pair of bright cat's eyes appeared at the window and Nell went to open it and let the poor creature in. A rush of cold air flew into the room. It was usually a little colder and windier down on the seafront and tonight was no different. The wind had been growing to almost gale force all day and whipped the fallen gold and red leaves around the streets and the pale grey sea into a frenzy.

'Nell,' Brenda moaned. 'Do close that window, please? It's absolutely freezing.'

'I'm just letting the cat in.'

'What cat? You haven't got a cat now?'

The small, skinny, grey furball hopped in through the gap and jumped onto the floor with an elegant leap. 'No, I haven't. I don't know who this boy belongs to. He started coming in about a week ago and I've been all around the block, but no one knows who he is. I think he's a stray.'

'Well,' Brenda bristled, 'you should take him to the vet or the RSPCA or something. He might be diseased.'

'He looks perfectly healthy to me,' said Cat, brightening a little as she patted her lap and the cat leaped up and made himself comfortable. 'He doesn't have a collar or anything, does he? And he is quite skinny, poor thing. What have you been calling him?'

'Mr Scrooge,' Nell answered with a grin.

For the first time since her mum's arrival, Cat smiled. 'Why Mr Scrooge?'

'Because its Christmas time soon and apart from me, and now

you, he hates absolutely everyone. Even Tom. He's a right old grump and as I'm getting into the Christmas spirit early, I thought it suited him. I don't know what he'll be like when I put the tree up.'

'You're not going to keep him?' asked Brenda, horrified.

Nell quite liked having Mr Scrooge around. She had been keeping an eye out for any lost cat signs, but nothing had been put out. She certainly wasn't going to send him back out into the cold until she was sure he had a home to go to. Nell had already conjured up several scenarios where the cat's owner – tall, dark and handsome – followed him into the hotel and when he and Nell locked eyes, they instantly fell in love … but so far, it hadn't happened.

'Nell?' Brenda barked as she once again fell into a dream. 'Are you going to keep it?'

'I don't know yet, I might do. I'll put some posters up and see if anyone claims him. If they don't, why shouldn't I?'

Brenda shook her head, her perfectly curled hair holding resolutely firm. 'What about your guests?'

'Apart from Mr and Mrs Limstock, I haven't got any, so it doesn't really matter right now.'

Cat was the first to reassure her. 'Things will pick up soon, Nell. Have you upped your advertising like we discussed?'

'Yeah, as much as I can afford to.' Nell plonked down into the armchair again. 'I've got a few regulars that have booked again off the back of an offer I emailed out, but no new people. I've got a meeting with a firm tomorrow to see if I want a proper marketing plan made up. The thing is, I know what the problem is. It's the Langdon Mansion.'

Brenda's head popped up from the file. 'Oh, it's lovely there. Very, very expensive. I've been told the accommodation and food are absolutely exquisite. And the service—'

'Mum!' Cat shouted. 'You're supposed to be supporting my friend.'

Brenda adjusted her shirt again. 'I'm sure this wedding fair will be absolutely marvellous, Nell, *if* you've organised it properly.'

Only Cat saw the almost imperceptible raise of Nell's eyebrow. 'I'm doing my best, Brenda. I've got all the stall holders sorted, I'll mention it at the business forum soon and I've been marketing it online and all around the local area. Hopefully, people will come.'

'I'm sure I'll be able to swing by,' said Brenda. 'I might even be able to get some of my friends to come.'

Nell knew that the reason she might attend was more to make the place a socially acceptable choice to all her well-to-do friends who thought of Holly Lodge as a poor substitute for the Langdon Mansion. A flash of annoyance stiffened her spine but with tension radiating off Cat, Nell kept her mouth shut. She took a chocolate biscuit from the plate she'd laid out for them and Cat did the same.

'Should you be eating that, sweetheart?' asked Brenda, looking at her daughter from the side of her eye. 'You want that corset to do up. And I hate to say it, but you've been filling out a little recently. I can see it on your face.' She gently cupped her daughter's face and affectionately tapped the end of her nose. Cat lowered the biscuit as Nell gulped in a breath ready to fight her friend's perfectly normal-size corner – and then Cat put the whole biscuit in her mouth in one go. An act of defiance Nell admired and copied, earning her the evil eye too.

After Brenda had harrumphed and turned back to the depths of her file, silence descended, the only noise the blissfully warming crackles of the fire and the slight rattle of the old sash windows in ancient wooden panes. Nell was beginning to worry her outfit for tonight wasn't going to keep her very warm, but she wanted to look nice and that won over comfort. Before long, Brenda was mumbling to herself, listing all the things they still needed to organise and sort out, Cat stroked Mr Scrooge who had become a tight ball of fur on her lap, and Nell waited for her next set of instructions.

Watching the leaves dance in the wind, she couldn't stop her brain wandering. After staring at the accounts all day and making some financial predictions based on her most recent takings, the awful truth was, that if she didn't secure some weddings off the back of this first one and the wedding fair, business was really going to suffer and that meant laying people off or even selling up. She didn't employ that many staff and if she sold up, she'd not only be selling her business but her home too and she loved Holly Lodge more than anywhere else on the planet.

A part of her wondered if that was such a bad thing – but even when she'd gone to university, she'd stayed at home rather than live in halls. Okay, so the beach of Swallowtail Bay was pebbly and not sandy, but that had never stopped her and Cat from sunbathing, and she loved hearing the echo of the tide as she fell asleep at night. She loved that she could get hand-made chocolates for the guests' pillows, special herbed sausages for the full English breakfast, and delicious pressed juices all made locally. Things like that were what made Holly Lodge an institution in the town, having been there for over twenty-five years. Each room was unique with a big, comfy bed covered in soft white sheets and pretty cushions; all had top-of-the-range showers or roll-top baths and unusual furniture that Nell had sourced herself from car boot sales. But what made the place truly unique was the personal service she offered, catering to people's different needs with genuine warmth and affection. Her aim had always been to create a luxurious home from home.

'Right,' said Brenda, lifting out a notepad and pen from her enormous handbag. 'Let's talk about china, shall we?'

'China?' asked Cat. 'Why China? I'm going to Tenerife on my honeymoon.'

Brenda rolled her eyes. 'No, Catherine. China as in china plates and cups and saucers, not the country.'

'Oh.' Cat took another biscuit under her mother's watchful

gaze. Brenda's eyes followed it from the plate all the way to Cat's mouth where her daughter took a big satisfying bite.

'Why did I agree to do this?' Brenda muttered to herself.

Neither Cat nor Nell were brave enough to point out that no one had asked, or even wanted her to help in the first place. She'd taken over arrangements as soon as Cat had said the word proposal and the Brenda Wilson steam train hadn't slowed down yet.

As Mr and Mrs Limstock waved from the other side of the lounge, trying to get her attention, Nell smiled and excused herself to Brenda and Cat. She may not have many customers at the moment, but while she had some, she'd give them the best service she could. And it meant she could top up Cat's gin while she was up. Something about Brenda's scowl and the set of her mouth told her she might need it before this planning meeting was over.

Chapter 5

In the dark evening light, Nell walked up the slope leading through the gardens of the huge, intimidating hotel, lit by Victorian-style streetlamps. Though it was a renovated manor house, to Nell it had none of the elegant feel of a stately home. The façade was the same, apart from a giant automatic door that seemed to suck the classiness away every time they opened and closed with their horrid swooshing noise. A sweeping semi-circle of steps led up to it, but all Nell could think was that they wouldn't be easy for anyone with mobility issues. Taken together, they ruined the whole look of the building. She much preferred the gentle ramp she'd installed that led to the modest front door of Holly Lodge. Or if they were after a grand entrance, then it had to be the other local stately home, Thornhill Hall that sat the other side of the bay.

Tom had agreed to meet her outside and Nell shivered in the little jacket she'd worn over a deep-burgundy wrap dress and tights. A flimsy patterned scarf did nothing to keep out the cold and it really was brass monkeys in Swallowtail Bay tonight. She ran the toe of her black suede ankle boot along the edge of a paving slab. The ground began to glitter beneath her feet as the moisture turned to frost.

Normally when she went out with Tom, she wore whatever she happened to throw on, which was usually her flared jeans, high-top trainers and a jumper, but the Langdon Mansion Hotel was one of those places that had an unspoken dress code. Her imagination had run a little wild, as it always did, and when she'd imagined this evening, she'd pictured women in fur stoles and slinky dresses with cigarettes hanging from their lips in long ivory holders. As they draped themselves over the furniture, elegantly suited men wandered about with tumblers of whisky on the rocks and everything was vaguely black and white. A slap of cold wind whipped around the face, waking her up. She closed her arms over her chest and waited, taking a moment to breathe after the meeting with Brenda. It felt more and more like going into battle rather than joyfully discussing different options for Cat's wedding.

'You should have gone inside,' said Tom, striding up the same slope she had a few minutes earlier. 'You must be freezing. Why didn't you wear your coat?'

'Because it's a parka and it wouldn't have gone with my dress. Do you like it?' She gave a little spin on the spot and immediately Tom's face flooded with affection.

'You look great,' he replied, wrapping an arm around her and kissing her cheek. He always had lovely, soft skin and smelled nice. 'It's better than one of your enormous jumpers.'

'Hey! Enormous jumpers are the best thing about autumn and winter. You can snuggle up in them. It's like wearing a duvet.'

Nell's mind turned inwards and before she could help it, she was seeing herself and the love of her life wrapped up in blankets in the lounge of Holly Lodge. She desperately wanted someone who understood her passion for the hotel, for the wedding business, and for making people feel special when they walked through her door. So far, boyfriends had understood at first, but their enthusiasm quickly faded when she couldn't make a date because it was a changeover day or she had a house full. That wasn't the case at the moment, but she hoped it wouldn't be long before her plans came to fruition and the wedding business took off.

'Shall we go in then?' Tom asked, nodding to the door.

'Yes, definitely,' Nell exclaimed. 'I can't feel my toes.' The horrid automatic doors parted as they climbed the top step and made their way inside.

As they stepped over the threshold, their eyes met and Nell knew he could read the fear on her face. She pushed her long golden hair back from her face.

The entrance hall was opulent, intimidating and huge. A long, wide, dark wood reception desk ran down one side, full of computer screens that popped up in front of suited-and-booted staff. On the same side, a little further along were the lifts, and opposite, between open doorways, were two different bars and crushed velvet sofas in deep purple. In the middle stood an enormous Christmas tree perfectly decorated like something from an interior design magazine. Twinkling lights wrapped around it in perfectly slanting circles. Expensive-looking glass baubles glittered and underneath sat a pile of flawlessly wrapped boxes posing as presents. Nell puffed out her cheeks and she and Tom stared around. It was so much grander than she'd imagined. As if to reassure her, he reached out and took her hand, holding it tightly in his.

'Are you okay?'

'Look at this place, Tom. How am I ever going to compete with this?'

'Nell, there's room in the market for everyone. You have a different customer base and a different offering. Don't compare yourself to here.'

'How can I not?' The realisation of what this place was actually like caused her stomach to knot in worry. 'I know my hotel's lovely but this is next level snazzy. How can I not compare myself to this?'

'Things will pick up, Nell. We just need to do some more

marketing.' He let go of her hand and placed his on the small of her back. She found its warmth and strength strangely comforting. 'Come on, it's almost eight – let's find the restaurant.'

They walked further into the entrance hall and past the Christmas tree to see huge festive red flower arrangements in giant silver urns. If Tom could get the contract providing this place with displays, he'd be made for life. 'You should give them your card and let them know you're a local florist. If you got their order, you'd never need another bit of business.'

'I'm not doing that,' he replied as they peered through the open doorways into the two different bars. One was like an old boys' London club and the other was an elegant cocktail bar with a shiny counter and high bar stools.

'Why not? It makes perfect business sense.'

'They probably have someone who provides the whole chain and besides, it would feel disloyal.'

Tom was the absolute sweetest, but she wasn't going to let him miss an opportunity like this. Knowing she had one of his business cards in her wallet, she veered off to reception.

'Where are you—' But she was gone before he could stop her. After giving it to one of the receptionists she came back to him. 'Why did you do that?'

'Because I'm not letting you miss on an amazing opportunity because of me.'

'But I'm snowed under as it is. I don't really need—'

'You can never have too much business and you never know what's going to happen. Their regular florist might let them down, or they might need something at the last minute, or they might recommend you to someone. It can't hurt for them to have your card.'

A small chuckle escaped from Tom's mouth. 'Well, thank you.' His voice chased away some of the cold lingering in her bones. Pointing at a sign, he said, 'Come on, the restaurant's down here. And my stomach's rumbling.'

At the end of the hallway he turned left, following the sign for the restaurant. The website said it was at the back of the mansion with views over the gardens, and Nell had to admit the aromas heading her way were delicious. There was a strong savoury base note over which she could smell something winey mixed with something sweet. As soon as Mr and Mrs Limstock had left for a day of sightseeing, she'd been working hard in the hotel, making the most of the quiet time to give it a big clean, and had even started wrapping Christmas presents after working on the brochure for a bit. She absolutely loved Christmas and spent ages choosing the right gift for someone and then wrapping it carefully, so every parcel had neat corners and a proper ribbon bow on top. The only problem was she'd got caught up in doing that and hadn't eaten much.

When they reached the restaurant, it was Tom's turn to be taken aback and his mouth hung open. Floor-to-ceiling windows lined one side, separated by giant columns. The larger tables had grand candelabras in the middle while the smaller ones had small silver holders with white candles. Giant silver snowflakes hung from the ceiling and everywhere were cascading silver and green flower displays. A gazillion staff clad in crisp black-and-white uniforms buzzed here and there carrying plates of food or clearing tables with the ease of experienced silver service, stacking empty plates on top of each other, all in the crook of their arms. Nell could only manage about three plates at a time. Maybe she needed to go on a course or something? Would her customers expect that sort of service?

This was all unfamiliar ground for Nell who was pretty positive and confident. Feeling unsure of herself only heightened her insecurities. After a glance at the guests, she also felt woefully underdressed. Tom clearly felt the same as they exchanged another worried look.

'Can I help you, sir? Madam?' A man with slicked-back hair in a shiny navy and yellow pinstripe suit sidled over. Nell noticed his suit trousers were drainpipe straight and stylishly short and he was wearing brown brogues without socks. All she could think was that he'd have cold ankles on the way home tonight.

'We've got a reservation,' said Nell, shoving Tom slightly forward as if it was all his fault. He almost stumbled from her forceful shove but regained his composure with a slight clearing of his throat.

'Yes, it's in the name of Barton. Table for two.'

Nell caught the man's name badge. Bryan. With a Y. Bryan led them to a weird, onyx-black sculpted workstation and swiped away at a computer hidden in its depths. 'Ah, yes, here we are.' He clicked his fingers – actually clicked them, which she thought was a bit rude – and a waitress appeared at his shoulder, her hands clasped behind her back and bolt upright like a soldier on parade. 'Tallulah will see you to your table. Enjoy your meal.'

Tom nodded his thanks and they followed Tallulah. She was young, probably only in her late teens, not that much older than Janie, Tom's apprentice in the shop, but she carried an air of confidence that even Nell as a grown woman struggled to feel at times. It was intimidating, as was the whole place. There weren't any 1920s cigarette holders or draping women, but she did spy some town councillors and the local mayor at one of the large tables. Nell waved as she went past and Linda, the mayor, waved back, her cheeks a little pink from a couple of glasses of Christmas cheer. Arnold, her husband, seemed to be enjoying himself too though he hadn't noticed Nell, being deep in conversation with the person opposite him.

They were seated next to a window and from the hotel's position at the steepest end of Swallowtail Bay, the graceful curve of the coastline splayed out before them. Punctuated with lights in varying shades of yellow and white they looked like sparkling Christmas baubles in the dark. Before long, the high street would look like a Christmas bauble when the lights were strung up and the giant Christmas tree was up. Nell loved the way they decorated the town, seeing all the lights as you walked through the traditional Christmas market.

Tonight, the sea was black and still, but a pale moon shone down from the deep inky blue of the sky and its reflection glittered off the water. A sea mist had begun to roll into the bay obscuring everything in its path and blurring the hard edges of the buildings. Tallulah asked if she could take a drinks order and Tom turned to Nell.

'Are you on the sauce tonight or driving?'

'Definitely drinking,' she replied, looking around her once more. The cutlery was more reflective than her mirror at home. She didn't get many nights off because it depended on when Zoe could work but as she was covering tonight, Nell wanted to make the most of it, plus she needed some courage. The odd gin and tonic normally did the trick.

'Then can I get a plain gin and tonic and a glass of house red, please?' Tom said. With a slight nod of the head, Tallulah disappeared off. 'I thought house wine would be the cheapest option.'

'Good idea. Have you noticed there's no music? Or is there? I think I can hear something.'

'You can, it's really faint, though. Something classical, I think.'

The faint sounds of Christmas chimes met Nell's ears. 'It's a bit boring, isn't it? I much prefer a cheesy Christmas bop or a cheerful carol. A bit of a *Ding dong merrily on high*.' She sang it a little too loudly and the table next to them sneered. Nell hunkered down into her seat as Tom studied her unimpressed expression.

'Is it the music or me making you look like that?'

'Definitely the music,' she replied, pulling herself straighter. 'This place is a bit scary. And fancy. But we always manage to have a nice time when we're together so despite the fact that this place makes me shaky, I am happy to be here with you.'

'You might want to tell your face that.'

She stuck her tongue out and they both laughed. Without fail,

46

whether they were clearing blocked drains at the hotel or having dinner at the pub, they always spent their time together laughing and joking. 'I'm just a bit worried. My restaurant's not even half the size of this and if the food here is good—'

'This isn't like you, Nell. You're normally much more optimistic. Are you sure there's not something else going on?'

Nell rolled her shoulders back, trying to relax, but the fact was her subconscious had been throwing up some weird thoughts lately. 'Do you ever feel like you've reached a turning point in your life? A crossroads?' Tom raised an eyebrow. 'Clearly not. Well, since I went wedding dress shopping with Cat, I've been doing some thinking.'

'That sounds dangerous.'

She flashed her eyes at him. 'I've realised that lately something feels different. This feels like a big, momentous time in my life with Cat getting married and the hotel not doing so well. I've been re-evaluating things.'

It wasn't that she was suddenly on the lookout for a husband because her best friend was getting married, but she did miss having some romance in her life and at this time of year she particularly wished for a love that was both powerful and romantic with someone who knew her inside and out. Someone to really get into the Christmas spirit with and spend long winter nights cuddled up to. Since going wedding dress shopping with Cat, the idea had been growing more and more that, though she would love someone to be with, until that happened she should make the most of being single and do all the things she'd wanted to do but hadn't.

'It's not that I don't want to fight for the hotel, you know how much I love that place, but I think I need to be realistic and figure out what I'll do if things don't work out because that's looking like a real possibility. It's heartbreaking because I love Holly Lodge, and maybe it's my defences going up, but I feel like I need to be prepared for the worst.'

'Hang on. You and reality have never been the best of friends—'

'We have when it comes to business.' She knew he was teasing and made her tone light to match it, but how could she make it clearer to him? 'You know in *You've Got Mail* when Meg Ryan loses her bookshop?' He nodded. She'd made him watch it so many times he knew that film as well as she did. 'She's fought hard for her lovely little bookshop, but lost, and now she has to figure out what she really wants to do. I feel a bit like that. I want to keep the hotel – it's my life – but what happens if I don't make it through this rocky patch? I'm going to do everything I can but maybe this is the time to make a change if ever I'm going to. The wedding fair's a good idea but it's a bit last-chance saloon and if the business doesn't start to improve soon, maybe I should do something else.'

Tom was looking really concerned now. 'What sort of change? Become a wedding planner or something? You do love weddings.'

'I hadn't actually thought of that.' She stored that idea away for later. 'If I have to sell up, I thought maybe I could do something big like go travelling. I've never been anywhere—'

'You've never wanted to go anywhere.'

'I might now. Oh, I don't know.' She drummed her fingers on the table. 'Lately I've been imagining visiting all the places I've never had the chance to with being tied to the hotel.'

'You and your imagination.' Tom's concern was fading a little. 'If that's what you want, have a holiday. I've told you before I can look after the place for you.'

'That's not quite what I meant.'

Tom sipped his drink and said, 'You always get like this when something's bothering you. Are you sure there's nothing going on? The last time you were like this you cut all your hair off in a pixie crop because the redecorating wasn't going as quickly as you hoped. You said it was because you loved what's-her-name's hair in that film you like—'

'Ginnifer Goodwin in *He's Just Not That Into You*,' she mumbled, knowing full well he was right.

'But really it was because you were stressed out that you were letting your mum and dad down by changing the hotel. Are you sure you're not stressed about Cat and Kieran's wedding? Or the wedding fair stuff?'

Sometimes, she really hated that he knew her so well. That haircut hadn't suited her at all as her ears stuck out a bit too much, and she'd been growing it back ever since. Luckily, she was partly yeti or something, because her hair grew very quickly. 'Maybe it's a bit to do with Cat too.' She told him about the wedding dress situation. 'But she knows her own mind and I don't want to press too much. I've tried a couple of times, but she just turns the conversation to something else.'

'Do you want me to have a word with Kieran?'

'No, don't do that!' The table nearby looked over again and Nell lowered her voice. 'Cat wouldn't want him to know anything about the dress. It's fine. I'll speak to her again and see if I can change her mind. I am excited for the wedding fair though. All those couples at the hotel will fill the air with romance.' It was going to be a magical day, but she really needed to get the brochure finished. It was only just over two weeks away, but all she needed was some photos.

As if by magic, a hand delivered two menus to the table. They were absolutely enormous A3-size sheets of thick, dark blue paper with indecipherable fancy gold lettering. The only thing her eyes could make out for sure were the enormous prices. Next to the small blocks of virtually illegible text were giant pound signs and extortionate numbers.

'How the hell am I supposed to read this?' asked Nell, manoeuvring her menu so she could see Tom over the top. He was squinting too.

'I know what you mean. I can barely make it out.' Nell popped her head up over her menu again to see Tom blinking at it. His eyes were the colour of russet autumn leaves with hints of amber and flooded with warmth. 'We can do this. We're grown-ups, we can read words. Even squiggly, upside down words.'

Nell laughed and turned her attention back to her menu. 'So, the first starter is basically a take on baked camembert—'

'But with weird cheese from Mongolia.'

They quietened as Tallulah delivered their drinks and Nell thanked her before taking a sip. It was nice, but a little watery and she wondered what brand of gin they were using, or if she'd been making hers too strong. She didn't have many but when she made one, she didn't always bother measuring. 'Next is … well, it's basically a scotch egg, isn't it?'

Tom guffawed. 'It really is. Except it's Himalayan breadcrumbs and a quail's egg. Why on earth do you need breadcrumbs from the Himalayas. I'm sure Asda ones are just as good. So, the third, veggie option is …'

'Carrot soup,' Nell exclaimed with a giggle. 'It's basically just carrot soup.'

'Umm, no it's not. It's small-farm, hand-grown, organic, French baby chantenay carrots roasted with a whimsical dressing and then made into a savoury liquid. What's a whimsical dressing?'

'I don't know. Maybe it tells you jokes before you eat it.' Nell chuckled and took another sip of her gin.

'What are you going to have?' he asked, rolling the gigantic menu up into a tube and placing it on the table. There wasn't quite enough room for it no matter which way he laid it.

'I think I'll go for the soup. I want to find out more about this whimsical dressing. You?'

'Baked cheese without a doubt. You can never eat enough cheese.'

Nell made a mental note to buy him a cheese-related gift for Christmas. Tom took a sip of his wine and scrunched up his face. 'What is it?'

'The wine's just a bit sharp.'

'Not as outstanding as you'd expect?'

'Not really. So, shall we try and decipher the mains?'

'Go on then.'

After a lot more giggling, the two of them decided what they would have just as Tallulah returned to take their order. They'd been given a lot of time to decide what they wanted and that was one thing Nell liked. They weren't pounced on as soon as their drinks had been delivered in an effort to get everything moving along. Nell hated it when that happened. If she opened the dining room of an evening, she'd have to hire a good chef first of all, but she'd also make sure the waiting staff gave people time to enjoy their time. Maybe she could hire different chefs for different evenings. Cat's caterer for the wedding was really good, and that way the menu could always be different. The chefs could decide the food and cost out what they need, then Nell could agree charges with them.

'What are you thinking about?' asked Tom. 'You've gone all quiet. Back in your imaginary world?'

'Ha ha. I was just thinking about chefs and how I could make the dining room idea work. I was thinking I could get a different chef every night—'

'Or just open a few nights a week.'

'Good idea.' Nell explained about the different menus, and from across the table Tom studied her. She pretended not to notice at first but when he was still watching her as she finished speaking, she said, 'What?'

'Nothing.' Tom ran his hands over the smooth surface of the tablecloth. 'You just … you always crinkle your nose when you're thinking.'

'Do I?'

Nell bit the inside of her cheek, feeling suddenly self-conscious. It was like they were on a date. Any girl sitting in her seat would be lucky to have Tom sitting opposite her. He was so kind and caring, and he blushed whenever he paid her compliments. It

51

was endearing, even more so because it really should have worn off by now as they'd been friends for so long, but he'd always been like it and Nell had grown used to it. She'd never seen him blush with his previous girlfriends though, now she came to think of it, which was odd.

'Okay, enough about work.' She shook her head a little to shake the mishmash of thoughts away. 'How're things with you? I know it's only been two days since I've seen you but how's Grandad Nigel?'

'He's an old rogue as usual.'

'Is he getting used to things now?'

'With his sight you mean?' A pained expression passed over Tom's face and he rubbed his eyes. 'He seems cheerful enough, but he wouldn't say anything in front of anyone else. I'm going next week to help decorate the place for Christmas. I was thinking of making some Christmassy-smelling decorations or something. You know, cloves, cinnamon, dried oranges. I mean, Grandad's not the only one there with vision problems – if anyone can't see Christmas deccies, it'd be nice if they can smell something.'

That was just like Tom. He was so considerate and caring and thought a little out of the box. Not many people would think about something like that.

'I'll come with you next Sunday if you like. It'll be nice to see Nigel again.'

'He'd love to see you too, and if you don't mind, I'll pop in and see him on Christmas Day before I come to you? Unless you want to come too?'

'Of course I want to come. I wrapped his present today.' Tom and Nell always spent Christmas Day together after a quick trip to the care home in the morning. Cat and Kieran would be on their honeymoon, Tom's parents had emigrated to Australia and Nell's stayed at the hotel in Dorset. Over the past few years, she and Tom had made their own celebrations, just the two of them, and sometimes guests if the hotel had bookings. As it was looking at being just the two of them this year, it was shaping up to be laid-back, easy and fun.

Their starters arrived, delivered by the surprisingly confident Tallulah, and Tom and Nell stared at them in surprise. His baked Mongolian cheese was a surprisingly decent size but covered in so much rosemary it looked like a forest had fallen onto his plate. Nell's soup was just that: bog-standard carrot soup with some flecks of green floating in it, served in a gold teacup on a shiny matching saucer.

'Is that it?' whispered Tom, pointing his bread knife at the cup and saucer.

Nell looked up, trying desperately not to laugh out loud. 'It's tiny, isn't it?'

'I could neck that in about three seconds.' She picked up her teaspoon and stirred her soup trying not to spill any as she lifted it to her lips. Just as she opened her mouth Tom's hand shot out. 'Don't.'

'What?' Nell followed Tom's horrified gaze to the teaspoon. Sitting in the head of the spoon was a curled black blob. Peering a little closer, her face fell into a grimace. 'Urgh, it's a spider! That's so gross.' She leaned forward, whispering, 'What shall I do? I can't eat the soup now. That's honestly made me feel sick.'

'You should tell the waitress.'

'What? I can't. I hate complaining. Maybe I can just say I didn't like it, not that that sounds any better.' Nell stared at the crumpled dead spider in her spoon, feeling slightly sorry for the poor thing. There weren't many nice ways for a spider to go, but she couldn't imagine being drowned in soup was one of them.

'You have to, Nell. What if someone else finds one in their soup? You'd feel terrible. It might be a one-off, but it might also mean their kitchens aren't quite as clean as they think they are. Someone could get proper food poisoning or something.'

'Oh no.' Nell laid the spoon, complete with arthropod accompaniment, on the gold saucer, which only seemed to spotlight it more. 'This sucks. I really hate complaining.'

'Do you want me to do it?'

'No, it's okay. Right, here goes.' Catching Tallulah's eye, she waited until the waitress came over. 'Umm, I'm really sorry,' Nell began, keeping her voice hushed. 'But I'm afraid I found a spider in my soup.'

The waitress's face registered shock and then disgust. 'I am so sorry, madam. I think I'd better get the deputy manager for you.' She darted away and a few moments later Bryan with a Y, the man in the shiny suit and cold ankles, arrived at the table. Tallulah had clearly briefed him because his brow was crinkled and he came over clasping his hands. Nell repeated what she'd said to Tallulah and Bryan peered at the spoon, picking it up and examining it.

'Madam, I sincerely apologise, I can't imagine how this has happened. I assure you that we have the highest levels of cleanliness in the restaurant. I can only imagine it fell from the ceiling when it was being carried out.'

It was possible, Nell supposed, but not likely. The poor thing definitely seemed sufficiently cooked to have been in there for a while. Even though Nell had tried to keep her voice low the other tables began to glance over and whisper amongst themselves. Bryan's eyes darted towards them then back again as they examined their own plates for wildlife. Still, Nell tried to be conciliatory. 'No problem. I run Holly Lodge. We don't do dinner, but we do breakfast and my cook's constantly cleaning everything to make sure there's no chance of something getting in.' She'd meant it in a nice, understanding way but Bryan sneered at the mention of Holly Lodge and embarrassment flushed over her neck.

'We do have a five-star hygiene rating, Miss Jones.' The fact he knew her surname even though she hadn't told him was disconcerting. Was it that they knew of Holly Lodge? She supposed they must know all their competition in the town. 'I can assure you nothing like this has ever happened before.'

At a nearby table, a woman was angling a phone as if she was recording the whole thing. Even the mayor was watching with her group of councillors. Nell's cheeks grew hot and she looked at Tom for support.

'I'm sure it's just a one-off,' he said to Bryan. 'But if we could maybe change Nell's starter to something else? And you might want to get rid of that batch of soup, just to be sure.'

Bryan eyed the woman with her phone, and suddenly his demeanour changed. He stood a little straighter and his expression hardened. 'There is another explanation. As the owner of Holly Lodge, you might have placed it there to sabotage us—'

'What?' Every muscle in Nell's body stiffened. 'Don't be absurd. Why would I do that?'

'We're well aware, Miss Jones, that your business has suffered since the opening of our hotel. You could have come here and placed that spider in your soup, so we lose business and even our hygiene rating. Or possibly you wanted a free meal. It wouldn't be the first time someone has tried something like this. Though they usually use one of their own hairs.'

Nell's temper flared. 'I would never do such a thing. How dare you suggest that I would? Do you think I found and kept a soggy arachnid, bringing it with me to dinner just so I could put it in my soup to try and discredit the Langdon Mansion Hotel? That is ridiculous.' She crossed her arms over her chest. It was clear that having realised who she was, Bryan was now trying to blame her rather than take responsibility for the oversight of his restaurant.

Bryan puffed out his skinny, wimpy chest. 'I'm afraid I'm going to have to ask you to leave, Miss Jones.'

Nell gasped in a breath. This was so utterly embarrassing. Her body felt like it was on fire, she was sweating and could feel how beetroot-red her cheeks were.

'Now hang on a minute,' said Tom, his voice edging towards angry. It wasn't something she heard all that often. 'We haven't done anything wrong. Your restaurant has allowed a spider to crawl into its soup and yet you're trying to blame us?'

Tallulah the waitress was looking on in terror at the furore in front of her and she suddenly looked much younger than she had before, more like Tom's Janie – just a young girl caught in a horrible situation. Nell felt instantly sorry for her. From Bryan's behaviour she could imagine he wasn't a very nice boss. One of those who was fine as long you were on the right side of them but get something wrong and you were thrown under the bus, especially if it caused him any problems.

'Let's just go,' said Nell, feeling the eyes of everyone on her. She'd never been so humiliated in her entire life and once she'd walked out of a public toilet with her skirt tucked in her knickers and shown half her bum as she walked down the high street. At the time she'd thought nothing could top that, but she was wrong, this definitely took the trophy for the most embarrassing moment of her life.

'Are you sure?' Tom asked. 'You've done nothing wrong, Nell. You shouldn't be bullied out of having your dinner here because they've messed up.'

Bryan sniffed and ignored the comment even though Tom shot daggers at him.

Trying to regain some of her dignity, Nell stood and grabbed her jacket from the back of her chair. 'I'd really rather just go, Tom. We can grab some fish and chips on the way home. My treat.'

As Tom passed Bryan, he turned to face him. 'You should be ashamed of yourself. You know full well Nell didn't place that spider there, you're just too embarrassed to admit it. That's despicable. And cowardly.'

As they left, with all eyes upon them, Nell felt Tom's reassuring hand on her back. It wasn't until they were outside in the cold, fresh night air that she felt able to breathe again and her cheeks began to cool.

'Well, that was horrible,' Nell said, wrapping her scarf around her neck. The awful automatic doors opened and closed as people inside walked past them.

'It was. Do you want my coat?' Tom asked as Nell shivered.

'No. I'm not actually that cold. I think it's just shock and shame.'

'Hey,' Tom said quickly, turning Nell to face him and taking her face in his hands. She loved the warmth of them. 'You have nothing to be ashamed of. They're the ones who should be ashamed. They've treated you so badly. I hope the mayor saw it—'

Panic flooded her face. 'I hope she didn't. What if she believes them?'

'No one would believe them. They were clearly lying to save their own skin. Much easier to turn the tables and try and blame you than tell the truth that they messed up. You heard him say about people trying to get free meals. I bet they've done this before, blaming customers rather than take responsibility for the meals they serve.'

Some of the tension released from Nell's shoulders and she tipped her head down. Tom did the same, resting his forehead against hers, and she enjoyed their closeness for a second.

'Shall we get those fish and chips?' he said as they stood there in the dark.

Nell lifted her head and nodded. 'Much better than – what was that beef thing?'

Tom thought for a moment and recited the menu. 'Full-blooded, Australian Wagyu beef strips in a flaked cheddar and chive pastry envelope.'

'So, beef Wellington in cheesy pastry?'

'Yep.'

As they strolled back into Swallowtail Bay, Nell threaded her

57

arm through Tom's, glad that even though the night had been horrible, she'd at least been with him. That always seemed to make everything better.

After ordering Tallulah to dispose of the spider soup, Bryan stomped into the kitchen.

'François? François?' He turned to the pot-wash, a young man not much older than Tallulah. 'Where is that piece of French … toast? François?'

'Out the back having a fag, I think.'

Bryan shoved his way past and into the small fenced back yard behind the kitchen. François was sat on a metal beer barrel, puffing away. 'François, you waste of bloody space. Did you know someone found a fucking spider in their soup? A spider, François! And it was enormous. It wasn't like a tiny money-spider you don't know is there until it crawls across your face. It was a giant fucking tarantula thing, its legs all curled in and gross.' He mimed it with his hands then felt a bit silly as the Frenchman cocked his head and frowned at him. 'It had been cooked in the fucking soup, François. What do you say to that? Some spider decided to have swim in the carrot soup, and you didn't notice. How the hell did it get in there? Did you clean the place from top to bottom last week like I asked? Because I know there was a spider's web in the corner of the room above the extractor. I saw it there and I told you to make sure it wasn't there this week.'

The Frenchman shrugged and answered in a heavy accent. 'It must have happened in the dining room. It cannot have happened in my kitchen.' The stocky chef threw down his cigarette and ground it out with his foot. Without looking at Bryan, he went back inside.

With a deep breath, Bryan strode through the kitchen, down the plush corridors of the hotel to the office he shared with Kevin, the manager. The deep pile of the carpet softened his stamping tread, but the slamming of the door could not be ignored. It echoed through the room and no doubt down the hall leading back to reception.

Kevin looked up from his computer screen. 'What's the matter with you? We're fully booked in the restaurant and the hotel, we're pretty much guaranteed to meet all our sales targets for November – life's good.' He sat back and clasped his hands behind his head, his bright white teeth shining in the light from his desk lamp. 'Why the long face?'

Bryan sat down, but just as his bum hit the seat he stood back up again. He couldn't figure out if he'd done the right thing or not. Normally he'd have apologised for any mistake and offered a free meal. That was the company policy. But as soon as she'd mentioned Holly Lodge and he'd realised she was the owner of the nice boutique B&B on the seafront, and seen that woman recording the exchange on her phone, panic had risen in him like a volcano about to erupt. They'd known the mayor was in tonight with all her cronies and as she was booked in to have her Christmas party there, they wanted to make a good impression, show how amazing the service was as well as the food. The company always started Christmas in early November knowing that people were already booking Christmas parties. If she was impressed, they might get some brownie points locally. The order from the top was that it was important to keep the local dignitaries on side. At the time it seemed his only option was to blame Nell and make out she'd put it there, but now he doubted himself and it was a feeling he didn't like.

'Oy,' Kevin demanded, as Bryan hadn't answered. 'What's wrong?'

Scratching his cheek, he told Kevin what had happened. All the humour fell from Kevin's face. He hunched forwards, his hands balled into fists and his jaw set. 'Shit!' After a second, he said it again and began pacing the room. 'Someone recorded it?' Bryan nodded. 'Shit.' Kevin ran a hand over his hair. 'Okay, let's not panic until we have something to panic about. If she doesn't post it anywhere, we're fine. We just pretend like nothing's happened and it'll all be forgotten soon. If she does, we'll have to do something to discredit Holly Lodge and pin the blame on them. Like you said, we make people think she did it on purpose to make us look bad because her business is going under. Sour grapes. That's what we'll say.'

The desk phone rang, and Kevin answered. 'What? They're checking out? Why?' Bryan watched on, and Kevin's eyes shot to him. 'Right. Offer them a free spa pass and ring me back if they say no.' He put the phone down and stared at Bryan, neither of them speaking as the room filled with apprehension. Two minutes later, it rang again, and Kevin listened closely. 'No, let them go. Just assure them that what Bryan said was true. They're welcome to go elsewhere if they want. They're probably not the type of people we want here anyway.'

'What was that?' asked Bryan, once Kevin had replaced the receiver, but deep down he already knew the answer.

'The Summertons just checked out. They said they saw what happened in the restaurant and don't want to eat somewhere spiders can get in the food.'

'Shit, Kevin, I'm sorry.'

Kevin shook his head. 'Don't worry, they only arrived this afternoon and haven't been happy since they walked into their room. They're in the one with the broken radiator and had already moaned. They were probably looking for an excuse to get out. When I spoke to them earlier, they said unless it was fixed, they weren't paying the full rate for staying. I could tell straight away they were serial complainers.'

'How long were they here for?'

'Three nights. It's no big loss. We'll fill those rooms in no time.' He leaned back, perching on the edge of the desk. 'But we have to do something. We can't just wait for more people to check out and there'll be some damage limitation to do if that woman shares that video. Is she a guest?'

60

Bryan shook his head. 'No just a dinner reservation. Someone from the town.'

Kevin nodded slowly, taking in all the information and formulating a plan. 'Knowing what these locals are like, they'll stick together and believe her which we don't want, even though she is telling the truth. We don't have the video so we can't edit it and use it to our advantage, making it look like Holly Lodge were playing dirty. We need to do something that makes Nell Jones look bad. It's all about reputation. If our reputation's better than hers, people will believe us. No doubt about it.' Bryan held his breath and waited for his superior to finish. As Kevin made up his mind, a sly smile came to his face. 'Don't worry. I know just what to do.'

Chapter 6

The next day, Nell was busy wrestling with the artificial Christmas tree in the lounge of Holly Lodge. It was a bit early to put it up, being only the eighth of November, but after last night she needed some cheering up and wanted it up for the wedding fair. It was important to make Holly Lodge the most amazing hotel at Christmas time, and show how cosy and warm and romantic it was: the perfect setting for a winter wedding.

Outside it was a damp and rainy day and a flock of seagulls swooped and swayed over the sea, but with the log fire burning and some Christmas tunes playing there was nowhere else she'd rather be. Wizard's 'I Wish it Could be Christmas Every Day' had been on three times in a row, and Nell munched a mince pie and drank hot chocolate while she worked. She couldn't help but buy mince pies as soon as they were stocked in the shops. She even loved the ones with icing on the top. They just tasted and smelled of Christmas and gave you a warm fuzzy feeling when you ate them.

Having changed the normal blankets and cushions to Christmassy ones embossed with robins, reindeers and festive patterns, Nell was beginning to feel a little more relaxed and able to shake off the embarrassment of the night before. She always went for natural decorations where she could, tiny traditional wooden ornaments being her absolute favourites, and Tom always made something to go over the fireplace. Sat cross-legged on the floor, she began sticking the different parts of the Christmas tree together. As much as she loved real trees, she'd invested in a huge but still gorgeous fake one last year for the hotel. It lasted longer and didn't need quite as much looking after; there were no pine needles to sweep up and no pots to water. She also had two smaller trees that went either side of the front door, but she'd get around to those later.

A small wooden box, more like a jewellery box, lay next to her containing her tiny wooden decorations. She always used them to fill in the gaps once all the baubles were up and there were all different types – snowmen, ice skates, a robin, a sleigh – anything remotely Christmassy, bought over the years. Each one had its own memory attached. Some had been bought on holidays with Cat, Kieran and Tom, and others by her family, but each one meant something special to her. Taking a break from the prickly boughs, Nell picked one up and examined it. These just smelled different to other decorations. The woody scent meant Christmas had finally arrived more so than anything else. Beside her was another old cardboard box full of baubles and another that held a collection of different sized nutcracker soldiers. She loved those too with their tall hats and bushy beards and they fitted in perfectly around the hotel, lining the hall and slipping into spaces, making every room feel Christmassy.

Despite last night's horrifically embarrassing dinner with Tom, one good thing had come out of it. A couple who'd been in the restaurant had decided not to stay at the Langdon Mansion, and had checked in to Holly Lodge instead. They'd arrived shortly after she and Tom had settled with fish and chips in the lounge. They had seen the whole spider-soup incident. Just remembering it made Nell shiver with humiliation at being asked to leave, and disgust that it had happened in the first place, but she pushed the horrid thoughts to the back of her mind and made an effort to focus on the positives. The Summertons had been incredibly nice and agreed that she'd been treated badly. Tom had been wonderfully indignant on her behalf and she loved him even more for his support. The Summertons loved their room and as they were here for a few more nights it meant a nice boost to Nell's income.

Nell checked her watch. Tom was arriving shortly to attend this marketing meeting she was having with a local firm. As business had slowed, she'd been tempted by their free consultation. As the Summertons were out for the day and had booked to eat at a local Indian restaurant for dinner, they shouldn't be disturbed. They'd wanted to eat at Holly Lodge if it was possible, and even after last night's debacle and the fact that her offering would have to be much simpler, it had made the idea of opening the dining room a little stronger in her mind.

With a satisfied sigh, the bottom part of the Christmas tree was finally together, and Nell began work on the middle section. She needed a big tree to fill the wonderfully large and airy lounge, but it was a giant pain in the backside to put together. Once it was up it always looked amazing and Nell beavered away, fixing up the bare tree, until a strange voice from the hallway caught her attention.

'Hello? Anyone there?'

Making her way out to the hall, she saw a man placing a small suitcase down by his feet before loosening his stripy scarf decorated with little snowmen. Nell took a moment to control the buzz of excitement. His large, well-built frame was encased in a black wool coat and the removal of the scarf showed a clean-shaven, chiselled jaw. 'Hi,' Nell managed to say. 'Can I help you?'

'I was hoping you had a room for a few weeks.' The American accent sent a little shiver through her. The Christmas music playing in the background broke into something orchestral and it was like the moment she'd been waiting for all her life. Her brain suddenly transported her to her dream where she was dressed in a wedding dress, walking down the aisle to this American god. And had he said a few weeks? Nell almost jumped up and down on the spot. 'Umm, yes, yes, I do.' She went to her little reception desk and opened the laptop to process the booking. 'It's £130 per night, bed and breakfast. Is that okay?'

'Sure, fine,' he replied, giving a killer smile that showed beautifully even white teeth. 'I'll need it for three weeks initially but if my work can stay under control, I might need to extend. I'm here seeing family.'

'Oh, how lovely.' Nell loved a man who valued family and friends. 'Can I take your name please?'

'Harry. Harry Decker.'

'Thanks.' Nell typed his details into her computer booking system while her imagination swept her back to their wedding day, him saying his name during the vows, gazing longingly into her eyes. She pressed enter on the keyboard and chanced a glance to find him looking around.

'This is a nice place. I'm surprised you're not fully booked at this time of year. Is it yours?'

'Yes. It was my parents'. I started running it after they moved away. I'm glad you like it.' She didn't bother telling him she was virtually empty in case he saw it as a reflection of quality, and she wasn't going to mention the Langdon Mansion Hotel in case he decided to try there instead.

'Awesome. I see you're getting ready for the holidays?' He nodded to the tree branch she'd placed next to her laptop.

'Yes,' she replied a little too loudly, regaining control of her voice. 'Oh, yes. I'm a bit mad for Christmas.'

'So, it'll be up for Thanksgiving? I appreciate that.'

'Well, that is the type of service we offer here at Holly Lodge. Is the room just for you or for you and your wife?' She tried to keep her voice easy and free but almost held her breath waiting for his response.

'My wife?' He laughed, tilting his head. 'No wife. Just me.'

She finished taking his details, saying silent prayers of thanks, and got the key for the room. She'd thought about getting those snazzy card jobs installed but the cost didn't seem worth it for the nine rooms she had. There was just a good stock of spare keys, plus master copies in case anyone lost theirs.

'Wow, an old-fashioned key.'

Nell flushed. 'Sorry. We're a bit low-tech here, but the beds are the most comfortable you'll ever sleep in. I can promise you that.'

'Then I'll look forward to a good night's sleep tonight. I don't know about you, but I can never sleep on planes.' Nell, who apart from some holidays to Spain and Ibiza hadn't really travelled much, mumbled an agreement and showed Harry up to his room. He looked around appreciatively, admiring the deep sage-green accent wall behind the large king-size bed. Every room had been designed with relaxation in mind and as soon as you walked in it felt calm. 'I can tell I'm going to be real comfortable here. Thanks.'

'You're very welcome. There's tea and coffee over there by the window and the bathroom is through there. There's a lovely view out towards the seafront as well.'

'Wow. It's beautiful. I love that you've kept the period features. You can't go wrong with a big ol' fireplace.' She was just about to leave when his deep voice called her back. 'Say, what should I call you? As we're going to be seeing a lot of each other, I should know your name.' Her ribs vibrated in her chest with the power of his voice.

'My name's Nell.'

'Nell.' He repeated it, nodding approvingly. 'That's a pretty name. Thanks for the room.'

She backed out of the door, closing it behind her, then blew out a breath that lifted her fringe. Now that was the type of visitor she liked: tall, handsome and staying for at least three weeks. As she walked down the stairs, she wondered what his chest looked like under the heavy cable knit jumper he'd been wearing, imagining a scattering of hairs on smooth, tanned skin.

At the bottom of the stairs, Nell grabbed the branch she'd left on the reception desk when Harry arrived. Feeling the most positive she had in ages, she carried on with the tree and was just thinking how she'd need to decorate the fireplace when, as if by magic, Tom arrived bringing with him some willow branches that he'd made into a beautiful display to go over the fireplace, studded with dried apple slices and cinnamon sticks. It was the fanciest potpourri Nell had ever seen. 'What's this?' she asked, as Tom secured it on the fireplace, resting it behind a couple of redundant bookends he'd grabbed from the bookcase.

'You're my guinea pig. And you always have something to go over the fireplace at Christmas. I thought this might be a nice change. I've gone along rather than up this year.'

'It's gorgeous,' Nell replied, immediately noticing the perfume filling the room. Not only was the place beginning to look a lot like Christmas, it was smelling like it too. Last year, Tom had made her a stunning display in a vase using white and red flowers; this was even more exquisite and would last all the way through until January. She marvelled at how creative he was. 'What made you think to do that?'

'I don't know really. I just wanted to do something slightly different. If you like it, I can do some for the bedrooms.'

'That would be great, they'll look amazing. And they smell absolutely gorgeous.' She ran her finger over the willow branches. Tom had kept some of them in their natural state but a couple he'd spray painted silver and it added a touch of festive sparkle.

Tom blushed as he always did whenever he paid her a compliment or she paid him one. 'How were the Summertons this morning?'

'Good. They're so lovely and they love the room. And I've just had some American guy turn up wanting a room for three weeks!'

She bounced onto her tiptoes. 'He said he's visiting family. I was really worried that once the Limstocks had gone I wouldn't have anyone here, but I've got two lots of guests! Two!'

'I told you things would pick up, didn't I? And we'll see what this fab marketing team have come up with in a bit.' Tom's voice dripped with derision as he puffed one of the Christmas cushions and sat in the armchair by the fire. He believed that Nell knew everything there was to know about the business and if she put her mind to it, she'd figure out the best ways to market the place. But she was feeling a bit insecure at the moment, particularly about herself and the future of Holly Lodge, which made it hard to look at things objectively.

'It's a free consultation to see if we want a full-on marketing package. I've got nothing to lose. We might learn something that neither of us would ever have thought of.'

'All right,' Tom said, sliding his coat down his shoulders.

'I do feel a little bit guilty about the way we left the Langdon Mansion last night though. I mean, I know the whole spider thing wasn't my fault—'

'And Bryan with a Y treated you appallingly.'

Nell nodded. 'And Bryan with a Y treated me appallingly, but ...'

'But?' Tom reached down and began unfurling some more of the fake tree branches ready to hand to Nell.

'But ...' She shrugged. 'I don't know. It feels a little bit like I've stolen their guests.' Tom shook his head at her and even though his gaze was kind, she bristled. 'What?'

'You just make me laugh, that's all. It's not like you went in there wearing a sandwich board advertising your hotel. We went for a quiet dinner, they treated you badly and *you* end up feeling guilty. You've always cared too much about other people.'

'I'm going to take that as a compliment.'

'It's a wonderful quality. It's what makes you different to ...'

When he didn't finish Nell looked up. 'To who?'

68

Tom kept his eyes on the tree and Nell couldn't understand why he was so embarrassed. 'To everyone really.' Then he brightened. 'Have we got time for a coffee before the marketing gurus arrive?'

'I think so. I'll go and make some in a second and get a tray ready for the meeting.'

Mr Scrooge appeared at the window again, rubbing his body against the pane asking to come in. Nell opened it and as Mr Scrooge climbed in, he gave one look at the half-built enormous fake Christmas tree and decided it wasn't worth his time before finding a chair to sit in. As he circled, getting ready to sleep, he gave Tom an evil glare and hissed when Tom reached his hand out.

'That cat must belong to someone,' Tom said. 'Though he's still quite skinny so he could be a stray.'

'I keep feeding him up every time he comes in. Actually, do you want to make some drinks while I finish this off? I don't want to leave it half done when the marketing people come. I don't mind it not being decorated but I'd like the tree pretty much made up if I can.'

Tom agreed and shuffled off to the basement kitchen to make some drinks. He came back a few minutes later with two cups and a plate of food for Mr Scrooge.

'You're such a softie,' Nell teased as she blew her tea to cool it.

On seeing the food, Mr Scrooge jumped down off his chair and hunkered by the fire, scoffing. Before long, the marketing people were due, and Nell flitted nervously around while Tom tried and failed to fuss the cat. Every time his hand went near Mr Scrooge, the cat would either recoil, bat it away with claws out, or hiss. 'Do you think he's been abused or something?' she asked, moving to the cat who allowed her to stroke him.

'Possibly. He seems quite happy with you, but he doesn't like men.'

69

'If that is the case that's really sad.' She leaned down and gave him another fuss. 'Isn't it, poor Mr Scrooge?'

Nell drank her tea and watched the waves dance together in the sea through the window of the lounge. The sky was a pale grey and rain tapped against the window. The watery late-autumn sun shone through the gaps in the heavy cloud and when it came through the window, she could feel the warmth on her face. In the holly hedge that surrounded the hotel, birds hopped in and out of the gaps, chirping happily. The very top of the Christmas tree wasn't quite finished as she spotted the marketing duo arriving. Once they were walking through the arced iron gate and down the front path, she rushed to greet them at her little reception desk in the hall. 'Hi, I'm Nell.' She held out her hand for them to shake.

A woman in her mid-twenties wearing the skinniest fitting jeans Nell had ever encountered, along with a luminous pink shirt and matching trainers, gave her a firm handshake. The man with her had lank hair pulled back into a man-bun and was wearing jeans that, as he walked towards her were so low slung, they barely covered his bum. A slim-fitting shirt had been tucked into the waistband and he wore very shiny blue shoes. His handshake was what Brenda would have described as wet and his fingers slid in and out of Nell's in a way that made her skin crawl. Still, she welcomed Nadia and the ironically named Manley into the lounge. Apart from her little reception desk, her office was mainly her studio flat in the basement, so the lounge would have to do, and given that at the time of organising it she didn't have any guests, she hadn't foreseen a problem. Luckily, Harry was still in his room, probably sleeping off some jetlag. In her mind, she repeated his name, replaying the American twang with which he pronounced it, then grabbed her notebook and carried on with the introductions.

Tom, she could see, was already amused as Nadia set up her laptop on one of the small coffee tables before standing and clapping her hands to get everyone's attention. 'Right, let's start by talking about you.'

Nell shifted uncomfortably in her chair. She was never very keen on talking about herself. 'What do you want to know exactly?'

'Well ...' Nadia was worryingly enthusiastic with her hands and Nell thought she might get accidentally slapped in the face if she got too close. 'You're the heart and soul of this business, Nell. We want to know all about you, Nell Jones, and Nell Jones's vision for the future.' Every time she spoke her hands flew around like she was directing traffic and the end of each sentence lifted up as if she were asking a question. The repeated use of Nell's name grated like nails down a blackboard. A textbook tactic to build a rapport with her and make this seem more personal, but really it was just extremely irritating. 'So, Nell, like, what's the hotel's USP? What's your USP? It all comes down to you, yeah? Like what is your ultimate vision for the future, for Nell ...' Her eyes darted to the screen of her laptop, checking her notes.

'My what now?'

Though Nadia's slightly manic grin remained intact, she took in a tiny breath of annoyance. 'Your vision for the future. So, like, where do you see yourself in five, ten years' time, Nell?'

'Umm, here. I suppose. Doing this.' She motioned around her. 'Maybe with a few more guests but ...' Two sets of eyeballs narrowed, telling Nell her answer was less than sufficient. 'I just want some ideas as to how I can market the place better, that's all.'

'Well,' began Manley, in the highest, reediest voice Nell had ever heard. It was so high even Tom jumped in surprise. 'In order to do that we need to know where you want your business to go. Where's it headed, okay? Where is Nell Jones going?'

'Ah huh,' agreed Nadia, nodding with such vehemence she looked like one of those bobble head toys you get on car dashboards. 'This stratosphere? The next stratosphere? Are we talking Mars level of ambition?'

71

Nell glanced at Tom, who, as well as enjoying himself thoroughly, had an annoying, I-told-you-so look on his face. This wasn't what she'd had in mind at all. She'd thought they'd have told her where was best to advertise and whether adverts in the local paper or the luxury retreats websites were more worth the money. She didn't realise she was going to be interviewed by trendy youngsters speaking a language she didn't understand. All she wanted was to make her hotel as successful as it could be. 'Umm, I just want to know where the best place to advertise is really. I've got reviews on HotelRater and I've got a website—'

'Wow,' said Nadia in a really patronising manner that made Nell's muscles instantly tighten up. 'I mean, it's a start but, I'll be honest, that is so basic.'

Seeing Nell's face, Manley cut in. 'But we all have to start somewhere. So good job.' He gave a strange, double thumbs-up and Tom stifled a giggle.

'True, true.' Nadia nodded again. 'But we can take you to the next level in luxury hospitality. If we do your marketing plan including an awesome new logo, top-quality photographs and deluxe marketing package, we can put you on Mars, Nell. Mars!'

Nell had no intention of going to Mars. All she wanted was to be here in Swallowtail Bay, just with more visitors.

'This place is fab, Nell,' Nadia continued. 'We checked out your website and you've made this place look good. There's top-quality design here.' Considering she wanted to remove Nadia from the building by her long dangly earrings, it was a compliment Nell was willing to take. 'You've got good reviews on HotelRater apart from that one from yesterday and—'

'What?' Nell shot a quick glance at Tom who, from the puzzled look on his face, didn't seem to know anything about it either. She'd never had a bad review in her life. All right, there might have been a couple that leaned more towards the moaning side than out and out praise, but no one had mentioned anything other than matters she couldn't control like bad weather, or an attraction being closed. 'What bad review?'

'Here, look.' Nadia sat down and loaded up HotelRater then turned the screen to face Nell and Tom. Nell read it slowly, taking in each word and a searing hot fire crept up her spine.

Some unnamed person, who had apparently stayed on dates they weren't prepared to specify, spoke about the poor food at breakfast (Mrs Meggett, who came in and cooked for her would be livid and rightly so, her full English breakfasts were to die for), they moaned about the quality of the beds, the moody and hardly ever there owner who never listened to anything they said. It was all so utterly preposterous, Nell didn't know what to do. She couldn't recall the guest or think who it might be; no one had ever complained to her. Her guests had always left with glowing compliments and big happy smiles. And she hadn't had that many lately, so she'd definitely remember these people by the sounds of it.

Then there was the video. Only one video was listed on the page linked to her hotel and she clicked to view it. Her stomach dropped to the floor and bounced back up again ricocheting off her throat. It was of her and Tom's attempt at dinner last night at the Langdon Mansion Hotel and being asked to leave. The Langdon Mansion had been tagged too. She felt sick. Her throat closed over and she had to push through it to swallow. That person who'd been angling their phone must have recorded the whole thing and uploaded it.

'Oh my God.' Nell sat back and pointed at the screen. Tom moved closer and placed his arm around her, trying to calm her down. 'Someone's posted that video from last night, Tom. Why would they do that?' Did they think it would expose the Langdon Mansion's shoddy treatment of her? Even if they did, she still couldn't figure out who'd left this review.

'It's the world we live in, I'm afraid,' Tom replied.

They both knew how damaging this could be. She came out

73

of it looking mildly better than the Langdon Mansion but there was still the possibility that people might think their accusation was true. They didn't know her or how honest she was, or how much she loved her hotel. And now this bad review had popped up, it really didn't help her situation at all. 'The whole wide world has seen me be asked to leave for sabotaging my competitor.'

'Being accused of,' Tom corrected. 'You did nothing wrong.'

'But it's the whole world, Tom. The whole wide world.'

Nadia turned the laptop back around. 'Umm, yar, it is the world wide web after all. That's the beauty of it, it doesn't matter where you are, you can find out anything about anyone, anywhere.'

Nell pinned her, channelling Brenda's death stare, and felt Tom's hand stroke small circles on her back. He must have seen she was on the verge of ripping out Nadia's throat then shoving her out by the scruff of her neck because he suddenly closed the laptop and stood up.

'I think we should call it a day,' said Tom, saving Nadia from a near certain death. 'Thanks for coming. We'll have a think about what you've said and come back to you, okay?' Nadia looked at Manley, shocked that their sales pitch hadn't worked. 'Yes? Good. Thanks. This way. Don't forget your coats.' Tom shepherded them out while Nell paced around the room.

Anger and annoyance were pulsing through her muscles. She began fiercely placing the branches into their designated slots on the tree to take her mind off it, pulling them into place and spreading out the fronds. When Tom walked back in, she couldn't look at him for fear he'd be nice, and she might cry. 'What the hell is that video doing online? Why do people feel the need to do that type of thing?' Tom began to help with the tree, gently easing out the branches that were higher up. 'Do you think I should email the Langdon Mansion and let them know?'

'Why would you do that?'

'Because they might not know it's been uploaded, and I want

74

them to know it wasn't me. We don't need any more animosity.'

Tom scowled. 'In my opinion, if they don't know, then that's just tough. They're the ones who come out of it looking bad.'

'Not to me. I'm so embarrassed, Tom.' Just thinking of it sent a prickle up her spine that danced on the back of her neck. 'And that's if people believe I didn't do it on purpose.'

'Of course people will know that.' Tom's voice was rising, and Nell could tell he was getting a little bit cross with her doubting herself again.

'But shouldn't I show some professional courtesy and let the Langdon Mansion know I didn't put it up there?'

'No way, Nell.' She widened her eyes at his forcefulness. 'They should be apologising to you, not the other way around. If this damages their reputation, that's tough luck on them. They shouldn't have been complete arseholes.'

That was true. 'Oh, shit! What if Mum and Dad see it?' Nell could feel a pinch in the skin around her eyes, and she played the conversation in her mind. Her dad calling full of disappointment and her mother in full crisis management mode. They'd be up here like a shot. She couldn't have that. She grabbed a bauble from the box and cradled it. 'All I want is to have enough visitors to keep my hotel open. I don't want to win tonnes of industry awards, I don't want to rule the world, or colonise Mars or whatever it was Nadia was talking about. I just want enough to pay the staff and stay open and make the guests I do have happy. Is that too much to ask?'

'No, it's not, Nell.' Tom reached his long arm around her shoulder and pulled her in close. 'Look, I've always said we can figure out this marketing thing ourselves. Let me do some research and we'll find the best places to advertise.'

'Okay.' It was time to pull herself together. 'I'm going to email HotelRater and see if they can take the video down. Until then, we've got the wedding fair to think about and we can explore this dining room idea some more.'

'That's the spirit. You just have to hang on in there through this rough patch.'

He gave her a squeeze and Nell relaxed a little. 'You're right. I've got some guests booked in so I'm going to make sure they have the best time possible and leave me glowing reviews. The Summertons are here for a romantic stay and I'm going to make their room lovely for them for when they get back.'

'But don't go mental. That's part of your problem. You always want everyone to have such a nice time you end up spending more than you make personalising everything, even down to the wine.'

She didn't tell him she'd spent ages this morning choosing some speciality liquor chocolates or that she'd brought a small bunch of red roses from the supermarket for the room (as well as grabbing those mince pies). Mr Scrooge rubbed himself against Nell's legs and she reached down, stroking his fur, which was warmed by the fire. It was becoming less and less coarse the more he came in. She really was developing a soft spot for him. 'Right, I'd better get this tree decorated. I've got the knit and natter group this afternoon and then Cat and I are meeting her caterer this evening.'

'Is Brenda coming?'

'No, thank God. She's got bridge with some women from the WI. Cat deliberately booked the meeting for when Brenda was busy and hasn't even told her about it.'

'What?' Tom feigned disbelief. 'You lied to the terrifying Brenda Wilson?'

'*I* didn't.' Nell confirmed with a cheeky grin. 'Cat did.'

Chapter 7

The fire burned in the grate and the smell of cinnamon and apple from Tom's fancy twig display filled the room.

'That was thoughtful of Tom,' Cat said, pointing to the wonderful display he'd made then settling back into the armchair she always chose. Mr Scrooge, who had left shortly after Nadia and Manley, had come back in some time ago and after eating an entire tin of tuna, had curled up on the windowsill. From the way he had devoured it, the poor stray was definitely getting better. Nell was so used to having him around, he was becoming like part of the furniture.

'It was. I don't think I know anyone as kind and caring as him.'

'Hey! I'm kind and caring.'

'You are indeed,' Nell confirmed. 'But I mean, a guy who's kind and caring. You also have a no-nonsense scary side.'

'That's the midwife in me. Sometimes you have to take charge to stop people panicking or getting overwhelmed by it all.'

Cat was sitting with a pink gin and tonic while Nell nursed a hot chocolate. They were the only things to warm her up on cold winter nights like this. While she sipped, enjoying the rich chocolatey taste, she brought Cat up to date on her eventful few days:

the dinner disaster at the Langdon Mansion Hotel, the lovely time she'd had with Tom afterwards as they walked back with their fish and chips, laughing at the ridiculous menu, and the spider-soup video ending up on HotelRater. She even managed a quick rundown of nodding Nadia and man-bun Manley who had tried to sell her a marketing plan based on NASA.

'Wowzers,' Cat said, after sipping her drink. 'At least it wasn't the other way around and someone found a fly in their breakfast here or something.' Nell gaped at Cat because the very thought was enough to turn her stomach. If something like that happened, she'd be mortified and certainly wouldn't automatically blame the customer. The thought that she'd have to have words with the formidable Mrs Meggett was beyond terrifying.

'I suppose you're right,' Nell replied. But even though the marketing meeting had been a complete waste of time, there had been one good point in the afternoon that followed.

Nell had finished the tree, placing the last tiny wooden decoration on it, as the knit and natter group made themselves comfortable in the lounge. She loved the knit and natter group and the way it brought different generations of women together. They'd been coming to the hotel since her mum and dad had owned it and Nell loved the feeling that Holly Lodge was a part of the community. She knew what they all had to drink and had prepared the trays with some festive biscuits she'd bought from the posh baker's in town. Some of the ladies were older and able to knit without looking at their hands, chatting away without dropping a stitch. Some of the younger ones enjoyed the chance to absorb the older women's knowledge as they discussed their children's ailments or difficulties in their love lives. More than once Nell had been on the receiving end of their advice when it came to men, even if she never asked for it.

When they'd settled, one of the grandmothers had mentioned something very interesting. The local primary school normally held its annual festive carol service in the school hall, but the roof was leaking and needed some urgent repairs. According to her, St Herbert's was searching for a new venue that wasn't going to cost them any money to hire, otherwise they'd have to cancel, and the children were heartbroken at the possibility. Nell had immediately been struck with what she'd thought at the time was a good idea and was eager to tell Cat all about it.

'The knit and natter group said St Herbert's Primary were looking for somewhere to hold their Welcome to Christmas service and I rang them and suggested here, and they said yes straight away! Isn't that awesome? I can clear the dining room and open the door to the lounge. If Tom helps me bring school benches over in his van, I reckon I can get the singers in the lounge here' – she gestured to where with her hands – 'and have everyone seated out there in the dining room. It's such a small school there's only one class per year and that only has twenty kids. I've planned out all the space already. What do you think? I'm going to sell hot chocolates and mince pies and all kinds of Christmassy treats. I reckon it could really help with takings. I need to do everything I can to get money in while the bookings are low.' Cat didn't speak and Nell worried she thought it was just another of her flights of fancy.

Nell knew herself well enough to understand that her imaginative nature made her prone to thinking things would always work out and sometimes they didn't. Like when she was a teenager and had decided the boy next door fancied her. In her mind, the chance meeting she'd engineered would end up in love at first sight. She'd trip up and fall into his arms, he'd catch her and from that point on they would be inseparable. What actually transpired was that she'd bumped into him accidentally on purpose trying to eat an ice cream in a coquettish fashion, and the ice cream had gone all over his T-shirt. That choir of angels she was sure were waiting open-mouthed to sing hadn't started because he'd been less than impressed and called her a stupid cow. Love had died instantly.

Incidents like this had been repeated throughout her life and she'd learned to manage her expectations, at least as far as the business went. At times though, she still couldn't stop her mind wandering to the day her true love would walk into her life, every moment like a romcom movie waiting to happen. Which reminded her, she still needed to tell Cat about Harry.

'What do you think, Cat?' Nell asked nervously. Even though she didn't have children herself and being an only child, she had no nieces or nephews to fuss over, she still loved kids' carol concerts. There was something about the madness and chaos of the homemade costumes that made it really feel like Christmas. And Christmas carols were always magical and made her cry.

'I think it's a great idea,' Cat replied. 'And it's a really lovely thing to do, which, given the time of year, is perfect. Well done you.'

Nell glowed at the compliment.

Heavy footsteps descended the stairs and Harry poked his head around the door. He was wearing a different sweater, thinner and tighter this time, and dark denim jeans. Nell noticed for the first time how his hair was a light reddish-brown, like the willow branches Tom had brought, but streaked with California blond. He wasn't from California, she'd just had a little fantasy about that involving him, half-naked in an undone wetsuit. The address he'd given her when she took the booking was New York. A city she'd longed to visit but had never got around to despite many drunkenly planned shopping trips with Cat. 'Hey, Nell.'

'Hi, Harry. Everything okay?' Seeing him again, his hair slightly dishevelled, sent a bolt of electricity into her heart waking it up. She hadn't failed to notice Cat's bewildered glance at this new and exciting unmentioned guest.

'Relax, everything's fine. The room is absolutely divine, and I just wanted to say you were right about the bed. As soon as I'd had a shower ...' Nell swallowed to stop herself from seeing him all toned and soapy. She could already feel herself blushing. 'I just couldn't keep my eyes open and it was the best nap I've ever had.'

'See, I told you. I'm glad you're feeling better.'

Cat's gaze flitted between the two of them.

'Well, I'm still pretty jetlagged so I'm just off to see my family for dinner then I'll be back for a good night's sleep. Evening, ladies.'

'Good night, Harry.'

'Good night,' Cat called enthusiastically and when he'd disappeared with a smile that could melt the coldest of hearts, she batted Nell's arm and burst out in a hearty giggle. 'When were you going to tell me about him then?'

'Harry? He's just a guest. He's staying for three weeks to see some family.'

'And all the flirting?'

'We weren't flirting. At least I wasn't.' Nell brushed a long tickly hair behind her ear.

'Oh no, no flirting with the tall, gorgeous American,' Cat teased. 'Blimey, we don't get many of those around here, do we?'

'No, we don't,' Nell replied, playing with the edge of the Christmas cushion she'd tucked under her arm.

'I'd make the most of it while you can.'

The words 'while you can' left a horrid feeling in Nell's chest but as Cat carried on, she ignored it. As much as she wanted to believe in love at first sight, she wasn't sure Harry did. Cat took her mind off things with tales of Brenda's latest exploits which included a strange new kind of face cream made from seahorse poo. They were just laughing about this when Niall, the wedding caterer, came in.

Niall Peters made the most incredibly delicious fancy food and Nell couldn't decide which aspect of the wedding she was most excited about; that this was going to be the first of many weddings held at Holly Lodge; that it was her best friend's wedding and therefore a joyous day when two of her very best friends became one; or getting to stuff her face with food made by an incredibly talented man. Niall walked in with a happy ease and arms laden with little white boxes that were sure to hold delicious food.

'Hey, ladies,' Niall said. 'You look very comfortable there.'

They were incredibly comfortable by the fire with Cat two gins down and nearing the end of the third. So far it had been more like a girls' night in than waiting for a meeting. The smell coming from the white boxes was like icing on the cake – the fanciest takeaway ever. Nell couldn't wait to dive in.

'I'm not late, am I?'

'Not at all,' Nell said, standing up. 'What can we get you to drink?'

'A coffee would be great, thanks.'

Nell already knew how he had it and went off to get him one. When she came back, Cat and Niall were looking decidedly cosy next to each other on the sofa. The meeting began and Nell watched Cat taste the food samples with mounting worry.

It wasn't that she was pretending because she didn't like them, or conversely, going over the top in her enthusiasm for the tiny cheesy vol-au-vents. It was more that the way she was behaving could only be described as flirtatious. Definitely, definitely flirtatious. And Cat hadn't flirted with anyone since she and Kieran had got together. To see her do it now was more than a little disconcerting.

'Niall,' Cat began, gently touching his arm, her hand lingering there for a moment longer than necessary. 'These are absolutely divine, don't you think, Nell? We definitely need to have these for the guests to munch on when they arrive.'

Niall leaned to the side to get his pen and notepad and knocked into Cat. 'Sorry. So, definitely the mini cheese soufflé vol-au-vents. What about something meaty?'

Cat gave a devilish smile and widened her eyes at Nell. 'I do like something meaty.'

Who was this woman in front of her? The Cat she had seen

only a few days before was as different to this one as could possibly be. Last night, Cat had seemed tired and fed up; this one was like Cat on Viagra. She looked the same and dressed the same, but a playful vixen had reared her head. Over the top of her hot chocolate, Nell eyed the situation with mounting concern. Was it her imagination or had Cat moved closer to Niall? No, it wasn't, and Niall too looked increasingly uncomfortable at Cat's proximity.

'What other things would you suggest?' Nell asked, trying to give the meeting some kind of focus.

'I do this fabulous chicken salad in a baby gem lettuce cup. It's one of my favourite light bites.'

'Light bites,' Cat giggled, and Nell looked at her like she'd gone completely insane.

'Let me tell you about them,' said Niall, pulling open another white box to show the tiny baby gem lettuce leaves piled with chicken, halved grapes and sprinkles of chopped walnuts. As he did, Nell studied his face, trying to figure out what was happening. Niall had one of those faces that wasn't really attractive until he spoke and his personality came through. At first his features seemed quite plain, due to a very square jaw and crooked nose, but when his love of food filled his face, his features softened. The crooked nose gave him character and hinted at a bad-boy past, while his stockiness and manly features gave the impression of security and protection. He wasn't Nell's type, but she was a bit worried that Cat had randomly decided he was hers, even though he wasn't giving any indication of being anything other than professional. 'I've made a sample. Here.'

Nell took one, hoping Cat wouldn't like it so they could hire a different caterer she wasn't going to flirt with, but it wasn't to be. Cat took a bite of hers and was rapturously enjoying the taste, making strange 'umming' sounds when Nell decided to intervene. Maybe Cat hadn't had much lunch. As a midwife, her days were unpredictable. She had mentioned how busy she was today with a woman on the verge, a couple who were overdue and a delivery that had gone swimmingly producing a gorgeous, squidgy pink baby girl. Perhaps three gins on an empty stomach had gone straight to her head. It was the only reasonable explanation for this weird behaviour. 'Shall we get some water, Cat?'

'Oh, Niall. Yum. This is amazing. We should definitely have this too.'

'Cat?'

Cat looked up in surprise and swallowed. 'No, thanks, Nell. I'm fine.'

Nell grabbed her arm and yanked her up out of her seat. 'No, you're not. You need some water and so do I. Come with me. Back in a minute, Niall. Make yourself comfortable.' *Just not too comfortable*, she added internally.

'Don't go anywhere,' called Cat over her shoulder.

Once they were in the safety of the basement kitchen and Cat had pulled herself onto the countertop, swinging her tiny legs, Nell took three glasses from the cupboard and poured some water into them from the cold filter in the fridge. 'What are you doing?' Nell asked, unable to contain herself any longer.

Cat pulled down the hem of her skirt and picked fluff off her bright purple thick woollen tights. 'I don't know what you mean.'

'Yes, you bloody well do. When did you start flirting with guys? You haven't flirted with anyone since you and Kieran first laid eyes on each other. You weren't even behaving like this the first time we met him. What's going on?'

'Nothing,' she said with a shrug. 'I'm just trying to enjoy my wedding preparations without my mother badgering me, that's all.'

Nell leaned against the countertop, her other hand on her hip. 'Well, do you think you could enjoy them a little less enthusiastically? You'll give Niall the wrong idea.'

'No, I won't. Oh …' She paused, her hand at her mouth. 'Do *you* like him?'

'Me? No.' The idea had never crossed Nell's mind actually. He wasn't her type. She wasn't exactly sure what her type was, but it certainly wasn't Niall.

'Or is handsome Harry more your thing?' Nell felt her ears grow hot, and shook her head, knowing full well it wasn't very convincing. 'I'm engaged to be married, Nell, I'm not dead from the waist down. I was just having fun.' Cat crossed her arms over her chest.

'You'll be dead from the neck up if you keep flirting, or I'll lock up the gin.'

'I didn't realise I was flirting like that, I was just trying to have a bit of silly fun, like we used to when we were younger, but I promise, I'll stop.' Cat's shoulders slumped down in a sulk. 'Why is everyone determined to make my wedding bloody miserable?'

'I'm not trying to make your wedding or its planning miserable,' Nell replied, gently touching Cat's knee. 'You know how much I love you. But you've been acting a bit weird. Is everything okay? Is your mum getting to you?'

Cat shrugged. 'A bit. I just wanted to enjoy myself while she wasn't here. She takes over so much when she's around, it takes all the fun out of it.'

'You're going to have to talk to her about this, you know. If she keeps making you miserable, you have to say something.'

'I know.' Cat hopped down off the counter. 'Can we get back to eating the food now? Mum's put me on a diet, and I've been starving all day.'

Nell tutted at Brenda's machinations. If Cat didn't speak to her, she was going to have to, and Brenda Wilson was almost as formidable as Mrs Meggett. The diet thing was the most ridiculous of all. Cat was happy as she was, and it wasn't for Brenda to say otherwise. 'Okay, let's go. You carry your drink and I'll take mine and Niall's, but no more flirting okay?'

'Okay.' Cat pushed open the swing door with her bum and they went back into the lounge to eat the rest of the delicious food, yet Nell wasn't totally satisfied. There was something deeper going on, Nell was sure of it. She had a feeling it was to do with this wedding dress business and if Cat wasn't going to stand up for herself, she was going to have to do it for her.

Chapter 8

Tom's Saturday morning ended up far busier than usual. After he'd arrived, he kept his coat on because the shop was so cold his teeth were chattering. He couldn't have the heating on too much as it dried the flowers out and lowered their shelf life, but he popped it on now to heat the place up a little. Settled at his workstation, he also pulled out some fingerless gloves.

The shop smelled like Christmas and orders for festive wreaths were coming in thick and fast. They were his speciality in the town, and he'd also decided to make a range of garlands like the one he'd made for Nell. The child within him had run riot and he'd begun a range of 'Santa Stop Here' signs using driftwood from the beach. He always loved using natural materials collected from the pebbly beach of Swallowtail Bay, though he drew the line at seaweed and anything that smelled remotely fishy. No one wanted that in their home at Christmas or any other time of the year. The first few mock-ups he'd made were looking pretty good.

Though he'd arrived there at a little before six-thirty, with the sky as dark as night and the sun still hiding behind the horizon, time flew by as he worked and the next time he checked the large clock on the wall above the flowers, he'd been there for almost

87

two hours. The shop was finally beginning to warm up a little and a pale white sky was visible through the window when Janie arrived at a quarter to nine. She came through the door looking like an Eskimo. Her eyes were only just poking out between the pink scarf wrapped over her mouth and the matching hat pulled down tightly onto her head. Her hands were covered in big fluffy mittens. Even though it was only her pale blue eyes that were visible, Tom could see she was as cheerful as ever from the sheer light and joy shining out from them. It was a pleasure seeing and working with her, and to Tom she was feeling more and more like a little sister every day. 'Morning, Janie. Bit cold at the bus stop, was it?'

'Freezing this morning,' she replied, unwrapping the layers. 'I thought my toes were going to drop off.'

'Well, I've got the heating on, so you'll warm up nice and quick. What do you think to this one?' he asked, showing her one of the driftwood Santa Stop Here signs as she readied herself for the day. A bright red, jolly Santa winked back at her.

'I love it. I think they'll sell out straight away. They're so perfect for Swallowtail Bay. The seaside meets Christmas. We should have a bucket of those out front.'

Tom stood back and admired his handiwork. Janie was right. It really was the seaside meets Christmas. He'd never thought of it in those terms, but she was definitely onto something there. Something a little bit different but still festive. She had a good brain for marketing. Maybe he should get her to look at the hotel stuff.

'I can't believe how cold it's got. Do you think it'll snow?' Janie asked with childlike enthusiasm at the prospect of the white stuff floating down and covering everything in a seamless blanket that called out to be stepped on.

'I don't think it's quite cold enough for that, but you never know. I did have to de-ice the car this morning so if the temperature keeps dropping, it might.'

When Tom had driven to the shop earlier that morning the pavement glistened under the lamplight. He'd sat in the car watching the windscreen de-frost which was actually helpful as it gave his eyes time to adjust to the dimness around him. He was going to have to go to the optician's soon but the thought brought with it an element of fear. The headaches were increasing in intensity and frequency and the thought that something was seriously wrong sprang into his mind and with it, panic. If something serious was wrong with him, like a brain tumour, what would happen to Grandad Nigel?

His parents had emigrated to Australia a decade ago and weren't going to move back to look after either him or his grandad. The thought of Nigel being left without any visitors, sad and lonely, like some of the people in the care home, almost broke Tom's heart. Seeing Janie's happy face as she began to gather things together for her first job of the day pushed the gloomy thoughts down and he blamed needing a sugar boost.

'Right, Janie, shall I make us a nice hot chocolate each? I've even stocked up on squirty cream and marshmallows and if you ask me, it's the perfect way to start the day.'

'You're the best boss ever.'

Tom left his tools, headed out to the back of the shop and made them hot chocolates, even using their Christmas mugs. His had a picture of a snowman on it and Janie's a llama in a scarf. After squirting as much cream on the top as he could manage without it being bigger than the cup itself and smattering the marshmallows all over the top, he took them out to where Janie was already working away. Tom returned to his own seat at the workbench to start the first wreath of the season. There were a lot of other things on the agenda for today. He also had three birthday bouquets to deliver, and some flowers for a big anniversary party, and he wanted to get the Christmas display planned for change over day next week. He always changed the window displays on a Wednesday when it was half-day opening. Though the number of shops only opening for half a day was dropping as new businesses moved into Swallowtail Bay.

The old place was regenerating before his eyes and the amount of walk-in trade was increasing year-on-year. He just wished it was the same for Nell and Holly Lodge. This whole video thing had caused him a sleepless night and he'd decided that when they met for a drink with Kieran and Cat at the hotel, he'd take his laptop, and hijack some of the wedding talk so they could research similar hotels and where they were advertising.

There was a whole day to get through first though. 'Right, Janie, shall we get some music on and kick this day's butt?'

'Definitely,' she replied with a giggle, already working on an order he hadn't even asked her to start on.

And as he turned on the radio his favourite Christmas tune was playing, 'Last Christmas' by Wham, which was surely a good omen for the day ahead.

With aching feet, Tom climbed into his van to begin the afternoon's deliveries. The morning had been pure madness. They'd had a number of people pop in to buy some loose flowers for vases at home and he'd taken a few more orders for gift bouquets. The shop had been filled with chatter from the moment they'd opened, so Tom was happy for the peace and quiet of the van.

The fresh air of the high street, crisp and clear, felt lovely after the heavy floral scent of the shop. Some of the stores like the chain coffee shops were already playing Christmas songs and were full of Christmas decorations. The smells of cinnamon hit him first and then savoury smells lingered too. The bakery was selling Christmas cakes and Christmas tree-shaped shortbread, decorated with bright green icing and he thought about grabbing himself and Janie one, but he was already running a little late. Some more of the smaller Christmas trees that were going on the sides of the buildings were up now, decorated with multicoloured lights. It wouldn't be long before it was all finished and Swallowtail Bay would be ready for Christmas. Though so much quieter than summer, the bay at Christmas time was just as special with everyone coming together to enjoy the season. Carol singers or brass bands were in the high street every weekend giving a wonderful soundtrack to your Christmas shopping. Which reminded him, he had some presents to buy.

Finally at his van, he hunkered down in his thick winter coat and pulled the collar up to keep his neck warm. Tom switched the engine on and turned the heater up, taking a moment to appreciate how comfortable he was leaving the shop in Janie's capable hands.

When he'd first taken on an apprentice, he'd anticipated doing a lot more teaching and training, but Janie had a knack. She'd learned the cash handling side of the business with ease and had come up with great ideas for new products and offers. Tom really felt he'd landed on his feet with Janie and planned to offer her a permanent job once her apprenticeship was over.

The frost of the morning had disappeared, and though the day was dry and clear with a soft-white sun shining down, it was bitter outside: a freezing stillness that turned cheeks pink and fingers blue. He pushed the clutch down but before he could put the car in gear his phone rang. Easing his foot back off, he fished in his coat pocket for his phone.

'Hey, Kieran, what's up, mate?'

'Are you busy?'

'I'm on deliveries. Why?' The line went quiet. 'Kieran? You still there?'

'Yeah. Umm, listen, has Nell said anything to you about Cat?'

'What about her?' Tom asked a little hesitantly. At dinner the other night, Nell had mentioned about the wedding dress, but she'd been adamant that Cat wouldn't want Kieran to know. He rested his free hand on the steering wheel, wondering what to say. Sometimes the four of them being friends could be a minefield.

'I just wondered if she'd said anything about the wedding. She's been really weird lately. Quiet and … I don't know … just not *my* Cat.'

Tom could hear the frustration and worry in his friend's voice. How could he ease his pain without giving anything away and betraying Nell's trust? 'Look, mate, it's probably just some wedding jitters. I've got them about my best man speech. Maybe organising the wedding is proving a bit much with Brenda on her back. I don't envy you your mother-in-law.'

There, that was a nice way of hinting that Brenda was getting a bit too involved. Tom felt secretly proud of himself.

Not normally one to open up with so little prompting, Tom was surprised when Kieran continued. 'Yeah, I get the impression Brenda's being a bit controlling. I've said I'll talk to her, but Cat won't let me. She doesn't want a row. And I keep asking to be more involved in all the organising and stuff, but Cat says it's her job to organise the wedding and she'll give me things to do as and when she needs to. I just feel like I'm not pulling my weight with it, even though she won't let me, and seeing her get so stressed out is hard, you know?'

Unfortunately, Tom didn't know because as much as he'd love a wedding, kids and all that lot, he'd never found anyone who could replace Nell in his affections. It must be so hard for Kieran seeing the woman he loved, normally so vivacious and bubbly, not enjoying the preparations for the most wonderful day of their lives. Tom knew he had a duty to reassure his friend, and maybe he could drop some hints to Brenda. She might not listen, but it was worth a try. 'I'm sure it's just a temporary bit of stress that will go as Cat and Nell get things sorted. The more they tick off the list, the more chilled out she'll get. I'm pretty sure it's Battle-axe Brenda winding her up.'

'Yeah, I suppose you're right.' Kieran sounded a little more cheerful, but reservation hung in the silence that followed. 'Okay, I'd better get on, but if you hear anything, you will let me know, won't you?'

'Sure,' Tom reassured him. 'But I don't really know what you think I'm going to hear.' There was no way Cat would be thinking of calling off the wedding. Nell would have mentioned something like that, even with everything else she had going on. It also comforted him that Cat and Kieran never stopped smooching when they were together. Even though Tom wasn't a relationship expert, he would have noticed if something had changed to wedding-cancelling degree, and as far as he could see, Cat was as in love with Kieran as ever, even if she was feeling the pressure of the wedding preparations.

'Just let me know anyway, yeah?' Kieran asked with the kind of sigh that took all the air from your body.

'I promise. It'll be all right, mate. Cat loves you and that hasn't changed. It's probably just her long hours and trying to organise everything so quickly.'

After hanging up, Tom was conscious that he was now running late. He loved the afternoon delivery session – the peace and quiet of the car and the moments of surprise and excitement when he delivered unexpected flowers. Those smiles were one of the best bits of his job and driving through Swallowtail Bay was always a pleasure. So many of the streets were lined with trees and there were even some Victorian boulevards with big walkways in the middle. Those walkways were covered in the remaining red and gold leaves that hadn't yet been blown away to wherever leaves go, and they looked beautiful. The car had warmed a little, but he was still cold and he shuddered, though he wasn't sure if it was at the temperature or his conversation with Kieran.

The main road that ran the length of the town and parallel with the sea, linked Swallowtail Bay to the two nearest towns. Driving along with the blue-grey sea beside you and salty sea air filling your lungs was enough to refresh even the gloomiest of souls. On a day like today, cold but thankfully not windy, the sea would be calm and serene, making a nice change from the wild, high waves they'd had recently. The first bouquet was needed over on the other side of town and Tom pulled his seatbelt on and began on his way.

Exiting the main junction off the high street and onto the long road that ran parallel to the beach, Tom checked right at the roundabout before pulling out. After moving a few feet, the honking of a horn penetrated the song he was singing along with, alerting him that something was wrong, followed by a loud crunch at the side of the van.

'Aargh!' Tom's body rocked to the left then shot back to the right, bashing into the van door as a scraping sound filled his ears. His seatbelt tightened at his neck, jolting him backwards into his seat. Instinctively, Tom's hand grabbed the back of his head and he heard angry voices growing louder and louder as someone knocked at his window.

'What the fuck are you doing?' A large angry man, his face red with rage, knocked again.

'I'm sorry – I—' Tom opened his door a little and the man stepped back allowing him to get out. His legs were wobbly, and he held on to the roof as he looked around. A tightening in his throat made him think he might be sick, and in vain he tried to control the swirling in his stomach. The man's people carrier had scraped the driver's side of Tom's van. His skin prickled as he realised he'd driven out too soon, causing the man to swerve away enabling them both to have a narrow escape. If he hadn't, it could have been so much worse.

'You just drove straight out of the junction. I've got kids in the car, mate – you didn't even look.'

'I did, I promise you. I looked both ways.' He glanced over and saw a woman at the people carrier checking on two crying toddlers in the back. Tom felt his eyes sting as worry and guilt hit him like a tidal wave. 'Are your kids okay? I'm so sorry, I don't know what happened. I did look and I didn't see you – I just didn't see you—' Tom's hand shot up and grabbed his hair as he tried to understand what had happened. The cries of the children calmed a little with gentle shushes from their mum, but Tom knew that the problems with his sight – problems that seemed to be growing more and more severe – could well be to blame for this. His peripheral vision was getting less and less clear, so it was entirely possible that even though he glanced left and right he simply hadn't seen them. The whiplash in his muscles began to tighten through his back and neck. 'I'm so, so sorry. I'll pay for the damage to your car.'

The man seemed to soften a little with Tom's clear concern for his children. 'All right, mate. Thanks. The kids are okay, just a bit shaken up, like us. Are you all right? You look a bit white.'

His kindness was almost too much for Tom to bear when he could have really hurt them, albeit unintentionally. 'I'll be fine. I'm really just so sorry.'

The redness was disappearing from the man's face as his anger abated, but cars were lining up behind them and the honking of car horns filled the air, for once drowning out the noise of the seagulls. The sea was calm today, and Tom wished his emotions were the same. Instead, they were more like the violent huge waves that had crashed onto the shore the last few days, dragging flotsam and jetsam with each one.

'Come on,' the man said, 'let's get over to the side and swap insurance details then we can both get on with our days, hey fella?'

Tom nodded. 'And let me give you and your wife some money to treat those kids to something. They must have had the shock of their lives. I'm so sorry. So sorry.'

'I appreciate it. Thanks.' He headed off to his car while Tom climbed back into the van ready to move off the roundabout and out of the way of the traffic. As he did, he sniffed loudly, and angrily wiped at the solitary tear escaping from his useless fucking eyes.

Chapter 9

Sat in Holly Lodge that night, Tom listened to Nell talking excitedly about the wedding fair and eating some more mince pies which she always became slightly addicted to in winter and then completely forgot about for the rest of the year. While he was glad to hear her being more positive, and for the genuine excitement to have come back in her voice, he was having trouble concentrating after such a difficult day.

The tree they'd put together had been decorated with Nell's favourite tiny wooden decorations that she'd been collecting since before they'd met. Between the glowing bright white Christmas lights, the small painted decorations twirled on little green strings and larger red and gold baubles dazzled with glitter. If he closed his eyes, he could pretend it was Christmas and that everything was fine. That it was him and Nell, sitting in Holly Lodge, snuggled under their favourite Christmas blankets (she liked the grey, Nordic-patterned one, he liked the one with reindeers on it) and watching the James Bond movie that was always on (his favourite was Roger Moore, hers Sean Connery). But every time he did close his eyes, he was unable to forget the sight of the woman comforting her terrified children. It had been imprinted on his brain and played out on the underside of his eyelids. Nell had put on some gentle Christmas songs and the music would normally have soothed him, but tonight nothing could penetrate the shroud of guilt he was wrapped in.

Nell's voice filled his ears, but the words all mushed together like song lyrics he couldn't quite make out. The accident earlier had played on his mind all day and he'd found that for hours afterwards his hands would shake, and he'd have to drop the scissors, secateurs or whatever it was he was holding. His body was trying to cope with the adrenalin pumping through his system and once it had he was hit with such a huge wave of tiredness he could have slept on the spot slumped over his workstation. The warmth of the fire in the large cast-iron grate permeated any remaining tension and for the first time that day, in the comfort of Holly Lodge, his whiplashed muscles relaxed. He'd replayed those few quick seconds over in his mind time and again just to check his own actions, and he'd definitely looked left and right before pulling out. The only conclusion he could come to was that he simply hadn't seen that people carrier and that raised the question, why?

'What do you think then, Tom?' asked Nell, taking a bite of another mince pie. How many had she had? He looked at the plate and saw three empty silver wrappers. He wouldn't put it past Nell to have eaten them all. He hoped Cat had eaten one because she was looking a bit worn out. Nell raised her eyebrows expectantly. Unsure what she was asking, he wondered whether to have a guess or just come clean about not hearing. He went with a guess.

'I agree,' he replied, hoping it was the right answer.

'You agree?'

'Yeeees?' he replied hesitantly. As Nell's expression changed, he knew he'd made the wrong call, evidenced by Cat and Kieran sniggering.

'You agree that I should pack up the hotel, move to Sweden and start selling that weird, smelly tinned fish they eat over there?'

'Hmm?'

'Busted, mate,' said Kieran. He and Cat were sat on the teal Chesterfield again and Cat was snuggled into his side, cradling a cushion. From her amused expression, he really was busted.

'Weren't you listening to anything I said?' Nell's eyes softened and her voice was full of concern.

'I was listening.'

She sat back with her tea. After taking a sip, she eyed him over the rim of her mug. 'What did I say then?'

'You said …' He hesitated and glanced at Kieran hoping for a clue, but Kieran was enjoying watching him struggle.

'Don't look at me, mate. It's normally me that gets caught out like that.'

'Yeah, it is,' Cat added, jokingly jabbing him in the ribs. 'Normally about wedding stuff.'

'I do not. I love hearing about wedding stuff but you're not telling me anything now.'

Tom's ears pricked up at the slight tension in Kieran's voice, though his mate was trying to sound jovial. Cat responded with a one-shouldered shrug. Her other was nestled into Kieran's side as they cuddled, so things couldn't be that bad, could they?

'It's just boring, detailed stuff. Do you really care what colour napkins we have?'

'No, but I want to hear you talk about it,' Kieran said. 'I want to know that you're happy and help make decisions when you're unsure.'

Cat pecked Kieran on the cheek. 'That's what I've got Nell for.'

Nell didn't look entirely comfortable and when his eyes met hers, it was clear they were both thinking about the wedding dress issue. Tom thought about saying something, but Nell changed the subject. 'So come on, Tom, what did I say?'

Lately she'd been preoccupied with the Langdon Mansion Hotel, so he plumped for that and the video of spider-soup. 'You said you were worried about those gits up at the Langdon Mansion Hotel and—'

'Thomas Barton, you weren't listening at all.' Nell cocked her head to study him, her eyes laden with worry. It made him feel guilty again and he'd had enough of that for today. 'I didn't say anything about the Langdon Mansion Hotel. I'm moving on from that horrifically embarrassing incident and thank you very much for reminding me of spider-soup. What I actually said was that St Herbert's Primary School are holding their Welcome to Christmas carol service on the twenty-ninth of November at the hotel and I'm really excited about it. Even though it might turn out like *Nativity* which I class as a romcom by the way.'

'Surely it's a kids' movie?' asked Kieran.

'Not to Nell,' Cat added, but her voice was fond rather than teasing.

'I love the romance in it though. And when the helicopter lands at the end, and all those children are amazing after no one believed in them and then the lovebirds get together.' Nell pressed a hand to her heart dramatically, but Tom knew that she really did love that film. They watched it every year without fail and it always made her cry. 'I love it.'

Tom tried to brighten and share in Nell's excitement. As he did, he found a little of his worry fall away. Her face glowed when she was happy like this. Her fringe and long blonde hair framed her face so beautifully, emphasising perfectly sized features. She'd rimmed her eyes with kohl liner tonight and he loved how it made them stand out. She fluffed her hair, pulling it forward. She thought her ears were too big, but Tom never had. 'The idea of the kids' concert is amazing.'

As little blurry dots danced in front his vision once more, Tom looked out into the dining room, hoping glancing away from the bright lights of the Christmas tree would help them clear. Through the large windows that ran the length of the external wall he could see out into the large gardens surrounding the house. The last few leaves rustled on the mature trees as the wind grew stronger. Most had fallen onto the grass. All the rain had made it a bright vibrant green and he could just make out the gorgeous shades of chocolate-brown, golden-yellow and crimson from the light spilling out through the dining-room windows. Soon, he and Kieran would be stringing up the fairy lights Nell always brought out and hung around the edge of the garden. She loved to look out and see them twinkling like stars. See, his eyes weren't that bad. If he could make out the different colours of the leaves, there couldn't be anything wrong. Perhaps earlier had just been a one-off freak accident. These things happened. Deep down Tom knew he was kidding himself. His head was beginning to pound again and as much as he loved being with everyone, all he wanted was to go and lie in a dark room. He clung to the fragile thread that maybe he'd had a migraine coming on and that had affected his vision. It certainly felt like a migraine now.

Nell shifted her chair closer to Tom's and her leg rested against his. She gently touched his arm. 'What's wrong, Tom? Are you sure you're okay? You don't seem yourself this evening. Is everything all right with Nigel? And you're quite pale. Have you got a temperature?' She placed her hand on his forehead and he enjoyed the coolness of her fingers and the affection with which she'd put them there.

The sudden urge to grab Nell's hand and wrap his fingers in hers pulsed through every fibre of his body. He fought hard, moving his hands and clasping them together in his lap. He wanted to tell her everything that had happened today and how worried he'd been about the kids in that car. How worried he was about his eyesight and the symptoms that were mounting up. He wanted to tell Nell how worried he was about Grandad Nigel and what would happen if he wasn't there to visit. But if he said the words out loud, he'd have to admit to himself and to the world the possibility that the dreadful thoughts had substance, and no matter how hard he tried, he just wasn't ready to do that yet.

'Nothing,' he replied tightening his hands. 'I've just got a headache. It's been a busy day.'

She eyed him suspiciously but decided not to press. 'Okay. Did I tell you that I've emailed HotelRater and asked them to remove that video as well?'

'Have you?' said Cat, sipping her gin. Tom suddenly realised just how tired she looked. Her job was hard both emotionally and physically, but he'd never seen it have this effect on her. Tom had hoped that tonight all Kieran's worries would be put to bed, but now, his own were mounting. Cat really didn't seem herself. She was quieter and more subdued. She also wasn't teasing him the say way she normally did. Kieran kissed the top of her head and she looked up at him in adoration. Maybe she really was just tired; she certainly seemed to still love him as much as ever. 'I'd leave it up there if I were you, Nell,' Cat continued. 'The Langdon Mansion come out of it looking worse.'

'I can't do that. I think it makes me look as bad as them. I'm sure it would be best for everyone if it just came down.'

'Okay,' Cat replied distractedly. 'It's your choice.'

Tom tried to lighten the mood. 'I think the school thing is a great idea. How did you get involved in that?'

From the look on her face, she'd already told him once, but Nell went through it again and this time he pushed his problems to the back of his mind and paid attention.

Bryan closed the office door behind him, happy to take a break from the madness of Saturday night at the Langdon Mansion Hotel. It was still busy even though they weren't fully booked. They should have been, but since that damn video had been uploaded onto HotelRater, the most visited hotel rating website, they had lost several dinner reservations, and even a few more in the hotel. Bryan was positive Nell Jones had uploaded that video. She must have known the woman who took the recording and got a copy or asked her to do it. Bryan was new to the area, having moved down for the job of deputy manager, but he'd heard that everyone knew everybody else in this place so it wasn't out of the realms of possibility that Nell had got the recording and was using it to save her business, because from his perspective, they came out looking far worse than she did. Either way, they were losing bookings and Kevin was fuming.

Already in the office, peering at the screen of his laptop with a scowl fixed on his face, Kevin opened his mouth to place a manicured fingernail in for a chew. Bryan had never seen Kevin chew a fingernail and the effect was disconcerting.

'Bry, I'm not happy at all about this situation.' He shoved his chair back and began pacing around.

The bright lights from all the hotel windows meant Bryan could see the gardens outside almost as well as in daylight. A great big bush of rhododendrons blew in the wind and though the branches of the tress were mostly bare, the last few leaves that held on tightly were forced off and carried away into the shadows.

'We've got to do something about this bloody video. The only good thing right now is that we've secured that massive holiday firm's Enchanted Ball. Find the Sun are huge. They're taking over the holiday business and if we hold this ball for them and do a good job, it could undo all the damage this bloody woman's done and make us one of their top recommended. To fit them in we're going to have to dump the mayor's party and that's not going to go down well locally.'

'When are you going to tell them?'

'Monday. I can't be bothered before then.' Kevin rubbed a hand over his perfect eyebrows.

Bryan nodded. 'What are we going to do about Nell Jones? I've heard on the grapevine that she's now hosting St Herbert's Primary School nativity play or carol concert, or whatever it is.

She's making herself the darling of the town. And that's in addition to this wedding fair that seems to be creating a buzz. I've had loads of people asking us when we're going to do one.'

Kevin's head shot round. 'How did you hear that?'

'My cousin goes to the knit and natter group she holds at the hotel and Nell was apparently quite open, asking them all if they thought St Herbert's would like to hold it at Holly Lodge as she's right nearby. Apparently, the hall roof has a leak.'

'I don't like this, Bry, I don't like this at all. The Summertons went from us to her, we've lost loads of dinner bookings because of her.' He shook his head. 'We need to discredit her as much as possible. I think we continue with the bad reviews on HotelRater, but I want to get inside that hotel of hers and see exactly how much of our business she's stealing.'

'How do we do that?' Bryan was a reasonably clever man, but he couldn't see how they could get inside the inner workings of her hotel. She wasn't taking on any staff, she didn't have that many on the books and the ones she had probably wouldn't be open to bribery. He'd heard that most of them had been with her since her parents ran the place and there was no substitute for family loyalty. Oh yes, he'd done his homework already and he told Kevin as much. His boss lifted his eyebrows, impressed.

'Well done, Bry. Good work.'

He really did wish Kevin would stop calling him Bry. He hated it. But he didn't want to get on his bad side. If Kevin was right about Find the Sun, he could find himself in a really good position when all this was done. 'So, what were you thinking?'

'What about sending someone along to this carol service? Surely, she won't know who's a parent at the school and who's not. If we can get someone in there they might be able to sneak a look at her reservations and report on how this event goes down with the local community, find out what they're saying about us and if they're talking about the video.'

'Good idea, but I'm afraid it can't be me because I kicked her out of the restaurant. She's seen my face.'

'It can't be me,' said Kevin. 'I'm too busy.'

'Then who?'

Kevin went to chew a fingernail but after examining it decided not to ruin the paintwork. 'Who served Nell that night?'

'Tallulah Jacobs. Why?'

'Damn it. She's just come in asking me if she can train for reception too and get some extra shifts. Apparently, her dad has just lost his job and her mum's stressed out about Christmas. She's got quite a few brothers and sisters. Maybe they go to St Herbert's Primary so it wouldn't be amiss for her to be there.'

A sudden flush of excitement filled Bryan. 'Shall I call her in? I mean, no one remembers their server, do they? I doubt they'd be able to recognise her.'

Kevin's smile was enormous, bright and white. He had teeth that seemed to be two sizes too big for his mouth and where he had them artificially whitened at an extortionate amount it made them stand out even more. 'Yes, get her in here. We'll pay her some overtime for it. There's no way she'll be able to say no.'

Bryan found Tallulah in the restaurant laying up a recently vacated table. He was getting heartily sick and tired of this classical Christmas music. It was so bloody boring. The playlist was sent down by head office and they were expected to play it throughout the public areas from seven in the morning until dinner finished and the last customer had left the restaurant. It was classy and elegant, Kevin had said, and Bryan didn't want to seem too lowbrow by disagreeing, so he put up with it. It didn't stop it appearing in his dreams though, or in the middle of the night when he got up for a wee. Tallulah almost dropped a fork as he neared and stood up, smoothing down her black skirt. 'Come with me, Tallulah, please.'

Before he led the way, Bryan saw the flash of panic in her eyes. His conscience pricked him then disappeared as he flattened his tie. Business was business. Tallulah didn't speak as she followed him down to the office. He opened the door, walking in before her, then waited. A polite smile was fixed on her face, but a redness had already crept up from her neck.

'Tallulah, come in please.' Kevin was all politeness and his big wide grin seemed as natural as it was ever going to. Any smile with teeth that could be seen from space would look slightly menacing. He was sitting on the front edge of his desk, in front of the chair he motioned for her to sit in. One leg was hitched up, the other resting on the floor for support. It made him look creepy, but Bryan wasn't going to say anything. Kevin had no sense of humour for jokes like that. Tallulah glanced at Bryan, her immediate boss, before gingerly lowering herself into the chair. Another flash of conscience told him he should let her know things were all right, that she wasn't in trouble, but he couldn't. Knowing Kevin, and even himself if push came to shove, there was every chance that if this backfired, she'd be under the bus before she had any idea one was coming. 'Thanks for stopping by, Tallulah.'

She hadn't had much choice, thought Bryan.

'We talked earlier about you needing extra hours and I said I'd consider it. Well, I'm happy to say that we have an opportunity for you.' Tallulah's eyes brightened and her shoulders relaxed a little. Bryan felt queasy as Kevin went on. 'It's not on reception but it's something very important to the business. We need someone to do some research on one of our competitors in the town.' Fear and confusion passed over her face, and Kevin raised his hand in a conciliatory fashion. 'Don't look so scared. It's nothing illegal or wrong. We just want to get an idea of what they're doing. You wouldn't want us to lose business and have to lay off staff, would you?'

'N-No,' Tallulah said, but she shifted uncomfortably in her seat. 'But I'm not sure I should—'

'Tallulah, Tallulah, Tallulah. You're a bright girl with lots of potential. You could really go far with this company if you work hard, and you're uniquely placed to do this job for me. I'll be paying you double time as you'll be working in the evenings. Let me explain some more before you give me an answer. You know that woman who put the spider in her soup? The woman Bryan had to ask to leave?' They'd put it about amongst the staff that that was what had happened, rather than François the chef being a lazy turd. Tallulah nodded. 'She got someone to take a video of the whole thing and she's uploaded it to HotelRater to make us look bad.'

'But didn't the spider fall into the soup in the kitchen? That's what Bryan said to Franç—'

'No.' Bryan stepped closer into the room. He should have controlled his temper that night. 'Tallulah, I conducted a full investigation and we established it didn't get into the soup here in the hotel. She must have put it there.' Tallulah's eyes dropped, suitably chastised, and Kevin continued.

'All we want you to do is attend this school carol service she's hosting and if possible, have a look at her reservations. See how busy she is. If you can't, fine. No problem. Just let us know what people are saying. Are they talking about her, or talking about us? Haven't you got little brothers and sisters at St Herbert's Primary?'

'Yes, sir.' As soon as she confirmed it, Bryan nearly punched the air and Kevin leaned back, resting his hands on his hips. 'I've got a younger brother in Year 4 and a sister in Year 1 but—'

'So, you'd be going anyway.' Kevin gave a chuckle that sent an odd sensation up Bryan's spine. 'Double time for going to an event you were already going to? That's not bad, is it?'

'No, sir,' Tallulah replied in a small voice.

'And after that, we'll see what extra hours we have on reception, shall we?' Tallulah nodded and looked at them both uneasily. 'Great.' Kevin's teeth gleamed. 'So, we'll catch up after the carol service. Until then, Bryan can give you as many shifts as he has in the restaurant. Right, Bry?'

'Sure thing.'

'Thank you,' Tallulah said, but having worked with her for a good few months now, Bryan could tell she wasn't completely on board with their plan. When Kevin leaped off the edge of the desk, she stood to leave, and Bryan opened the door for her.

After she'd gone, Kevin congratulated them both on a job well done, but Bryan wasn't feeling as easy about the situation as he thought he would. He sat at his desk and began working on the rota for next week, putting Tallulah's name down as much as possible, but he didn't like the uncomfortable tightness in his stomach. Perhaps he'd pulled a stomach muscle at the gym this morning. It couldn't possibly be a scruple. His father had warned him about those.

Chapter 10

Nell responded to the latest email cancellation with a sigh and all her recent positivity went with it. What a crappy way to start a Monday morning. Normally, Nell didn't mind Mondays. She didn't mind any day she woke up in her little flat, ready to start the day in her hotel. She had a lot of sympathy for people who woke up feeling terrible because they were off, probably in the rain, to a job they hated. Nell had been there herself so every day she got to be her own boss in her own gorgeous hotel, was a gift. A gift that was rapidly being taken away from her.

Another bad review had popped up on HotelRater and as a result, a last-minute booking had cancelled. Yet again though, Nell couldn't place the guests or recall any of the conversations mentioned. She was sure they'd never stayed with her and wondered if they'd tagged the wrong hotel. There must be Holly Lodges up and the down the country, it wasn't an unusual name. Feeling a bit of her enthusiasm come back, she carried on.

A sip of tea helped to restore her a little more, but it was all very confusing. She'd never had two bad reviews in a whole year before and now there were two in the space of a week. She'd have to email HotelRater again but was pretty sure there wasn't much they could do. That was the point of sites like that. They were

108

open for people to post honest reviews and the admins had already refused to remove the video of the spider-soup incident. She'd have to think of something else, maybe another local event she could host to make up for the lost income. And there was the restaurant idea she'd been costing out. She closed the spreadsheet and shut the lid of her laptop.

From her spot in the dining room, she looked out of the large conservatory windows at the back of the house. It was far too cold to work from her little reception desk in the hall and as Harry had been the only guest in there for the last half an hour, she'd moved there clad in her favourite massive oversized jumper and second favourite pair of jeans. The jumper was pink and fluffy and had little sequin stars on it. It was her favourite tasteful Christmas jumper. She'd held back slightly feeling that if she put on one of her crazy full-on musical Christmas jumpers in mid-November, everyone – and by everyone she meant Harry – might think she'd gone mad but nothing would stop her edging stealthily into Christmas. The lounge had already been decorated and she'd replaced the centrepieces on the dining-room tables with mason jars full of tiny silver baubles with a long, tapered silver candle. What she needed was some more of Tom's displays to go along the windowsills. They would really make everything feel festive.

She was a bit worried about him at the moment. He hadn't been right on Saturday night and it wasn't the first time he'd mentioned a headache. Maybe he was working too hard? Or maybe she was relying on him too much for moral support and it was stressing him out. They'd always been so honest with each other. A friendship that had grown from solid roots. She'd even fancied him a little when they first met. The thought amused her now she came to think of it. But then he'd got a girlfriend fairly quickly after starting uni and it hadn't been long till she'd begun dating a boy from one of her lectures. It hadn't lasted more than two weeks but by then, because they hung out together so much, they'd fallen into the friend zone. She just wanted to know that he was all right though. Maybe she could ask Kieran.

Casting a glance at Harry, who was sipping his Earl Grey and reading the paper, she pulled the sleeves down over her fingers and got back to the task at hand. There were a couple more things to work through before Tom arrived. Her mum and dad would be calling soon for their regular catch-up and Nell wanted to be able to tell them everything was fine. She'd have to mention the spider-soup video and, eyeing her tea, decided something stronger might be in order before that conversation took place.

Mrs Meggett, breakfast chef extraordinaire, bustled out into the dining room and began to clear away the last few remaining breakfast things. 'Why on earth do people eat this horrible muesli stuff?' She always called it 'moozli' and said it like it was rat poison and not the darling of the health conscious. Nell loved the odd way she pronounced certain things. She also said 'croyzonts' instead of croissants and it was guaranteed to brighten up any miserable morning. 'Give me a full cooked breakfast any day of the week. I've had one every day since I was old enough to stand at a stove and it's never done my arteries any harm.' Packing away the unopened mini boxes of cereal into a large wicker basket, she gripped the handles and carted it back off into the kitchen. Harry glanced at her over the edge of his paper.

Nell hoped against hope they'd get some more bookings soon because if she didn't, she'd have to cut Mrs Meggett's hours and the thought of doing that right before Christmas made her sick to her stomach.

The scrape of a chair drew her attention from the computer screen and a second later Harry was sitting at her table. He wore a beige turtle-neck sweater and whereas it made most men look like they had double chins, man boobs and middle-aged spreads, all this one did was gently underline his firm jaw bereft of even a hint of shaving rash. 'She's really somethin', huh?'

'She really is,' Nell replied. 'But I don't know what I'd do

110

without her. And no one cooks as a good a breakfast in the whole of the county.'

'That I can believe. So, Nell, the best hostess in the whole of Great Britain, I'm definitely going to be here for Thanksgiving, so where's the best place to find all my home food comforts? I'm talking, a giant stuffed turkey, good ol' American gravy, not this strange brown stuff you guys seem to like. I mean it's delicious but American gravy is kind of different. Then I gotta have sweet potato pie—'

Nell could listen to him speak all day, and as he listed the dishes he had to eat with a childlike glee, Nell's imagination whisked her off to a house complete with white picket fence on an American prairie. Together they were cooking a Thanksgiving feast. She was even wearing a chequered apron which in normal life she'd burn before wearing and was pulling dishes from the oven. It was one of the scenes she loved most in any Hallmark movie.

'Nell?'

'Yes?' she replied, suddenly brought back to reality.

'Do you know anywhere I can get food like that?'

'Umm, not really. Sorry. There aren't many restaurants in Swallowtail Bay that do all-American stuff.' Then she had an amazing idea. 'If you're not seeing your family that night why don't I cook for you here? I mean, if you fancy it?' She felt her cheeks colour under his intent yet quizzical gaze.

'You'd do that for me?'

'Yeah.' Nell tried to pretend it was the type of offer she made all her guests. 'If you wanted to.'

'That'd be amazing.' He sat back and began wagging his finger at her knowingly. 'See, I knew you'd be the best hostess in the whole of Great Britain as soon as I walked in that door.' He took a big sip of his tea. 'I gotta go. I'm being taken to somewhere called Halebury Castle today. Am I gonna love it or hate it?'

'Definitely love it. It's beautiful.'

'Great.' He grabbed his coat from the back of his chair and slung it across his broad shoulders. 'Have a wonderful day.'

'You too.'

Just then, Tom's cheerful voice echoed through the hall as he pushed open the front door and trilled a greeting. She heard the kerfuffle as they passed each other, giving greetings and goodbyes in equal measure.

'Morning Tom,' Nell called. 'I'm in the dining room.'

From the sound of his voice today, he was back to his normal cheerful self and that was reassuring. Tom walked through the open doorway and as he did, Nell giggled. An enormous wreath framed his face and he was pulling silly model faces.

'Blimey, who's that for?'

'You, of course.' Tom continued turning his head left and right and pouting making Nell laugh even more.

'Me?'

'Yeah.'

'But you don't normally deliver my wreath until the first weekend of December.'

Tom struck a final pose and laid the wreath on an empty table. 'I know but you don't normally put your decorations up this early, so I thought I'd get your wreath done and on the door to cheer you up.'

Nell picked it up, admiring its beauty and the skill it took to make one. It was wonderful. A perfect circle made with fir, pinecones, cinnamon sticks and dried orange slices. At the top there was a red velvet ribbon tied into a bow and at the bottom there hung two small pieces of driftwood that he'd painted silver and in black fancy lettering written 'Holly Lodge'. 'Tom, it's amazing. This is definitely your best one yet.' Nell felt her heart glow on seeing his reaction to her compliment.

'There's one last thing we need though.' He helped her lay the wreath on the table. 'Wait here.'

Nell wrapped her hands over her chest, ready for his final

touch. He did the same thing every year and it had become their own little tradition. Tom left, pulling his secateurs from his pocket as he went. When he came back Nell bit her lip from the pure joy running through her system and stepped back as he studied the sprigs of holly he'd snipped from the hedges outside. She watched his face as he found the spots he'd kept just for those pieces. That he'd thought of her so intently when making it, warmed her up from inside and her hands dropped from across her chest. Recently, having Tom around was giving her a strange feeling at times, like when they were together her soul was stronger and she was more ready to take on the world. Theirs was truly a timeless friendship. The fine lines at the corners of his eyes scrunched together and he pursed his mouth a little as he concentrated. After a second, he stepped back. 'Ta da!'

'It's amazing. Thank you.' For some reason she felt more than just a hug was needed and holding on to his shoulder, she stood on tiptoe and kissed his cheek. Tom's eyes shot to hers and the importance of the moment they were sharing reflected in them. Feeling embarrassed because she didn't normally say thank you like that, she turned her eyes to the wreath and ran her fingertips over the ribbon. 'This'll be just the thing to welcome my special Christmas guests.'

'Your what?'

'I had this amazing idea. I'm going to offer a deluxe Christmas romance package complete with flowers, chocolates and wine. There'll be a lower rate for in the week and I'll charge a bit more for weekends. And as an added extra I'm going to supply a small gift for each guest. I'm going to make each room super Christmassy too. I can't afford a tree for each one, but I was hoping I could have some garlands like you made for the fireplace. On the tea trays, I'll leave hot chocolate sachets and a little jar of marshmallows so people can make hot chocolates in their rooms.'

'That's a great idea.' As the awkwardness of the moment was forgotten he carried on. 'How did you think of that?'

'Let's get a drink first, then I'll tell you. I let my tea go cold.' She didn't mention it had gone cold while she'd been busy gazing at Harry. As a rule, she didn't really talk to Tom about her boyfriends. He was a typical loyal and true friend – a bit like a big brother – and the men she mentioned were never quite good enough for her. But to be fair, she'd always been the same when it had come to his girlfriends.

'Again?'

'Yeah, you know what I'm like. Why don't you make yourself useful and put that on the door while I make the drinks?'

Tom followed her down into the basement and went to the maintenance cupboard while she headed into the kitchen. Before long, he'd finished and shaken off his coat, and Nell had returned with the tea. They were back in the dining room as a weak and watery sun shone between the bare branches of the trees. For a second, Nell admired the twisting beauty of the boughs, tapering from thick stems to small reaching fingers, naked and bereft of leaves. Strong winds had left them stark and empty. *Empty*. The word rang around her head like an alarm going off and for a second, she reflected on how that was how she felt at times lately. Empty. Maybe that was why she was disappearing into her own world more and more. She'd been prone to it since sitting her exams at uni. It was a coping mechanism and one she'd at first thought she'd grow out of, but she hadn't. Sometimes she wished she could and at other times it helped more than anything else.

'So, what's the deal?' Tom sipped his tea and grimaced. Nell liked hers super strong, like builder's tea. She let it brew until weird bits started floating on the top. Tom liked his the colour of wheat. The trouble was Nell tended to get side-tracked doing or thinking about other things and both cups ended up exactly how she liked them. She pulled her chair in a little closer to the table.

'I've lost another booking, and another bad review has come up on HotelRater—'

'Really? Who? Was it that couple who wanted an ergonomic mattress because he put his back out shagging?'

Nell rested her chin in her hands. 'I don't know who it was and honestly, I have no recollection of the things they're moaning about.'

'Like what?'

'They say there was a lack of free toiletries in the room when they arrived, but no one's ever mentioned that to me, and I always check the rooms before people check in making sure everything's perfect. I don't think I'd have forgotten that.'

Tom gazed over the top of his cup. 'That's not really a reason to complain either. You just come down and ask for them, don't you?'

'Yeah and no one's ever done that. I always check they're there. And that's just the start. They talk about rudeness from staff, ignoring requests for extra pillows and the place being dirty and dusty.'

'This place is spotless. Mrs Palmer would be mortified if she heard that.'

'I know.'

Mrs Palmer was Nell's cleaner and a more disciplined, thorough woman had never been seen. She had a system and it was thanks to that system nothing was ever missed. She regularly cleared the cobwebs, cleaned the skirting boards, wiped the paintwork and door handles, and did all those jobs Nell wouldn't even think of.

'I'm going to email HotelRater to see if it's possible these people tagged the wrong hotel, but I don't think it'll do anything. Anyway, I need to come up with some more ideas. The dining room thing is going to take a while to sort out and though I hope Cat's wedding will help get some bookings, not many people get married this time of year so even with the wedding fair, I'm really looking at next year – summer, more likely, or even the year after – before I get any returns on that. I thought I could use some Valentine's decorations in the rooms for that romance touch and with some Christmassy bits it should work well. Actually, could you do some small wreaths for the room doors? I'll pay for them of course. I'm costing out everything else and I think it'll work. I thought about what you said and I'm not going to go overboard on the gifts. I'm going to have a budget that I stick to, but I can still make things personal and special.'

'Sounds good to me.' Tom took another mouthful of tea and pulled a face.

'You don't have to drink it if it's that bad.'

'It's fine.'

'No, it's not,' she laughed. 'You look like I'm pouring vinegar down your throat. I'll make you another one in a minute and I promise I won't get side-tracked.'

Tom laughed. 'I really don't know how you manage to forget you're making tea. It's the most important drink in this country. What were you thinking about this time?'

'Nothing.' Nell could feel herself blushing. She didn't want to admit that once she'd poured the hot water onto the teabag, she'd thought about kissing Tom on the cheek and his delivery of the wreath. Her romantic brain had turned it into a wonderful scenario for her and a vague version of Harry, but it had been strange. While the face was a weird mix of Harry and Tom, the personality she felt was most definitely Tom's. It had made her feel a bit ... odd. 'I went looking for biscuits and got distracted.'

'Okay. Oh, listen. I wanted to ask you something about Cat.' Tom's voice now carried a serious tone. 'I had a call from Kieran the other day and he said she seemed different. You know, really, really stressed. He wondered if she'd said anything to you. I know you told me about the dress, but do you think things have got worse? They seemed happy enough the other night but ... I don't know.'

Nell shifted uncomfortably. She opened her mouth to tell him about Cat flirting with Niall, but Cat had sworn she didn't realise she was flirting and Tom was right, the other night Cat had been

116

a bit quiet but she was still cuddled up with Kieran and they seemed happy. Was it worth burdening Tom with something he couldn't talk about? Weighing it up, it wasn't worth stressing him out and he was already nervous about his best man's speech. 'Said anything about what exactly?'

'I don't know. The wedding? Her mum? Kieran said she wasn't herself.'

With an effort, Nell assembled her thoughts into a tactful but non-worrying answer. 'I think she's just a bit stressed with Brenda. She's normally a force to be reckoned with but lately she's gone into overdrive. I'm sure Cat will be fine. Though she did text me yesterday and even though she hated them before, she's changed the party favours from traditional sugared almonds to little Christmas present-shaped chocolates. I've now got to source them online and try and get them at a reasonable price. I could do without it with only a month to go, and I don't know why she's changed her mind, but I guess it's a bride's prerogative.'

'Sounds fun. Okay, if you're sure everything's all right.'

Just then, Harry strolled back into the dining room and Nell's heart fluttered at this unexpected treat. 'Can you believe I forgot my wallet?' he said, laughing, in his wonderful American accent. 'What a dope. Hey, Nell, while I'm here, where's a good place to take my family for lunch? I want some proper British food but something classy. Where would you recommend?'

'The Fisherman's Wharf is nice. It's down on the seafront. I'd definitely recommend there if you like fish.'

'Good job I do then, thanks.' He stepped away but paused before he left. 'Oh, and you're looking really pretty today. I meant to tell you earlier. I like that sweater. It makes your eyes sparkle.'

And on that bombshell, he left. Nell didn't hear compliments like that often and her chest tightened. Tom stared at her like they'd just had a fleeting visit from aliens.

'So who's the new guest?'

'That's my American who's staying for three weeks. I did tell

117

you about him.' She hadn't told him how handsome and charming he was though.

'Oh right.'

'What?'

Tom's face clouded over. 'Nothing. He's just a bit in your face, isn't he?'

'He asked for a restaurant recommendation. All my guests ask for that. It's not exactly in your face.'

Tom harrumphed as a gust of wind whipped around the house, rattling the windowpanes and shaking the bushes in the garden. Nell and Tom watched the world outside, glad to be indoors in the warmth of the dining room. A light drizzle tapped against the window and onto the stone path that led down to the holly bench. While there were a few benches dotted here and there, the holly bench was at the bottom of the garden and her favourite place to sit in the summer. When Tom continued, he quickly changed the subject. 'Grandad Nigel wanted me to check you're still coming to help decorate the care home. He said he was looking forward to seeing you.'

'Yes, of course. I wouldn't miss it for the world.' She loved seeing Grandad Nigel. He was cheeky and a bit of a rebel in the care home. 'I've got a little present for the old boy too.'

'Don't tell him that, he won't let you leave. That reminds me though. Have you got any spare Christmas decorations?'

Nell cocked her head to one side. Tom was so mad about Christmas he normally had enough decorations for every room in his house and then some. Many a time he'd ended up giving the overspill to friends or turning the flower shop into some kind of floral Christmas grotto. All it needed was a jolly fat Santa. As for her, she'd put out everything she had and needed more if she was hosting this carol service and offering a romantic Christmas retreat. 'Not really. Why?'

'Tracey, the care home manager, texted me to say she'd been in the loft and most of their decorations are so old and tatty she

118

can't use them. I've got a box I can bring along. I didn't know if you had any spare. She's in desperate need of donations because they don't have the budget to buy any.' Giving up on his tea he pushed his cup away. 'Between you and me I think she spent all her decorating budget on Halloween when she frightened all the residents half to death with that life-size talking butler. The only person who wasn't scared was Grandad and that was only because he couldn't actually see it. He could hear it all though. Said it was the noisiest thing he'd heard since the Blitz.'

Nell giggled. 'I'd love to help but I can't afford to buy any to donate out of the business account. Not with doing this romantic Christmas escape idea. I might be able to get some out of my own money. It's not like I've got loads of Christmas presents to buy and I've already got most of yours and wrapped them too.'

'Really?' She nodded and another strange moment passed between them. She wondered if Tom felt it too because he was beginning to blush, but she couldn't quite figure out what it was or what it meant. Nothing was different between them, was it? 'You don't need to buy anything. I'm sure we'll think of something. I'll bring some greenery along with me too. I've got some left over from the wreaths I've made so far.'

'There's an idea,' said Nell.

'Another one?' Tom teased. 'Don't hurt yourself.'

'Ha ha.' But while he might tease, she'd just had another great idea to boost her business. At least, she thought it was a good idea. 'How about we host a wreath-making session here? Not massive ones like you made me but smaller ones, and then we can decorate the care home with them? I'll still come on Sunday and help you decorate with what they've got and then we can top up with some of the wreaths made here afterwards.'

'But there'll be loads. If everyone makes one each what will we do with what's left?'

Nell shrugged. 'I don't know. You could sell them and donate

119

the money to the care home? Tracey's always going on about wanting to get the residents out and about a bit more, and I'm not that far from them. We can do it here in the dining room.' She motioned around at the large redundant space they were sitting in. She really needed to get more use from it and what better way than to invite the older generation. Maybe she could convince the choir of St Herbert's Primary School to stop by for a little carol singing practice. That would really put smiles on the residents faces.

Tom was nodding faster and faster the more she spoke. 'And I tell you what,' he replied, now as excited as she was. 'I bet I could get our lovely mayor along. She owes me a favour after I heavily discounted her wreath for the town hall. It might raise your profile a bit locally and show the Langdon Mansion Hotel, and anyone else who didn't know it already, that you're not the type of person to put spiders in their soup.'

'I like it,' she replied, over her mug.

'I'll ring Tracey now and see when she's free.' Tom stood and found his mobile in the pocket of his coat. He dialled and leaned on the back of his chair as he spoke. From her place as spectator, the conversation seemed positive but there were some long silences where Nell couldn't discern what Tracey was saying. Finally, Tom rang off. 'Are we on?' she asked, pressing her hands together in prayer.

The grin that gripped his face was mirrored on her own, but she still hung on until he said the words. 'Yep. We're definitely on.'

'Yay!' Nell jumped up and grabbed hold of Tom, pulling him into a tight embrace. For a second, she felt his cheek press into her own and a surge of affection shot through her body. The force with which she'd grabbed him knocked him a little off balance and she held on to his arms to stop herself falling too. Instinctively, his hands went around her waist. They righted themselves and for a fleeting moment she didn't want him to let go.

Then she remembered it was Tom and told herself not to be so stupid. Tom was blushing furiously too.

After ensuring her feet were both flat on the ground, Nell brushed her clothes down, feeling more self-conscious than she ever had before. Harry liked to remind her, she was British, and there was only one thing to do in embarrassing moments when you're British. She cleared her throat. 'More tea?'

Chapter 11

The clean, cold November air seeped into Tom's bones no matter how many layers of clothes he had on. Under a pale, watery sun, it was the perfect day to decorate the care home and bring some warmth and festive spirit to the residents. They were generally a happy and congenial bunch aside from the one or two curmudgeons who liked a moan, but overall, the residents were always up for a bit of Christmas fun.

The care home, located in the middle of town, was equidistant from Tom's house and Holly Lodge and he'd been able to roll out of bed as late as possible which he'd needed after another headache had come on last night. He'd gone to bed early and this morning, the pounding behind his eyes had faded and he was feeling much better.

Stepping out of his van, Tom shivered a little and pulled his coat tighter around him. He'd even worn a woolly hat and gloves; anything to keep him warm against the wind. As he began unpacking all the stuff for the care home – the spare decorations he had left over; tinsel, baubles and all the stuff from the shop he'd set aside – his mind wandered to the American staying at Holly Lodge.

How was a man like Tom supposed to compete in the world

of women when there were men like that? Superhero lookalikes that if he stood next to them, he'd look like a weedy nerd. Nell's eyes had sparkled when she'd seen him. A sparkle that he'd give absolutely anything to see in her beautiful round eyes, but a horrible sinking feeling told him that wasn't ever going to happen. 'You look so pretty today,' he said to himself in a terrible American accent, then scoffed. He'd told Nell she looked pretty hundreds of times, but her eyes never lit up like that when he said it. And yet, when he'd caught her as they'd nearly fallen over, it felt so right to him – so perfect. Like his were the only arms capable of holding her as lovingly and carefully as she deserved. Nell was prone to flights of fancy and almost believed in the romcom movies she watched, but Tom had read enough true stories to know that sometimes, people did meet coincidentally and fell in love. As long as that didn't happen with her handsome American guest, he thought. Tom shrugged a box forwards as Nell pulled up, parking next to him. The gravel crunched under the wheels of her car, then under her boots as she climbed out.

'Good morning,' she sang happily. It was wonderful to hear her so positive after the rough week she'd had. She'd always loved her life, but these bad reviews were making her restless. It was understandable, but he wished he could reassure her. Jealously, he suspected some of her good mood was due to the American. Under her giant Russian-style faux fur hat and with her flared jeans sticking out the bottom she looked like she'd stepped out of a 1970s fashion magazine. Her hair was curling in the slight dampness of the air and shiny lip gloss drew his eyes to her lips, but her face fell as she spotted the side of his van. 'What happened to your van?'

Tom's shoulders tensed. He should have parked in the corner next to the big prickly bush so she wouldn't have seen it, but he'd been excited at the prospect of Christmasifying the care home and too busy finding a space big enough to open the back doors fully to think about it. 'Oh, that.' He kept his voice calm. 'Just a little prang on the roundabout last Saturday.'

'It doesn't look like a little prang. It's scraped right through your logo.'

How right she was. It had scared him to death, and he hadn't slept properly since for fear of what might have happened and as his health worries intensified. The thought of the kids in the car, scared and shaken, still filled him with guilt a week later. His throat closed over at the memory trapping the fear and worry deep down in his belly. Nell ran her hand over the rough metal. He'd have to take it to the garage and get it sorted out. What would people think if he kept driving around town like that? A scraped-through logo didn't exactly speak of a florist who took care. And Janie had been amazing when he'd got back and mentioned briefly what had happened. She'd immediately dived into his filing cabinet and pulled out the insurance details for him in case he needed to call them. Her age, cheerful demeanour and happy-go-lucky attitude belied a spot-on business sense and organised mind which had been exactly what he needed in his frazzled state.

'Hang on,' Nell said, scowling. 'Did you say last Saturday? Why didn't you say something when we were at the hotel that night?'

'Just leave it, Nell, okay. Like I said, it's just a prang. How's the hotel?'

Suspicion writ large on her face, as his tone was entirely unconvincing. 'The hotel is absolutely fine, thank you and don't change the subject. As soon as I saw you in the hotel, I knew something had happened. You were really weird Saturday night. You were so quiet.' There was the slightest edge of annoyance to her voice because he hadn't confided in her, but it softened almost immediately. 'Why didn't you just tell me? I could have helped.'

'I don't know. It just slipped my mind,' he lied.

'How can it have slipped your mind? This was quite a "prang".' She made speech mark signs in the air with her fingers.

'Why are you doing that?' he asked teasingly, trying to lighten the mood.

'Doing what?'

'Making the bunny rabbit ears in mid-air.' Nell scowled, unimpressed. 'Nell, honestly, it's fine. I just don't want to talk about it, okay?'

'Why not?' Normally, he'd tell her everything and not just brush it off, so he knew this was an unusual response, but he just couldn't bring himself to go through it all right now. 'If it was just a prang, you've got nothing to be ashamed of. These things happen all the time. It could have happened to anyone.'

Tom took a deep breath and asked again if she'd let things be. He'd been stupid not to just tell her about it. Hiding it had made things so much worse. He should have known Nell would need to know everything so she could make him feel better. Tom had an enduring love of Christmas and had been so excited this morning. Now it was all leaching away and being replaced with guilt and shame. She'd hate to know he felt like that, but he just couldn't bring himself to open up. The fear inside him was too strong. You didn't have to be a genius to know it was an unhealthy response, but one he didn't have the strength to fight this morning. 'Can you help me unload some of this lot, please?'

'No, not until you tell me exactly what happened.' Even though she shivered as the cold wind whipped around the sides of the van, she crossed her arms over her giant parka, defiant and unmoving. At least she tried to cross her arms over; the coat was so big she didn't quite manage it.

'It's freezing out here, Nell. I'm not standing in a car park in the cold explaining again.'

'But you haven't explained anything at all.' Her arms fell back to her sides. 'I'm not trying to nag you, I'm worried about you. Come on, Tom, talk to me. Don't shut me out. Who else was involved? You looked so pale the other night. Why don't you want to talk about it?'

'Because it was my fault,' he replied sharply. As he'd imagined and feared, Nell's face registered first shock and then unease. She'd be disappointed in him – he was disappointed in himself – and he hated it. Forcing his fingers underneath his hat he scratched his head. 'I checked before pulling out, but I didn't see anything.' Tom snatched up some willow branches from the boot of the van. 'Look, I really don't want to talk about it, Nell, okay. I feel terrible enough as it is.'

He knew he should tell her about all the other things that were going on with his sight: the swimmers, the time it was taking for his eyes to adjust to darkness, the accidents he'd had in the middle of the night when he'd bashed into things walking to the toilet. And of course, the headaches. They were the most worrying thing.

'Okay,' she replied, her voice quiet, accepting the matter was closed. She moved beside him and placed her hand on his shoulder giving it a squeeze, then drew it down his back. It was supposed to be a friendly gesture but his feelings for Nell surged at her touch. He so wanted to turn around and let her hug him, but it was getting harder and harder to be close to her knowing she'd never feel the same way. 'I'm here if you need to talk though, Tom. You're my best friend. And I know you, don't beat yourself up, okay? Accidents happen all the time.' Maybe he was projecting his own disappointment onto her as she didn't seem to blame him. He nodded but didn't turn around and was grateful to hear her voice happy and cheerful once more. 'What do you want me to take then?'

Tom tried to put some life back into his voice and drag himself out of the bad mood. 'Can you bring that box and I'll carry some of this heavy stuff.'

'Okay. Wait, is that a tree?'

This time he found some of his Christmas spirit returning. 'Yeah. It was on sale and I just couldn't resist. I might need to buy some more baubles.'

'I love that you love Christmas so much.' She leaned gently

into his shoulder and rested her head there. The smell of her perfume carried on the wind and the familiarity of it calmed him.

'You do?'

'Of course. I always have. It's one of my favourite things about you.' Lifting her head and stepping away, she said, 'Shall I tell you my favourite Christmas joke?'

The final remnants of tension floated from his muscles. 'Go on then.'

'What do Santa's elves learn at school?'

'I don't know, what do Santa's elves learn at school?'

'The elfabet!' Tom rolled his eyes. 'Do you see? Because they're elves and they learn the elfabet. It's like the alphabet but for elves!'

'Nell?'

'Yes?'

'Stop talking and take that box.'

Both grinning and with arms laden, they walked inside.

Tracey was busy bustling around, settling her residents in the TV room and finding jigsaw puzzles and activities for them. It was hot with that stuffy, slightly damp warmth that comes from having the radiators on full blast, and after stashing some boxes in the corner of the room, Nell and Tom immediately began to strip away their outer layers.

'Hello, you two,' said Tracey. 'We're all really looking forward to this, aren't we, guys?' A few members of staff lifted their heads and waved a greeting. 'A bit of Christmas sparkle will cheer us up a treat.'

'Well, you know Tom' said Nell. 'Nothing stops him at Christmas time.'

Putting the exchange outside behind them, he beamed. 'Yep. Mr Christmas is here and ready to get to work.'

'Is that my grandson?' Nigel's voice boomed from the corner of the TV room. Edith was sitting beside him as usual.

'It is, Grandad. I'm just coming over.'

'And where's that lovely young lady of yours?' Tom cringed. Grandad loved a massively unsubtle hint.

Nell bounded over and planted a big kiss on his cheek. 'Here I am, Nigel. You're looking well.'

'Am I?'

'Yes, you are.' She adjusted the brown and red plaid blanket on his knees. 'And I got you a present.'

'Lucky me. Anything good?' He shifted, sitting up a little. Tom found a chair for Nell and one for himself, carrying them over and putting them in front of Nigel.

Nell ran back to her handbag then handed Nigel a tin of his favourite biscuits. They were hideously expensive Italian ones: handmade affairs from an artisan baker in town. Nell had made the mistake of buying them for his grandad one birthday and the old boy had acquired a taste for them. She'd already eased the lid open a little so he could get to them easily, which was typical of her kindness.

'I think I know what this might be. You always bring the best treats, Nell.' He opened the box and sniffed in the delicious scent of the almond biscuits.

'Hey!' said Tom. 'I'd like to remind you that I smuggled in your favourite sherry last year.'

'Tracey found that within two minutes of it being on the property, boy,' Nigel said with a grump. 'She put me on more stingy rations than I had in the war. I think there's still some left actually.'

'I did not,' Tracey shouted, coming over and pausing with her hands on her voluminous hips. 'Cheeky devil. I let you have more than was good for you.'

'I'm 87, what's the point in being good?' Though his eyes were cloudy and unseeing, there was still a life to them that spilled out encouraging those around him to feel the same way.

'Tom,' Tracey continued, 'I've added our decorations to your pile, but we haven't got much. I'm a bit worried the rest of the place is going to look like a bit of a poor effort.'

128

'Not by the time I'm done,' Tom replied. 'This isn't even half of what I've got in the van. And I brought a tree. It's a fake one, but it's nice and big and I thought it'd go well in the TV room. There's plenty of stuff for everywhere else.' He pointed to the boxes they'd brought in so far and Tracey's eyes lit up.

'Let's crack on then, shall we?'

With a sweet peck on Grandad's cheek, Nell followed Tom, leaving Nigel to enjoy his biscuits. The decorating began and Tracey put on a CD of Christmas songs on the old stereo in the corner of the room. Tom glanced at Nell from time to time and was pleased to see her enjoying herself. There were one or two moments when he caught her looking at him, but his heart didn't sing at the idea. He knew it was only because she was worried after the car accident.

After decorating the TV room with a beautiful garland over the fireplace, paper chains made with the residents hanging across the ceilings, and tinsel over the picture frames on the walls, all they needed was the tree. They loved getting the residents involved and many enjoyed a singsong while hanging up a bauble. There was a lovely sense of friendship in the care home and Tracey was a wonderful, caring manager, encouraging everyone. Tom decided he'd have to get Tracey a present for Christmas too, not just the box of chocolates he'd got her last year. He wanted to get her something special. They all worked together to get the lights up around the ceiling, and some star-shaped willow decorations he also planned to sell in the shop, laughing and joking with Nigel and Tracey as they did so.

Nell broke off at one point to have a bop with one of the livelier residents and her laughter rang out as he twirled her around the floor, the spectators clapping along in time to the music. Tom's foot was tapping too, as everyone had such a good time. When it came to hanging the final lot of baubles, Nell and Tom placed them on a tray and handed them out to the residents so they could each place one on.

Just as he finished hanging the last decoration on the tree, Nell came to stand beside him. 'What were you and Edith chatting about?' he asked.

'She was just telling me about her husband and how they met. He was a soldier in the Second World War, and they married halfway through it, worried they might not get a chance at all. Don't you think that's awful. Imagine meeting the love of your life and them having to go away and you thinking you might never see them again?'

A dreaminess had come to Nell's eyes and Tom knew that, though her eyes were open, they were only seeing the world in her head. For as long as he'd known her, her vivid imagination and empathetic nature had always taken her into her own little universe. The trouble was the real world never quite measured up.

'Can you imagine how awful that is?' she repeated when she'd joined them again.

'I can. Scary too.'

'When I get married,' Nell began, toying with a skinny bit of tinsel Tom had discarded, 'I'm going to have—'

'A massive shiny diamond as big as your head?'

'No.' She nudged him playfully with her arm. 'I want a small round solitaire. Gold, not silver. Something quiet and simple and elegant and beautiful.'

'Like you.' The words had escaped his mouth, unbidden, and he blushed.

Nell eyes widened in surprise. As she recovered, she bit her lip. 'Simple? Thanks.'

'I meant – I meant …' He wanted to say elegant and beautiful and as she laughed at his stuttering, her eyes sparkled like they had when she looked at Harry. Or had he imagined it? Just wishful thinking on his part.

'You can stop digging now, Tom. It's fine.' But a blush lingered on her cheeks.

Leaving him standing there, tongue tied and hot, Nell went and sat down with Grandad Nigel who had demolished a third of the biscuits.

'Did you actually share any of those?' asked Nell.

'Of course I did. I gave one to Edith.'

'Just one?'

Tom loved watching them together. Grandad Nigel was almost as fond of Nell as he was of him. And that Nell was equally as fond made his heart full.

After hanging the last bits of bedraggled tinsel onto a picture frame, Tom joined them. 'Have you still got room for your lunch? Tracey will kill you if you don't.'

'I'm not afraid of her,' Nigel replied, puffing his chest out a bit. Tracey's voice carried across the room.

'You should be.' She came to join them, carrying a tray of mince pies. 'Don't say I don't treat you lot. Mince pie, anyone?' Tom and Nell shuffled backwards as the residents descended on the tray. They knocked into each other and when she turned to him, happy and content, that sparkle was there again. They'd bashed into each other hundreds of times over the years, but today the lack of distance between them seemed charged with a new, different energy. Tracey's words, muffled as she ate a mince pie, cut through. 'It's not looking too bad in here, but the halls are a bit bare as are most of the corridors.'

'With the wreath-making event on Wednesday,' said Tom, 'I think we'll have enough to do a nice display in the hall.'

'The residents are so excited to be making their own and some have promised them to their own families. Isn't that lovely? What a brilliant idea, Nell.'

'Thank you,' Nell said, 'but it was Tom's idea too.'

'Mostly yours though.'

'They're off again!' shouted Grandad Nigel. 'Honestly, you're like a honeymoon couple, always being nice to each other.'

'By the time we've done that,' said Tom, swiftly moving the

131

conversation along, 'we'll have more than enough, and I've got a couple of garlands that went a bit wonky. You can have those if you like?'

'Wonky garlands? Gee, thanks.' She and Nell giggled.

'They're fine. It's just one's missing a couple of berry clusters and the other I thought I'd picked up silver spray paint and I'd actually picked up neon pink so it's ended up with a bit of a weird hue where I tried to cover it. It's barely visible, but I can't sell it.'

'Okay then,' Tracey said with a grin. 'Bring me your wonky garlands over the next few days. Let's get some more lights up, shall we?'

Finally finished, Tom stood back with Nell. The feel of her body against his filled him with such warmth he was sure it was radiating out of his eyes. She met his gaze. What he wouldn't give to have a smile like that to wake up to every day. To roll over and watch those thick lashes lift and happiness fill her face at the prospect of being with him. But it was too much to hope.

'Edith, are they staring at each other again?' asked Nigel, causing Nell to study her fingernails. Tom squeezed his jaw tightly shut as they shifted apart.

'Anyone for a little Christmas sherry?' Nell asked, looking around mischievously. 'I think Nigel's got some to share.'

'Traitor,' the old man mumbled as a wonderfully loving smile plumped his old whiskery cheeks.

Chapter 12

Nell flitted around the dining room full of nervous energy. The care home residents were coming over any minute for the wreath-making. Too edgy to sit still this morning, she'd caved into pressure from Brenda and put some posters up around town about Mr Scrooge, including a picture of the little scamp and the number of the hotel in case anyone wanted to claim him. She really hoped they didn't. Mr Scrooge was so at home at Holly Lodge now. In the evenings he curled up on her lap and had even taken to following her into her basement flat and sleeping on her bed. She'd taken him for a check-up at the vet's who, after checking for a microchip, had given him a clean bill of health apart from being under-nourished, and sent her away with some flea tablets that he'd happily gobbled down when she wrapped them in ham.

On a long table underneath one of the large windows in the dining room, the snacks were laid out. Casting her eyes over the display, made even more Christmassy by the tinsel she'd woven between them, Nell was sure there were enough to go around. She'd roped Niall into coming over and making treats for the wreath-making and he was doing a great job. His chocolate bark, made of milk chocolate with white chocolate swirls and cranberries studded in, was proving a big hit with her and she had to make an effort not to eat it all. Then there were truffles, chocolate peppermint cookies, traditional coconut ice and much more besides. Nell imagined the residents' faces when they came over.

After breakfast that morning, Nell had said goodbye to Harry who was off to see his family. His mother lived in the bay and had been poorly recently. Nell hadn't pressed for details, but it seemed she was on the mend now and had been the reason for his unplanned trip over. When he'd told her, a tingle had run from the top of her head to her toes that he'd travelled at the last minute to see her. He hadn't even made a hotel reservation which was how he'd ended up at Holly Lodge. 'Was it fate?' she wondered. Those amazing coincidences that somehow brought two people together, so their lives intertwined. It was like *Serendipity*. A very underrated film in her opinion. She hoped that the person his life had intertwined with was her.

While Niall was in the kitchen working away, Nell shoved on some Christmas music to set the scene and couldn't resist dancing away as she adjusted the urns of water, glasses and cups she'd laid out. She'd prepared some coffee and hot water for tea and pulled out the best milk jugs for the milk. Pinching a chocolate truffle from one of the plates, Nell adjusted the biscuits on another and the mince pies on their glass cake stand. The smells coming from the kitchen were divine and making her stomach grumble even though she'd already had about five chocolates. The mayor was coming too but they had no idea what time. Nell's mind flew back to that night at the Langdon Mansion Hotel. Hopefully the mayor wouldn't mention anything after having seen everything that night. It had taken a while to get over the embarrassment, but Nell was thinking about it less and less as her plans for the business began to move forward. It was only two days until the wedding fair and she was incredibly excited for that.

She heard a van pull up out front and went to the window to see Tom jump out, back to his usual happy self. That scrape he'd been in wasn't sitting easily with Nell. A horrible tightness settled in her stomach that something was wrong, but then he bounded in with his usual enthusiasm and she found it hard to reconcile the way he had always been so honest with her with the idea that he had a secret. Perhaps she was worrying about nothing – just her brain being overly dramatic as usual.

'Hey, you,' he said, bashing his cold hands together. 'This place looks good. You ready to help me unpack?'

'Yeah, of course,' Nell replied, determined to make the day wonderful and fun for them both. She followed him out and they unloaded the van. He'd brought a small polystyrene wreath for everyone to decorate as well as boxes of tiny pinecones, reams of ribbon, different-coloured foliage and all manner of adornments like stars, bells and tiny sparkly Christmas trees. Seeing it all set out, Nell jiggled up and down on her toes in excitement. This was going to be such a wonderful event, but her excitement was in danger of vanishing as the terrifying Brenda and Cat unexpectedly walked in.

'Thomas,' Brenda said, arms outstretched. He glanced at Nell in alarm and she bit her lip to stop from laughing. 'Thomas, how lovely to see you.'

'Lovely to see you too, Brenda.'

Brenda air-kissed his cheeks then surveyed him, casting her eyes up and down over his frame. Nell saw him swallow. 'You don't look well. What's the matter with you?'

'Nothing. I promise.' He ran his hands through his floppy hair. Nell glanced back at the window wondering if the light was different today as it reflected the different blond colours in his hair. It was something she hadn't really noticed before. Frown lines were etching deeper and deeper into his forehead as they aged and the crow's feet at the corner of his lacklustre eyes were reaching longer. He looked tired and careworn, like he wasn't sleeping well, and the tightness in her stomach intensified.

Cat followed behind Brenda like a teenager who had just been told off. Her punky pink hair was so at odds with her downtrodden demeanour, Nell could only wonder what Brenda had been moaning about now.

'Brenda,' Nell said, in a bid to save Tom. 'What are you doing here? You're not here for the wreath-making, are you?'

Brenda adjusted the lapels on her long coat. 'Cat and I have had a little chat about the buffet, and we think we need to make some changes.' Nell looked at Cat. The corner of her mouth had lifted in resignation. 'Yes. When Cat told me Niall was going to be here for this event of yours, I thought it was the perfect opportunity to talk to him. I can't do this evening; I'm going to the cinema with the women's union.'

'Is that the same as the WI?' Nell asked. It wasn't exactly the point, but Brenda's social life was a whirlwind of confusing clubs.

'No, it's not.' Brenda gracefully moved her bag from one arm to another. 'They don't make jam.'

'Hey, Cat,' said Nell. She'd told Cat in good faith about the wreath-making event and about getting Niall in, knowing that Cat would keep it quiet. What torture had Brenda used to get it out of her? Or maybe Brenda had heard it somewhere else. The event had been talked about in town and the local paper had even mentioned it. Worryingly though, she'd thought Cat was working today and knowing how she loved her job and her patients, she was surprised to see her. 'I thought you had patients to see today?'

Cat cast her eyes down. 'I moved a couple of appointments to help Mum out. Where's Niall?' she asked, brightening a little.

'He's downstairs in the kitchen.' Cat seemed suddenly far more alert and happier to be there. She made to move off, but Nell grabbed her arm. 'But he's working, preparing some more snacks for the wreath-making. You can talk to him in ten minutes once the residents are here and we've got started. Until then, please can you two wait in the lounge? Brenda, can I get you a tea or coffee?'

Brenda's face was a picture of repressed disapproval, her lips pursed together in an unattractive line. She clearly thought she could come in and roam around the place like she owned it, and while Nell didn't mind Cat doing that because they'd been friends for so long, Brenda was too apt to find fault. After the last few 'helpful' comments, Nell didn't let her anywhere unaccompanied anymore. 'Tea, please. Earl Grey, but I don't suppose you have it.'

'I do,' Nell replied happily and motioned to the lounge for them to make themselves comfortable.

Brenda and Cat plonked in a seat by the window while Nell and Tom began laying out everything on the tables. They didn't have quite enough scissors to go around and only two glue-guns, but Tracey had suggested Tom was in charge of those. She didn't need a health and safety disaster on her hands with residents gluing their fingers together or to anyone else for that matter.

Just before the minibus arrived, Niall popped upstairs with another plate of truffles and more chocolate bark. Though Cat thought she hadn't noticed, Nell saw the way she sat a little straighter when Niall walked in. Since Kieran and Cat had got together at uni, no man or woman had ever got close to either of them. That she was seemingly interested in Niall in the run-up to her wedding was extremely worrying. It wasn't like Cat at all, but she was still refusing to change her mind over the dress and Nell didn't want to mention it anymore for fear of them falling out. Was this playful behaviour a superficial front for her feelings over the dress? Or was there some other underlying unhappiness that Nell was yet to identify? Deep down she was sure Cat wanted to marry Kieran from the way she was around him. She was back to her old self whenever she was with him, happy and affectionate. It was all very confusing.

'Hi, Niall,' Cat said, getting to her feet and walking into the dining room as he laid out some more food. 'How are you?' Nell watched her linger by Niall's elbow.

'I'm good. You look nice today.' He leaned in closer and Nell edged over to make sure she could hear. 'I'm sorry your mum didn't like the buffet choices.'

Cat glanced behind her, checking Brenda wasn't earwigging. 'The only reason she didn't like them was because we made them without her. It's not your food, she'd have found fault with whatever we chose.'

'Mums, hey?'

Niall had been friendly enough, but Nell needed to keep everything on track for the care home. 'Niall? How's the mulled wine going?'

He turned to face her. 'Fabulous. The whole kitchen smells like Christmas. I'll bring it up as soon as the mayor arrives. Just pop down and let me know, or text me, okay?' He made his way back downstairs to the basement kitchen and Cat was forced to sit with her mum in the lounge.

A minibus arrived out front and half of the residents slowly emerged from the side. Never had Nell been happier to have installed the gentle, easy-to-walk-up ramp that led to her front door. Running to greet them, Tom followed behind. 'Hi everyone, come on inside it's lovely and warm, and we've got treats and hot chocolate and mulled wine.'

Tracey bustled over. 'After we've unloaded this lot we'll head back and get the rest. Everyone's so excited.'

'Is Grandad Nigel here?' asked Tom, looking around.

'Not yet – he's on the next run.'

Tom nodded, but for some reason seemed reluctant to move and he blinked in the daylight. After a second, Nell said, 'Tom, shall we head back inside and start settling people at the tables?'

'Yeah, yeah sure.'

Once they were moving, he relaxed again, and she slid her hand into his and gave it a squeeze. He looked down at her and the concern on his face sent a sudden wave of a deep, heavy, unnamed emotion down her spine. 'This is going to be awesome. So, is everyone doing one each?'

'Yeah, or if they've got bad sight they can work with a partner. I'm guessing Grandad will work with Edith.'

'I'm so looking forward to this. Aren't you?'

'I am,' he replied. 'Is Harry around today?'

'No, he's out with his family again. I think it's so sweet, don't you?'

'Hmm.' But she could tell he didn't agree. She got a strange feeling that maybe he didn't like Harry, but had no idea why. He'd been perfectly pleasant to Tom on the few occasions they'd met.

'He's my only guest right now.' When he'd come down from his room that morning, they'd had a quiet moment in the dining room together. He'd been excited about Thanksgiving dinner and there'd been such a spark of electricity between them Nell was sure she'd burst into flames if he stayed much longer. Tom stared at her and the way his eyes pierced kept her imagination at bay. 'I'm hoping to get a few more soon from this December romance deal I'm doing.'

'I hope so too. I didn't expect Brenda to be here.'

'Me neither.' At least Cat hadn't been flirty this time and until she knew for sure there was something to worry about, she wasn't going to tell Tom. He had enough on his plate with the accident and getting his van fixed up. 'I'm not going to let Brenda ruin today's fun, though.'

'Good, but I have to say she's the reason I'm so terrified of my best man's speech. I've known velociraptors with less bite, and I can already see her glaring at me from the top table as I speak.'

'Maybe we can spike the punch and get her sozzled before it all kicks off.'

'Now that's a plan.' Tom laughed as they walked back inside. 'Nice jumper by the way.'

Nell smiled at the fake compliment. She knew the enormous Christmas jumper was a bit shapeless, but she loved it nonetheless. It was warm and cosy and had a giant penguin wearing a hat and scarf on it. She'd had it for ages, and it was one of her favourites. 'Where's yours, Mr Christmas?' He opened the front of his coat to show off his own Christmas jumper bearing a Christmas tree with light up baubles. As he switched it on, the tiny decorations glowed and so did she. 'I love it.'

The second lot of residents arrived about five minutes later, including Nigel and Edith.

'Well, this is a grand idea, Nell,' he said as he was guided past.

'Thanks, Nigel.' She gave him a kiss on the cheek and Tom took his arm.

'This way, Grandad.'

In the dining room, the joyful sound of chatter was growing. The residents began to enjoy themselves, settling into seats and digging through the piles of adornments in front of them. Nell made sure everyone was comfortable, finding cushions from the lounge and extra blankets, making sure they were tucked in tight around their legs. She even threw a couple more logs on the fire in the lounge and whacked the heating up, despite Brenda's protests. By the time everyone was beavering away with their wreaths, Holly Lodge was filled with Christmas music, laughter and noise.

When Nell knew everyone was settled and she wasn't needed for five minutes, she made Brenda and Cat tea and nipped into the lounge to tell them they could head downstairs to see Niall. Cat moved so fast even Brenda was surprised and Nell followed them downstairs, determined to keep an eye on things for as long as possible. As soon as the mayor arrived, she'd come back up, but for now she wanted to see what was happening with Cat and Niall.

He'd been right about the kitchen. Where the mulled wine simmered away it smelled like Christmas. The metal worktops were covered in extra plates of truffles, mince pies, Niall's signature chocolate bark and other delights, and Nell filled with that excitement so particular to the festive season. A feeling of exhilaration, anticipation, hope and love.

'Wow, Niall.' Cat was so close to him Nell was surprised she wasn't in the way. 'This place smells amazing. Can I steal a coconut ice?'

'Sure,' he replied.

'Darling.' Brenda stepped forwards. 'Do you really think you should? I mean, we've talked about this already. No one wants to be a tubby bride.'

'She'll be beautiful,' Nell interjected. Niall looked down at petite Cat from his grand six-foot height. His gaze lingered on Cat for a second longer than was strictly necessary, but Nell wasn't sure if it was just to let her know she didn't need to listen to her mother or because he was secretly hinting he fancied her. 'So, what are we here to discuss?' Nell asked, taking charge. She didn't have a lot of time to waste with the mayor arriving soon and she didn't want to leave Tom managing everything upstairs either.

Brenda pulled out the dreaded wedding file. 'I'm not sure the buffet choices are really suitable.'

'In what way?' asked Niall, leaning over the counter. To his credit, his tone was one of professional enquiry and not at all judgemental which Nell's would have been. She and Cat had been excited about the menu when they'd had the initial tasting and thought there was something there for everyone. Niall had even asked if he could use it as a sample menu for the wedding fair so it couldn't be that outlandish.

'I think we need a few different things. I know Cat has strange tastes but I'm not sure mini pumpkin pies and Mississippi mud macaroons are the sort of thing Aunty Phyllis would like.'

'But if it's what Cat wants …' Niall let the sentence trail away and everyone turned to Cat. Nell's heart lurched for her friend. Her mother's eyes were boring into her pulling her one way, and Niall's sweet gaze, trying to help her stand up to Brenda, pulled her another.

141

'I think Mum's got a point,' Cat said meekly. 'I might have got a bit carried away with what I like and not thought about my guests.'

'But it's your wedding,' Nell pointed out, earning the death stare from Brenda. Nell used her friendship like a suit of armour and continued. 'Cat should have what *she* wants on her wedding day.'

But Brenda was not to be derailed. 'Nell, darling, when you finally get married, you'll understand exactly what I mean. Until then, let's just carry on with some common sense, shall we?' If Brenda's helmet-hair hadn't offered indestructible protection, Nell would have hit her with a saucepan. Instead she looked to Cat who was trying her best to catch Niall's eye like an awkward teenager; Nell hoped it was to let him know she was sorry for Brenda and not another attempt at flirting. She tried one more time to help her friend have the wedding of her dreams.

'Cat, you loved the idea of the Mississippi macaroons and you said they were the best thing you'd ever tasted. And you said pumpkin pies were a dead cert.'

'Nell, it's fine,' Cat replied sternly. 'I don't mind.'

Maybe divide and conquer would work. 'Cat, can you just help me find that cocktail idea we were working on? It's in my living room. Niall could you just top up the mince pies upstairs? I'm sure they're going down a treat. And Brenda, while we do that why don't you have one of Niall's amazing chocolate truffles?' Nell took one off the platter and shoved it into Brenda's face. She looked horrified like the calories were already jumping out and turning parts of her body into fat. Nell took Cat by the arm and led her into the living room of her tiny flat.

'We weren't working on a cocktail idea,' Cat said, folding her arms over her chest. 'What are you doing?'

'Cat, I love you. So please don't be mad at me but you've got to stop letting your mum bully you so much. It's like the mum in *What's Your Number?* who keeps saying she won't come to the wedding if her ex-husband's there—'

142

'Just for once will you stop with the romcom movies, Nell,' Cat exploded. The vehemence in her voice nearly knocked Nell over. 'Life isn't like a romcom movie. It's not just a giant misunderstanding that somehow rights itself in the end.'

Nell's cheeks stung like she'd been slapped. 'Maybe not, but Brenda's taking over everything, telling you what you can and can't have at *your* wedding and undoing all the decisions you've been so sure of. You've got to stand up to her.' Cat didn't respond, just dropped her eyes to the floor. 'Maybe Kieran should come with you next time. I know he wants to be more involved in the wedding.' At the mention of his name Cat lifted her head.

'Kieran? He wouldn't know where to begin in planning a wedding.'

'But he'd be there to back you up against your mum.'

'She's just trying to help.'

'I know, darling.' Nell stepped forward and took Cat's hands, but they hung limply in hers. 'But she's not helping, is she? She's making you miserable. She's planning a second wedding for herself, not your one. Every decision should be about what you and Kieran want and no one else. I mean this in the nicest possible way but stop being such a wet blanket before you end up having a wedding for her and not you. It's not like you. I don't know where the real you has gone lately.'

'What do you mean *the real me*?' Cat fired back, yanking her hands away and wrapping them over her chest once more. 'I'm right here. I'm just trying to be considerate of other people's feelings, that's all. Which is more than I can say for you right now.'

Nell didn't want to fight and figured the wet blanket comment had been a bit too much. 'Cat, I'm sorry I—'

'Just let me make whatever decisions I want for *my* wedding, okay? And if I choose to have a quiet life then that is my choice and you should accept it.'

'I just want you to turn up on your wedding day and look around and see everything you've ever wanted, that's all.'

143

'I'm a grown woman, Nell. I know what I'm doing. Maybe Mum's right. When you're planning your own wedding, you'll understand.'

Quietly gasping in a breath, Nell closed her mouth. From Brenda the remark hadn't hurt but from Cat it was like a knife in her back. She briefly thought about challenging Cat on her flirting with Niall, but she'd been much better today and had sworn that she hadn't realised she was doing it before. Nell decided not to mention it now as the atmosphere was tense enough. 'But what about Kieran? It's his wedding too. What does he want?'

'Kieran wouldn't have a clue. Look, I love him, but he knows about gardening and flowers. He doesn't know about planning a wedding.'

'I think if you give him a chance—'

'Oh, just mind your own business, Nell. You think you know everything about romance and weddings and love because you've watched some movies, but you don't. You're supposed to be my friend and friends support each other.' Cat spun on her heel and flounced out of the flat back to the kitchen.

Nell remained in her small living room, shell-shocked. She and Cat never argued, and even if they did it was in a jokey fake manner and they always managed to come to some agreement in the end. This was totally new, and Nell didn't like it one bit. Just then her phone beeped with a message. It was Tom. The mayor had arrived. Rolling her shoulders back and taking a deep breath, she decided to leave Cat and Brenda to it and get back to her event.

As she walked through the kitchen to see Cat very close to Niall, Nell said, 'Niall, could you bring the mulled wine up, please? The mayor's here.' Then let the door swing shut behind her.

Though she hadn't been downstairs long, the wreath-making was in full swing when she came back up. They were looking lovely and all so different. An older lady, who had a real eye for it, had made one of dark red ribbon and studded it with silver pine cones and tiny sprigs of holly. Others were more traditional and full of festive greenery. So many joyful faces greeted her it felt like Holly Lodge was full of life, love and Christmas spirit. It was just a shame it hadn't reached the basement.

'Ah, there you are,' said the mayor, Linda Armstrong. Her long, thick grey hair was tied back in a messy plait and fixed with a velvet scrunchy. As it was an informal occasion, she'd worn wide-legged suit trousers with a high-necked jumper and three or four long necklaces adorned with giant coloured stones.

'Mayor, how are you? Isn't this lovely?' From the corner of her eye she saw Niall bring up a large silver bowl full of mulled wine with a ladle sticking out the side.

'It certainly is. How wonderful to see so many of our elderly citizens out and about, socialising and enjoying some festive fun.'

'Speaking of which,' said the mayor's consort, 'might have a little drop of that mulled wine. Looks delicious.' Nell and Tom exchanged glances. Arnold Armstrong enjoyed his wife's role as mayor as much as possible on account of all the free booze he was provided with. He was a lovely man but could sometimes over-indulge. Now, he helped himself to a ladle full, plopping it into one of the small glass cups provided. 'Ah, lovely. You'll have to give me the recipe for this, Nell. The best mulled wine I've ever tasted. And I've tasted a lot recently.'

Linda fired a warning glance at her husband, then surveyed the room. 'This really is just wonderful to see, Tom. Thank you for inviting me. These wreaths are going to be beautiful. Whatever will you do with them all?'

'I'm not really sure to be honest. Some will go back to the care home to decorate there and I know some of the residents have promised theirs to their families, but there's going to be more than I thought. I'd anticipated some people wouldn't want to do it, but everyone's been so excited I've got more than I bargained for.'

Linda leaned in. 'If you've got any spare, I could use them

around town. We've got lights but there are a few strategic points I could hang a wreath. And a wreath made by some of our local residents in one of our local hotels would mean so much. I think we could do a whole marketing campaign about it. What do you think, Nell?'

'That sounds great.'

Arnold came over with another glass of mulled wine. 'And it'd get you some local publicity, dear, wouldn't it?'

Linda carried on. 'And I understand you've got the wedding fair this weekend and you're hosting St Herbert's Welcome to Christmas carol singing in a week's time?'

'Yes,' Nell replied bouncing on her toes. 'I'm going to be busy. I'm really looking forward to them both. I've never done anything like it before.'

'I know the headteacher of St Herbert's and she is so thrilled the night can go ahead. She was so worried all the children's hard work would be in vain. You've saved the day.'

Nell could feel how cheesy her grin was, but she didn't care. It felt amazing to be thought so well of. 'A few of the older kids should be coming along at three to sing some carols. I hope you'll stay for that. We thought the residents would like it.'

'I'm sure they will.' Linda's forehead wrinkled as she frowned. 'If only all our hotels were as welcoming as yours, Nell. It's lovely that you're such a part of the community. It's just a shame that some seem to think they're too high and mighty to deal with the riff-raff.'

Tom and Nell both looked at each other in confusion, but it was Nell who asked the question. 'Is everything all right, Mayor?'

Linda sighed and took a glass of mulled wine provided by Tom. He poured another and handed it to Nell. The strong smells of deep, rich red wine, orange, cinnamon and clove filled her nose.

'I was hoping to hold a winter wonderland Christmas party for my fellow councillors and everyone who works on the town council, and it was supposed to be held at the Langdon Mansion Hotel, but they've since told us they can't accommodate us because there was a booking error.'

'What sort of booking error?' Nell asked.

Linda shrugged. 'I don't know, but they're now making a big thing of the fact they're holding a huge event for a travel company and it just happens to be on the same night as our do was.'

'What are you going to do?' Tom asked.

'I guess I'll have to cancel. There aren't many venues that aren't booked up already.'

Nell spotted Tom flashing his eyes at her, but she couldn't figure out what he wanted. She looked around, checked her top for mulled wine dribbles and at last, admitted defeat. She gave her head a slight shake to show she hadn't the slightest idea why he was wiggling his eyebrows at her. With a slight shake of his head, Tom gave in to her cluelessness. 'What about holding it here, Mayor?'

'Here?' Linda looked around taking in the size of the room. 'I'm not sure the dining room will be big enough.'

Nell finally caught on to what he was saying and grinned. 'But we can open the double doors so the lounge and dining room are both open and the same for the conservatory so this will all make one huge space. Look.' She strode over to the lounge and showed the mayor how the doors folded back. Nell pulled the doors closed again. 'And behind you.' In excitement, Nell jogged to the conservatory, weaving between staff from the care home, and folded the doors back there. The air was a little cold and a couple of grumbles sounded around her. Nell closed them quickly and went back to the mayor. 'It's what I'm doing for my friend's wedding next month. In the lounge, we can remove all the armchairs and coffee tables so it's another standing space, or just place seating around the edges. And we can place smaller tables around the edge of the dining room for refreshments and set up a bar in the conservatory. The conservatory is like another room too and if it's dry, we can even set up some heaters in the garden because that's a lovely space too. My favourite spot is down the path to the tall holly hedge at the bottom. There's a bench there and a few more dotted around.'

'And if you have a winter wonderland theme …' Tom started to speak then paused, squeezing his eyes tightly shut. Worry inched its way down Nell's back, but then he opened his eyes again, carrying on as if nothing was wrong. 'We could decorate each doorway making them into a snowy Narnia-like arch. I can twist willow and fir branches up and we can pin some holly sprigs. You won't see it isn't one big space.'

The mayor looked between them both, and Nell could see they were beginning to convince her. 'But what about food?'

'Just let me know your budget,' said Nell excitedly. 'And what sort of thing you'd like, and I'll sort it out. All the food today is made by a local caterer called Niall Peters. Try some of the chocolate bark.' She grabbed the platter and held it out for her. As the chocolate melted in her mouth, the mayor's eyes closed with pleasure and Nell could tell the deal had been sealed. 'What do you think?'

'I think it's a wonderful idea,' Linda replied. Nell could have kissed Tom. She glanced at him with that idea in mind and an image of her lips meeting his flew across her brain. A strange feeling rose through her chest and into her heart. With his usual impeccable timing, Grandad Nigel decided to say something embarrassing.

'Are those two being lovey-dovey again?'

As much as Nell loved Nigel, he really needed to get it out of his head that anything romantic would ever happen between her and Tom. They were friends, that's all. So, what was this strange niggling at the back of her mind?

With a loud bang, the door to the basement bounded open and Brenda came storming out with Cat stomping along behind.

Luckily, they bypassed the dining room and headed straight down the hall towards the front door.

'Excuse me a moment,' Nell said to the mayor and ran off to see what was happening.

'You're turning into a bridezilla, Catherine Wilson. I never thought it of a daughter of mine but there, I've said it.'

Nell's mouth nearly hit the floor, especially when Cat responded vitriolically. 'Ha! Bridezilla? Chance would be a fine thing.'

'I don't know what you mean.'

They left the building and Nell watched them climb into Brenda's car and speed off into the distance. Nell turned and walked back into the house, seeing Niall come up from the basement looking shell-shocked. 'What happened down there?'

'I'm not really sure,' he said, scratching the back of his head. 'One minute Brenda was talking about mini chocolate macaroons and the next thing I know, Cat's gone off on one saying that's exactly the same thing as the Mississippi macaroons she wanted and her mum was just trying to take over as per usual. Then she demanded the Mississippi macaroons be re-instated and told her mum that the pumpkin pies were going back on the menu and if she didn't like it, she could not bother coming to the wedding.'

Nell blinked. 'Cat? Cat said all that?' So, it seemed she wasn't just shouting at Nell at the moment. Nell was beginning to seriously worry that this wedding wouldn't be going ahead and the idea that she should talk to Kieran moved up in her mind.

'I couldn't believe it. I didn't know where to put myself and Brenda looked like she wanted to stab me. I was only trying to give Cat some backup. I've met some intimidating mothers in my time and can normally help everyone reach a compromise, but Brenda's ...' He didn't finish the sentence. 'Sorry I shouldn't be saying anything about my clients.'

'She's not your client, Cat is. And don't worry, I know what you mean. That stabbing expression? Her face is always like that.

149

You're not in any real danger. I'd better call Cat and see if she's all right.'

'Can you tell her I'm sorry and I hope she's okay?'

'Sure,' Nell replied. Having heard Niall speak she felt a little reassured that he wasn't encouraging Cat to flirt, which meant it was all coming from her. After their row, would Cat even pick up if she called? She'd been so angry at Nell.

On a day when so much had gone right, she should have been happy, dancing for joy that her hotel was full of people and becoming more and more important to the town this Christmas, but if she lost her best friend in the process, it hardly seemed worth it.

At just after three, six of the older children in the choir of St Herbert's Primary turned up. Tom and Nell settled everyone in the lounge with drinks and refreshments when the children started to sing. The faces of the older residents softened as they watched the children perform a few carols, clapping and saying 'bravo' when they'd finished. Even without accompanying music they sounded beautiful and Nell found herself tearing up. Tom was by her side and when she looked up at him, he gently wiped an escaping tear away with his fingertips. When his skin touched hers she suddenly felt like everything was right with the world. He'd never done that to her before and her throat tightened unexpectedly.

She sent the kids away with a goody bag full of Niall's treats and began tidying up the dining room and all the leftover things. But as her sense of success faded, reality came crashing in. Her relationship with Cat was going south, the pressure of the wedding was beginning to tell on everyone, and the wedding fair would be a disaster if her only couple were on the verge of splitting already. She just hoped today was a moment of madness for her best friend – something that would pass quickly and quietly. If it wasn't, and the wedding didn't go ahead, more than just the future of Holly Lodge was at stake.

Chapter 13

'Welcome to Holly Lodge. Thank you so much for coming,' Nell said from her little reception booth in the hallway as another loved-up couple arrived. Crowded with people who'd come for the wedding fair, there wasn't much room in Holly Lodge. Nell was buzzing with energy. Tom rushed through the door and shook off his coat, stuffing it behind her tall reception desk that was more like a lectern. Thrilled and relieved in equal measure at how well things were going, she wrapped her arms around him, pinning his arms by his side. 'There's so many people here already.'

'I know,' he laughed. 'I can't believe how busy it is, especially for a Sunday. Sorry I'm a bit late. I had to umm, sort something out.'

'Is everything okay?'

'Yeah. It was nothing serious.'

Nell had never known Tom to be late to anything, but after the accident with his van, she didn't want to press. 'I've saved you the best spot obviously. You're in the lounge near the Christmas tree, next to The Love Heart Boutique.'

'Brill. I'll just grab some bits from the van. I've bought different-sized bouquets and buttonholes.'

'I'm sure people will love them. You're the best florist in town.'

151

'Don't say it too loudly or you'll upset the others.' He motioned to the other Swallowtail Bay florists who were setting up in the dining room.

All the doors that separated the lounge, dining room and conservatory had been opened so Holly Lodge was one large, open-plan space. It was absolutely full of anyone who might play a part in someone's wedding. There were different caterers, bridal shops from nearby towns, and florists (none as good as Tom, obviously, but she had to be fair) and even Hetty, the most amazing local event planner, was here. If anyone was struggling to know where to start, she'd surely have everything sorted for them in a matter of weeks. She'd even prepared some wedding checklists to hand out and Nell had nabbed her own copy, certain it would come in useful for Cat's wedding. That was if Cat's wedding went ahead, she thought, before quickly dismissing the gloomy idea. Everyone had tiffs and even pre-wedding jitters and hopefully by now Cat would have calmed down.

Where Nell was, in the entrance hall, she'd laid a small table in front of her little booth stacked high with Holly Lodge's glossy wedding brochures and little biscuits Mrs Meggett had baked. Next to them was a supply of takeaway cups and a small urn of hot chocolate. If someone didn't want a hot chocolate, there were tea and coffee urns set up in the conservatory, but space was at a premium. It was a vibrant autumn day with a clear blue sky and a bright golden sun. When she'd seen it this morning, she couldn't help but feel excited. Sunshine always made the world better, but the air was still frosty, reminding you that Christmas was just around the corner as it nipped at your nose. She'd debated long and hard about what music to play on the small stereo system in the lounge, wondering if something classical or jazzy was better for a wedding fair, or if something Christmassy was best. She wanted the place to feel cosy and festive, so had compromised and put on Michael Bublé's Christmas album. With the place now fully decorated and only a week to go until December started, Nell was bursting with festive fun. It really added to the magical celebratory atmosphere.

As she'd expected, romance was palpable in the air. It was almost as if she could reach out and touch it. Chatter filled the air and before she knew it Tom was back with his flowers. 'What time are Cat and Kieran coming?' he asked as he rushed into the lounge to take his spot. 'Hi, Hetty. How's life?'

'Really good thanks, Tom. We've got big plans for next year.'

'Glad to hear it.'

Nell spoke to him from the doorway. 'They should be here any minute.' She didn't want to talk about their problems in front of anyone else so kept her concerns to herself. It would be the first time she'd seen Cat since their argument and despite thinking it through more times than was good for her, she still wasn't sure what to say to get them back on track. Over the last week she'd picked up her phone ready to text, then put it down again, unsure what to say. She'd even watched *Bridesmaids* just to see the scene where Annie and Helen make up, hoping it would give her some pointers. She'd cried through a lot of it, which had been therapeutic at the time, but now she was nervous and still didn't have a clue what to say.

A large group of women arrived, chattering and giggling, and Nell welcomed them, motioning for them to go through to the lounge and begin looking around. The wedding fair had only been open for half an hour and it was already jam-packed. A sure sign that she was on the right track with this idea. Zoe would be arriving soon to cover reception and greet everyone, allowing Nell to mingle and show people around the hotel and up to the rooms if they wanted to see them. Tom had made her some more garlands and with all her decorations for the romance package every room looked great. She'd even gone a little overboard in the honeymoon suite and it was absolutely stunning. If anyone was on the fence about a winter wedding, they wouldn't be after seeing that.

With Zoe's arrival, Nell was free to start mingling. 'Let me know if you need anything, Zoe,' she called over her shoulder as she headed off. Tom's table was busy as he presented the different styles of bouquet he could offer. He had pictures of some of the others he'd done so they could see the different seasons. His summer bouquets of hand-tied, bright yellow sunflowers and white camellia were particularly show-stopping, perfect for a country wedding. And she remembered one he'd made the year before for a spring wedding of a dozen dazzling tulips in blush-pink, pale lavender and peach tied with twine. Of all of his creations, Nell couldn't draw her eyes away from the Christmas ones he had on show today. She adored the deep, velvety red and dove-white roses mixed with white-tipped pine-cones and gleaming red berries. Then and there she decided she'd have a winter wedding when she got married. There wouldn't be snow – a white wedding would be too much to ask for in rainy old Britain – but deep down she knew her heart belonged to Holly Lodge and it was here she'd want to marry her soul mate.

Moving around the room, Hetty was animatedly chatting to a couple, making them laugh. She exuded confidence and Nell decided to roll her shoulders back and channel some of that kick-ass spirit. Today was going to be great, she could feel it in her bones. The Love Heart Boutique had brought a couple of large catalogues full of wedding dresses. Nell couldn't resist a little look at the gowns and spied the one Cat was to wear, reminding her of how much she wanted her best friend to be happy.

The dining room was busiest of all as that's where Niall and the majority of the vendors were. Nell took a moment to enjoy the sight before her and snapped some pictures on her phone in case she needed some marketing photos later.

'Hey.' The voice beside her was small but she knew exactly who it was and turned to see Cat. Kieran had his arm around her waist but let go when Nell, overcome with emotion, stepped forward to hug her best friend. As it turned out, no forethought was required as the words tumbled out of their own accord.

'I'm sorry about the other day,' Nell said quickly. 'I shouldn't have moaned at you. You're right, it is your wedding. I just want you to be happy.'

'I'm sorry too,' Cat replied into her shoulder. 'It was Mum. She really got to me on the drive over with all the don't eat this, don't eat that stuff and I took it out on you.'

Kieran backed off. 'I'll leave you ladies to it.'

'Where are you going?' asked Cat.

'I thought I'd go and see Tom and talk about buttonholes.'

'I've already decided on the buttonholes.'

Kieran shifted slightly and Nell's nerves began to bubble once more. Cat was clearly still cutting Kieran out of the decision-making process. 'Okay, then I'll ask him what we're having.'

'Why? You don't know anything about flowers.'

'Actually,' said Kieran, quite kindly considering Cat had just completely disregarded the fact he was a gardener, 'I know quite a lot about flowers, but don't worry, I won't change anything.'

Nell took Cat's hands, eager to continue their reconciliation. 'Are you okay? I've been so worried about you, but I didn't want to call when you were working because I know how busy you are and I thought about texting, but I wasn't sure what to say.'

'It's fine. I should've texted you and apologised for being a complete baby and having a tantrum in front of everyone.'

'It's forgotten,' she said, happiness rocketing through her. 'And you weren't a baby. You were standing up for yourself. Your mum's face was a picture. It was exactly like that time we took her to that play for her birthday and unbeknownst to us, the actors kept getting naked.'

Cat laughed. 'That was one of the best days of my life. Every time one of them came on in all their glory, bits everywhere, she'd huff and study her programme—'

'Or tut at us for giggling. I'm sure she thought we'd done it on purpose.'

'I don't think I've ever seen her so embarrassed.'

'Not since you got a caution at uni for stealing traffic cones.' They were talking as easily as they always had, and Nell relaxed.

'The other day, she didn't speak to me at all on the way home in the car. When she pulled up at my place, I thought she was going to push me out rather than stop.'

'Has it done any good? Has she got the message you want to make your own decisions for the wedding?'

'She's backed off a bit, but I'm not sure it'll last.'

'We can hope. Want to have a look around with me?' Nell craned her neck to check where Kieran was and as the crowd had disappeared from Tom's table, she could see them chatting, but it wouldn't be long before he was busy again.

'Sure. Where's Harry today?'

'He's gone to see his mum again.'

'That's sweet.'

'Isn't it?' She ignored the gleam in Cat's eye.

'He's very attractive.'

'I suppose so,' Nell joked.

'Just don't go getting ideas, Nell, okay.' Cat's voice was soft, but her words made Nell's stomach lurch.

'Ideas about what?'

'You and him. I know he's cute but he's from New York and he'll be going back soon, and you live here. I know you love a love story, but this is real life.'

Not wanting to disagree and risk falling back into arguments, Nell nodded her understanding. They wandered around the rest of the dining room and came to a stop at Lexi's spot. Lexi worked at Raina's Café in town but was also a huge fan of vintage dresses and very gifted at making them. She'd brought a small rail with her and on it had hung some gorgeous vintage-inspired gowns. There were a couple of slender Sixties-style ones, but Cat gravitated towards the Fifties ones. One in particular stood out to her, the full petticoat pushing the other dresses to the end of the rail as if it was calling out for attention.

'Can I see that dress, Lexi?' asked Cat. As Lexi pulled it out, Cat checked over her shoulder and Nell had a horrible feeling it was to make sure Brenda wasn't around to stop her.

She pulled out the beautiful mid-length gown. The tight fitted top came down in a deep plunging V-neckline and a silk-ribbon wrapped around the waist, fastening into a small bow at the back. It was a champagne satin overlaid with lace and Nell could see the longing in Cat's eye. Her fingers reached out to touch it but whether out of respect for the dress or fear of her mother she drew her hand back.

'You can touch it,' Lexi said gently. 'I always like to feel the fabric. You want to know it's good quality.'

'That's fine.' Cat thrust her hands into the pockets of her jeans. 'It's beautiful.' The sadness in her voice resonated through Nell, pounding on her heart and willing her to help. If she could afford to, Nell would have bought it for her on the spot – but she also didn't want to risk having another row by mentioning the dress situation again, and time was running out to get a new one with only three weeks to go. On the table in front of them were white and silver long-sleeved gloves, shorter wrist-length ones, and pillbox hats with tiny veils. Everything needed to complete a vintage-bride look. Nell decided to draw Cat away before she became even more depressed.

They moved back towards the lounge and Kieran joined them, placing a kiss on the top of Cat's head as she pressed herself into his side. It was nice to see them happy. Cat looked up at him but there was a pinch at the sides of her eyes, and it was then Nell noticed the amount of concealer she'd used to hide the blue tinge of tiredness. To give her an energy boost, she grabbed four of the small chocolate brownie samples Niall had on his table and thrust them under Cat's nose. The heavy chocolatey aroma made Nell's mouth water and by the look on Cat's face it was doing the same to her as she began to munch away happily.

She was just taking the last one when Nell spotted Brenda's grey helmet-hair in the crowd. Two ladies accompanied her with similar uncompromising styles and fearful expressions, but as Brenda drew near, she was saying uncharacteristically nice things. Nell knew it was an effort to make her humble boutique hotel socially acceptable to the types of people Brenda mixed with – social climbers who were part of the tennis or bowls club. Knowing she would disapprove of Cat shoving brownies in her face at an unseemly rate, Nell stepped in front of her friend, obscuring her from view and as a warning, said loudly, 'Brenda! I'm so glad you came.'

Cat ducked down and finished off the last of the brownie bites. Brenda clearly didn't trust this unusually cheerful greeting and narrowed her eyes. 'Nell, how lovely. What a fabulous job you've done here. It's certainly extremely popular, isn't it?' She stressed the extremely for the benefit of her friends. Eyeing Kieran, who was too tall for Nell to shield, she said, 'Kieran, darling.' And gave him a kiss on the cheek. 'Where's Catherine?'

'Here I am,' she said, standing up. 'I was just tying my shoelace.'

Seeing a spot of chocolate near her mouth, Nell panicked and dived in between mother and daughter. 'Brenda!' she shouted in a high-pitched squeak. 'I – I – I absolutely love your dress.'

Well aware that everyone was staring at her as if she'd gone mad, she tried to signal to Kieran that Cat had something on her face using her eyebrows as semaphore flags. Brenda tried to side-step around her, and Nell forced herself in front and grabbed hold of Brenda's lapels, pretending to feel the fabric. 'It's such a lovely jacket. And it matches too – how marvellous. Where did you get it? I'd love one like that for my new role as wedding planner.'

Brenda gave an embarrassed chuckle as she tried to remove

Nell from her person, easing off her vice-like grip. Thankfully, Kieran had somehow caught on and grabbed Cat's face planting a whopper of a kiss on her lips and frightening the poor girl half to death.

'Young love,' Brenda joked to her friends, but her embarrassment at this public show of affection was clear. Kieran stepped away and relief swept over Nell as the chocolate crumb was now stuck to his cheek. 'Oh, Kieran, have you been at the free samples again? It's a good job you have such a physical job.' She handed him a tissue but before he could use it, Cat reached up and gently wiped it from his cheek.

'Darling.' Brenda Wilson was not the type of woman to admit to a family feud, and it seemed that, in front of her friends, all previous disagreements were forgotten. Whether that would continue in private, Nell would find out later. Brenda cupped her daughter's cheek. 'You look a bit tired. Were you on nights last night? Cat's a midwife,' Brenda said over her shoulder to her friends.

'Yes, we know,' one of the women replied, obviously having been told before.

Brenda ignored the slight note of irritation. 'Such a noble profession, isn't it?'

'Lates, not nights.'

'Well, make sure you get a good night's sleep tonight. No one wants to be puffy-eyed on their wedding day.'

Worried that things might go south fast, Nell said, 'Was there anything specific you and your friends wanted to see, Brenda? Tom's in the lounge and Niall's just here. He's even got some sample menus and tasters.'

At the mention of tasters, the women accompanying Brenda left her and headed in Niall's direction. Without even a goodbye, Brenda hurried to catch up.

As time wore on, Nell was soon caught up answering questions about Holly Lodge and even roped Cat into explaining how she was going to have the place set up for her wedding. Taking down names and addresses, Nell arranged some appointments for the New Year for people to come back and talk more about their weddings. She could have punched the air but didn't, knowing she'd look like a total idiot in the still crowded hotel.

By late afternoon, the crowds disappeared, and the vendors packed up and left in dribs and drabs. Brenda left on good terms with Cat, even if it was just for the sake of appearances. When the last business owner had departed, Nell told Zoe to go home and thanked her for all her hard work. She wasn't going to make her stick around for the clear-up, it was going to take a while.

In the aftermath, Nell, Tom, Cat and Kieran were having a cup of tea in the lounge before she tackled putting all the furniture back and an epic hooverthon to clean up all the cake crumbs and debris on the floor.

'Well,' said Nell, 'I officially declare the Holly Lodge wedding fair a success. I had lots of enquiries and I've even got some people coming back after Christmas to chat some more.'

'I'm – I mean *we're* really proud of you, Nell,' said Tom and Nell took a moment to admire the light in his eyes at her success.

'Very proud,' Cat added. To be back to their normal friendship was the icing on the cake.

A noise in the hall had Nell halfway out of her seat when Harry stuck his head in the doorway, back from a day with his family.

'Wow, looks like your wedding thing was a success. Great job, Nell!' Enthusiasm filled his features, brightening his already blue eyes, and she felt that rush of attraction that ran in her veins whenever he was around.

'Thanks, Harry. Nice day?'

'Yep. We went somewhere called Thornhill Hall. What a place. Wouldn't mind somewhere like that myself.'

'Did you want a drink or anything?' She hoped he'd say yes and join them, even though Tom was scowling. She really couldn't figure out what he had against her polite, handsome American guest. It wasn't like he'd ever been rude or complained about anything. Not like these other mystery guests whose reviews kept appearing on HotelRater.

'No thanks. I think I'd like a soak in the tub and a good book on that amazing bed of yours. I mean …' Colour flooded his cheeks. 'The amazing bed in my hotel room. I'll be going out again in a few hours anyway.'

Nell clenched her stomach muscles tight to stop the fluttering inside her as she imagined him naked in the bath. Had that been a Freudian slip? Had he been imagining her in bed with him? The thought that he might have been thinking of her in that way made her hot. Retaining some professionalism, she said, 'Well, I'll be down here if you need anything.'

'Sure thing.' And with a kind of salute he said goodbye.

Nell watched him go, knowing Cat's eyes were on her but she didn't look for fear that everyone would see the hope in her face.

'Who salutes when they say goodbye?' Tom said. He was getting a bit grumpy again and she wondered if it was another headache coming on.

'Cool people, mate,' Kieran teased. 'I only salute when I see a magpie.'

'And that's not weird at all,' Nell replied. 'Do you salute magpies, Cat? I've been known to curtsey at cats before, but I don't normally salute magpies.' Cat giggled just as Mr Scrooge appeared at the window, tapping with his paw. Nell jumped up to let him in. 'Hey, my little pussycat. Welcome home. Did you have a nice day out?' She turned to see everyone smirking at her. 'What?'

'Do you think you're getting a bit too attached to him?' asked Tom.

'No,' Nell lied. She was getting far too attached to him and with every passing day hoped no one would claim him but didn't fancy admitting it. After teasing Kieran just now he wouldn't fail to tease her back. 'I just like him, that's all.'

161

'No takers yet then?' Nell shook her head. Tom held his hand down and surprisingly Mr Scrooge didn't immediately back away or scratch him to death. 'Seems he's getting used to me.'

'And me,' said Kieran. Mr Scrooge curled up by the fire that was now roaring in the grate and Nell had to force herself to move from her comfortable chair.

With a great sigh she said, 'Okay you lot, if you're not helping then off you go. I've got a lot to do before I can relax for the evening.'

'What movie is it tonight?' asked Cat, knowing Nell would be curling up on the sofa and watching a romcom.

'After today and given the fact it's nearly Christmas? It's got to be *Love Actually*. The wedding scene with Keira Knightley when everyone starts singing 'All You Need is Love'… Perfect.'

Cat nodded approvingly. 'Good choice.'

'Want to join me?'

'No, thanks. It's my only night off so me and Kieran are cuddling up and watching a movie too.'

'Not a romcom though,' he added. 'Unless I can count *The Fast and the Furious* as a romcom.'

'Definitely not,' Cat and Nell said in unison.

'What about you, Tom?' Nell asked. He was scrunching up his eyes and opening them slowly. He did it a couple of times and Nell's worry began to grow again that he was getting another headache. It had been deafening in the hotel at times today so it wasn't that surprising. 'Tom?'

'Yeah?'

'Are you okay?'

'Yeah fine,' he answered, stopping blinking.

Nell cast a glance at Kieran and Cat, but they were snogging and didn't seem at all worried. She was happy to see them back to normal and hoped the blow-out with Cat and Brenda had cleared the air, but the worry over them was replaced with worry over Tom. Maybe he had something in his eye. 'Did you want to watch a movie with me tonight?'

162

'Oh, umm.' He considered for a moment. 'No, thanks, Nell. I'll help you clear up but then I'll be off. Bit worn out after today.'

Feeling unusually disappointed that he didn't want to stay, she stood up. 'Go on then, lovebirds, you two go and let me get started.'

'We'll help you tidy first,' Cat said. 'We're not leaving you with all of this.'

'Are you sure?'

'That's what friends are for.'

With Michael Bublé's velvety voice singing Christmas tunes, Nell and her friends put her hotel back together, and she was left feeling more positive than she had in months. Things were finally starting to turn around and she even had Thanksgiving dinner with Harry to look forward to in only a few days' time. There was a lot to prepare for that too. She wanted to create something special for him. Not a scene from a movie exactly, but with the twinkling lights, the Christmas decorations and the fire burning, it was sure to be a magical evening and one that catapulted their relationship forward into … well, into something, because right now it wasn't anything at all. She just knew this was the thing to stop him thinking of her as just a hostess and as a woman. The idea sent longing through her body causing the tired aches to intensify.

With a contented sigh as she hauled furniture up from the basement, she daydreamed of another wonderful fantasy where Harry was madly in love with her and her guests joined him in calling her the greatest hostess in the whole of Great Britain. Cat might have said that life wasn't like a romantic movie and Nell knew that deep down, but there was no harm in believing. Maybe one day her daydreams would come true. There wasn't actually anything wrong with hoping you'd find a love that made you fizz with excitement every time you saw that person. And her daydreams had never hurt anyone before. It's not like they would now, either. There was no one to hurt.

Chapter 14

Though Tom was thoroughly enjoying adding even more things to the Christmas window display of the flower shop, slotting in a couple of poinsettia in bright red pots tied with giant gold bows and wooden nutcracker dolls standing proudly to attention, he shivered having gone outside in just his jumper, too preoccupied to find his coat.

He'd seen the exchange between Cat and Brenda and heard all about Cat and Nell's argument. At least the wedding fair had brought them together again and been a huge success too. It was nice to see Nell looking content again. Even if she did still beam a little brighter when Harry was around.

Then there was Kieran. As his best friend and best man at his wedding, Tom had a duty to check on his mate. Kieran had told him what Cat had said at the wedding fair about the buttonholes, but he had no idea how to actually support his friend. Cat was constantly making all the decisions, and Kieran was too worried about starting a row to say anything much about it. Cat was normally fun and lively, but this behaviour was worryingly erratic. Laid-back Kieran had always steadied her, brought her down to earth, he was her perfect counterpoint, but if she was shutting him out, what exactly did that mean?

At the back of Tom's mind, he worried that if things carried on as they were, and Cat continued to push ahead as she was, she would end up so stressed at the idea of marrying Kieran, she'd jilt him at the altar. He hadn't voiced these fears to his friend. It would be too much right now and apart from that one episode at the wreath-making, and Nell mentioning that Cat kept changing her mind on the more minor details, nothing else had happened. Now she'd given Brenda a flea in her ear maybe she'd back off. Unfortunately, all this drama had taken the edge off how successful the wreath-making event had been for Holly Lodge. He'd so wanted for everything to start coming together for Nell, but it seemed life liked to throw more obstacles in her way than an episode of *Ninja Warrior*.

Stepping outside into the cold air, he examined the window display again. It had a lot of height, but it needed framing more. The two tall nutcracker dolls at the sides were doing a good job but it needed a little more. He still had tons of holly as there were more wreath orders to fill and a holly wreath hanging down from the centre would finish it off perfectly.

Back inside, shivering from not wearing his coat, he settled at his workstation to begin. The Christmas music was in full flow now it was the end of November and he and Janie could often be found having a bop and a singsong. Without his permission, Tom's thoughts ran to Nell. Her dinner with Harry was coming up on Thursday and it weighed on his shoulders. Swimmers flew across his vision, blurring everything before him and a sharp pain shot through his finger. 'Ouch!' He blinked but the squiggly dots made it hard to focus, and they were all he could see against a background of red. 'Shit!' He'd cut himself with the secateurs. He hardly ever cut himself. The tiny lapse in concentration combined with the pesky swimmers getting in the way of his vision and he'd split open his finger.

'Oh no,' said Janie, coming up behind him. 'That's deep, Tom. You'd better go to the hospital and get it checked.'

His vision cleared and his eyes focused on the deep gash in the pad of his left index finger. 'It's fine, I'll just wrap it up and shove a plaster on it. I'm sure it's not as bad as it looks.' He squeezed it tight to stop the bleeding, wincing as pain shot through the length of his finger and into his hand. 'I'm sure it'll stop in a minute.'

'I really don't think it will,' Janie continued, grabbing some tissues from the box on the worktop and wrapping them around the wound. Almost immediately the tissue became red and sodden. 'I think that might need stitches. We can do the deliveries when you get back. I can't wait till I've passed my test then I can help you with those.'

Tom looked at his finger again, now twice the size with the tissues around it. He squeezed even harder trying to stop the bleeding determined to avoid a trip to the local hospital. After grabbing a few more tissues, he pulled the wet ones off, and saw for himself how deep the cut really was. It would definitely need gluing or stitching. With a sinking feeling, he realised Janie was right; he had to go but at least the shop was in good hands. He was the liability lately, not her.

'Do you want me to call you a taxi? You can't really drive with that.'

Tom thought about calling Nell, but she was busy sorting out her winter romance package and he didn't want to get in the way. She'd had enough downers recently without worrying about him and his clumsiness too, especially after the car incident. If she knew about this as well, she'd start getting suspicious. 'I'll call Kieran. I'm sure he'll be able to drop me at Minor Injuries.' He pulled his phone from his back pocket and made the call.

After hanging up, he sat for a moment feeling dizzy and light-headed. He'd never liked the sight of blood, that's why he hadn't followed his dad into medicine and become a doctor. It was funny how he'd fallen into floristry quite by accident after taking a short-term job following university. It had been to help a family friend over the Christmas period, but he'd absolutely loved it. Some of their friends had taken the piss but Kieran hadn't. As a gardener he loved flowers just as much as Tom, just in a different way. Tom had fallen completely in love with the wonderful mix of art and science in floristry and never looked back. In all the time he'd been working he'd only cut himself a few times, and never before like this.

Kieran bustled through the door within about five minutes of Tom calling. 'All right, Tom, what have you done, mate?' Tom showed him the wrapped-up finger and changed the soaking wet tissues once more. 'Geez, that's bad. And you look a bit peaky. Janie, have you got any biscuits or anything?' Janie nodded and went to grab one while Kieran helped Tom into his coat.

'I'm all right, Kieran, honestly. Blood just makes me a bit squeamish. If you drop me off at Minor Injuries, I'll just sit there until they see me then get a taxi back.'

'No, you won't,' he replied, his eyebrows lifting to the brim of his woolly hat. It always made Tom laugh how when Kieran was caught frowning, he could look so severe and even a little thuggish, but inside he was a giant teddy bear. 'I'm not just leaving you there. I'll wait with you and bring you home. Come on, though. Best get that seen to.'

Janie shoved a handful of biscuits into Tom's free hand and he tried to reassure her as she stared at him in concern. 'Don't worry, Janie. I won't be long.' As he left, he felt guilty for putting her through it, and for leaving her alone in the shop for God knows how long yet again. 'I really am sorry about this, Janie. Just serve the customers who come in needing stuff for today and make notes of everything else. I can sort those out tomorrow, okay? You don't have to do everything. Hopefully, I'll be back within an hour.'

Kieran scoffed. 'An hour? At Minor Injuries in winter? You're having a laugh, aren't you?'

'Don't worry, boss,' Janie said with her usual chirpiness. 'I'll manage fine.'

Knowing she would, Tom reluctantly allowed himself to be led and bundled into Kieran's van. It was lovely and warm where he'd had the heater on, and Tom was glad of it. The truth was he was feeling a little shaky and cold. He clipped in his seatbelt and cradled his bad finger inside his jacket like a tiny baby. With his good hand, he nibbled on a biscuit, hoping the sugar would stop his legs feeling like jelly.

Kieran pulled away then nodded at Tom's hand. 'So, what happened?'

Tom's initial reaction was to just pass it off as bad luck, or a moment's lost concentration, but his worries had been mounting for months, getting steadily worse with each passing day and carrying that weight alone was becoming harder. With the prang in his van and now this, Tom felt the alarm bell ringing in his brain louder and clearer than ever before, and knew it was time to come clean. After a heavy sigh he said, 'I've been having a few problems with my vision for a while.'

His friend's brow wrinkled in concern. 'What sort of problems?'

'Little bits floating across my eyes, difficulty seeing in the dark and particularly during that weird half-light you get at dusk. It takes ages for my eyes to adjust and if I don't stop and stand still while it does, I end up missing my footing.' He paused, feeling the keenness of Kieran's glance. 'And I keep getting headaches. Bad ones. I think it's because I'm straining my eyes but ...' He didn't want to finish the sentence and say out loud how worried he truly was.

'Have you been to the doctor's?' Tom shook his head. 'The optician's?' Tom shook his head again and looked down at his finger. 'Why the bloody hell not?'

If only he had a good excuse. He couldn't say, 'I've been too chicken shit to face up to the fact that something might be seriously wrong.' It sounded pathetic. Kieran's voice was a little softer, but not by much.

'Well, you'd better tell the nurse at Minor Injuries everything when she sees you.'

'I will,' Tom replied. 'I know I have to now.'

'I'll be checking,' said Kieran. 'Even if I have to interrogate her as soon as you're out.'

The world of Swallowtail Bay passed by as they drove to the hospital in the larger nearby town of Halebury. They followed the long road that ran parallel to the seafront and Tom watched the rough sea froth at the crest of each wave. Finally, the beach and its line of weather-beaten beach huts, some decorated with festive fairy lights, gave way to fields enclosed in tall hedges. Rounding a bend in the road they saw Thornhill Hall, tall and stately on the horizon, then the small roads were replaced with larger, busier ones.

Twenty minutes later Kieran pulled into the hospital car park and tried to find a space. Even though it was only a small hospital it was amazing how busy it was. The bigger hospital that had an Accident and Emergency department was almost an hour away in the opposite direction. When he stepped out of the car into the cold fresh air, Tom felt a shiver run through him that intensified the pain in his finger. A kind lady on reception took his details and asked him to sit down. The biscuit had helped a little with the shock and he wasn't feeling so wobbly, but he still felt cold and now, very tired. A headache began to pound at the back of his eyes and as he looked outside, he was glad he'd told Kieran the truth. The afternoon was grey and dark and by the time they emerged the purple-blue half-light would be falling. He didn't want to trip over in front of his mate as he pretended everything was fine, but now Kieran knew he'd be able to give him a minute without feeling self-conscious.

'So how was Cat last night?' asked Tom as he plonked down into a plastic chair in the waiting area. Looking around he saw couples holding hands, comforting each other and sharing nervous laughter, joking to pass the time. A spindly Christmas tree had been set up in the corner of the room next to the kids' play pen. How he wished Nell was there with him. She could always make him laugh and lighten a heavy atmosphere like this one. Her dreamy nature made her incredibly empathetic. He'd give anything to rest his head on her shoulder right now, close his eyes and have a nap. He was so tired.

Kieran pulled off his beanie and scratched what little stubble had grown on his head. 'I just don't know what's going on with her, mate. She's never been like this before. You know what she's like normally – wild, fun, a bit mental – but since all this wedding stuff she's changed. She either withdraws completely and doesn't talk to me, or she's really defensive and moody. I've told her I'll come with her to these wedding things. I'd like to, you know, it's my wedding too, but she doesn't want me there. And I've told her we can run off just the two of us and get married abroad if she'd prefer that.'

'And does she?'

'No. She wants to get married at Holly Lodge. Partly for her, partly for Nell. She doesn't want to let Nell down.'

'Nell would understand.' Tom knew she would. Kieran brushed some dried mud from the thigh of his old work jeans. 'I feel for you, mate, I really do. Not least because the prospect of having Brenda Wilson as a mother-in-law is absolutely terrifying.'

At this he laughed. 'I just want to marry Cat and I don't care where, or how, or when for that matter, but Brenda seems to have all these ideas about what *should* happen and it's rubbing off on her.' He crossed his huge arms over his chest, the thick, heavy checked shirt buckling at the seams. 'I'm glad she stood up to her mum. It was about time, but now she's worrying about the fallout from that too.'

'Nell was distraught they had a row. I'm so pleased they made up.'

'Cat too. I told her just to call and it'd be fine, but she said she was too embarrassed. Good old Nell just came straight out with it and they were all over each other within two minutes of us walking into Holly Lodge.'

'It's a shame you're not joining us for Christmas Day this year.'

'Yeah, we'll miss you too. Only a bit though. We'll be sunning ourselves on a white sandy beach while you're freezing your tail off with Nell at Holly Lodge. Or you could cuddle down by the roaring log fire.' Kieran wiggled his eyebrows and the tension eased for a moment.

'I've told you not to wiggle your eyebrows suggestively at me.'

'You said not in front of your staff.' He continued to wiggle his eyebrows up and down and Tom chuckled as his name was called by a tall, thin nurse with deep wrinkles and a stern voice.

As soon as Tom made his way towards her, feeling slightly like he was in trouble, her features transformed from stern to kind. 'That looks nasty, my lovely,' she said, holding the door open for him. 'Let's get that seen to.'

The small treatment room was tightly packed with a bed, a desk, various bins and cupboards stocking everything the nurse might need. 'Have a seat, my love and let's have a look.' Tom let the nurse pull his hand towards her and watched through a half-closed eye as she unwrapped the blood-soaked tissue. It had mostly stopped bleeding but as she examined the depth of the wound it started a little more. 'So how did you do this?'

He kept his eyes away from the cut, staring out of the window at the branches of the trees rocking wildly in the wind. What he wouldn't give for a glass of mulled wine and a mince pie by the open fire at Holly Lodge right about now. 'I nipped it with secateurs. I'm a florist and I just caught myself.'

She must have sensed his hesitation or the note of untruth in his voice and looked at him over the top of his finger. He knew he had to carry on before he changed his mind and tell her the whole truth even though his stomach had tightened like a muscle in spasm. The thought of Kieran coming in and telling her for him, which he would do given half a chance, made him own up.

'I've, umm – I've been having a few problems with my sight … and some headaches.' The nurse immediately glanced up then dropped her eyes back to his finger. After a moment she got up finding supplies to clean the wound.

'What sort of problems?'

Gathering his courage before it could desert him, Tom sucked in a deep breath and told her everything.

Leaving behind the small treatment room and entering back into the large and still busy waiting area, Tom exhaled a deep breath, pushing tension from his lungs. As soon as Kieran saw him, he shoved his phone into his pocket and stood up. From Kieran's reaction, Tom knew he looked as pale and shaky as he felt. With a faint smile, he hoped to put his friend at ease, but the relief from his deep breath was fleeting and his internal organs turned to stone.

'What did she say?' asked Kieran, concern flooding his eyes.

Tom scratched the back of his head with his right hand. His left index finger was now wrapped in a white bandage. 'She said that it was a deep cut and needed a couple of those stitches that look more like stickers. She put about three on and told me to be really careful in the future.'

'And what about the – you know—' Kieran waved his hand in front of his face like it was some kind of magic trick. 'The eye thing.'

The fact his friend looked idiotic waving his hands in front of his face like some terrible dance move should have been amusing, but Tom swallowed. 'She's referred me to a consultant and I've got to have some tests. What will I say to Nell? If it's on a day I'd normally see her, she'll get suspicious.'

'Will you stop worrying about Nell for two minutes?'

'I'll have to lie to her and tell her I'm doing something else. You'll cover for me, won't you?'

'Of course but why have you been referred for tests, rather than told to just go to the optician's? What does she think it is?'

'She didn't say.' Tom's headache pounded harder. 'When I told her all about the symptoms, she asked me to hang on and rang the Ophthalmology department at the big hospital to speak to someone there. She looked deadly serious when she was talking and she just ummed and nodded when they spoke to her. Then she put the phone down and in a calm voice told me that they'd advised her to make an emergency referral. I should get a phone call or letter in the next few days with a time and date have some tests done. When I asked what they'd said, she just told me that it could be something or it could be nothing, but they'd like to see me to find out. And given I've had a couple of accidents she wants it to be sooner rather than later.'

'What do you mean a couple of accidents? This is the first one, isn't it?'

'Umm …' He'd conveniently forgotten to mention the prang to Kieran and Nell had saved his blushed by not mentioning it too. 'I had a bit of a prang in the van a couple of weeks ago.'

'What? Why didn't you tell me?'

Tom plonked down on one of the seats in the waiting area again and Kieran sat next to him. 'I didn't want to face it, and now it seems there really could be something wrong it makes me feel sick.'

'You need to tell Nell.'

'No way.' Tom stared at his friend. 'She's had so much going on. This is the last thing she needs.'

'Stop worrying about her and worry about yourself, Tom. Nell's a grown woman and she doesn't need mollycoddling. I know she's always off in a dreamworld or watching those blimmin' romcoms, but she cares about you and she'd want to know. She'd want to be there for you. You could even be a big strong boy and tell her how you feel.' He was trying to tease but Tom felt far too emotional to laugh or joke.

'And get a pity date because I might have a brain tumour or something? No way. My health might be in doubt, but I've still got my pride. And besides, she's having this dinner with Harry tonight. She hasn't stopped talking about it.'

Kieran clapped a hand on his shoulder. 'You're hopeless, you know that? Come on, mate. You don't know it's anything bad. Like the nurse said, it could be nothing. Don't stress yourself out until you know. Let's go to the pub. We'll call in and close the shop on the way.'

Tom saw it was pitch black outside. 'How long have we been here?'

'A couple of hours.'

'I'm really sorry, mate. I've screwed up your whole afternoon.'

'Don't worry about it. I've gone up loads of levels on Candy Crush while I was waiting.'

Finally, Tom was able to lift the corners of his mouth. 'I was more worried about Janie than you.'

'I'm sure Janie's done fine on her own. She's a good girl.'

'I'm sure she has. I don't know where I'd be without her.'

Kieran wriggled his coat back on to his shoulders. 'So come on, you really look like you need a drink and some time to take things in.'

Though there was a slight tinge of relief that he'd taken the first step, Tom couldn't help but worry. An image of the nurse's face when he'd mentioned the terrible headaches flew across his mind, and he began to worry that he didn't have time to take things in. Now, he worried he didn't have a lot of time left.

174

Pulling the turkey crown from the oven, Nell blew her fringe up to cool her hot face. Finally, it was Thanksgiving, the night of the American feast she'd been mentally preparing. She'd reluctantly made mashed potatoes instead of roast because that's what all the Thanksgiving menus she'd read online had. She'd made a sweet potato pie but didn't particularly like the idea of the sweet orange flesh mixed with sugar and breadcrumbs on top, but still, if it was traditional, she was going to cook it for Harry. For dessert she'd got one of the bakers in town to make a pecan pie. She wouldn't have known where to start with that so cheated. Not that Harry would mind. He seemed such an understanding guy.

In the dining room, she'd laid a table with stars-and-stripes serviettes and a little American flag and Harry was meeting her there at seven when he got back from visiting his family. She'd changed from one of her enormous oversized jumpers into something a little bit cuter, sticking with jeans so she looked laid-back, but teaming it with a sheer top. She'd even done the smoky eye make-up she'd been practising for the mayor's party to bring out her eyes. She just hoped the steam from the turkey hadn't melted it all off. It was so hot in the kitchen she was glad they were eating upstairs where it was cooler. She'd texted Cat a picture of her make-up, and Cat had replied with a much-needed confidence boost but had reminded her that he was just a guest and she shouldn't build it up into anything else. Though Nell knew Cat was right the words had stung. It was all right for Cat who had been with Kieran for ages and was in general, a practical, no-nonsense sort of girl. Nell just wasn't like that. Yes, she was a bit flighty sometimes, but she liked to think of it as optimistic and open to possibilities.

At ten minutes to seven, Nell took the foil-wrapped turkey upstairs along with a big jug of pale, weird-looking gravy. It smelled divine, but having grown up on the dark, beefy British stuff, it was going to take some getting used. The next trip saw the mashed potatoes and sweet potato pie. Looking at the spread, she'd made more food than two people could ever eat. She hoped he was hungry.

Harry walked in as she was lighting the candle. She'd dimmed all the other lights, giving the dining room a romantic atmosphere. The rest of the hotel was empty until those who had booked her new romance package arrived. Despite the bad review, she'd put up the advertisement today and already had a booking off the back of it. They were arriving tomorrow for a last-minute getaway and Nell was excited at the idea of creating the perfect weekend retreat for them. It had reminded her why she loved running Holly Lodge.

'Now, this is why you're the best hostess in the whole of Great Britain, maybe even the world,' Harry joked as he tossed his coat and scarf onto a vacant chair. 'This looks and smells amazing.' Nell flustered but was secretly pleased her hard work had paid off. When he looked up at her, he paused. 'Wow, you look beautiful.'

'Oh, thanks.' Feeling self-conscious, she pushed her hair back behind her ear. Having laid out all the food on one of the other tables, Nell said, 'Come and help yourself. I've made way too much.'

Harry leaned over her shoulder, examining the feast. 'This looks so good. I can't wait to dive in.' He was so close she could see the slight wrinkles at the sides of his eyes. They were having a moment and Nell tried to think loving thoughts, hoping her feelings would be revealed through her gaze. He examined her face for a moment then stepped away and began loading his plate. Unsure what to make of his response, she began filling her plate too.

As they sat at the little table, just the two of them, butterflies pranced in Nell's stomach as Harry laid a napkin on his lap. Every time they chatted a fire sparked within her. There was something in the air between them tonight she was sure, and from the way Harry was looking at her intently from under his long thick eyelashes, she was sure he felt it too. Who knew where this one dinner might lead? Now was her chance to find out some more about the handsome American who'd walked into her life three weeks ago.

'So, I have some great news,' Harry began loading his fork. 'My business is behaving itself, so I need to extend my stay by at least another week.'

'That's brilliant.' She ignored the little voice that told her his being here for longer didn't mean he was suddenly going to stay indefinitely. 'I'm sure your family are pleased.'

'They are. And so am I, even though I'm missing New York like crazy.' He took a bite of his food. 'This is delicious, Nell. You're a great cook. Now I'm really feeling Christmassy.'

'Thanks. New York must be amazing at this time of year.' She placed some turkey in her mouth, pleased it was juicy and not dry. Mrs Meggett would be proud. 'I've never been but I'd really love to go.'

'Oh my gosh, Nell, you would love it. It really is amazing. You should come visit me one day. I don't know about you, but I feel like we're … you know … friends.'

'I do too,' she replied shyly and could feel herself blushing.

Did he mean friends or *friends*? Whatever he meant, the evening was going better than any scenario she'd made up in her head. 'If I hadn't got this other booking you could put me in your suitcase and take me with you now,' she joked.

Harry eyed her before placing a forkful of food in his mouth. After swallowing he said, 'Is everything okay with the hotel, Nell? I mean, don't get me wrong, I've had a great time and I think the place is amazing but, I've noticed that sometimes you kind of zone out and you don't seem that happy.'

Adding some more gravy to her plate, Nell considered how to respond. If she were to stay in professional mode she would deny there was anything wrong, big up the hotel and pretend everything was fine, but she'd had her regular business phone call with her parents and they'd been less than impressed with the current situation. Not angry or blaming, just disappointed, and Nell had felt it keenly. Her mother was going to email her a list of suggestions to boost business even though she'd probably already thought of most of them. The person she'd wanted after talking to them was Tom, but she didn't like to bother him in the middle of the day.

'Come on, Nell. I can tell something's going on. Talk to me.' His voice was soft and kind and as he reached out across the table, resting his hand over hers she felt heat run up her arm. 'Is it that guy? What did you say his name was? Tom?'

'Tom?' Confusion marred her features.

'Yeah, I just kind of assumed you and he were … a thing. You're so close.'

'No. No!' She was so shocked at the suggestion she replied an octave higher than intended. 'We're just friends.'

'Oh, okay. Sure.' He took his hand away and began to eat again. Nell wished he'd put it back.

Was Harry scoping out her relationship status? Seeing if she was single? A shiver danced through her. Though she knew he wasn't married from when she'd checked him in, she asked, 'What about you? Is there someone in New York waiting for you to come home?' Inside she grimaced. That sentence had sounded so much better in her head. Out loud it sounded brash. She might as well have said, 'If you're single, fancy a hump?'

Harry's face suddenly darkened. 'There was someone – Emma – but we broke up about six months ago. Since then I've been so focused on work that I haven't even thought about my love life. Being here though, it makes me think that however successful I am, something's lacking somewhere.'

Nell glanced up and he was looking straight at her. Was he implying she'd been what was lacking? 'I know what you mean.'

It was something she was beginning to think about more and more too. She spent so much of her time working on the business, thinking about the business, dreaming about the business that romance only ever happened in her head. The relationships she'd had hadn't lasted because they didn't understand the commitment she'd made to the hotel and because after a while the flowers, the chocolates and the general romance had disappeared. Harry's eyes had taken on a pained look that dulled their brightness.

'I'm sorry,' Nell said. She really wanted to reach out and wipe the hurt from his face. Whoever Emma was had been a lucky woman and a fool to let him go.

'That's okay. What about you? I can't believe a girl like you is single.'

'Oh, I am,' she confirmed, half-happy, half-resigned. 'I've had a few relationships, but they just didn't work out.'

'I see.' Harry sipped his wine. She'd put a bottle of red and a bottle of white on the table, unsure what he liked. He'd opted for red. 'So, if it's not Tom or some other guy, then what is it that makes you seem so sad sometimes?'

A silence descended, and Nell realised that it was horribly quiet when they stopped talking. She leaped up from her chair. 'Let me just put some music on. I hate sitting in silence and normally

179

have the radio on low. Otherwise this place feels really big and kind of intimidating.' She hadn't changed the playlist from Michael Bublé and he was back crooning away. The perfect soundtrack to their romantic Thanksgiving dinner. With music playing, she sat down again.

An amused look washed the pain away. 'Come on, Nell. You can tell me.'

Why was she hesitating? Was it because she didn't want to spoil the evening with talk of miserable things, or was it because she normally talked about these things with Tom or Cat? Unsure, she took a sip of her wine. 'It's just the hotel business is a bit slow at the moment. At least for me. With the Langdon Mansion being so amazing, it's knocked me for six.' Harry smiled at the Britishness of the phrase. And then there was Cat's wedding and this business with Tom. She was sure he wasn't telling her everything at the moment but for some reason held back from saying anything about that to Harry.

'So why don't you do something else? Go travelling. Come to New York.'

There was a note in his voice she couldn't quite place. Was it an invitation? Before she could stop herself, her mind had swept her away to New York with Harry. One of those wonderful airport scenes where he was running through a terminal unable to let her leave until she promised she loved him too and would follow him halfway around the world. 'You could come and stay with me.'

Nell's head shot up so fast she went dizzy. An explosion of excitement tingled every nerve in her body. That didn't just sound like an invitation, that *was* an invitation. 'Could I?'

'Sure. I could show you a proper New York Christmas. The Rockefeller Centre, ice skating, eating a hot dog on a street corner while snow falls.'

'It sounds amazing,' she managed to say.

Outside the sky was clear and cold with sparkling stars but

the chance of snow was slim. She could almost feel the flakes falling onto her skin and settling in her hair as she pictured herself in New York City. The pull of excitement and the tantalising possibilities of a new future were beckoning her, calling her to be reckless and try something new and crazy – to make a change – but just as quickly the feeling faded as Cat's words came back to her. Was she getting caught up in another fantasy? Another dream? She did get swept up in the idea of things, romanticising them, making them out to be something they weren't. Did she really want to leave Holly Lodge? Would she have a future with Harry if she didn't because she was fairly certain he wouldn't want to stay here. Or maybe he did as his family were in the bay, and his mum had been sick. Maybe this was the thing to bring him back to Britain. There's always that moment in a movie when two worlds collide, maybe this was hers and Harry's. The little voice in her brain told her she was doing it again, making stuff up to suit her circumstances but she ignored it. 'I couldn't go anywhere until after Cat's wedding. Even for a holiday.'

'Sure,' he replied with a shrug.

Oh … that wasn't as enthusiastic a response as she was hoping for. Maybe it was disappointment. She was finding it hard to read him.

Nell finished her dinner with Harry making chit-chat about his job as an IT consultant and his newfound love of Swallowtail Bay. She was pleased to hear his mum was on the mend since her operation. 'This place is great, Nell. I can see why you might not want to leave. I watched the most stunning sunset the other night. I've never seen anything like it. I mean the skyline of New York is something special but the colours here are incredible – yellows, oranges, pinks, purples – amazing.'

'The colours are spectacular here,' Nell agreed as they pushed their plates aside. It was time for dessert, and she grabbed the pecan pie and served them both a slice. Normally a chocolate girl, it was nicer than she expected. Harry enjoyed it too. 'You know, I travel a lot, Nell and you're different to every other hotelier I've met. You're special.' He waved his dessert fork at her. 'Don't ever forget that. I mean, how many would have done something like this for their one and only guest?'

Nell spooned some pudding into her mouth in stunned silence. Was she special? She'd never really felt that special deep down inside. In truth, as exciting as the idea of being whisked away to New York was, even if it involved romantic airport scenes, she really did love Swallowtail Bay and her little hotel. Times were tough right now but with everything she was doing there was no way this funk could last forever. Tom had been saying that for ages, she thought, and she suddenly pictured the way he pushed his hair back from his face. Always on the right side, never the left.

Glancing around, she saw Mr Scrooge settled by the fire. There'd been no calls about him yet and she found herself relieved. If the opportunity arose, which it seemed it had from Harry's subtle invitations, could she really bring herself to leave? In her dreams, she'd imagined feeling different in this situation. Instead of unmitigated excitement and longing to be with handsome, sweet Harry, an uncertainty was growing in the pit of her stomach that she couldn't explain.

When dinner ended, they settled into the lounge. The room was beautifully warm and cosy with the fire burning and music playing, and Nell tapped her foot and hummed along. After a coffee and a lull in conversation, Harry stood up.

'Come on, best hostess in Britain. Let's dance.'

Fizzing with excitement, Nell stood, and he took her in his arms, twirling her around the lounge in between the tables. He was a really good dancer and there was no awkward shuffling or stepping on each other's toes. It felt so incredibly special and more romantic than anything else she'd experienced. Allowing every sense to be immersed in the moment, her confused thoughts vanished, and with her hand on a strong bicep she felt giddy and light. As the song ended, he pulled her in and dipped her. She met his eye and refused to look away letting him know of the attraction growing inside her, but he simply drew her back up. Still standing, Harry gave a great yawn.

'I am exhausted. I think I'll head to bed. Thanks for a great Thanksgiving. It's been amazing. It felt like home from home.'

'Oh, you're welcome.' Surprised at his sudden wish to leave, Nell didn't really know what else to say. Harry walked up to her and gave her a peck on the cheek. She could smell his aftershave and enjoyed the feel of his lips on her skin, but once again she wasn't feeling quite how she thought she would.

'Good night, Nell.' Harry gathered the coat he'd abandoned when he walked in before heading up the stairs to his room.

With a huff at the rather abrupt end to the evening, Nell headed back into the dining room to clear up the remains of their feast. Instead of wholly romantic, the evening had been strange and confusing. He'd asked her to visit him in New York, hadn't he? That must mean something, but when she said she couldn't come till New Year he'd not seemed bothered at all. Nell knew she had to stop her brain going into overdrive. It often coloured her interpretation of reality and left her disappointed when things didn't go quite how she'd imagined they would. Once again, reality hadn't measured up to her hopes. Worst of all, she had a feeling it was something to do with her. Something she was doing, or not doing.

Stacking the dirty plates and serving dishes, she made her way to the basement kitchen. Turning on the tap and piling the dishes in the sink, she wished her brain would include all the practical bits as well as the romantic ones. If it did, it would have imagined the amount of washing up she had to do. In which case, she'd have suggested they eat out.

Chapter 16

The next day, as the late afternoon sun shone bright and low in the sky, Nell moved the last of the chairs from the lounge down into the basement. The one problem the hotel had was that there wasn't much storage, so she was having to stack them in her flat and in the corner of the kitchen where Mrs Meggett was just finishing her baking marathon. Nell had thought about hiring Niall in again to provide some refreshments for St Herbert's Welcome to Christmas carol service, but she'd instead roped in Mrs Meggett who as well as making an amazing cooked breakfast, also baked delicious cakes.

When Nell walked in with another chair, Mrs Meggett's large round bottom jiggled as she pulled another tray of mince pies from the oven then danced around to the Christmas songs playing on the radio. 'They smell delicious, Mrs Meggett. Are there many more to cook?'

She rested one hand on her hip and wiped her rosy cheeks. 'Only a few more trays of mince pies and a few more of ginger-bread. Lord, my feet are killing me.'

'Oh, Mrs Meggett, you've worked so hard today. I'm so grateful for your help. Let me make you a cup of tea. Have a sit-down for a minute.' Nell put the chair down and patted it.

184

Mrs Meggett checked her watch and the timer on the oven and decided she had five minutes to spare. 'Go on then.' Her body flopped down with a sigh. 'Oomph. And I've still got to decorate all those bloody gingerbread men. Honestly, men are the bane of my life at the moment.'

'Is Mr Meggett not behaving himself?' Nell asked as she popped the kettle on.

'Not on your nelly, Nelly, and he never does.'

Nell gathered the cups and turned to rest against the counter. Only Mrs Meggett called her Nelly and she didn't mind it one little bit. Platters of already cooked gingerbread men and women lay on the counter from the work she had done that morning. They were expecting twenty-seven children in the choir and their parents, plus the teachers and any other families from the school who wanted to attend. It was likely they were going to be jam-packed, but Nell had studied the geometry of the place and mapped out how it was all going to work. She'd installed some tables at the sides of the dining room and conservatory piled high with treats. She'd also borrowed some old-fashioned gym benches that brought back more bad memories than good, so there was enough seating and, if necessary, people could even stand on them to ensure they could see.

Spying the gingerbread and the bags of sweets Mrs Meggett had to decorate them with, Nell had an idea. 'Mrs Meggett, why don't we save you a job and not decorate the gingerbread men at all?'

'What do you mean, dear?'

'Well, we're not putting out the food until after the carol concert, so why don't we lay out the gingerbread men and all the things to decorate them with, and the kids can do it themselves? If we put the mince pies and the tea urns on the other table, they'll be safe enough.' The kettle began to boil, and Nell stood up to make them both a cup of tea.

'What about the hot chocolate? We still haven't decided what we're putting that in.'

'Instead of putting out two tea urns we can use one and keep the other for hot chocolate. I don't mind topping them up more regularly. What do you think? Then people can help themselves to toppings. I've got peppermint candy canes, squirty cream and marshmallows. We can shove it all alongside and I bought paper takeaway cups for the wedding fair, so there won't even be washing up.'

'Sounds like a plan to me, my dear, but are you sure you haven't spent more than you're likely to earn. You know how you get – and I mean that nicely – but you do go a bit overboard on the extra touches.' She held her hands up, palms facing outwards. 'It's your caring nature coming out and it's very admirable, but you can't go spending more than you make or you won't make any profit.' The oven beeped and Mrs Meggett leaped to her feet to check the mince pies. The kitchen was filled with the aroma of Christmas spice and sweet, sugary pastry.

Move over, Mr Kipling! thought Nell as she brought over the tea. 'I only need to charge about fifty pence for each drink and mince pies and though I wanted to do the gingerbread for free, the school's offered me some money to cover the cost of the ingredients. They would have been providing refreshments too, so they just paid me to do it instead.'

'Well, it sounds like you've got it all sorted. Right, I'll slurp this and get back on.'

'Me too. I've got my first guests for my Christmas romance package arriving today and I want to make the room really special for them. And there's more to do down here first.'

Mrs Meggett cleared her throat.

'And I know not to go silly on the details. Tom's already told me.'

'Good. At least one of you has got some sense,' she said affectionately.

After the refreshing tea, Nell's next job was to add some more decorations to the lounge so when it was viewed from the dining room, it would be the perfect back drop for the children. She left Mrs Meggett and the chair and went back to the dining room. Standing and looking into the lounge with the door folded back, Nell imagined all the children there. The Christmas tree was to the left, the fireplace to the right, though she wouldn't light it until after just in case of accidents. The garland Tom had made for the mantelpiece framed that side of the room but there was something missing. She needed something to fill the large elegant sash windowsills and thinking of what she could use, decided to recycle a couple of the empty boxes from the kitchen. She had some wrapping paper left over from her recent present buying and a couple of tantalisingly giftwrapped presents would finish things off nicely.

Nell set to work but stopped when Harry walked in, his hands in his pockets. A cream sweater ran ever so nicely over his broad torso. She felt her breath hitch a little with the force of his presence. After last night's dinner, she'd been confused at how the evening had gone, but she'd put it down to tiredness sapping her good mood. She needed to let the Christmas spirit fill her with excitement, just as it normally did.

'What's going on here then?'

'I've got the Welcome to Christmas carol service tonight by the local primary school.'

'That sounds fun. And what is that smell? It definitely smells like Christmas in here.'

Nell glanced up from her present wrapping workstation in the lounge. 'Mrs Meggett's been making mince pies and gingerbread men for after the service. It does smell good, doesn't it?'

'Reminds me of home,' Harry replied wistfully, sitting next to Nell on one of the few remaining armchairs in the lounge. His trouser leg rode up a little revealing a hint of athletic calf. Nell approved; she didn't like men with skinny chicken legs.

'Feeling homesick today?'

'Yeah. I never told you last night, did I? I come from a big

187

family. You know about my mom, but my dad moved to the States when they got divorced and as I went with him only coming back for holidays, I wanted to come back and be with her. But back home, we always have a big family Christmas with my stepmom. She has a large family.'

Last night, they'd chatted quite happily but she realised now that quite selfishly, the conversation had been focused on her and not him. She hadn't asked as many questions as she wanted to and there was still so much to find out. 'I bet you'll be glad to get back at the end of the month in time to celebrate with them.' She looked around for the scissors and Harry handed them to her, his fingers brushing hers.

Suddenly, he rose from the chair. 'I'd better get going. I've got some things to do. Save me a mince pie, okay?'

'I will.' Nell watched him go as her imagination once again went into overdrive. Suddenly, on his last day with her, he was begging her to come to New York, to sell the hotel and build a life with him there. Or he was asking her to extend his stay while he set up an office here, oh, and by the way, he was madly in love with her. Lost in myriad scenes that would have made any romantic comedy Oscar winning, Nell felt the day speed by.

In between setting up the lounge and dining room and making trips to the kitchen, Nell made sure the room was ready for her new guests. With excitement she sprinkled rose petals over the duvet, placed a vase of red roses on the table, along with a box of chocolates and a bottle of prosecco. She even wrote them a little card welcoming them to the hotel, that she placed on the table in the room. Within minutes of returning to the dining room, her guests arrived. The young couple, who were extremely happy with their room, really appreciated the special touches she'd added. They were even happy about the carol concert that night, feeling it added to the charm rather than causing them any inconvenience. Nell promised to save them a gingerbread man each and left them to enjoy themselves hoping she'd get a good review to balance these strange bad ones.

Mrs Meggett left later that afternoon, tired but satisfied, her work done. The afternoon light turned from a clear whiteness to a pale, shimmer and darkness rapidly followed as Tom, her moral support for the night, arrived.

'God rest ye merry gentleman, let nothing ye dismay,' he sang in a great baritone voice.

Nell laughed. 'I'm more of a 'I Wish it Could be Christmas Everyday' kind of girl.' She did a little dance on the spot as she sang it.

'I can't wait for tonight,' he said, taking off his coat and gloves. Suddenly he sucked in a breath like he'd hurt himself.

'What?' Nell asked, checking him over. Her eyes came to rest on his left hand. His index finger was wrapped tightly in a bandage. He must have caught it when he took his coat off. 'What happened to your hand?'

'I just nipped myself, it's fine.' He sang the next line of the Christmas carol. 'So what do you need me for?'

Nell eyed the finger once more. It was an occupational hazard in his job, and he seemed so jolly she didn't want to bring his mood down. If she was a florist, she'd probably have lost most of her fingers by now. 'The choir are arriving at 6 p.m. for it all to kick off at 6.30 p.m. The head told me that people will start to arrive from 6 p.m. because they love to get there early. Can you help me with the tea urns? I've brought them up, but I need to fill them. If I fill them first, they're too heavy to get up the stairs. I've labelled the one that's for hot chocolate. We'll put the mince pies out now and the gingerbread will go out after. I thought the kids could do a decorate-your-own kind of thing, so I've got everything in bowls to come out once the singing has finished.'

'Any more mulled wine? I quite fancy a drink. I've come straight from work.'

'No. Sorry.' She watched Tom move around and could see the amount of pain he was in with his finger. Two things didn't seem right. Firstly, Tom had had two accidents in the space of about a week and secondly, he was crazily cheerful. Unnaturally cheerful. The type of cheerful people put on when something was worrying them, and they wanted to convince the world and themselves they were fine. 'Are you all right, Tom?'

'Yeah. Fine. Why?' He'd answered far too quickly, and she didn't feel reassured in the slightest. Tom began to talk of inane things and the subject seemed to be closed. If she pressed too hard, he'd clam up and she'd never get anything out of him, so she carried on with the setting-up and they laughed and joked together, and sung carols.

At five minutes to six, the first of the choir started to arrive and within ten minutes they were all there clad in their school uniform. The tiniest was in reception class and looked like a pretty china doll, the eldest, at 11, thought himself too cool for school, but their headteacher soon had them all in line.

Nell explained where she'd set up and the treats she had in store for afterwards. Even the 11-year-old was excited at the prospect. Another couple of teachers arrived bearing a makeshift nativity scene and Nell directed them to where it could go next to the Christmas tree. A small manger containing a dirty, slightly bald doll took centre stage and next to it they positioned something that was supposed to look like a donkey but was actually more like a rhinoceros. From the centre window they hung a north star that kept veering off to the west.

'What a beautiful setting,' the headteacher said. 'This is lovely. Much better than our cold, draughty, not to mention damp, school hall.'

'When will it be fixed?' Nell asked.

'Not for another few weeks yet. You know how these things are. We have to get lots of quotes for the work then the board has to decide who to give the job to. It's not like the old days

190

when we could just get a local builder to do it, or someone's husband.'

Nell didn't know when the old days that she was referring to were. The head didn't look more than 40 and had beautifully glossy, long, dark hair. She seemed far too young to have the experience a headteacher needed, but when she spoke all the children listened.

'If you don't mind,' the head continued, this time speaking to Nell, 'I'll stand in the hallway and welcome all the parents in then once we hit six-thirty, I'll come and get the kids started.'

'Lovely,' Nell replied, glad that she knew what she was doing. She and Tom stayed in the dining room offering a second welcome and helping with any seating problems. 'Where were you yesterday by the way?' Nell asked Tom. 'I kept ringing you. Janie said you disappeared mid-morning, not telling her where you were going and didn't get back till four. What were you up to?'

It had been four days since Tom had cut his finger. To now have him disappearing off without telling Janie where he was going, and being cagey with her, was worrying.

Tom stared, caught off guard by the question. 'All right, Sherlock Holmes,' he teased. 'I was out.'

'Doing what?'

'I umm, went to see Grandad Nigel.'

'No, you didn't because I called him, and he said he hadn't seen you either. So come on, where were you?' The idea that Tom had lied to her stung; what could be the reason for him not telling her the truth?

'Just out.'

'Why won't you tell me?' She tried to say it in a jokey manner.

'Shush, people are arriving.'

'Fine, but you're telling me later.'

With an effort, she left her inquisition of Tom to welcome the first few arrivals. By six-thirty the room was full with parents, teachers and other pupils and an air of excitement buzzed around them. Despite her fears, she'd been able to fit everyone in which boded well for the mayor's party. The choir fiddled and fidgeted with anticipation, waving nervously at parents. Nell scanned the room and her eyes found the young couple who had checked in earlier and the way they watched with such appreciation told her how happy they were. With Harry as well, that meant she had seven empty rooms, but with her offer running she hoped she'd have some more guests soon. Then she spotted the waitress who had served her and Tom at the Langdon Mansion Hotel. Her neck grew hot as she recalled the embarrassment. She didn't think the shame would ever totally leave her. It seemed to have stained her blood and seeped into her bones. Though Nell smiled to try and show she wasn't an evil con artist after a free meal, the young woman turned nervously away. She clearly felt as uncomfortable as Nell did and Nell decided a wide berth would be the best plan for both of them.

The head stood up in front and all the chatter died away to an expectant silence. 'Good evening, everyone. Thank you so much for coming along to St Herbert's Primary School's Welcome to Christmas carol concert. I'm so excited to hear our wonderful choir. I know the children have been working extremely hard on their songs so without further ado, let's welcome St Herbert's choir.'

She walked away clapping and the children lined up in the lounge. Nell stood back, proud of the time she'd spent that morning moving the tree and decorating the windowsills. The children were framed beautifully. Standing tall in three rows with the three tiniest children in front, they gave big cheesy grins and fiddled, crossing and uncrossing arms, clearing throats, tightening ponytails. Their music teacher walked in front of them and Nell's stomach churned with nerves for them and her. The music teacher nodded to an assistant who was stationed in the corner with a laptop Tom had helped connect to her speakers. He clicked a button and 'Jingle Bells' began to play out. Nell stood at the back of the room with bated breath and the children, in between nervous coughs and some rocking from side to side, began to sing.

Their voices were quiet at first, but they soon warmed up and Nell found herself surprisingly moved. She glanced around for Harry, but he hadn't made it back and a passing moment of sadness swept over her. For the next song, a traditional carol sung without backing music, tears formed in her eyes and she steepled her hands in front of her face. There was something so wonderfully pure, heartfelt and clear in their voices and joy filled the room.

Overcome with happiness, she wiped a tear from her eye as a handkerchief flicked into her line of sight. It was Tom. Trusted, wonderful Tom and she took it before resting her head onto his shoulder. His arm wrapped gently around her waist and he gave a soft squeeze but the look in his eyes wasn't as happy as she expected. Tom loved Christmas and kids, but his excitement was dulled. His expression was clouded with concern and something else she couldn't understand. It was almost like loss or grief and she had no idea why that would be. Her body responded to her worried thoughts by tightening her chest.

A crescendo of music drew her attention and from behind the children she could just make out a skinny black tail weaving its way through the rhinoceros-donkey's legs. Mr Scrooge must have come in through the open front door and was trying to find his spot by the fire. Nell took in a breath and pointed him out to Tom. 'Shit. Mr Scrooge has got into the nativity.'

'You can't disrupt the children,' Tom whispered. 'You'll just have to leave him and hope he settles somewhere and goes to sleep.'

With bated breath they watched Mr Scrooge sniff and roam through the makeshift nativity scene. Only a couple of the children noticed though the cat remained oblivious. He rubbed himself against the legs of the manger almost sending it off balance, turfing baby Jesus out, then gave the rhino a very odd look and made his way back to his little corner. If anyone started sneezing or coughing like they were allergic she'd have to run and get him and take him down to the flat, but so far no one had.

Together they enjoyed the rest of the concert and when the headteacher stood to thank everyone for coming, Nell rushed to the kitchen to start bringing up the mince pies and gingerbread men, along with the decorations and bowls of icing to make things stick. Before she left the kitchen, she put a mince pie on a small plate and left it to one side for Harry, then doubled back and put two more on another tea plate for her and Tom to enjoy after everyone had left. He definitely deserved one for always being there for her. Sometimes she really did take it for granted.

Nell walked back through the door and into the dining room with the platters of gingerbread men. 'Now for all you kiddies, I've got some delicious gingerbread men who need decorating. Who wants to help me?' She was met with a chorus of excited cheers. Tom looked on and the sadness seemed to have disappeared from his eyes. 'And for the adults I've got mince pies and hot chocolate with cinnamon stick or candy cane stirrers for a bit of extra festive fun. Enjoy yourselves!'

On her way back to the kitchen, Nell spotted the waitress again, chatting to one of the parents. She must have had younger brothers or sisters there. Grabbing another couple of platters of mince pies from the kitchen counter, she went back up the stairs, pushing the door with her bum and as she came through, the waitress was near her laptop at the little reception desk in the hall. Nell couldn't tell what she was doing but she was peering around behind it. Luckily, the laptop was always closed, though she'd think twice about leaving it there in the future. 'Can I help you?' Nell asked, keeping her voice light and airy. Startled, the young girl stood bold upright and her cheeks turned pink.

'No, thanks. I was just … umm, looking for an earring.'

'They're both in your ears,' Nell commented dryly.

'I mean the backs. One of the backs has come off. Never mind, though. Thanks.' And like a frightened rabbit she darted back into the throng.

Nell scowled but shook her head and went in to deliver the mince pies. The place was so wonderfully full and the teacher in charge of the laptop had put on some more Christmas songs. Excitement hit the festive air and seeing the place so full made Nell bounce on her tiptoes with joy. As it was now the very end of November it was basically the start of Christmas and no one could fail to be filled with the joy of the season or say it was too early to celebrate. Taking a break, she found a quiet corner and sipped her hot chocolate.

'Here,' said Tom, brandishing a hip flask.

'Naughty,' she replied with a giggle. 'Where did you get that?'

'I know where Mrs Meggett keeps hers.'

'Brandy? Or whisky?'

'Brandy.'

'Yum.' She took a sip of the drink and took a moment to enjoy the velvety sweet warmth in her mouth. 'It's been brilliant tonight, hasn't it? I've loved every minute of it.'

'Me too.'

'What was wrong with you earlier?' she asked, watching him carefully looking for clues and any signs he was lying.

'When?'

'When you handed me your handkerchief? You looked so sad.'

'Nothing.' He shrugged. 'I was just worried about you getting all teary.'

'I can't help it. There's just something about children singing Christmas carols that gets to me.'

'I know,' he replied knowingly. She really did love the fact that he knew her better than anyone. She took another drink of her hot chocolate.

'Their voices always feel like the true sound of Christmas. I

195

don't know what it is about them, but they carry all the excitement of believing in Santa and everything being magical. The world's just a more wonderful place on the build-up to Christmas. Even the cold doesn't feel as bad. What?'

Tom was studying her in a way that felt unfamiliar, yet comfortable. Almost ... exciting. 'I love how your brain works.'

'Do you? I'm not sure it works very well at all. I wonder if I've got so caught up in dreams, I've lost focus on the hotel and that's why business has suffered.'

'I don't think so. It's inevitable the market has changed with the Langdon Mansion opening up. I think you've coped well.'

'That means a lot.' Whether it was due to the wonderful night they'd had or the festive atmosphere, his words meant so much to her that they continued to reverberate through her head causing a strange sensation in her heart. 'Now everyone's mingling, are you going to tell me where you were yesterday?' Tom sighed at her questioning. 'Is it a secret woman?'

As she said the words, she'd meant to tease but the thought of it was like someone stabbing her in the heart. She'd never really thought about it before, but it was the same way she'd felt whenever he got a new girlfriend. Until she got used to them that is, but even then, the feeling faded rather than disappeared completely. She had to stop being so protective of him.

'It's not a woman. I was umm ... Christmas shopping.'

'Secret Christmas shopping? I'm liking the sound of that.' Tom smiled but it was tense. His smiles were normally so wonderfully uninhibited his whole personality shone out through his face. Wherever he'd been she hoped he had a nice time, though she wasn't sure he had from his expression. It was hard for her not to press, but she knew she had to be patient even though that wasn't a trait she'd been blessed with.

Once the gingerbread men and mince pies were gone, the rooms began to clear, and everyone left in a flurry of activity. It was like snow going from one or two flakes in the air to a huge whirlwind of white. One person left then everyone else had gone in the space of five minutes. Before long the hotel was empty with just her and Tom present. It didn't seem Harry was going to arrive any time soon which was disappointing. She'd been so sure he would. But she had Tom and that was all she needed. Tom's words that he loved how her brain worked rebounded in her brain causing a strange feeling in her chest. Nell surveyed the carnage the children had left in their wake. 'Shall we have a mince pie before we start the clean up?'

Tom glanced at the empty platter. 'They've all gone. And so have the gingerbread men. I think there might be one with one ear and half a leg missing if you don't mind a mangled one.'

'I wouldn't mind a mangled one at all, but the mince pies haven't all gone actually. Wait here.' She sped off to the kitchen and came back with the ones she'd saved. 'Just for us.'

They shared the mince pies in the lounge, sitting on the floor by the now lit fire, the golden glow lighting their faces. The pies were delicious, as Nell knew they would be. The pastry flaked in her mouth and the sweet, light dusting of sugar on the top gave some crunch. A strangely expectant silence formed between them.

Usually they talked about anything and everything, never running out of things to say or laugh about. A few times Tom looked on the verge of saying something but then changed his mind and turned his eyes back to the flames. She could see from his expression that his mind was occupied but whether it was the heavy tiredness she also felt, or another matter, there was no way to tell. If she asked, he wouldn't tell her until he was ready and if their friendship had taught her anything over the many years they'd known each other, it was that she had to wait. However hard that was.

Chapter 17

December

Walking down the high street amongst the wooden stalls of the Christmas market, Nell, Tom and Kieran chatted happily. It was Saturday night and Nell had taken a break from the hotel. After the stress of the last few weeks she really needed a night off and Zoe had agreed to cover her again.

Above them, the strings of Christmas lights twinkled against the blackness of the dark, cloudless sky and on the sides of some of the buildings small Christmas trees jutted out, their multicoloured lights aglow. Nell felt like she'd entered a magical fairy tale. The shops of Swallowtail Bay were open late, and their golden lights shone out from wide windows, highlighting pretty Christmas displays. Red tinsel framed giant stars that hung down and spun in the air, and glittering fairy lights made every shop sparkle and shine.

The artisanal shops were Nell's favourite. They had a cheesemaker who did the most amazing Christmas gifts (she'd have to try there for Tom's); a wine seller, and old-fashioned bakers and butchers, and seeing them open tonight, busy with chatter and laughter, made the place seem even more special. The Bake House, an amazing local bakery that had proved so popular they'd just opened another shop in Halebury, had a queue out of the door. In between the stores lining either side of the high street were small wooden huts like a traditional German Christmas market selling all manner of ornately carved and brightly coloured decorations, as well as traditional German food. The town was buzzing with life and happy, smiling people ambled past her.

The small blue-grey cobbles of the high street were already shimmering as a heavy frost settled. The night was cold and clear and by morning the world would have a light dusting of white. It wouldn't be snow, but it would at least make the world look like something from a Christmas card. The chilly air nipped at Nell's cheeks and she pulled her thick knitted scarf higher to help keep warm. With the sea crashing and roaring just a few streets away, both fierce and soothing in its rhythm, it was wonderful to see so many people about. The delicious aroma of rich Christmas spices, boozy mulled wine and sweet cookies and pastries warmed her senses. Her stomach bubbled with excitement like a child at the wonder of it all. Christmas really was the best time of year.

Further down the road, in the middle of the market, a small brass band were playing Christmas songs complete with a few singers. In matching Santa hats, they collected money for charity and Nell watched as the people who passed them mouthed the words to songs or sang along. Couples snatched kisses, children wiggled and danced, and everyone was merry. Even though it was only the start of December, Christmas spirit was everywhere, and everyone seemed to be embracing it making the most of the short time they had to enjoy it, especially if like her, you looked forward to it all year round.

They stopped at a stall and Kieran grabbed a traditional German potato pancake filled with gooey melted cheese, and munched happily. Cat was sadly absent. She'd told Kieran she wanted to come but her mum had called a last-minute meeting about the wedding. Nell hadn't been invited but it seemed something else wasn't quite right and Brenda was getting herself involved. Nell missed her best friend so much and her worry ebbed and flowed like the tide depending on how Cat was behaving. They'd had a few snatched phone calls but even those had been focused on the wedding as Cat was now ordering Nell to change the colour scheme for the party balloons and ribbons to go on the chairs. She could only imagine Brenda was forcing it on Cat because Cat had been perfectly happy with the silvery blue they'd chosen at the beginning of their preparations. Nell didn't want to question Cat's decisions, but she was torn between keeping their friendship trouble free and the duty she felt in helping her get the wedding of her dreams. Kieran had spent the first half an hour of the evening telling her how he wanted to be involved but Cat just wouldn't let him. Nell desperately wanted to see Cat face to face but tonight was Cat's only night off and with her night shifts, it wasn't to be. Kieran dribbled melted cheese down his chin and Nell snapped a photo to send to Cat. Hopefully this would cheer her up.

'This is delicious,' Kieran mumbled, and Tom and Nell burst out laughing.

'I'm after the roasted chestnuts down there,' said Tom. 'I always have a bag of those at Christmas time. Nell, have you seen the wreaths dotted around?'

The leftover wreaths had been placed at the ends of benches, on some of the shop doors and a few even hung from long red ribbons down from lampposts. They added to the traditional feel of Swallowtail Bay. There was nothing overly fancy about the decorations. Classic round, twinkling lights hung across them, zigzagging from building to building. A large Christmas tree stood proudly at the bottom of the high street. It wasn't enormous like the one in Covent Garden, or the one in the Langdon Mansion Hotel for that matter, but it was perfect, and everyone gathered around, admiring the baubles and decorations that hung on its full, bushy branches.

'The whole town looks great,' she replied. 'You should be so proud, Tom.' As she stepped backwards, she spotted the waitress from the Langdon Mansion Hotel and St Herbert's Welcome to Christmas carol service. The one who had been a bit shady about her earring and had lingered around Nell's little reception desk. The girl spotted her too and paused then darted her eyes away. She looked so awkward, Nell went to speak to her. It was about time the air was cleared and she told the girl that she hadn't deliberately put a spider in her soup, but before Nell could get near, she virtually ran away and was lost in the crowd. 'That was weird.'

'What was?' asked Tom.

'I just saw the waitress from the Langdon Mansion again and she just looked … I don't know … like she was avoiding me?'

Tom checked the crowd then returned his gaze to Nell. 'Why shouldn't she avoid you? She doesn't know you and you keep making crazy eyes at her.'

'I am not making crazy eyes!' Nell exclaimed. 'Kieran, am I making crazy eyes?'

Kieran stepped closer and still munching on his potato pancake, examined her face. 'Do the face you did just now.' Nell did and Kieran scowled. 'Sorry, Nell. Definitely crazy eyes. You look like a nutter.'

'Huh,' she huffed. Though she did her best to immerse herself in the festive fun, she couldn't help but feel that she'd enjoy it more if she hadn't read what she'd read that morning. 'That's a bit mean considering I've had yet another bad review.'

She'd checked HotelRater that morning to see if the video had been taken down, but it hadn't and to make matters worse she'd been met with a new bad review.

'Another one?' asked Tom.

Kieran took a few steps away and brought a large bratwurst

from another little wooden stall, eyeing it lasciviously, then shoving it in his mouth with childish delight. 'Bwhahshw hishtiun.'

Nell tried to decipher what he was saying but couldn't. 'I'm sorry, what?'

'Oi! Didn't your mum ever tell you not to talk with your mouth full?' Tom said. Nell loved that he was enjoying himself. He'd been so stressed of late; it was nice to see him joking again.

Kieran swallowed and was finally able to say, 'But isn't that the third one?'

'Yes, it is, Kieran. Thanks for keeping count.' Nell rolled her eyes and Kieran looked abashed then stuck the sausage back in his mouth.

Tom stood at her side. 'What was this one about?'

'Frustratingly, it's another random one I can't place. I genuinely think they must be moaning about some other Holly Lodge and tagging me by mistake.'

'Have HotelRater got back to you yet?'

Nell shook her head as she shuddered in the cold, even in her enormous parka. 'I'll email again on Monday. God knows what Mum and Dad will say this time.' Tom lifted his eyebrows enquiringly. 'We had a catch-up the other day and they were not impressed. They weren't mean, but you know how they like to point out all the things I need to do to turn things around. It just makes me feel even worse. They're threatening to come down if things don't pick up. The only thing that's keeping them away is the wedding business. I've had some enquiries and I'm keeping them posted.' She didn't bother mentioning her conversation with Harry about going to New York. She didn't want to stress Tom out even more and he definitely wouldn't approve of her leaping off on holiday with someone she barely knew. Even she wasn't sure now if it was an actual offer or a vague thing said in the heat of the moment.

'Wow,' said Tom.

They turned to see Kieran having demolished his sausage, now eating an iced doughnut with red and green sprinkles. The man had hollow legs. 'Be careful or your wedding suit won't fit, porky,' she teased, mimicking Brenda and her obsession with slimness.

'Hey! I burn enough calories doing my job.' Licking his fingers, Nell and Tom giggled.

'I want to go to Stella's stall, she's doing gorgeous wooden Christmas decorations,' said Nell, shoving her hands deep into her pockets. Even her fleecy gloves weren't keeping the tips of her finger's warm tonight. 'They're my favourite type.'

Stella had come to Swallowtail Bay in the spring and turned around the fortunes of Old Herbert's Shop. It was lovely to see her tonight in one of the little wooden huts, selling the wonderful Christmas decorations she was stocking. She was also recently engaged and beginning to plan her wedding. Nell hoped that if Cat and Kieran's wedding went well, she and her fiancé, Miles, might think about booking Holly Lodge.

'Come on then.' Tom placed a hand at the base of her back and guided her forward. It felt different somehow, but it was nice to have her Tom back.

The three of them wandered over and Nell perused the little wooden snowmen, big fat Santas, gingerbread men and robins. There were all manner of sizes from enormous ones to sit on windowsills and bookshelves, to little ones with tiny green ribbons for hanging on the tree. 'Stella, these are amazing.'

'Thanks. I couldn't resist them. I just love them, and they're all made locally.'

'Really? I love that. Look at that little nutcracker one, Tom.' Nell pointed to it in the corner of the stall.

'Where?'

'There.' She pointed at it again and watched as he tried to focus his eyes but still hadn't spotted it. 'Look, there.' She picked it up and showed it to him.

'Oh, that one,' he replied, giving a chuckle. 'Sorry, I thought you meant a different one.' The laugh sounded hollow and forced, carrying a hint of a lie. As far as Nell could tell, he'd turned his head in the right direction but just hadn't seen it and it was the only nutcracker there. Nell frowned but decided not to say any more as he seemed a little embarrassed. Unable to resist the festive temptation, she purchased one to hang on the tree at Holly Lodge. She had a little tree in her flat but as she spent most of her time in the hotel itself, the tree in the lounge got all the attention. Just as they were walking away, Tom stumbled, and Kieran caught his arm.

'You all right, mate?' he asked, and Nell became instantly aware of the concern on his face. Normally, Kieran would have cracked a joke or teased Tom. Nell felt her chest tighten, closing over at the base of her throat.

'I'm fine, I'm fine.' Tom reassured them, standing straight. 'I just stubbed my toe on a cobble.'

He hadn't though. Nell had seen it all. He'd done that thing where you stepped and lifted your leg higher than necessary and then because the ground was lower than you thought, you kind of crumpled down. Maybe he needed glasses. That would explain the headaches too. He really should go to the optician's and she hoped it wasn't ridiculous manly pride keeping him from doing so. Worryingly, Kieran's concern seemed like he thought it was about more than just needing the optician's. His face had lost all fun and satisfaction at his food and taken on a ghostly look. Tom suddenly brightened but it was faker than the Christmas tree at Holly Lodge. 'Oh look, there's the roasted chestnut guy. I'm going over. Anyone coming?' Tom stalked off, his hands in his pockets, head down.

'Yeah,' replied Kieran enthusiastically, having recovered enough to still be a bit peckish.

'In a sec,' Nell answered. 'I'll just put these bits away.' In reality, she had no intention of squashing the lovely decorations she'd just purchased into her tiny cross-body bag, she wanted to speak to Kieran and pulled him back by his arm as he tried to walk away. 'Kieran?' Her voice rang with worry. 'What was all that about?'

'What?'

'You know exactly what. That! Tom and that whole couldn't see the decorations thing, and then stumbling over his feet. I've never seen him do anything like that before and your face was ...' She tried to find the words.

'What was my face doing?'

'You looked ...' She continued to search her brain for the right word but the only thing she could come up with was, 'Scared. You looked scared.'

'No, I didn't. He just tripped.' Kieran shrugged. 'He's fine.'

A person dressed as an elf collecting for charity walked past them. After giving them some money, Nell said, 'Well, I don't believe you. And where was he on Thursday?'

Kieran paused like a rabbit in headlights and Nell raised her eyebrows expectantly. So Kieran did know where he was. 'He was at an appointment – with a supplier – just a meeting with a supplier.'

'Ha! No, he wasn't—'

'Oh, no that's right.' She could tell straight away Kieran was lying because he kept pushing his beanie hat down onto his head so it almost covered his eyes, and he shifted his feet. Now Nell was really worried. Why hadn't Tom told her where he was going. 'Ah, that was it, he was writing his best man's speech. He's really worried about it. He just wanted to be alone to do it.'

'You're the worst liar in history, Kieran. There's no way he'd take a day off work to do that. He told me he was Christmas shopping, but I don't believe him.'

'I must have got the wrong day then. Yeah, I've muddled it up.' He was turning redder by the minute. 'I must have. If he says he was Christmas shopping, he was Christmas shopping.'

Though Nell felt bad for putting Kieran on the spot like this, she was becoming increasingly worried about Tom and that he wouldn't tell her what was going on just added fuel to the fire. She really had tried to be patient and wait for him to tell her, but as her worry mounted so did her curiosity. If she knew what was going on, she might be able to help and she hated the idea of him struggling with something alone. 'No, he wasn't, Kieran, he's lying. I can tell.'

Again, Kieran pushed his hat further down onto his head as if that would help him hide. 'Maybe he was Christmas shopping for you and that's why he kept it quiet.'

'Why would he do that?' She gently placed the decorations in her bag. 'He'd never leave Janie alone in the shop just so he could go Christmas shopping and especially not knowing we were coming here to a fabulous Christmas market. And,' she emphasised the word, 'you know perfectly well he gets so excited about what's he bought someone, he tells them straight away.'

'Maybe he wants to get you something extra super special.'

'Why? That still doesn't make any sense, Kieran. I just know he wouldn't leave the shop for that. They're so busy right now.' Clearly finding her interrogation unbearable he tried to walk around her, but she stepped in front of him. 'Kieran, what's going on?'

'Nothing—'

'Kieran, I can tell you're lying. Please, I just want to help. If Tom's worried about something I want to make him feel better.' Kieran tried to respond but she cut him off. 'I love you to bits but you're a terrible, unconvincing liar. You're covering for him and I'm starting to worry something is properly wrong. Something's going on and if you don't tell me what it is, I'm going to go and ask Tom why he's suddenly being weird, lying to me, and can't seem to see prop—'

Completely panicked, Kieran glanced at Tom then back to Nell. 'Nell, wait—'

Under the barrage of words, he'd turned bright pink. She waited but he didn't finish the sentence and just opened and

206

closed his mouth like a fish. 'Right I'm off—' Nell began to walk off.

'Tom loves you,' Kieran blurted.

Nell's stomach tightened like someone had slapped her around the face, which in effect they had. 'What?'

Kieran stopped looking like a rabbit in headlights and now looked like he'd accidentally dropped a bomb – a bomb that had taken half her world with it. 'Nothing,' he said quickly, trying again to shuffle away.

'What are you talking about, Kieran?' She glanced at the roasted chestnut stall and saw Tom being served. He'd be back any minute. She had to know for sure that she'd heard him correctly. The words Kieran had let slip so hastily were buzzing around her head.

'Look, I was never supposed to say anything but surely you must have guessed by now?'

Nell's eyes couldn't focus. Everything she looked at didn't seem real and even the noise of the band faded in her ears. Her heart thudded hard in her chest as if it didn't want to be ignored anymore. 'You mean like a friend, yeah?'

Kieran shook his head. 'You must have known.'

'Why would I have known? And what did you mean by now? He's had girlfriends, I've had boyfriends. How was I supposed to know he felt like that about me?' She felt a little bit queasy with the stress of it all. All the smells that she'd loved when they arrived were too much for her overpowered senses.

'Oh, come on, Nell, he's been in love with you for years. The way he looks at you must have told you? Or have you really never noticed? The way he's always been there for you? The way he always *tries* to be there for you whether you want him to or not. There's …' He counted on his fingers. 'Three things for starters.'

Nell stared at his held-up fingers. 'How do you manage to run your own business?'

'Cat helps me with the counting,' he grumbled.

Even a deep breath of the cold night air didn't help as she tried to come to terms with a tiny sentence that had shaken her world. It stung her throat like she was coming down with something. The lights overhead dazzled rather than romantically framing the moment. 'Tom's in love with me? Me?' Kieran nodded, a small smile pulling at his mouth. 'Does Cat know?'

'No. Tom swore me to secrecy.'

Nell really wished Cat was there with her right now. Her best friend would be full of advice and help her navigate this strange situation. What was she supposed to do? How did she act around him knowing that he was in love with her? With her! What did she say? Cat had always grounded her, doing her best to stop her turning everything into a fantasy and helping her see things as they really were. Never had Nell needed her so much.

'He's coming over,' Kieran said, quickly. 'Act normal.'

Normal? Normal! What was normal? Knowing her own mind, normal for Nell would be imagining a life with Tom – a snowy declaration of love, a kiss under the mistletoe – but she was too shocked to do anything. For once, her mind had frozen and wasn't sweeping her away to another world. That could only mean one thing – it wasn't right – they weren't right. It wasn't to be. So why did that thought make her feel so sad?

Tom came over, oblivious to how Nell's world had just been blown over in the icy chill wind and she suddenly realised that she'd stopped feeling cold the moment Kieran had said those strange unexpected words. Shock normally made you cold but something about Kieran's secret made her feel the exact opposite. She felt warm and … safe? Unsure how to describe it, she focused on the ground. Tom munched happily on his bag of roasted nuts.

'Now these taste like Christmas,' he said, tipping the bag and the dregs of them into his mouth, as normal as he ever had been. 'What's the matter with you two?'

'Nothing,' Nell said, followed swiftly by Kieran.

'Nope, nothing at all, mate. Nope. Nothing.' Nell widened her eyes at him, warning that he was overdoing it.

For her though, everything was wrong, because now, absolutely everything was going to be different, and the mixture of surprise, happiness, joy and fear rolling around her head weren't helping at all.

'Shall we look at that stall over there?' Tom asked, eyeing them both. 'I like the look of their big wooden stars.'

'Okay,' they both agreed hastily and as Kieran walked ahead with Tom, Nell shuffled along behind, trying to understand the strange feeling in her heart and the tightening in her stomach. Everything had changed. Even the back of Tom's head looked different, but still her imagination didn't fire like normal. She only saw them sitting together in the hotel lounge, the light from the fire lighting his face as he pushed his hair back as usual. They were laughing yes, but it was normal, as things always had been. It wasn't crazily romantic like her usual romantic fantasies. If she couldn't love Tom the way he loved her, how did she let him down gently? And how could they stay friends after something like that?

Bryan tore apart the pages of the report, flicking a paperclip up into the air. It landed in his tea with a splash and he sighed deeply. That pretty much summed up his day so far. Find the Sun were really starting to take the piss with their demands. They were supposed to be having a huge Christmas bash – Christmas! – with Christmas trees, snowmen, reindeer, elves, that sort of thing. But no. Find the Sun were making the most extreme and silly demands he'd ever had a customer make. As a travel firm with 'sun' in the title they wanted waitresses in bikinis and sombreros – he was yet to have that conversation with his staff and might actually have to hire in models to serve as he couldn't imagine some of his chubbier employees in swimming costumes and speedos. They also wanted fifteen-foot palm trees instead of Christmas trees

209

(still decorated with tinsel) and they'd already had a blazing row about removing the Christmas tree from reception. He'd left that one to Kevin. To his credit, Kevin had calmly explained that they had a hotel full of guests and dinner bookings for people who wanted to feel Christmassy and so, for the sake of the rest of the hotel guests, the tree in reception was staying put. Given the extortionate amount they were being charged it hadn't gone down well. Bryan had yet to source the palm trees. Then there was the menu. They wanted buffet food from all over the world. François had sworn first in English, then as fury overtook him, resorted to his native language.

But the thing that really got Bryan's goat, was that local news and gossip was all about Holly Lodge and Nell Jones and the amazing things she was doing for the town by hosting local events. Even the mayor, rather than cancel her do, had moved it to Holly Lodge and the Langdon Mansion's reputation locally had taken a battering. Apparently the bad reviews weren't slowing her down. Every week they checked the number of hits on the spider-soup video and it was still going up. If only they'd been able to get hold of the woman who posted it and edit it first. To make matters worse, there'd been an increase in the number of bad reviews of the Langdon Mansion Hotel, particularly the restaurant. Kevin was firefighting with the top brass and reassuring Find the Sun that they were the ones to stick with, but they both knew that if this big event didn't go without a hitch, there was every chance he and Kevin would be transferred to some hotel in the back of beyond or simply sacked.

Kevin came into the office and sat on the edge of Bryan's desk. Bryan hated the way he did it. He also hated the way Kevin pulled up the drainpipe trousers of his suit to reveal his hairy calves. 'So, I've just seen Tallulah.'

'Oh yes,' Bryan raised his eyes. He didn't enjoy the pang of guilt that shot into his brain when the young girl's name was mentioned but he couldn't stop it happening.

'She said the carol concert thing was packed and everyone was impressed with Holly Lodge. It seems Miss Jones has had some more bookings. Some bloke's staying for a good few weeks while he visits family and she's doing lots of offers too. Everyone was talking about how we'd let down the town because they mayor's party had been dropped.'

'Tallulah got all this from a few mums at a carol concert?'

'No, you idiot.' Bryan didn't like being called an idiot but bit his tongue. If he insulted his boss, he'd be sacked on the spot. Kevin didn't like to be challenged. 'She's heard a lot at the school gates when she's gone to pick her brother and sister up and just general chit-chat in town too. Our name's mud. The only good thing is that she's heard Holly Lodge is still in financial trouble. Nell Jones is hoping that a wedding she's holding for her best friend just before Christmas is going the be the saviour of her business.'

'So, what do we do?' asked Bryan.

'I think,' Kevin said with a malicious glean in his eye, 'we get someone at that wedding and sabotage it.'

'What? Isn't that going a bit far?' Though Bryan tried to swallow down his fear, his voice dripped with it.

'I don't think so with the damage she's done to our reputation.'

For the first time, Bryan wished they'd never started this campaign against Holly Lodge. Everything seemed to be spiralling out of control and a tiny, annoying part of his brain told him it was his fault. But it was too late. Without a doubt, if head office found out what they'd been up to, Kevin would blame him for everything, denying any involvement and leaving him out to dry. Bryan had no choice but to go along with it now. There was no turning back.

'If we can tell the bosses that our only real competition has gone under,' said Kevin, 'and we've got a monopoly here, there's every chance they'll overlook the video and the recent bad reviews, and we can keep our jobs.'

'But what about the number of complaints we've had? They'll know about those as well.'

'Only the ones that go direct to head office.' Kevin shrugged.

'But …' However hard he tried Bryan was having trouble grasping things. 'We're supposed to report on all complaints we receive here, face to face. Formal or informal.'

'Do you want to keep your job or not?' Kevin snapped. 'If we keep a lid on the smaller, minor complaints we're getting here face to face—' Kevin mimicked the way Bryan had said it and he felt the tiny hairs on the back of his neck stand on end '—and pull the Find the Sun event off without a hitch, we won't be looking at the sack, we'll be looking at bonuses.'

Still reeling from his mockery, Bryan stayed calm. 'So how do we get someone into this wedding?'

'I've already thought of that,' he said smugly. 'She's hired Niall Peters as the chef and I know his business partner who takes care of staffing. I'm going to make sure Tallulah is included on that list as a favour.'

'Tallulah? Don't you think she's done enough? She's only a girl.' That damn scruple was flicking his conscience into life again.

'What are you, her skint father? This is the last thing she needs to do, and I've promised her a whacking great Christmas bonus if she can.'

'The mayor's ball is before that. Can't we send her there rather than to a wedding and ruin someone's day?'

'There's that conscience again, Bry.' Kevin wagged a finger in his face. 'And anyway, Tallulah's just seen her in the town, and said she's sure Nell recognised her. It's too soon for her to work the party. Nell Jones will figure it out. We need to wait until this wedding. By then she'll have forgotten who Tallulah even is. The girl's plain and easily forgettable. Plus the wedding will be more impactful. She can – I don't know – destroy a few decorations, knock a couple of bottles of wine over, chuck a fly or two in the soup.'

Byran's mouth had gone all dry. This was all spiralling out of control. Tallulah was just a young girl desperate for money. If his mother could see what he was doing, she'd be absolutely appalled. He knew that by letting this continue he was letting himself down and Tallulah too. But what could he do? Kevin's enormous bright white teeth and tight smile were slightly menacing, and he really didn't want to go back to working in second-rate hotels with damp and bug infestations. 'Okay,' he agreed quietly. 'If there's no other way.'

Chapter 18

On Monday morning, Tom sat in the consultant's waiting area at the hospital. He hated hospitals. Hated them with a vengeance. It was the smell. That awful disinfectant smell. If they smelled of flowers, or something much nicer people probably wouldn't get as nervous. It was just so … clinical.

Last Thursday he'd had an appointment here for some tests and somehow, he'd snuck away without Janie or Nell knowing even though, the next day, she'd quizzed him at the carol concert. He'd managed to palm her off with a rather flimsy excuse and she'd been too kind to press him further. Kieran knew and had thankfully covered for him. He'd wanted to tell Nell, especially when he'd seen the concern in her eyes, but it would have spoiled the carol concert and he still couldn't form his concern into words.

Kieran had driven him here today after Tom had been advised not to drive until they knew what was wrong. Kieran had agreed fully, advising Tom in no uncertain terms that driving with, as he put it, 'wafty eyes' was a really bad idea considering he'd already had one accident. As grateful as he was for his friend's support, Tom had asked him to wait in the café. He just couldn't stand the sympathy radiating off him. All it did was make him worry even more. After all, he'd managed to get through all the tests on his own and now he was at last going to get the results. With any luck, the heavy weight in his stomach would be gone in the next half an hour and he could maybe get some glasses to sort things out and then his life would return to normal. He sat forwards, both arms resting on his knees, his scarf dangling from his hands. Though he kept telling himself that, he couldn't quite believe it.

Tom sat back, having read the notice board in front of him several times. He now knew the importance of having your poo checked for signs of bowel cancer when you were over 60; that, surprise, surprise, smoking wasn't good for your health; and he also knew that in the UK they ate below the required number of portions of fruit and vegetables per day. Maybe he'd be told to eat more carrots, he mused. If only.

The consultant was running late which he'd expected, knowing how busy and understaffed the NHS was, but it wasn't helping his nerves. He'd been waiting an extra half an hour already and Kieran kept texting asking what was happening. Had he gone in yet? What had they said? Was he okay? Tom's last reply had been a bit sharp and he knew he'd owe Kieran a pint by the end of the day, but the questioning was just too much for his stressed-out brain. Hopefully soon they could celebrate that he was okay after all, though the headache he'd had last night, that had caused him to go to bed at seven and lie in a dark room, reminded him the chances were slim. The hand of panic gripped him again inching up his neck and tightening the skin at the back of his skull.

The door opened and his consultant, Mr Carrington, asked him to come in. Mr Carrington's long slim face gave a polite and welcoming smile that Tom tried not to read too much into, but his nerves were tingling with worry and anticipation. He suddenly needed a wee and wished he'd gone earlier, but he hadn't wanted to risk missing his name being called. Mr Carrington rounded to the other side of the desk and Tom sat opposite. He wrapped his scarf around his hand then unwound it again.

'So, Mr Barton, how have you been? Any more headaches? Any other problems?'

'A few more headaches, everything is much the same as last week.'

'I see.' He typed on his keyboard and clicked the mouse, checking some details. Then he turned and his calm eyes focused on Tom. 'Well, we've had the results of your tests and I'm afraid to say you have a condition called Retinitis Pigmentosa.'

Tom tried to take in the words, but his brain had stuck on the phrase you have a condition. It meant something was actually wrong and vomit sprung up into his throat. He tried to swallow it down and catch up with what Mr Carrington was saying. 'It's a hereditary degenerative eye condition where the cells of the retina die and that affects a person's peripheral and night vision. It can sometimes affect the central vision as well.'

'Right.' Tom wound the scarf around his hand again, tighter this time, as if focusing on the discomfort would stop him panicking. 'What does that mean exactly?'

'I'm afraid that, as has already started, your eyes will find it difficult to adjust to the changes in light levels at night, and over time you will lose your peripheral vision altogether. When I talk about some cases losing their central vision too, if that should happen you will unfortunately—'

'Be blind.' The words had tumbled out without him realising. It was almost as if his brain was trying to understand by verbalising it, but he couldn't take it in. He couldn't go blind. He didn't want to go blind. His life would change forever if he went blind. How would he drive? How would he work? How would he live? How would he see the sunrise? Visit Grandad Nigel? See Nell's face?

Mr Carrington's patient and steady voice broke through the panic. 'I'm very sorry, Mr Barton. I know it's a lot to take in.'

'What – what can we do about it?' Surely there was some kind of treatment to stop it. Drugs? Tablets? Laser beams fired into his eyes? Robot retinas? Modern medicine could cure virtually anything, couldn't it? The room was suddenly ridiculously bright even though it was grey and rainy outside, the light too strong and penetrating, illustrating how his eyes were useless now.

'I'm afraid there aren't any treatments for it at the moment.' Inside, Tom's body crumpled. 'But it is a field of study that's being taken very seriously. What we can do is monitor your condition and help you adjust as it worsens.'

Tom forced his next question out through his dry, scratchy throat. 'How long will it take?'

The consultant gave a sympathetic shrug. 'I'm afraid there's no way of telling. It could be months or years. We'll monitor you closely from now on, but there's no way to predict.' He leaned forward a little, clasping his hands together on the desk. 'I know it seems like the end of the world right now, Mr Barton, and it is going to be a huge adjustment, but it really isn't the end. A lot of people continue to lead perfectly normal lives by making changes to their lifestyles.'

Tom replied with a nod of acknowledgement, but his breath froze in pure terror. A future that he'd thought looked normal now looked anything but. He wasn't too ashamed to admit he was frightened. He was petrified. What would his business look like if he couldn't see? He couldn't cut and arrange flowers, that was for sure. Would he need a guide dog or a white cane? He could feel his confidence ebbing away as gloomy thoughts ran through his head and the fear of how different everything would be penetrated his soul. 'You said hereditary?'

'Yes.' Mr Carrington nodded. 'That's why I was asking about your family background in our last meeting. You mentioned your grandad. I think it's likely he has the condition too. I'd definitely advise contacting the RNIB. They're an amazing support and will help you come to terms with the diagnosis. They can also give you lots of advice as to how you can make adjustments to your home and workplace so you can continue as normally as possible. I'm afraid you won't be able to drive anymore and will need to inform the DVLA. Did you have any other questions for me?'

Probably, Tom thought. Only his brain couldn't function enough to form any. He shook his head.

'Well, if you do think of anything, I'm happy to help. We'll be in touch shortly to arrange your next check-up appointment, okay?'

Tom nodded and stood up, taking the hint that the appointment was over. He could feel a headache coming on, but this wasn't the usual type caused by his eyes, this was a stress headache. His stomach lurched with queasiness and though he was clenching his jaw to keep his emotions in check, a stinging in his nose spread to the back of his eyes. 'Thanks for your time, Mr Carrington.'

'Take care, Mr Barton.' The consultant rose and the two men shook hands before Tom left.

Closing the door softly behind him, he noticed he'd wrapped the scarf tightly around his hand again. Tom slumped down into a waiting-room chair. He was aware of the receptionist stepping out from behind the desk. She went to the water machine and filled a small plastic cup then, to Tom's surprise, she came over and handed it to him. 'Here you are, love. Have a minute.'

She'd probably never know it, but that small gesture of concern meant everything to him in that moment. The bottom had fallen out his world and everything he'd ever hoped and imagined was sliding down a big dark hole, forever lost to him. It felt like his life was over.

Taking a deep breath, he tried to regain some perspective. Others had it far worse than him and he hadn't been told he had an incurable brain tumour which was something he'd genuinely feared. He sipped the water, feeling the coldness slide down his throat. Calming down, Tom felt more able to find Kieran though his hands were trembling. He took his phone off silent and saw he had some more messages from his friend who was only down the corridor, clearly as worried as he was. Tom went to find him, thinking that they could go into town and get a coffee to steady his nerves and give him some energy to figure out how he was going to cope with the rest of his life. There was no way he could think about anything like that on his own right now. Thanking the receptionist for her kindness, he stood on shaking legs and made his way out of the waiting area.

He made his way to the café feeling wobbly and almost faltered seeing the troubled look on his best friend's face. Kieran went to the vending machine and bought them both a coffee. When he brought them over, Tom wrapped his hands around the thin paper cup. He still had a plaster on his index finger though it wasn't as huge as the previous ones. It was just a normal plaster now.

Looking at Kieran, he suddenly realised he might never see Cat and Kieran's kids, if they made it down the aisle, that was. Then his heart almost stopped beating. He'd never see Nell's face again. A face he'd always wanted to cup in his hands, to kiss her lips and let her know just how much he loved her, how special she was and how different. To give her one of those romantic moments she loved in movies. Though it hadn't ever really been on the cards for them, he felt the loss of the chance even more keenly.

'So, what did the doc say?'

Tom's eyes met Kieran's and he told him the news.

'Geez, mate. I'm so sorry.' He shook his head. 'Have you called Nell yet?'

'No.'

'Nigel?'

Tom sighed. 'No.'

'You have to. You know that, right?'

Tom stared at the dark liquid swirling in his cup. Kieran was right, he did have to tell his grandad and Nell too, but until he'd figured out how his life was going to work from now on, he didn't want to worry them. And there was Janie to think about.

An overwhelming urge to make the most of the time he had to do the job he loved consumed him. What would happen to his business if he couldn't do the deliveries? If he couldn't see to make the designs and if he couldn't do the actual accounting? Janie was proving to be very gifted, but she was young to handle so much responsibility and it was still responsibility he wanted to bear. When it came down to it, he wasn't ready to give it up. He needed to get back to work. He'd left Janie alone in the shop enough already over these last few weeks.

That night at the Langdon Mansion Hotel, Nell had mentioned that her life seemed to be at a turning point. He hadn't really understood at the time, but he did now. Only he hadn't expected such a major one. 'I'd best get back to the shop,' he said, standing.

'But you've hardly drunk your coffee,' Kieran pointed out. He reached out and grabbed Tom's sleeve. 'I know it's not the nicest coffee in the world, but come on, mate, take a minute. If you want to shout, cry … whatever, I don't mind. I'm here to help.'

'Sorry. I just – I just want to do something normal. I think I'll head to work.'

'Work? Really?' Tom nodded. 'If you're sure.' He let go and swigged some of his coffee before standing up. 'Want me to come round tonight and we'll watch the footie?'

Watch the footie. Even that phrase was like a knife plunged further into his chest. How long would it be until he couldn't actually watch anything? All he'd have was the sound and audio descriptions. 'No, thanks, mate. I need some time alone to get my head round this. Do you mind if we just go? I can't stand this smell anymore.' The aroma of disinfectant was even more pungent here. Or maybe it was him. Whatever it was, it was making him queasy.

'Of course.' The teddy bear side of Kieran was coming out

again as his voice rang with unease. 'I really don't like the thought of you going back to work after such a shock. Why don't you come and hang out with me?'

'Honestly, I think it's for the best.' Tom realised he was wrapping his scarf around his hand again.

He was lucky to have such a friend. Someone who'd stick with him through thick and thin and already had for years. He knew Nell would be supportive too when he told her, but he just couldn't deal with that yet. She'd hug him and being in her arms would only intensify the pain of everything he was about to lose. There had never been much of a chance of them getting together, but it was like the last vestige of hope had gone with his diagnosis. The only thing he could deal with was getting back to the shop. He might even give Janie the afternoon off. After all, she'd covered for him enough, she deserved it. And he'd make sure to give her a surprise Christmas bonus in her pay packet this month. She was a good girl and if he was looking at winding up the business and finding something he could do even when his sight failed, she'd be out of a job.

As they left the warmth of the hospital and stepped into the cold December air, Tom again felt the whole of his life sliding away: all his plans, all his dreams, all his hopes for the future were fading with his sight. He'd never felt so low in his entire life and it was only going to get worse, but he had to push those feelings deep down inside and bury them. There were only five days until the mayor's Christmas party when he and Nell would be turning Holly Lodge into a winter wonderland and less than two weeks till Kieran and Cat's wedding. He had to keep it together until then.

As much as he could on the drive back, he studied the world of Swallowtail Bay before he wasn't able to see it anymore: the rolling green fields surrounded by high hedges; the way the coast appeared on the horizon and then ran alongside as you drove into town. He tried to memorise the endless noise of the seagulls,

221

remember the way they soared on the wind, gliding effortlessly.

The sea was blustery today, violently crashing onto the shore – destructive. Something about it matched Tom's mood. Before long, they entered the hustle and bustle of town and seeing the glittering Christmas lights hung all along the promenade made a lump form in his throat. Being surrounded by Christmas decorations made it all seem worse somehow. Receiving this news at any time would have been awful but getting it at Christmas – at the most magical time of the year – made it even harder to bear. Every decoration reminded him that at some point he'd be like Grandad Nigel, unable to see anything at all.

What would Christmas be like when he couldn't see? Would it still feel the same? It was the start of December, traditionally the time they got the Christmas tree out. At some point there'd come a time when he couldn't put the tree together with Nell at Holly Lodge or decorate it. The stinging in his nose returned as tears tried once more to take over. The town was busy with early Christmas shoppers and the tree at the bottom of the high street sparkled in the dull light.

Looking around he felt all his Christmas spirit vanish. It wasn't the most magical time of the year for him. It was the most horrendous.

Chapter 19

Saturday came far too quickly, and Nell had roped in all her friends to help rearrange and decorate Holly Lodge ready for the mayor's party that evening. To set the mood, she had cheesy Christmas music playing as loudly as she could get away with and set up a tea tray for them all with gingerbread men, mince pies and lebkuchen. There was more than enough to keep them going. Cat had taken the day off work, and Kieran and Tom were joining them later.

The thought of seeing Tom for the first time since Kieran told her how he felt about her – how he'd always felt about her – made her more nervous. It had been a relief not to see him as often as usual this week, but she was still worried about him. Since Monday he hadn't really spoken to her. Whenever she'd called, he'd been dashing off to see Nigel, or been working late into the evening. Though she had some guests, she'd also pretended to be busy with preparations for the party, and somehow had managed to avoid him without it being obvious. She just needed to figure out how to act around him first.

Nell wondered now if that was why he'd been so distant lately. Maybe as it was Christmas and they were both single he was feeling lonely. The thought that he wanted her made her both excited and scared in equal measure. Over the last few days, she'd spent the time trying to imagine a life with Tom, but her brain refused to budge. It made her feel guilty that she couldn't picture anything, because it meant only one thing – she didn't want him the same way she'd wanted other men.

To save her from herself, Nell shifted her attention onto Cat, who'd just come through the dining-room door. Holding onto the news for nearly a whole week had been the hardest thing she'd ever done, but Cat had been working long hours again, and whenever they'd talked, she'd had wedding things to discuss. Nell hadn't wanted to hijack those discussions with something like this, especially over the phone.

'Hey,' Cat said quietly, full of trepidation. Nell could immediately see she felt guilty for changing her mind on some more of the wedding details. The latest thing had been the fairy lights. Cat had originally wanted golden rather than white lights framing the dining room to give a more golden glow. Brenda had wanted star-shaped bright white ones. Both Nell and Cat had agreed and fought for the golden lights and it had all been settled until a day ago when Cat had changed her mind. They'd had a small disagreement because there was only a week to go until the wedding, but Nell had been forced to back down when it looked like they might end up rowing. Seeing Cat now, Nell jumped up and took her in a hug.

'Hey, are you okay?' Nell said into her cheek, then planted a big kiss.

'Yeah. Listen, sorry I got a bit narky with you again. It was work.' She slumped down in the chair and Nell immediately grabbed her a mince pie and gingerbread man and put them in front of her. 'I had a mum have a really difficult birth and it got to me.' Cat pushed a hand through her hair. 'We nearly lost the baby. It was just awful.' Nell studied her friend's tired face. She was tearing up at the memory and Nell hugged her again. That explained so much. The importance of lights did pale in comparison to a newborn baby's life hanging in the balance. Maybe Cat's job was reminding her what was important and what wasn't. If she'd chosen to have the same lights her mum wanted, was that a big deal? Nell decided to stop being so judgemental and let Cat make her own decisions. The responsibility, worry, fear and adrenalin must have been a lot for her to bear. It wasn't an easy job with long hours and so much pressure. She literally had lives in her hands. Tiny ones. If she could handle that, she sure as hell could handle decision-making for her own wedding. It was time for Nell to take a step back.

'I'm so sorry, darling. Why didn't you tell me?'

Cat wiped a tear away. 'I think I was still processing it all. Sometimes I'm so busy dealing with the emergency that it's only after that things really hit me.'

'Does Kieran know?'

'No.' Another tear escaped. 'I just didn't want to talk about it at all.' Nell nodded her understanding. 'And Mum's been bloody awful. I'm really sorry for being a bridezilla.'

A rush of emotion charged through her as she pictured Cat keeping a panicking mum calm and helping a tiny baby. 'I'm sorry. I should have been more supportive instead of just charging in and getting on my soapbox. Forgive me?'

'Forgive me?' Cat said with a smile.

Nell nodded. 'Let's forget about it all and get started on the decorations. There's tonnes to do and it's about time we got excited for your wedding! Can you believe there's only a week to go?'

'Not really,' Cat said, a slight sadness to her voice. 'It's gone so quickly.'

'It's been a learning curve I can tell you.'

The only good thing about Brenda's interference was that she'd learned a lot about dealing with last-minute changes and found suppliers who can deliver quickly. They were now on a special list on her computer. 'But I can't wait to see you and Kieran tie the knot.'

'Me too. So what's been going on with you this week?'

'Actually, I have got something to tell you.'

'Oh? What's that? Something wedding-related, I guess.'

As Cat took off her coat and got comfortable at the table prepared with scissors, Sellotape and white paper to make snowflakes and stars, Nell took a deep breath and told her about Tom.

Cat paused from cutting out her paper snowflake. 'Tom's been in love with you all this time? What? That's insane. I mean, we've known each other for over ten years. Why hasn't he said anything before now?'

Nell manhandled some silver ribbon while in the background Kylie whispered her shopping list to Santa. 'I've no idea. I can understand him not saying anything when he had a girlfriend or I had a boyfriend, but there have been times when we've both been single, and he still hasn't made a move.'

'Maybe he isn't sure what you'd say and if you said no that would be—'

'Horrendously awkward and beyond embarrassing?'

Cat giggled. 'Like, crazy awkward. I mean, how would you even talk to each other again. Yuck.' She shuddered at how humiliating the whole situation would be.

'Yes, thank you,' Nell replied with a smile, throwing her hand through her un-brushed hair. 'Do me a favour though, don't ever become an agony aunt. You're more agony than aunt.'

Cat snickered and went back to her snowflake, turning the paper as she cut, her tongue poking out a little from the corner of her mouth. When she'd finished, she placed it down, took a bite of her gingerbread man and washed it down with a sip of tea. 'I can't believe Kieran never told me. He's normally rubbish at keeping secrets.'

'It must have been hard keeping this from you, but it's probably a good thing. If you'd found out, you'd have told me within about two minutes. You won't be mad at him, will you?' As everything at last seemed to be settling down between Kieran and Cat and there'd been no more flirtations with Niall, Nell didn't want anything to cause problems now.

'I'm not.' Cat looked like the thought wouldn't ever occur to her. 'I completely understand. You've told me stuff and asked me not to tell, and you've helped me hide my shoe obsession from Kieran for years now.' After finishing the gingerbread man and moving onto the mince pie, she said, 'The question is how do you feel about it?'

Nell looked earnestly at her friend. 'I just don't know. I mean, Tom's a handsome guy. In fact, I think he's got even better with age.' A tiny tingle started somewhere in the vicinity of her heart, but it could easily have been indigestion. 'And he's sweet and kind and funny, but I don't know. For a while now I've wished for someone who knows me inside out—'

'Which Tom does.'

Mariah Carey belted out 'All I Want for Christmas is You' and Nell's chest tightened with the sentiment. 'Yes, but I've never looked at him in *that* way before.'

'Try it now,' suggested Cat. 'It's not that much different to me and Kieran. Except we figured it out a lot sooner than you two.'

'Oh, so you're turning this into a competition, are you?' Nell had missed this sort of gentle teasing with her friend.

'Here,' said Cat, resting her mug on the table and cupping her fingers around it. 'I've got an idea. Close your eyes and imagine you're on a beautiful sandy beach—'

Through one eye, Nell said, 'What's wrong with the pebbly one we have here in Swallowtail Bay?'

'Just do it!'

Both of Nell's eyes popped open. 'Considering you're always telling me to stop living in my imagination, this feels a little hypocritical.' Cat glared. 'All right, I'll do it, but I've tried imagining myself with Tom and I can't. My mind just doesn't want

227

to go there which can only mean one thing, can't it? We're not meant to be together.'

'And how does that make you feel?'

'Sad?' She'd posed it as a question because she wasn't sure herself. Was it sadness she felt because she couldn't return Tom's feelings? Sadness that if they did get together, they'd have wasted so much time? That final thought sent a shock through her, but her heart and head were such a mix of emotions she didn't know what to think or feel.

'The trouble with you is that you've let your imagination set standards for how romance and relationships should be and then reality can never measure up. You've convinced yourself it's all bunches of roses and love notes and romantic candle-lit dinners, and while things might be like that to begin with, real love and real romance isn't about those grand gestures.' Nell listened intently, knowing full well Cat was right. 'Real love is running you a bath when you've come home from work frazzled and absolutely knackered. It's knowing your favourite takeaway or brand of gin. It's buying you the extra soft tissues when you've got the flu even though you think they're a bit of a rip-off. They're the things that really matter, not roses and picture-perfect movie moments.'

Now Nell came to think of it, Tom had done some of those things for her. Not the bath thing, but he always knew what she wanted from the Chinese. Once, he'd even gone out in the middle of the night for some throat spray because she had tonsillitis and when he'd returned, he'd also brought her delicious expensive chocolate ice cream too. Had she been letting her imagination run away with her for so long she'd missed the real love right under her nose? Was that what had been happening with Harry too? Because what she felt for him didn't seem as solid or as anchored in her heart as the feelings she had for Tom. The realisation felt like the ground shifting beneath her feet and how she understood her emotions shifted with it.

'Come on, close your eyes and let's do this exercise,' Cat demanded. 'It's a visualisation technique I use to help my mums handle labour pains, but I want to try something. Okay?'

'All right.' Leaving behind the crackling fire burning in the grate and the smell of cinnamon and orange from the festive willow garland over the fireplace, Nell did as she was told and pictured the long, sandy beach. In her mind, the white sand was unbroken by footprints and a calm, bright blue sea glimmered in front of her.

'Now picture the sun setting in the sky creating a beautiful orange sunset.'

Cat's voice was surprisingly soothing, and Nell retreated into her imagination and the wonderful beach, leaving behind all conscious thought. She could almost feel the heat on her face, the sand beneath her toes and the gentle breeze ruffling her hair. She pictured herself in a floaty sun dress, rather than the bright red Christmas jumper she was currently wearing, her hair loose about her face.

'Now picture the man of your dreams walking towards you. It can be your TV crush, or that hunky American who's staying.'

Nell giggled but kept her eyes closed. 'You do this with your mums? Don't their husbands mind?'

'I told you I want to try something and you're normally the one away with the fairies so keep those eyes closed.' She did as she was told and Cat's low, relaxing voice continued. 'You're standing on the beach and he comes towards you. He's walking slowly, smiling.' Nell felt the corners of her mouth mirroring the imaginary smile. 'He gets closer and closer until he's right in front of you. Don't look at his face yet. Then he wraps his arms around you and kisses you.'

With burning cheeks, Nell's breath hitched in her throat. The kiss was intense, full of love everlasting but there was excitement and passion there too. 'Now, without opening your eyes describe him to me.'

229

'He's got lovely hair the colour of sand. It's longish, but not girly. And he's got gorgeous eyes with a few crow's feet at the side that make him look distinguished and when he smiles little frown lines appear on his forehead.' As realisation dawned, Nell gasped. 'It's Tom! Oh my gosh, Cat! He looks like Tom.'

Cat sat back, full of satisfaction. 'Looks like Tom or is Tom?'

'It is Tom.' Nell's mouth fell open as it suddenly dawned on her how much she loved her friend and *how* she loved him.

All those times she'd felt weird when he had a girlfriend. It wasn't concern that they weren't right for him, it was jealousy. The little moments they had together, like when they nearly fell after he'd called Tracey to organise the wreath-making. She'd known her life was at a crossroads but had thought it was all down to the business, but it hadn't been. It had been her feelings for Tom changing too. Maybe as she'd started facing the reality of her business failing, she'd been forced to live in the real world and leave the daydreams behind. It had been the catalyst for her to see things as they really were. Letting go of the ridiculous expectations she had of how things should feel and how things should be, had allowed her to open her heart for Tom. He'd always been there at the centre of her heart. Always. Only the timing had never been right for her to notice. Was that why he didn't propose to the last one? They'd all been so sure he would.

'What's going on here then?' asked Harry, striding into the dining room where the girls were sitting. He pulled up a chair, grabbed some scissors, and began cutting out a snowflake.

Nell didn't know how much he'd seen or heard, but strangely she didn't care. She didn't care what he knew or thought because as handsome as he was, he wasn't the one for her. She knew that now. All her made-up scenarios were just that – made up. They weren't real and her feelings for him had been entirely imagined. It was as if a winter wind had blown through Holly Lodge, taking her flights of fancy with it. Nell realised that her previous relationships hadn't lasted not because the romance had died away but because they just weren't meant to be. They weren't anything compared to what she felt for Tom. It was time to gain control of her imagination.

Nell turned to him and said, 'We're setting up for the mayor's party and needed to finish off some more snowflakes. They're going to hang from the ceiling at different heights, so we create a winter wonderland.'

'Sounds amazing.' His eyes flickered but Nell's heart failed to flutter.

'Oh, and anyone from the hotel is welcome to come. So, if you're at a loose end tonight, feel free to come down and join us.'

'I might just do that,' he said with a glance that before would have caused a wobble in her kneecaps. This time she admired the rugged set of his features, but it was nothing more than an aesthetic evaluation. 'So, listen, Nell, it turns out I'm flying back on Monday.'

'Oh, okay,' Nell replied and again, found that her heart didn't stir even once. No feeling of longing had gripped her, no sense of loss inspired by an imagined teary goodbye. Her heart didn't belong to Harry or anyone else. The only concern she had was that the hotel would then be empty. It would be full next weekend with Cat's wedding, but she really needed some midweek bookings to get enough money to pay the month's wages. 'I hope you've enjoyed your stay. I'll get your bill all prepared. It's been lovely having you here.'

'And you are the best hostess in the world,' he replied, standing up and giving her a kiss on the cheek. 'Have fun tonight.' Harry left, leaving his star half-cut.

Once he'd gone, Nell resumed her cutting and Cat said, 'That settles it, you know.'

'What does?'

'Harry might as well have been a tiny old fat man for all the dreamy eyes you gave him. It shows that you are well and truly in love with Tom. And that soppy grin tells me so too.'

Her heart fluttered uncontrollably at the thought of him. 'But what do I do now?'

'What do you mean?'

'Do I tell him or not?' Nell peered over the top of her scissors and Cat stared back, distinctly unimpressed.

'Of course you tell him. Why wouldn't you? Especially as you already know he feels the same way. You're not going to get rejected. It's a hundred per cent guaranteed love.'

'I don't know.' While she had the assurance that he had feelings for her, she didn't know if she was brave enough to make the first move and tell him so. Could she? It was the twenty-first century, she reminded herself. All she had to say was one or two short sentences, she could manage that. They'd be out and over within a few seconds.

'You could do it tonight,' Cat suggested. 'At the party.'

Tom had arranged for the party to be here, and something felt right about doing it tonight in the middle of the winter wonderland they were creating together. Their very own winter wonderland here at Holly Lodge. Nell glanced at Cat. 'I will. I'm going to. I'm going to say it. I'm going to say, "Tom, Kieran told me you have feelings for me, and I love you too."'

With a squeal Cat jumped up from her seat, Nell jumped up from hers and they hugged each other until she could barely breathe. Then Cat's expression became deadly serious. 'But do me a favour?'

'What?' Nell asked, slightly worried by her gaze.

'Change out of that horrendous shapeless jumper?'

Nell rolled her eyes. 'I was going to wear something slightly more glitzy to the party.'

'Good. Because seriously, that jumper makes you look like a bright red sack of potatoes.'

'Remind me again why you're my best friend?'

Tapping her chin with her index finger, Cat pretended to think of a reason. 'Oh, I don't know. Maybe because I helped you realise you're in love with Tom?'

'Okay I'll give you that one.' A huge smile filled Nell's face and her heart throbbed in her chest.

As the fire roared in the grate and the smell of Christmas surrounded her, Nell thought of all the great romcom endings she loved. For all the ones where the guy finally confesses his love, she always loved the ones where the woman said it first. There was no way the night couldn't be magical because tonight, she was going to leave the daydreams behind and embrace a real life with the wonderful man who loved her.

Chapter 20

The rest of the day passed incredibly quickly. Cat and Nell had left only a few chairs in the lounge and a few tables at the side of the dining room to be used for snacks and bowls of Christmas punch. She'd folded bright white tablecloths over them, sprinkled on silver glitter and wound lights around the edge, and all she needed were Tom's garlands to continue the Narnia-like feel. A bar had been set up in the conservatory and she'd hired a barman who'd be arriving later.

Hearing Tom's voice resonate through the hall, Nell jumped and turned to Cat in panic. For some reason, she brushed down her jumper and retied her hair in a ponytail. Pointless really, because Tom had seen her in far worse states than this. 'Hi,' she said with a strange little wave, her voice unusually high and squeaky. Seeing his face with fresh eyes and a heart that finally knew itself, she realised just how attractive he was. It was almost as if, because they'd begun as friends, she'd taken his face and personality for granted. Seeing him now sent a shock through her that tingled her fingers.

'Hey,' Kieran replied, giving Tom the side eye. The weight of the world seemed to be pressing on Tom's shoulders and his eyes were tired and dark.

'Hey, Tom,' Nell said again. Even saying his name felt different on her tongue. In his arms he carried the beautiful arches he'd created with fir branches, baubles, tinsel and strategically placed bits of holly because they didn't want to stab anyone.

Finally, Tom realised she'd been speaking to him. 'Hey, you. You okay? Nervous?'

'Yeah, really nervous.' She brushed her hair behind her ear.

She felt like an awkward teenager. Her world had shifted like a tectonic plate causing an earthquake. His face seemed different tonight. She saw his kind eyes that now held her spellbound; hair the colour of wet sand that she'd never thought about running her fingers through and now couldn't think of anything else; a smile that she'd seen a million times but now started a fire in her belly. How had she not *seen* him for so long?

'It's going to be fine,' he said, nudging her and together they began to decorate Holly Lodge.

But as the day moved on, even with Christmas bells ringing out through the music, and the taste of sugar and spice to keep them going, something was clearly off. Nell had tried to be normal around Tom and he'd been his usual self, but he'd been overly cheerful and somewhat preoccupied. Once everything was done, the boys used one of the hotel rooms to change in and Nell and Cat used her flat.

'There,' Cat said, pinning Nell's hair up and fiddling with a little bit so it curled down. She stood back and placed her hands on Nell's shoulders before kissing the top of her head. 'You look gorgeous.'

Nell had given herself a swipe of red lipstick to go with her silvery, long-sleeved maxi dress and high heels. Standing up, she took a moment to enjoy the feel of the dress as it swished around her ankles. Cat looked super chic in black, wide-legged trousers and a cute, black wrap-top. When she stood back with her hands in her pockets, she looked like a model with her long pastel-pink hair hanging loose about her face. 'I can't believe your mum wanted you to wear that awful shapewear stuff. You look amazing just as you are.'

'Wants, not wanted. She's still going on about it and the dress she's hoofed me into isn't exactly forgiving. But let's not talk about it tonight, okay? Tom and Kieran are waiting upstairs, and tonight is a special one for you.'

The sudden thump of loud music pounded on the ceiling and the deep base note of a classic Christmas bop-along summoned them upstairs. Nell's stomach fizzed with excitement. Tonight was definitely the night to tell Tom how she felt. Everything about it felt right and that enchanting Christmas magic was in the air. Mr Scrooge was asleep on her bed having had an extra-large meal of cat food and Nell could hear him purring in his sleep. With a quick tickle behind his ear, she said, 'Let's go then. I don't know about you, but I'm super excited.'

They exited the flat and walked through the kitchen. Niall was there, putting the finishing touches to an array of buffet food and classic Christmas treats. The steel surfaces were covered in all manner of delights: platters of salmon blinis, tiny puff pastry cheese bites, cocktail sausages in different sauces. There were Christmas-tree-shaped cookies, mince pies with pastry snowflakes on top, platters of truffles and piles of profiteroles. He looked up from adding fiddly bits of gold leaf onto some truffles.

'Ladies, you look gorgeous. I hope you'll save me a dance later.' He winked at them, but having worked with him for a while now, Nell knew he was just friendly and not flirting.

'If you're lucky,' Cat replied and stole a truffle from one of the plates giving Niall a wink as she did so. All Nell's feelings of ease and assurance began to fade. Niall laughed and went back to placing on the gold leaf, while Nell shuffled Cat out of the kitchen. Hopefully, she was just being friendly back.

As they climbed the stairs, Nell saw Tom at the top. He had a suit on, which wasn't like him at all, but it fitted his tall frame well. He was standing with his hands in his pockets, chatting to

Kieran. When his eyes fell on Nell, her heart fluttered like a butterfly fighting a strong breeze as he gave her a comedy double-take. She climbed the last few steps but at the very top the long skirt caught, and she crashed forwards headfirst into Tom's chest.

'Ooomph!' Tom exclaimed as she collided into him. 'Steady there.'

'It's these bloody shoes.' She righted herself and looked down at the sweet silver T-bar heels she'd chosen. They were striking, but having got used to running around in trainers all the time, she'd forgotten how hard heels were to walk in. Tom laughed and she felt herself blush. 'Not very elegant, am I? And I bet I've ruined my hair.' She patted the pretty up-do Cat had done for her and it seemed to be mostly in place. Instantly, as Tom stared down at her, she realised that his hand was around her waist. Before, she wouldn't have given it a second thought, but now it was like all her nerves were on fire. Where it lay felt suddenly very sensual and she was sure once more that she didn't want anyone else's hand to ever take its place. She looked back at Tom, hoping for a sign that she could press on and tell him she felt the same way, then his hand dropped.

'I'm just going to check the archways are still intact.' And he walked away back into the dining room.

Cat turned to Nell in confusion and Kieran quickly headed into the dining room after him. A cold shiver ran over Nell unsure what to make of his sudden departure but, glancing at her watch, she realised she didn't have time to linger, there were final preparations to make.

Linda, the mayor, and her husband, Arnold, along with a large group of councillors all arrived. Nell welcomed them and enjoyed their gasps of surprise as they walked into the transformed ground floor of Holly Lodge.

As they went into the dining room it was like entering a different world. White and silver paper snowflakes hung from the ceilings on silver ribbons, stars were pinned to the walls and everywhere was like a true winter wonderland. In the lounge, framed by a beautiful snowy woodland archway, was the Christmas tree, and throughout the ground floor into the conservatory were smaller potted fir trees. They'd been left plain, and the vibrant green leaves and heady scent of pine added to the wonderland theme. Along the bottoms of the walls were strings of fairy lights and the room glittered and sparkled. 'Oh, Nell,' Linda, the mayor exclaimed, hand on heart. 'This is just lovely.'

Arnold, her husband, helped himself to some of Niall's special Christmas punch that sat in giant glass bowls on the table between pots of traditional candy canes. Arnold took two and hooked them into his mouth like giant fangs then tapped Kieran, who was facing the other way, on the shoulder. Kieran turned and though not impressed, gave an indulgent laugh.

'Excuse me a moment,' Linda said and walked to her husband. Nell stifled a giggle as Arnold then did the same to one of the councillors and Linda hit him with her clutch bag.

The music filled Nell's soul and she began to sway with the rhythm. 'Is it what you wanted?' Nell asked once Linda had come back. 'I mean, I know it's not as grand as the Langdon Mansion but—'

'Nell,' Linda said, taking her arm. 'It's wonderful. It's even better than the Langdon Mansion because this is what Swallowtail Bay is all about. You've hosted so many local events this Christmas that have made a difference to our community. St Herbert's would have had to cancel if it wasn't for you, and those old folks at the care home so enjoyed their day.'

With her kind words, Nell finally started to relax as another councillor came over to congratulate Linda on her choice of venue and then both slipped away to grab a drink. The night began in a clatter of music, dancing, laughter and enjoyment. Nell hadn't felt so happy, so light and so free in a long time. If she could host events like this on such short notice, and if the weddings took off, there was every chance the hotel would be fine. In the corner, she found Tom and Kieran sharing a joke, but Kieran was laughing more than Tom who still seemed distracted and tense. 'Hey, guys. Having fun?'

Tom's eyes flashed over her, and it sent a thrill through her body, but then his face clouded again. It was almost undetectable, just a change in the brightness of his eyes, but she spotted it. 'Yeah. The place looks good.'

'Do you want to get something to eat?' she asked Tom, hoping to get him on his own.

'No thanks.'

'Oh, right.'

'I'm just umm … going to get another drink.' Tom walked away, leaving Nell hurt and confused. She glanced at Kieran who nervously shuffled after him. That was without doubt the shortest conversation they'd ever had. Had she said something wrong? Done something wrong? Offended him in some way? Maybe he had another headache. Cat was suddenly at her side, happy and jiggling about.

'Come and dance, Nell.' She dragged her onto the dance floor.

They wiggled away to another classic Christmas song, though she noticed the way Cat glanced at Niall when he came to top up the food and punch. Nell didn't know how much Cat had drunk but she was already sailing firmly towards tiddly. After a bit of a boogie, Nell's feet were killing her when Niall brought up another plate of nibbles and Cat left her on the dance floor alone to go and get some.

'She's really enjoying herself, isn't she?' said Kieran, suddenly appearing at Nell's shoulder, but underneath the happiness there was an unease, and she worried where this conversation was heading.

'She is. It's nice to see. I think it's being away from Brenda.' *But not far enough away from Niall*, she thought as Cat sidled over and chatted to him while he filled up the snacks. Nell hoped she was just being pleasant, maybe trying to set the relationship right after the flirtatious start. If Cat was drawing some boundaries, that could only be a good thing, but the way she touched his arm was like a warning flare going off in her mind.

'Hmm,' Kieran agreed. 'She seems very happy with your choice of caterer.'

Nell gave him a sideways glance. Was he blaming her for Cat's behaviour? The resigned and heartbroken expression on his face killed any ire she might have felt at the remark. 'Kieran, Cat loves you. I think all this ...' She cast her arm out as if trying to grab the right word from the air in front of them. 'All this weirdness is because Brenda's got her so stressed out with the wedding. And she told me today work's been tough too.'

'She didn't tell me that.' Kieran bristled, and surprisingly carried on talking. While Nell was glad he was opening up to her, he'd normally talk like this with Tom and she wondered why he wasn't. 'Why is she shutting down on me? She used to tell me everything. I'm not even sure she wants to get married anymore.'

'Don't say that, Kieran. It's not true. She does want to marry you. She texted me the other day about changing the colour of the party favours. She wouldn't be doing that if she didn't want to marry you, would she? She wouldn't care what colour they were if she wasn't planning to go through with it.'

As Niall disappeared back to the kitchen, Cat came over. 'What's up, honey?'

'Nothing,' Kieran mumbled. The strain was clear on his face and after a big swig of his beer, he walked out into the conservatory and on into the garden. They watched him go, Nell consumed with guilt that she hadn't been able to reassure him more.

'What's up with him?' Cat asked. 'Grumpy git.' Nell turned and from Cat's reaction, her surprise clearly showed on her face. 'What?'

'Cat, don't you see Kieran's worried that you're flirting with Niall or that he's flirting with you and it's upset him.'

Cat's eyes widened in surprise then narrowed accusingly. 'Did you tell him about that first time I was a bit … over the top because you said you wouldn't. You did, didn't you? How could you, Nell?'

'Of course I didn't tell him. And I'm sure you didn't mean anything just now, with Niall it looked—'

'What?'

Nell tried to keep everything under control. 'I think to Kieran it looked a bit off. And because you've been changing your mind about wedding stuff and not talking to him, he's worried you don't want to marry him.'

'Oh, for heaven's sake. I am allowed to change my mind about things. Honestly, between you, Kieran and my mum, I wish I wasn't getting married.'

'If Brenda's still being difficult, let us help you talk to her and sort it out. You don't have to do everything on your own, Cat.'

'I don't want to do this now, Nell. This is a party and I'd really like to enjoy myself for once.' Cat stalked off into the throng of people and disco lights and Nell lost her in the crowd. Feeling the heat of the exchange in her cheeks she went into the garden to cool down.

The night had started off so well and now it was falling apart. This morning with Cat had felt like old times. Nell knew this short-tempered, changeable version wasn't the real one but the real one was getting buried deeper and deeper and if that continued, she'd ruin her whole life. Nell took a moment to stare at the dark, starry night. A thick cloud passed over the brightest star and Nell wrapped her arms around her to keep warm in the still, cold air. The lights strung around the garden made her feel slightly warmer as her affection for the place replaced some of her worries. From the corner of her eye she saw Tom sitting in the conservatory, his head dipped, toying with his beer bottle. Seeing her chance, and needing to rest her feet, she went and sat next to him.

Being close to him filled every one of her nerves with antici-pation and a longing to reach out and touch him. 'Hey, you,' Nell said, gently leaning into his shoulder. 'Are you okay?'

Tom's eyes searched her face and from their lacklustre appear-ance she could tell that something was wrong. 'I'm fine,' he replied with a shrug and began to peel the label from his beer.

Hoping that his anxiety came from thinking her feelings weren't returned, Nell decided to speak. Willing her heart to stop beating so fast, she absorbed the magic from the Christmas music, the twinkling fairy lights and winter moon shining down on them. 'Listen, Tom, I wanted to talk to you about something.'

'Oh?' His shoulders stiffened.

'It's not bad. At least I don't think so.' She gave a nervous laugh, but Tom didn't look like he wanted to hear anything. He wasn't looking at her so much tonight and she missed it, but maybe her news would change that. 'So, Kieran told me that—'

'Listen, Nell. I don't mean to be rude but if Kieran's been moaning about Cat and Cat's been moaning about Kieran, I just can't get involved in it right now. Okay? They ...' Nell shook her head trying desperately to get the words out, but he hadn't stopped talking. 'They're old enough to sort things out for themselves and I've got enough on my plate. So just leave them to it, all right? You can't solve this one for them. It's not a movie, it's real life.' And with that, he walked away.

Nell remained where she was, wrapped in a thin, hollow silence. Had he known what she was going to say and decided he didn't feel that way about her after all? Was that why he'd given that out-of-character monologue then stalked off inside? Nell felt tears sting her eyes and a few escaped down her cheeks. She wiped them away and tried to stop her lip from wobbling. Arnold, the mayor's husband, stumbled out into the conservatory completely sloshed. His teeth had turned almost black, stained from the decadent red wine punch and there was a purplish line around his lips. It was a good job they didn't have any live flames because if he'd neared one, he'd have gone off like a rocket. 'Nell Jones. Nelly puddles. Nelly the elephant.'

'Oh, geez.' Nell rolled her eyes. If he started singing the song, no jury would convict her for her actions. Arnold swayed towards her, attempting some kind of samba, throwing himself too far one way then the other. His glass of punch sploshed onto his shirt leaving a horrid red stain like a gunshot wound.

'This is the best shindig we've ever been to. Lovely atmosphere. Lovely food. Good booze.' He raised his now empty glass and looked at it in confusion, clearly unaware of how it had become empty.

'I'm very glad you're enjoying it, Arnold. Merry Christmas.'

'Merry Christmas to you too, Nelly the elephant.' He lurched forward to give her a kiss on the cheek but the vision of his black teeth and purple lips lunging towards her were too terrifying for words.

'Oh, baby Jesus,' she cried, dodging sideways and shooting to standing. Luckily, Harry was close by.

'Nell, I've been looking for you. You owe me a dance, best hostess in the world.'

She'd never been so happy to see the handsome American and not because she'd kind of fancied him before the Tom epiphany. Taking her hand, he led her to the dance floor. She glanced around but couldn't see Tom, Cat or Kieran anywhere. Tom was so tall she normally spotted him in an instant. He must have left without saying goodbye and as she imagined Kieran and Cat leaving in a row, her heart sank within her chest.

'So, I can't believe tomorrow's our last night together and I'll be heading back to the States.'

He held her in a strong embrace as they slid to and fro, but it felt alien. 'You must be looking forward to going home.'

'I am. But there is one thing I'll miss.'

'Oh, and what's that? Don't tell me it's our fine British weather?'

He gave a loud barking laugh that drew the attention of the

people near them. 'No, it's not. It's the prettiest, most brilliant hostess a guy could hope for.' Before Nell knew what was happening, he had spun her out, twirled her back in and dipped her in a first-class ballroom dancing move. His head moved closer, smile wide, perfect teeth in full view. Big red flashing sirens were going off in her head. *No, no, no, no, no!* She pulled away, shell-shocked and unsure what to say. She didn't want him to kiss her. She wanted Tom to kiss her.

From the corner of her eye she saw Tom staring at her in disbelief. He hadn't left. He hadn't gone without saying goodbye. But now he did, stalking off without saying a word.

'What's wrong?' Harry asked, pulling her up.

'Harry, I'm sorry.' Nell pulled herself free and left him on the dance floor to chase after Tom, but by the time she made it to the front door he'd gone.

In the street in front of Holly Lodge, the chill wind wrapped around her, penetrating the thin material of her dress and she felt icy cold through to her bones. Even the blood running through her veins was like a frost on her skin. Just the other side of the road the sea washed onto the pebbled beach, hitting the rocks and pulling them under. The tears that fell stung her face, burning her cheeks with embarrassment that Harry had done that, and frustration that Tom hadn't given her the chance to tell him how she felt. Everything was a mess. Tonight had been a horrible mixture of the business finally making headway while the rest of her life fell apart. Why? Why did life always have to be like that? If her feet hadn't hurt so much, she would have stamped them in a temper.

'Want to tell me what all that was about?' The American accent told her immediately who it was.

'Harry, listen.'

Urgh, this was awkward. Why did Harry have to tell her how he felt tonight? Of all the nights he'd stayed, why now? And how to reject him kindly? She hadn't turned yet, worried that he was

244

right behind her and if she did, they might be so close that he tried to kiss her. Ironically, after wanting to picture herself with Tom and being unable to, she could see every moment of this scene playing out. Nell gave herself a mental shake knowing she was making up romantic scenarios again. Well, she wasn't doing that anymore. All the times she'd imagined him whisking her off to New York, leaving all the problems behind, but now she knew Tom had feelings for her, or at least had before tonight, her heart wasn't excited at the prospect. She braced herself for a difficult conversation and turned to face Harry. 'You're such a nice guy, Harry, and I'm sorry if I've led you on—'

'Wait. Wow. No—'

'No?'

'No.' He held up his hands like this was the last thing he expected her to say and a burning embarrassment crept up her spine. 'Did you think that I – I mean we – us—' Harry waved his hand between the two of them.

'Well – umm …'

Oh, dear. Yes, she had thought that. She'd thought that and a whole lot more besides including soapy bath scenes and other intimate scenarios during the quieter moments in the day. She wondered if he could read the thoughts in her mind because he was staring at her in mounting concern and she was sure her skin was going to burn off she was so hot. Even her ears were hot and she thought that only happened to dogs.

'Nell, I'm sorry but …' He scratched the back of his neck his cheeks turning pink in the lamplight. As well as humiliating herself, she'd embarrassed him too.

In all her life, Nell had never actually been slapped, but this was how she imagined it to feel and her cheeks stung as their burning heat met with the cold Christmas air. After staring at Harry's horrified face, she realised the pain was nothing more than a shocking level of embarrassment. 'So, you didn't mean that—'

'No!' He said it so quickly it was almost insulting.

'Oh.'

Thankful that he wasn't going to kiss her, but still cringing for thinking he'd want to when he so clearly didn't, Nell stared at the ground. It was another freezing night and the pavement glittered beneath her feet. She tapped her fingertip against the holly hedge trying to feel something other than shame. Yet again, she'd lived in her imagination rather than in reality, seeing things that weren't there, creating feelings that didn't really exist for either of them. At least now she could explain to Tom that what he'd seen was nothing more than a kind, caring man trying to make Nell smile, not a swoon-worthy dance move, designed to sweep her into bed. It was no wonder he thought that after the way she'd gone on about Harry. She rolled her eyes, even more annoyed with herself.

'Nell, I'm so sorry you thought …' He gave a helpless shrug. 'You're great, but you're just not my type.'

Would this feeling ever go away? Nell wondered. The awkwardness was seeping into her blood and bones. She wanted to run inside and hide under her duvet with Mr Scrooge but as a grown-up she wasn't allowed to do that sort of thing. Now she looked like some manic woman who just assumed all men fancied her and wanted to jump into her bed. 'It's fine.'

'I mean, you're lovely and sweet and kind but—'

'Still fine,' she said as her mind took her back to the Thanksgiving dinner she'd prepared for him. Another wave of humiliation hit her like the waves hitting the beach and panicked by its ferocity she added, 'I just get a bit caught up in my own world sometimes.'

Why had she said that? Now she sounded even more of a psychopath. Going around making things up in her head. He'd call the police if she said anything else like that.

'Yeah. I realised that pretty much as soon as I met you. But if I did come on to you, I think your friend Tom would have something to say about it.'

'So, you noticed too?'

Harry nodded. 'I think you're about the only person who hadn't, but it wasn't my place to say anything. Even if I had, I'm not sure you'd have believed me. I'm sorry if he got the wrong idea tonight, I was only trying to save you from that other guy. But Nell,' he took her hands gently in his, 'you are definitely the best hostess a guy could ever ask for.'

'After the night I've had, I'll definitely take that compliment.' She laughed at the ridiculousness of the evening and scratched her forehead, still prickling with the indignity of it all.

'There is something special about you. A spark. A passion. I saw it when you talked about your hotel. Don't ever let that go out, okay?'

'Okay,' she agreed but it felt very much like any spark was about to be blown out by the breeze building around Holly Lodge.

'Come on, best hostess in the world, you should go and finish this party.'

He let her go first, and they stepped back inside through the high, black metal gate that led the way to her gorgeous little hotel, but she couldn't help glancing behind her just in case Tom had come back. Her heart sank when no one appeared through the darkness and the chances of him doing so now were slim to none. Despite the pain in her feet and the ache in her heart she trudged back inside and prayed the rest of the night would pass drama-free. Thankfully, there were only a couple of hours to go.

Chapter 21

The ringing of Nell's phone woke her up early Sunday morning. Knowing that she'd be up till the small hours cleaning and putting the lounge and dining room back together, she'd arranged the luxury of a lie-in with Mrs Meggett. The decorations had been left in place – she wasn't Wonder Woman and couldn't clear it all single-handedly – and besides, it added to the Christmassy feel. By the time she'd fallen into bed at about three in the morning she'd been tired through to her bones, yet sleep hadn't come easily. The look on Tom's face when Harry had danced with her haunted her every time she closed her eyes. If only she'd been able to tell him how she felt.

In the cold light of day, she doubted she'd find the courage again and from last night's exchange there was every possibility he'd changed his mind, or maybe Kieran had got the wrong end of the stick. With a sigh, she scrambled around for her phone. The only good thing about winter was that the darkness lasted longer in the mornings so she hadn't been disturbed by sunshine or the seagulls cawing, but now, a pale light crept in through her curtains and the smell of bacon wafted in from the kitchen, waking her up a little more quickly.

Frowning at her phone in confusion, and with a pang of worry she saw it was Cat. Swiping to answer, Nell edged up onto her elbow and Mr Scrooge, who was curled at her feet, woke and stretched.

'Nell?' Cat sobbed. All she could hear was sniffing, crying, and breath gulped hysterically.

'Cat? What is it?' Dread settled in her stomach. Please don't let it be what she feared most. *Please don't let her and Kieran have split up and the wedding be off.* More sobbing followed her question and then out of nowhere there was a gigantic wail. Nell moved the phone back from her ear for a second as the shrill sound reverberated off her half-asleep eardrum. 'Cat, honey, calm down. You need to tell me what's wrong. I can't help if I don't know what's happening.'

'Can you meet me in town?'

Nell swept her legs round and out of bed. 'Sure. When?'

'Ten minutes?'

Ten minutes! She didn't even have clean pants on, but if her friend needed her, then she would be there, even if she went in pyjamas or without pants. 'Okay. Where?'

'Can we meet at Raina's? I'm nearly there now.'

Thank heaven Swallowtail Bay had caught up with the rest of the world and the shops had started opening on Sundays. 'Sure, I'll see you there in ten minutes.'

'Thank you, Nell.' Cat sniffed again. 'I love you.'

Nell's trepidation surged again. Cat very rarely got this upset and for her to say 'I love you' after their exchange last night alarmed her, sending goose bumps over her skin. 'Love you too, honey. I'll be there in a few minutes.'

Nell jumped out of bed, threw on some clothes and made her way to the back entrance of her flat. That way she could avoid the kitchen and Mrs Meggett. As much as she'd adore one of Mrs Meggett's amazing breakfasts right about now, she loved a chat and Nell wasn't very good at escaping them. She'd get waylaid and right now Cat was her one and only priority.

Climbing into her car, Nell's phone went once more but this time with a number she didn't recognise. 'Hello?'

'Hi, is that Nell Jones?' The voice was male.

'It is. Can I help you?'

'I saw your posters about the black cat. Ours went missing about a month ago and we've been looking everywhere for him. We live the other side of the bay. Is it okay if I come this afternoon to see if he's ours?'

Nell's heart sank even further in her chest, shrivelling with pain. She didn't want to lose Mr Scrooge. She liked having him around. She'd begun to think of him as *her* cat, cuddling up with him at night, but she couldn't keep him if he belonged to someone else. It wouldn't be right. Swallowing the lump in her throat, she said, 'Yes, of course.'

'Thanks. Is three o'clock okay?'

'Yes, fine. See you then.'

Nell drove down the long road that ran the length of the seafront, sucking in her emotions. Last night's episode with Tom, her worries for Cat, and now facing the loss of Mr Scrooge, made it all feel hopeless. In between the little wooden beach huts, she spied the sea, a calm blanket of pale grey, barely distinguishable from the sky above. The windscreen steamed up from her warm breath mixed with the freezing air inside, and as she entered the town centre where houses, already decorated with looming inflatable Santas, snowmen and reindeer, gave way to pubs, shops and boutiques, she drove around the main roundabout – the one where Tom had his accident – and on towards the car park.

Being reminded of his so-called prang also reminded her of the accident with his finger, and of his strange behaviour last night. He hadn't been around as much and when he had he'd acted so differently. She'd seen in his eyes that something wasn't right. All she wanted was to talk to him and find out what was bothering him and explain about Harry dancing with her. Her cheeks flushed again with the discomfort of embarrassment. But speaking to Tom would have to wait until she'd dealt with Cat. Nell swerved the car into the first available parking space and shot out. After throwing money impatiently into the machine, she stuck the ticket on the window and walked around the corner to Raina's.

Cat, her eyes puffy, her beautiful pink hair tied in a messy ponytail and remnants of make-up smudged under her eyes, sat at a table in the window. She looked devastated, like her spirit had been broken. With a quick check for Brenda, who thankfully was nowhere to be seen, Nell ripped open the door and threw herself into the chair, grabbing hold of Cat's hands and squeezing them tight. 'Whatever has happened, honey? We can fix it, okay? Is it the wedding?' Cat nodded and Nell felt her face fall as her fears broke the floodgates. 'Is it off?'

Cat's head shot up, completely horrified. 'What? No!'

'Thank God. Then what the heck's happening?'

'I stood up to Mum.'

'You did?' Nell couldn't believe what she was hearing. 'I want to know everything. Actually, wait, we need tea for this.' She nipped to the counter and ordered two teas and a large slice of an amazing-looking chocolate mousse cake from Lexi. She looked fabulous in a Fifties-style dress with her dark hair swept into a headscarf. A small Christmas tree at the end of the counter had been decorated with all sorts of homemade decorations. There was a star made out of lolly sticks and snowmen made from toilet roll tubes and cotton wool. It was wonderful. Nell guessed some of the decorations had been made by Lexi's kids and in her mind, she jotted a mental note to run an event for kids next year. Before long she was back at the table and Lexi followed with the plates of cake and sweet vintage pots of tea.

'So, what happened?' asked Nell, her voice full of pride that Cat had done what they all knew she needed too. The lights in the window behind Cat twinkled against the grey gloom as she shrugged off her coat.

Cat wiped her eyes with her sleeve. 'So, after we rowed last night, Kieran and I left.'

'I'm sorry if I was harsh,' Nell said, cupping her tea.

'No, you were right. I was being stupid. It's just that with Mum passive aggressively controlling the wedding—'

'It's more kind of aggressive-aggressive.'

'Exactly. With Mum being a giant control freak I just got so stressed out. She was moaning about everything and going on and on at me until I changed things. She'd say things like, *"I just think you should reconsider blah, blah, blah"*. She'd even ring me up when she knew I was working. Part of me thought it was because she knew I'd agree to get her off the phone.'

'It must have been so hard for you.' Nell took her hand and squeezed it.

'I know I should have stood up to her at the start, but I didn't and it just kind of snowballed from there. I love Kieran so much, but when I was …' Nell could see she was struggling to say the words out loud. Tears formed again in her eyes and her face washed with guilt. 'When I was being silly with Niall, who didn't flirt with me by the way, he's just really friendly and tried to make me feel better about Mum, I just felt like my old self again. Last night I really didn't mean to flirt. But when you said how it looked to you and Kieran, you made me realise how stupid and selfish I was being. When I said yes to marrying Kieran it was honestly the happiest day of my life and I've never wanted anything more. Then Mum started stealing all my enjoyment of it and everything else in my life. She'd argue with everything – literally everything – down to my bloody underwear. I want to wear my own pants on my wedding day. Is that too much to ask?' She took a sip of her tea, both of them too caught up in this moment to even think about cake. 'Last night when Kieran told me how scared he was that I didn't love him anymore, I knew I'd let things go on for too long. I love him and I'd never hurt him. This morning, I told Kieran that I wanted us to go and visit

Mum and tell her that we're going to have the wedding we want, and she can't control it anymore.'

Relief and surprise caused Nell's emotions to swell. 'And how did that go?'

Cat looked up, her eyes welling with tears again. 'About as well as can be expected. She called me an ungrateful child, told me she was doing all of this to help me and that if I wasn't going to appreciate her, she wouldn't help anymore. Dad had to basically physically restrain her and now she's stomped off to bed with a headache. I never wanted to hurt Mum and maybe if I'd been stronger right back when we went wedding dress shopping, I'd have set the tone and stopped us all getting hurt. Her heart's in the right place but she's taken it all too far. Even Dad told me I'd done the right thing. He said Mum was tying herself up in knots too.'

'And how's Kieran now?'

Happiness spread over Cat's face as she beamed. 'He's really pleased. He said he wanted to help but he was too afraid to get involved and I kept pushing him away. I told him I was worried that if he got involved then the wedding prep and our special day would turn into a warzone. Mum has been pretty terrifying. But we're going to do it together now. We're going to go back through the list of what's been organised and make sure we're happy with it. As the wedding is at the hotel, and you know what we like, we were kind of hoping we could sort most of it between the four of us. I know there's only a week to go, do you think we have time to put things right?'

'Of course we do,' Nell replied enthusiastically. It would be a challenge, but if they all worked together there was no reason why not. But the four of them also meant Tom and she had no idea how to talk to him or what to say at the moment. 'I love you, you crazy bird.'

'I love you, too. I'm sorry I've been such a pain in the bum.' Cat pulled her cake towards her. 'How did it go with Tom?'

Nell sighed heavily. 'It didn't. He was weird and standoffish last night. It was like he wanted nothing more than to get away from me. Then he saw Harry dancing with me and just left. And you're right by the way. I've been living my love life in my head instead of in reality. I don't know why. It just seemed safer somehow.'

Cat eyed Nell then her cake, but didn't take a bite. 'I think your imagination is a wonderful thing, and we all love that about you, but like with me and Mum, it's about taking control and not letting it control you.'

'You're so wise,' Nell teased. 'So, what's first on the wedding list?'

Cat forked a tiny piece of the chocolate mousse cake into her mouth and savoured it. Nell did the same, waiting for her response. 'The one thing I don't think I can fix – my wedding dress.' Cat pushed the plate of delicious food away. 'I shouldn't really be eating this, the bloody thing is tight enough as it is, even with my horrendously unsexy suck-it-all-in-and-not-let-me-breathe underwear.'

'Why can't we fix that? Can the dress be let out?' Cat shook her head and Nell knew she'd been right, that this was one of the main causes of the problems they'd had. Nell believed that every time a bride talked about her wedding dress, she should be excited to wear it and have a dreamy expression on her face. Whenever Cat had talked about hers, she'd scrunched up her face like she could smell something foul. The purchase of the dress had been the start of things going wrong. Nell remembered the day they'd all gone shopping and though she'd mentioned her reservations, there'd been no talking Cat into changing her mind or telling Brenda no. 'Cat, do you actually want to wear your dress? After everything you've gone through with your mum, now's the time to get the wedding you want and that means every aspect of it.'

'I hate it,' Cat answered quickly without a hint of hesitation.

'Absolutely hate it. I mean, I'm sure it would look lovely on someone else, but it's too long for me, the bodice is so tight it makes the tops of my arms look enormous and then it's all massive at the bottom and it weighs a tonne. I won't be able to get on a toilet in it and I can't even imagine wrestling with that bloody underwear and the twenty-seven million layers of net and ruffles every time I need a wee. And once I've had a drink I need a wee every five minutes. But it's been paid for and my last fitting is later today.'

'You could re-sell it. If you had your way, what type of a dress would you like? You loved the vintage one Lexi brought to the wedding fair, and the one you tried on at the shop. Your eyes sparkled when you saw that one.'

Cat glanced at Lexi, their gorgeous vintage-dressed waitress. 'I'd adore a Fifties-style dress. I've always loved them. They're so simple and stunning and elegant. That one of Lexi's was perfect, and I'd only need a small net underneath so it poofs out a little bit. Did you see those cute pillbox hats she had on the table? The ones with the little veil? And the little gloves?' Nell suddenly saw the dreamy, faraway look in Cat's eyes she'd hoped for and called Lexi over.

'Hey, ladies, what else can I get you?'

'Lexi,' Nell said, 'Do you still have that wedding dress Cat loved from the wedding fair?'

Lexi's eyes brightened with excitement. 'I do. Are you interested, Cat? I thought your dress was all sorted.'

'It is – I mean – it was. I'm making some last-minute changes and I've realised it's not really me. Do you think that one of yours would fit me? And I'd love one of your little pillbox hats with a veil.'

Lexi's trained eye roved over Cat, assessing her measurements.

'I'll pay for it,' said Nell quickly.

'No!' Cat interrupted. 'You don't have to do that.'

'I want to. You're my best friend. It can be my wedding present to you. What do you think, Lexi?'

Lexi smiled and put her hands on her hips. 'I reckon with a bit of tinkering it'll fit you like a dream.'

'Thank you so much, Lexi. You're amazing.'

'I finish work at one. Can you come over this afternoon and we'll do a fitting? Looking at you though, I'm pretty positive it'll only need minor adjustments to the top.'

Cat was bouncing in her seat with excitement and her eyes misted with tears again. Nell pushed the plate of cake back in front of her and, genuinely happy, Cat forked in a massive mouthful, and this time ate it with glee.

Chapter 22

Sunday afternoon, Tom stood outside the care home, trying his best to muster some courage and go in to see Grandad Nigel. Last night, after the party, he'd fallen off the kerb and twisted his ankle while marching home and if he ever needed a sign that he had to stop being such a wimp and tell his grandad what was happening, that was it. Now, facing the big white building, the front door decorated with a wreath he'd made them, he couldn't help the anxiety weighing his body down. He didn't want Grandad Nigel worrying about him, he didn't want him thinking he wouldn't be able to visit or pay for his care. He wanted Grandad Nigel to know he was safe and well and enjoy his later years.

Tom would have given anything to be able to delay this news until the New Year. Ideally, he'd never have to tell Nigel something like this at all, but his cards had been dealt and the sooner it was out the better. Who knew how much worse his sight would be in January? Fear almost strangled him as he prepared to ruin his grandad's Christmas with bad news and worry. Tom didn't normally feel the cold this much, but today, he couldn't get warm and his teeth were almost chattering. The longer he stood there, the harder it became to move his legs and step inside. Giving himself an internal shake, he put one foot in front of the other and moved.

The wreaths hung high on the entrance corridor wall. Their pine scent filled the air along with cinnamon, cloves and dried apple. Tracey was on duty, as usual, and she bustled around behind the little office station at the other end of the TV room.

'Hello, love,' she said, when she saw him. 'How've you been keeping?'

Difficult question. 'Not too bad, thanks, Tracey,' he lied. There was no point in telling her the truth just yet. He had to tell his grandad first.

'Oh good. Nigel's in the TV room with Edith.'

Tom slid his scarf from around his neck and his thick, heavy coat from his shoulders, hanging both over his arm. He ran a hand through his hair, and walked towards his grandad, nerves mounting with every step. Nigel and Edith were chatting away and Tom didn't want to disturb the happy scene. Everything would change the moment he said the words and once he had, there was no going back. His grandad had a bright smile and his unseeing eyes shone. He seemed happy enough even though he was blind, but he was 87, and these sorts of things were to be expected at his age. It was different for Tom who had so much of his life ahead of him and longer to cope with being different and less able than other people. He hesitated. It was going to be so hard to say the words out loud, but he'd come this far.

'Hey, Grandad. All right?'

Nigel spun his head towards the sound of Tom's voice. 'Tom, my boy. What's wrong? You're asking me if I'm all right, but I can tell from your voice you're not.' Even though his grandad couldn't see him, Tom dropped his eyes.

'There is something I need to talk to you about, if that's okay?'

Fear flooded Nigel's features. Edith patted his arm and stood. 'I'll leave you boys to it.'

'Come on then, boy. You'd best sit down.' Tom took the vacated seat, placing his coat and scarf next to him. The din from the giant TV had seemed so loud when he'd walked in, turned up high for those residents who were hard of hearing, but now, as the moment approached and he concentrated on his words, all noise faded into the background. 'So out with it, boy.'

This was it. This was the moment that he had to admit his health wasn't great and that it might ruin the rest of his life. Worse than that, it might impact on Nigel's life too, and he really didn't want the old man to worry. He'd had years of worry – worry that came from living through a war, and the worries of everyday life – and now, at his age, he deserved to relax and enjoy himself. But there was no way around it now the consultant had confirmed a diagnosis and it was already beginning to affect Tom's life. He had to man up and just get the words out.

'I've been having a bit of trouble with my eyesight recently, Grandad, and I went to see a doctor – well, a consultant actually.' Nigel cocked his head, listening intently. 'He told me that I had a condition called Retinitis Pigmentosa.' He took a deep breath, but Nigel didn't speak, letting Tom go on at his own pace. 'It means I'm going to lose my peripheral vision completely and possibly go completely blind.'

Nigel kept quiet, taking in all that Tom had said. For Tom, there was a fleeting sense of relief that the words were finally out, but watching his grandad's face and trying to gauge his reaction was heartbreakingly difficult, knowing he could be changing his grandad's life as well as his own. A resident shouted out, 'Melon balls,' in answer to the game show they were watching on the TV, shattering the bubble of silence between them. On any other occasion, Tom would have found it funny, but then Nigel reached out and took his grandson's hand, holding it tightly. 'How long, boy?'

'They can't tell me.' The stinging in his nose and throat took his breath away as he held back tears. Nigel's thin, papery skin felt cold over his hand. 'It's a degenerative condition and everyone's different. It could be months or years. I just don't know. But I don't want you to worry about anything, Grandad, okay? I'll find a way to pay for the care home even when I can't work anymore. Mum and Dad pay half and I won't stop paying my bit, even if I have to sell the shop. You won't have to leave. I promise.' He was speaking quicker and quicker and when he finished, he was glad that it was all out yet reticent of the repercussions.

'Now hold your horses, boy.' Nigel's voice was strong and forceful. 'I don't care about where I live. I mean I like it here, and even Tracey isn't that bad at times.' He raised his voice for the last part of the sentence so Tracey could hear him.

'I heard that!' she shouted from her place behind the desk. 'No mince pies for you, young man!'

Grandad chuckled. 'Young man? Ha!' But then his face and voice lost all humour and became serious once more, lowering his voice again. 'Tom lad, all I care about is you. Since your mum and dad decided to emigrate – and I don't begrudge them going off and making a life for themselves – it's been just the two of us, hasn't it? You're all that matters to me. Now, what's the state of those eyes at the moment?'

An unexpected grin appeared on Tom's face at his words. He was always to the point but never cruel. 'I find it really hard to see in the dark and when the light changes. I get headaches and I've already started to lose some of my peripheral vision.'

'So, what can we do about that? Have you contacted the RNIB? There's lots of things you can do to make life easier for yourself. Tracey's helped me beyond measure.' He sounded like an advert for visual impairment. 'Actually, that gives me an idea.'

'What?' Tom asked, slightly concerned at what that idea might be. As long as it didn't involve Nell, he'd probably be okay with it.

'Tracey? Tracey?'

'Oh, no, Grandad,' Tom said quickly. He wasn't quite ready to have everyone know yet, but Tracey was already bustling over. 'Grandad, I don't think I want to share the news with anyone else—'

'Rubbish,' he replied. The matter wasn't up for discussion.

'Yes, my lovely, what can I do for you?'

'Now, Tracey.' Nigel's voice rang with sincerity and fondness. 'You've helped me and lots of others with bad vision – or no vision – as is my case. What can we do to help our Tom here?'

'Oh?' Shocked, Tracey turned to face Tom. He sighed, scratched his head and then explained everything, swearing her to secrecy until he'd told the others closest to him: Cat, Nell and his parents. 'Oh, Tom, I am sorry, love. But it's not the end of the world, believe me. You can use magnifiers for your close-up work, we have those for some of our residents. You can get thin plastic ones that you carry around for reading things on the go and then there are quite high-tech ones for workstations that don't move at all. I saw them on a video on YouTube once. We don't really need those here, but you might want one for work. And you need to find ways of storing your tools, so you know exactly where everything is. Could you wear safety gloves to make sure you don't hurt yourself? You do a lot of cutting with very sharp objects, don't you? So that might be an idea. Make sure your walkways are clear and that your staff know not to put things there. You can get fabulous little stick-on lights now and you can put them everywhere so you can make sure anywhere you need extra light, you've got it.'

Tom sat there silently marvelling at this wonderful lady. She went about her business everyday caring for people, probably unappreciated, but was like an encyclopaedia of helpful tips and she wasn't even an expert. Hearing her talk, he felt his hopes rising and a pin prick of light rupture the dark future he'd pictured before him. Spying the Christmas tree in the corner – the one he and Nell had decorated – a little hope and joy of the season returned to him. Tracey continued, and Tom appreciated that her voice wasn't sympathetic or pitying. It was strong, practical and professional. 'I'd definitely get in contact with the RNIB and they can come and do a workplace assessment to help you.'

'Thanks, Tracey. You're amazing. I really appreciate your advice.'

'No problem, Tom.' Her gaze was soft and motherly. 'Once you've got your bearings it won't seem so grim. I promise. I've seen it time and time again, here.' She motioned around her, and Tom saw only happy faces before him. Though they were a different age group to him, and many of their problems were the result of advancing years, he supposed it wouldn't lessen the loss of freedom they felt, and yet, they were all content. He just had to make adjustments and if he did, he might even have years left. Janie would pass her driving test soon he was sure, and then she could do deliveries too. Maybe he could make her deputy manager? She was young but so full of ideas and he loved working with her. Suddenly there seemed to be any number of possibilities in front of him.

'You're a wonder, Tracey,' Nigel commented.

'Oh, stop that flattery, you. It doesn't mean you've earned back your mince pies.'

'Worth a try,' Grandad mumbled.

Tom knew of all her residents she was very fond of Nigel and his cheeky ways. 'I've got to get back to the desk but if there's anything I can do, Tom, just ask, won't you?'

'I will, Tracey. Thanks.'

Nigel didn't speak for a moment and then he asked the question Tom had been dreading. 'So, what does Nell say about all this?' When he didn't reply, Nigel's voice turned stern just as it had when Tom was a boy and he'd broken something in Grandad's house from charging around playing pirates. 'Tom?'

'I haven't told her yet.'

'Why not?' It was a good question, and one he'd avoided thinking about as much as possible.

'Because she's got enough to worry about with Holly Lodge and the bad reviews and Cat's wedding.' It was the excuse he'd constantly told himself and it had worked well so far, but it didn't convince Grandad.

'Who have you told?'

'Only you and Kieran.'

'Interesting.' Grandad Nigel paused. 'And why did you feel you could tell us and not Nell?'

'I don't know. I just don't want her feeling sorry for me.'

'What? Utter rot. Because you've been too busy feeling sorry for yourself, you mean.' Tom felt his mouth drop open. Nigel began patting his hand. 'Enough of this silliness and self-pity. It's time to start getting your life sorted out, Thomas.' The use of his full name meant he was really in trouble. Grandad had always been this way. He was of a generation that had been forced to deal with and do so much, there wasn't time for self-pity, and it was an attitude Tom admired. 'Having someone empathise or even feel sorry that you're going through something horrible, isn't a terrible thing. It means people care and they want to be there for you. Don't you think people want to be there for you, boy?'

'Yes,' Tom mumbled.

'Speak up, lad.'

'Yes,' he replied more clearly.

'So, now you've finished with the excuses, what's the real reason you haven't told Nell? Time for honesty now, lad.'

Tom shrank from saying the words out loud. With everything he'd been brave enough to say already today it made him feel silly, but Grandad was right. It was time for honesty. 'Because I love her, and I don't want her being upset. And I really regret that I've never told her before now how I feel about her.'

'Is the prospect of telling her really that scary? What's the worst that can happen? If she says no standing to the side of you, you won't even see her expression.' Momentarily shocked into silence, Tom then erupted into laughter. 'But seriously, lad, how would you feel if you don't tell her before your sight fails? Don't you want to see the look on her face when you tell her you love her, and she tells you the same?'

Tom had never thought about it before, but Grandad was right. He did want to tell Nell, and if there was even the slightest chance she felt the same way, he had to try. Closing his eyes he made a Christmas wish that she might love him as much as he loved her. And there was only one way of finding out. He had to tell her before it was too late.

Cat and Nell departed the café with hugs and a list of things for Nell to sort out so the hotel was ready for the wedding Cat and Kieran had originally wanted. Back at Holly Lodge, she'd begun ticking things off in an attempt to keep herself occupied and not think about the prospect of losing Mr Scrooge, or whatever his name really was.

With Harry now gone after a quick, professional goodbye, the hotel was silent. Nell felt incredibly lonely and wanted more than anything for Tom to be there with her. Another bad review had landed and with it, the loss of any chance of securing some midweek bookings before the wedding. She'd tried calling Tom to talk to him about Cat and the crazy phone call this morning, but he hadn't answered. Even with several voicemails, he hadn't responded. He'd been so angry with her at the party. With a heavy heart, she heard someone enter through the open front door and a voice call from the hallway. Leaving her list, she went to see the man who had phoned about Mr Scrooge.

He stood awkwardly, his hands in his coat pockets. The smaller Christmas trees she'd placed either side of the front door framed him but her festive cheer was absent.

'Good afternoon,' the man said.

'Hi,' Nell replied with professional friendliness. 'You're here for Mr Scrooge, aren't you?' She kept the tears from her eyes by plastering on a detached smile.

'Mr Scrooge?'

'Oh, sorry, that's what I've been calling him. The black stray.'

'Ah, yes. We called him Charcoal.'

'Right.' It was a nice name but somehow Mr Scrooge seemed to suit him better. 'He's in the lounge.' Nell had kept him next to the fire, tempted by another large bowl of food. She loved seeing him there, curled up and purring. The man followed her, but Nell could scarcely breathe. He knelt down by Mr Scrooge who worryingly didn't hiss or flinch as he had with almost everyone else. Did that mean he recognised the man and this was the moment he was taken away from her?

'Hello, there,' the man said stroking Mr Scrooge's head. He gently caressed the cat's ears and Mr Scrooge pushed himself into the man's hand. After petting him he stood, a sad look on his face. 'He's lovely, but he's not Charcoal.'

Relief flooded through Nell, then guilt because the poor man still hadn't found his cat. 'Have you tried looking on the Swallowtail Bay Facebook group for lost pets? There was another black cat on there when I checked to see if anyone had lost Mr Scrooge.'

'No, I haven't. I'll do that,' he replied, a little cheered. 'Charcoal does like to disappear for days at a time. It's just never been this long before.'

'I'll keep my eyes and ears open and if I hear anything, I'll give you a call. I've got your number.'

'Thanks, I'd appreciate it.'

The man left and Nell sat down next to Mr Scrooge, stroking him in relief, listening to his serene slow purr. She was going to keep him. Brenda might have suggested she give him to the RSPCA but there was no doing that now. She loved the little thing and wasn't going to let him go. When Mr Scrooge had first entered her life, she'd imagined a tall, handsome stranger coming to claim him and falling instantly in love, but when the man had called, her imagination hadn't fired once. She was changing and for the better, she was sure.

An image of Tom's face came to her, and with it a determination to tell him how she felt filled her once more with hope.

Chapter 23

The day of the wedding finally arrived but Nell hadn't yet changed into her bridesmaid's dress. She'd been around the hotel three times making sure everything was perfect. This was her final pass through before she spent time with Cat who was using her flat to get ready. Holly Lodge was booked out with wedding guests and the whole place was wonderfully busy. If only she could get at least a couple of weddings a year it would make such a difference to her future. Another bad review had come in and it had ramped up in intensity compared to the others. This time, some of the descriptions could only have been of her hotel but she still couldn't place the guests or their concerns.

As she checked everything one last time, she saw Tom's wreath on the front door. He'd been absent all week, and Nell still hadn't had the chance to tell him that she loved him. That she felt the same way about him as he supposedly did her. They'd never spent this much time apart and absence was certainly making the heart grow fonder in her case. She'd texted and though his messages had been friendly enough, he'd claimed being busy with work which she could understand given the time of year, but there'd been an emptiness to his words that she hadn't read before.

Shaking off the worry because she'd see him later, Nell

concentrated on the matter in hand. She had a wedding to host today as well as bridesmaid duties to fulfil and she wanted to make sure everything was perfect, especially as only a week ago the wedding didn't look like it was going to happen at all. It had been made slightly easier by Cat cancelling the bridesmaid dress Brenda had chosen for Nell and telling her to wear whatever she liked. She'd gone for another maxi dress, plain dusky-pink this time with a pretty sequin pattern on the top half.

The ceremony was to be held in the lounge. The comfy armchairs had been cleared out and normal chairs lined up for the small number of guests. Cat and Kieran were going to be married next to the twinkling Christmas tree, in front of a roaring log fire with Tom's beautiful willow garland decorating the mantelpiece. Despite Brenda's protests, Mr Scrooge had been allowed to stay and was asleep on the hearth. As the cat was now officially hers, Nell had popped a collar on him with a giant red bow tie. He looked smashing, getting fatter and healthier with every meal and his fur was becoming soft and fluffy.

In the dining room, the tables were put together in two small rows and covered in bright white cloths. A whole team of waiters and waitresses hired by Niall, were laying them up with sparkling glasses and gleaming cutlery. All the chairs had thick silver-blue ribbons tied around them, fastened into bows at the back. That was the original colour Cat had chosen then changed her mind. In the centre of each table stood a small Christmas wreath made from fir, holly with red berries, and a single cream pillar candle in the middle, ready to be lit. Around the edge of the room, strings of fairy lights sparkled and silver and blue balloons bobbed in the air. In the evening, when everyone had been ushered into the conservatory, tempted with mulled wine and mini mince pies, or relaxing in the lounge, the dining-room tables would be cleared so everyone could dance. They'd planned it down to the last detail and Niall was going to brief his staff. Taking a leaf out of Hetty the event planner's book, Nell had created a timetable and assigned jobs to people, so everyone knew what they had to do and when. This was definitely something she'd do for all the weddings she hosted. There was no way she'd rely on her memory to make everything perfect.

Feeling satisfied, Nell went downstairs to see Cat. Passing through the kitchen, she recognised the waitress from the Langdon Mansion Hotel and the Welcome to Christmas carol service. Frowning, Nell hung back while Niall briefed everyone, running through the order of play and the amazing level of service he expected. When he'd dismissed them, Nell nipped over. 'Niall, who was that young girl with the dark hair in a high ponytail?' He looked nonplussed. Clearly hair descriptions weren't his thing. 'The really tall girl, pretty but looked absolutely terrified.'

'Tallulah?'

Nell thought back to that horrible night at the Langdon Mansion Hotel, she was sure the maître d' had named the waitress who'd shown them to their table. She ran through the memory again and nodded. 'Yes Tallulah. Did you employ her?'

Niall shook his head. 'Not exactly. Philip, my business partner organises the staffing. She's not one we've had before but don't worry, I don't take anyone slacking, and no one will let you down.'

'Thanks.' But as she left the kitchen, she couldn't help feeling a little disconcerted. Perhaps the poor girl had left the Langdon Mansion. It hadn't seemed the nicest place to work. Putting the matter to the back of her mind, Nell went into her flat.

The dress fitted Cat like a glove with only a slight adjustment on the bust. There was absolutely no need for painful underwear and Cat surveyed herself in the mirror.

'Happy?' Nell asked.

'So happy,' Cat replied. She twisted left and right letting the skirt and pastel-pink petticoat that matched her hair, move around her. Her eyes were sparkling and dreamy just as Nell had hoped they would be. She quickly changed into her own wedding outfit and strappy shoes. She wasn't sure how well her feet were going to cope with the day ahead but wearing flats wasn't an option until later. Cat called over her shoulder. 'Let's see you then.'

Nell gave a twirl. 'Ta da!'

'You look gorgeous. Much better than your normal ugly jumpers.'

'My jumpers might be ugly, but they are very warm. I've turned the heating up full whack and the fire's blazing in the lounge so we shouldn't get cold in our flimsy dresses.'

An unexpected knock at the door made them jump and Cat hid behind the full-length mirror. 'If it's Kieran, tell him to go away, he can't see me before the wedding.'

'Calm down,' Nell replied, laughing. 'It's probably just Janie delivering the bouquet.' Nell opened the door and stood back. 'Oh, hello, Brenda.'

'Nell. Am I allowed to see my daughter?'

Glancing over her arm at Cat who had now come out from behind the mirror, she nodded and let her arm drop. Brenda walked slowly inside in her lilac, mother-of-the-bride dress and enormous hat. All the joy had been sucked from the atmosphere and in the small basement flat the air felt thick, heavy with Brenda's perfume. When Brenda's eyes fell on her daughter clad in the vintage dress, complete with a pink petticoat and tiny pillbox hat perched jauntily on her head, Brenda's mouth fell to the floor. 'Catherine, you look beautiful.'

'Thanks, Mum,' Cat replied uncertainly.

'I just wanted to say ...' Brenda needed a minute and perched on the edge of Nell's bed. She was pleased she'd made it for once, instead of leaving it all rumpled. Caressing a tissue in her hands, Brenda looked up. 'I'm sorry if I made you miserable, darling. I really was only trying to help. I didn't realise I was making you so unhappy. I didn't mean to take over. I just got a bit carried away. Your dad has told me to stop being such a goose and come and make it up to you before you actually walk down the aisle.'

Cat softened at this uncharacteristic show of emotion. 'I know this isn't exactly what you had in mind for me, Mum. I know it isn't the Langdon Mansion Hotel, but it's where I want to get married.'

'I know.' She nodded. 'And Nell?'

'Yes?' Nell prepared herself for the firing line.

'It looks beautiful upstairs. You've done a wonderful job and everyone who's staying here says how lovely it is.'

'Thank you,' Nell said. 'Now, if you guys aren't going to murder each other, I'll leave you to it. I need to check everyone knows what they're doing, and the celebrant should be arriving soon.'

Brenda stood up and walked towards Nell who now feared she'd pushed her luck a bit too far and the ferocious Brenda was going to smack her legs, but instead Brenda hugged her and kissed her cheek. 'Thank you, Nell, for being there for Cat.' Nell hugged her in return and left them to begin her role as host.

As Nell reached the top of the stairs two familiar voices swarmed around her. Tom and Kieran were chatting happily with some of the guests who were staying at the hotel and got the pleasure of being at the ceremony first. Tom, she imagined, had been the one to put on some choral Christmas music and the world of Swallowtail Bay felt truly magical. Entering the dining room, she saw him, handsome in his suit and tie, a tiny sprig of holly in his buttonhole. Kieran, too, appeared happy and excited but it was the man Nell loved she couldn't take her eyes off. As her heart soared, she realised he hadn't taken his eyes off her either and the thrill was almost too much for her senses. The celebrant was admiring the set-up, and as Nell checked the clock, she could see there was only half an hour to the ceremony.

'You look lovely,' Tom said, coming over to her. The sound of his voice rumbled around her heart.

'Thanks, you look very handsome too.' She was suddenly blushing. 'Very presentable.'

'Good,' he laughed and fiddled with the knot of his tie. 'The place looks great, doesn't it? You've done brilliantly.'

'We all have.' Nell decided she had to act normally, just as she had before she'd known. If she didn't, they were going to be stuck in this awful bubble that only she seemed to be feeling. 'So, are you going to tell me why you've been avoiding me all week?'

A pained look flew across his face. 'I'll tell you later, okay?'

'Okay,' she replied hesitantly. At least he was going to tell her soon. She'd always known that if she waited, he'd tell her when he was ready. Now she came to think of it, it was funny how her brain hadn't gone into overdrive creating scenarios about this secret. Tom clearly had a good effect on her. 'Should I be worried?'

'Nah,' he replied, but she wasn't sure she believed him. 'Come on, people are arriving. Let's seat them and get this show on the road.'

'I've saved us two seats at the front, we're both on Cat's side, but it doesn't really matter, does it?' The photographer Cat had hired was circling, snapping pictures and Nell couldn't wait to see how they came out. Everyone was enjoying themselves and perfectly relaxed as they took their seats. Cat had already said she was welcome to steal some for the wedding business.

When she received the nod from the celebrant, Nell went down to collect Cat. With a quick knock on the door to the flat, a flutter of excitement bubbled in her tummy. The week had been manic with all the wedding changes Cat had wanted, and though Nell had been more than happy to do it, she was glad the moment was finally here. She couldn't wait to see her two friends make this commitment to each other.

'Come in,' Cat said.

As Nell opened the door, Brenda left; mother and daughter seemed to have put the last few weeks behind them. 'Are you ready?'

'Yep. Let's get up those stairs. My man is waiting.' Grabbing her bouquet, Cat paused as she drew level with Nell. 'Thanks for sticking with me.'

'What are friends for?' Nell replied, taking her in a hug. 'Come on, your public awaits!' Nell grabbed her own small bouquet of white roses with silver pine cones and quickly followed Cat out of the flat.

Giggling with excitement they made their way through the kitchen to the sweet looks of the staff and Niall. At the door to the ground floor, Nell paused, looking through the glass to make sure everyone was seated. They exited to where Cat's dad was waiting. Nell stuck her head around the door to the dining room and gave Tom a quick thumbs-up. He turned on the music and as Cat wanted, Nell walked down the aisle first to a choir singing 'Silent Night' in Latin.

The choral voices filled the air with a magical Christmas enchantment and Nell smiled at everyone she passed, especially Mr Scrooge who was still asleep on the hearth in his bow tie. As she looked ahead, her eyes fell on Tom and suddenly it seemed it should be her wedding day, walking down the aisle to him, but not in a fairy-tale romance conjured in her mind. This time, it was something solid and real. The flood of emotion reinforced to Nell that he was the only one for her, and she'd been blind to it for so long. She'd wished for a love that was deep and rich, formed from strong bonds, and that was what she had with Tom.

Cat was right, romantic gestures were all well and good but real love was looking after someone through thick and thin, knowing their needs and wants and always being there for them. How had she not looked at him in *that* way before? If she had, she definitely would have fallen for him sooner. He was the best man in the world as far as she was concerned. Handsome, funny, clever, and when he smiled his kindness spilled out through his gorgeous eyes.

At the end of the aisle, next to Tom and Kieran, she turned, and they all watched as Cat arrived. When Cat appeared on her dad's arm, tears of joy took Kieran. It was wonderful to see that Cat was finally completely comfortable in herself, happy and ready to commit to the man she loved. When she reached the front, Cat was so full of joy she didn't just hand over her bouquet, she wrapped Nell in a giant hug, then held Kieran's hand.

Nell and Tom sat down as the celebrant made an introduction, welcoming everyone. In front of the assembled crowd, Cat and Kieran giggled, shyly glancing at each other like it was the first time they'd met. The log fire crackled and burned in the grate, and the Christmas tree twinkled beside them. Nell glanced at Tom and resisted the urge to take his hand. When his leg rested against hers, she felt a fire burn through her veins. Then Cat and Kieran exchanged vows and the celebrant called the witnesses to come and sign the register. Nell and Tom also had that honour. Whatever had happened with him recently, the look Tom gave reassured her he still felt the same and a world of possibility lay before them. But as she had to switch back into hostess mode as soon as the ceremony was over, she was going to have to wait just a little bit longer before she could tell him.

With the register signed and more Christmas carols ringing out, the guests threw white snowflake confetti over Cat and Kieran as they exited into the dining room. The waiting staff, including Tallulah, were lined up ready to serve glasses of champagne to the guests and Nell took one for her and Tom. Tallulah was still looking incredibly nervous and something about the whole situation didn't seem right. As Nell thought back over everything that had happened since that evening at the Langdon Mansion Hotel, her mind reached an unhappy conclusion.

Apart from the last one, each bad review had followed a run-in with Tallulah. That couldn't be a coincidence and given how she'd tried to look at her little reception desk, Nell suddenly filled with anger. How could this young woman do something like that to her? And why? Nell hadn't blamed her for the incident in the restaurant, but maybe Bryan with a Y had. She wouldn't have put it past him. Maybe Tallulah had been told off or disciplined and she blamed Nell for it. Nell checked Cat and Kieran were cheerfully chatting with their guests and pulled Tom to one side.

'What's going on?' Tom asked, righting himself as she yanked him sideways.

Nell tried to surreptitiously signal towards Tallulah. 'The waitress!' she hissed.

'What waitress?'

'The one from the Langdon Mansion Hotel. The one who served us that night. It's her.'

'So?' Poor Tom looked utterly confused. She wasn't making herself very clear.

'She served us that night then I got a bad review. Then she came to the St Herbert's thing and the next day – guess what? I got a bad review. I saw her at the Christmas market, and she blanked me, then the next day – boom! – bad review.'

Tom leaned his head down and whispered into her ear. 'You think it was her?'

His breath tickled her neck and she shivered, forcing her mind onto the matter at hand. 'Yes.'

'Why would she do that?'

'Maybe we embarrassed her. Maybe she got blamed for it or something. Maybe she's pissed off at me for making a fuss that night. I don't know but it can't just be coincidence, can it?'

Cat's voice carried over Nell's right shoulder. 'What are you two whispering about?'

In panic, Nell spun to face her, but Cat was oblivious, grinning in bliss. Kieran clamped a hand on Tom's shoulder. 'Nothing,' Nell replied, faking nonchalance. 'I was just asking Tom to turn the music up a little bit.'

'I need you two for photos now, so come on.' Cat grabbed Nell's hand, pulling her along to the garden. It was a beautifully dry day and heaters had been installed so it could be used as an extra space. Photos were taken of them all in front of the holly bushes, hung with lights, and the huge oak tree in the garden that Nell had surrounded with giant storm lanterns. While Cat and Kieran had photos with their parents, Nell pulled Tom back inside to hide behind the Christmas tree and discuss Tallulah further.

'What are you going to do?' asked Tom, trying to look as inconspicuous as possible which given his height, wasn't that easy.

In her frustration, it was difficult to think. 'I'm going to bloody well tell her where she can shove her bad reviews.'

'And when are you going to do that?'

Nell was just about to bluff and bluster some more, but as the bright lights of the Christmas tree reflected in Tom's eyes, she felt her anger fade away. She could kick herself that she'd never examined his face properly before. Everything about it was perfect. His eyes studied her as if he knew every inch of her personality. No one knew her better than he did, and she didn't want anyone to. She'd been so blind. And here they were, hiding behind the Christmas tree, her face just centimetres from his. Her breath caught as she studied his mouth. She was so tempted to blurt out that she loved him but hiding behind a Christmas tree while she uncovered a conspiracy against her hotel wasn't exactly perfect timing.

'Nell?' he asked again. 'What are you going to do?'

In order to stop staring at his face, she fiddled with a bauble, making sure it was facing the right way. 'As soon as she goes downstairs, I'm going to follow her and talk to her. You have to cover for me with Cat and Kieran. I won't be long.'

'Are you sure you want to do this now?' Tom asked. 'Why not just let it go and come and enjoy the wedding.'

'I can't risk it. What if she messes up the wedding somehow? What if she makes up a bad review for it and I don't get any wedding bookings? All our hard work would have been for nothing. No. I'm going to kick her out and I'll serve if I have to. Niall's got plenty of staff. I'd only have to help out a bit which wouldn't look weird to Cat anyway.'

Just then, Tallulah went downstairs to top up a plate of mince pies and Nell slipped out from behind the tree before she was caught in the enchantment of Tom's eyes again and shouted 'I love you' right in his face. Down in the kitchen, Nell came to a stop at Tallulah's side.

'Tallulah, I know what you're up to and I think you should go.'

The girl turned, a mince pie crumbling as her grip on it tightened. Nell felt guilt rise up but reminded herself she was doing this to keep her hotel and livelihood, and to ensure her best friend's wedding was perfect. After everything they'd been through to get here, she wasn't going to let it go south now.

'What's going on?' asked Niall, coming over. He was red from the heat of the kitchen and the fast pace of the work.

'Niall, this girl has been putting up fake bad reviews of Holly Lodge ever since she served me at the Langdon Mansion Hotel. She's trying to ruin my reputation and I bet she's here today to do the same for my wedding business.'

Tallulah's hand, still clutching the mince pie, trembled. Nell had imagined a confidence and bravado that she'd have to knock down to get to the truth, but now tears were forming in the poor girl's eyes. Her face was turning red and splotchy, and with a gasp of air she crumpled down in a heap.

'Oh my God!' Nell shouted and immediately helped the girl back up. 'Niall, can you get some water, please? Here, come with me and sit down.' Nell, overwhelmed with guilt that she'd been so blunt, worried she'd done it again – made stuff up and not based things in reality. But she was sure this wasn't a coincidence. She led Tallulah to her flat and forced her to sit on the edge of the bed. 'Are you okay?'

Tallulah wiped her face.

'Look, I'm sorry if I was mean. I was just so cross that I thought you were the one behind the bad reviews—'

'It was me, sort of. I'm so sorry.' She sobbed. 'I'm so, so sorry.

276

I didn't write the reviews – that was all them – but they wanted me to spy on you. I didn't want to, but they made me.' She took a huge breath in and then cried out.

'Who's *they*, Tallulah?' Though Nell's spine was rigid with indignation, she tried to remain calm.

'I didn't want to do it but they told me if I didn't, I wouldn't get the extra hours I need and Dad's just lost his job and Mum doesn't know how she's going to afford Christmas and—'

'Shush now.' Nell rubbed Tallulah's back, realising exactly what had happened. The girl kept talking, needing to get it out of her system.

'As soon as they found out I had a little brother and sister at St Herbert's they made me come. They wanted me to look at your bookings, but I couldn't bring myself to do it.'

So that was why she was at her reception desk looking for an earring. Nell felt her anger rising again; this poor girl had been used and abused. 'Who exactly is *they*, Tallulah?' she asked again. 'Who's making you do this?'

'Kevin and Bryan, the managers at the Langdon Mansion Hotel.'

'Is that Bryan with a Y? The restaurant manager?' Tallulah nodded. 'And which one's Kevin?'

'He's the one with the bright white teeth that look like they're trying to escape every time he opens his mouth. He's really mean to everyone.'

These horrible men had bullied her because she was young and working hard to help her family. That was absolutely despicable, and Nell put a protective arm around her shoulders.

'They wanted me to sabotage the wedding – ruin the food, or the music, or something – but I haven't.' She looked at Nell with wide eyes. 'I wouldn't. If my mum ever found out I'd done something like that, she'd be so ashamed of me.'

'Oh, sweetheart.' Nell rubbed small circles on her back, trying to calm her down. 'Tallulah, I'm so sorry. They've put you in such a horrible situation, haven't they?'

Where tears had washed her make-up off, Tallulah looked so childlike. With a gentle tap, Niall came in with the water. Unsure how much he'd heard, Nell smiled and said, 'Just a misunderstanding, Niall. I confused Tallulah with someone else and I've apologised to her. I feel terrible.'

The young girl stared at Nell. She clearly couldn't believe that Nell was covering for her. Then she turned to Niall. 'You're so kind, Nell, but I have to tell the truth. She wasn't mistaken, Niall. She was right. My bosses at the Langdon Mansion Hotel conned your partner into hiring me so that I could ruin this wedding and ruin Nell's reputation.' She pulled her shoulders back and sat a little straighter, regaining some of that professional expression Nell had been so impressed with. 'If you want to fire me, that's okay. I deserve it. And tomorrow I'm going to quit working for the Langdon Mansion. I can't keep doing it. They're just horrible to everyone and they sneer at the customers behind their backs. I hate it there.'

Concerned, Niall handed Tallulah the water then spoke to Nell. 'What do you want me to do, Nell? It's your wedding, so to speak.'

Poor Tallulah was so mortified and strung out by the whole thing, she'd suffered enough, and Nell could understand what a difficult position she'd been put in. She didn't need punishing any more than she'd been already. 'I think we can probably forget about the whole thing, as long you promise not to actually ruin the wedding.'

'Or my food,' Niall added firmly, but with a slight teasing edge to his voice. 'And, listen,' he added, 'we've got a lot of jobs lined up over the Christmas period. I'm sure I've got more than enough hours and you've been really conscientious so far. I've been very impressed.'

Tallulah's tears began again. 'I can't believe you're all being so nice to me.'

Nell gave her shoulders a squeeze. 'That's what Christmas is for, isn't it? Now, I've got a wedding to get back to, and there are guests requiring mini mince pies before you serve this delicious meal.' Nell returned to the wedding and Tallulah and Niall to work. That was one problem solved, and she'd deal with the Langdon Mansion Hotel later. How? She wasn't actually sure just yet. She'd talk it through with Tom and they'd come up with something together. Maybe now she could get that blasted video taken down, or at the least those made-up bad reviews.

Chapter 24

In the dining room, Brenda was just calling everyone to order and asking them to take their seats for the meal after being upstanding for the bride and groom. From the conservatory, Cat rolled her eyes at Nell. The mother of the bride couldn't quite stop herself from taking over a bit, but she had accepted all the changes in good spirits, so they let her carry on. Nell sat down, ready to enjoy the dinner Cat and Kieran had wanted but hadn't been allowed before. After the giant meltdown, when Kieran had got more involved in the wedding, Cat had asked him about the wedding breakfast, and they'd agreed on Kieran's favourite of chicken pie and mash. When the plate was put in front of them, Kieran and Cat looked at each other with such bliss that even Nell felt it.

All through dinner, Nell glanced at Tom and every time she did, he was looking back at her. Her spine tingled and she found herself fidgeting with the napkin on her lap. She'd never felt self-conscious around him before, but everything was different now in an exciting and amazing way. Tom shuffled nervously in his seat as the meal went on and Nell knew why.

'You'll be fine,' she said, referring to his best man speech.

'How am I supposed to do it with Brenda giving me evils all the time?'

'She won't. Unless …' She left the word hanging in the air just to wind him up.

'What?'

'You're not going to tell that story from when the four of us went to Ibiza are you? You know, the one where Kieran decided to sing 'Live and Let Die' on the piano in that bar.'

Tom started laughing, his eyes crinkling attractively at the corners. 'I'd forgotten about that. Shame he can't actually play the piano. It would have been a decent rendition if he could.' He took a sip of his drink and Nell rubbed his shoulder.

'You'll be great, I promise.' As he stared into her eyes a choir of angels sang from the Christmas carols playing in the background. It was like one of those moments she'd always imagined. Her longing to tell him tugged at her heart once more but she couldn't blurt it out in front of the strangers on the table and with his best man's speech hanging over him. While she didn't want the moment to be like something from a romcom, she wanted it to be perfect for them.

Cat's father's speech was wonderfully emotional and welcoming, and he thanked Nell for turning Cat's second home into such a wonderful venue. She felt herself puff up with pride. Then Kieran began his speech. He remembered to tell Cat how beautiful she looked, tearing up a little as he did so, which set everyone else off crying, then he thanked Tom. As Kieran spoke, Nell's skin prickled. He choked up but it was the mention of Tom going through his own things right now that made Nell sit up. Tom flushed to the roots of his hair but from the way his jaw tightened, Nell could tell he was feeling emotional too. Kieran drew his speech to a close, so she didn't get a chance to ask Tom what he was referring to as it was his turn to speak.

Tom pulled a few cue cards from his pocket as he stood. 'Thanks Kieran. I'm pleased to see that although you forgot to wear pants that time at university, you've remembered to put some on today for your wedding.' Everyone chuckled and Nell watched him visibly relax. 'And I'm pleased to see that you remembered to say how beautiful Cat looks, because she does. She looks amazing. You've made a good choice of wife there, Kieran. And if I may say so, Cat's decision to lower her standards has been a blessing for you, because you are seriously punching above your weight.'

There was more laughter and a few 'hear, hear's, and Tom really got into the swing of things. He had to check his notes once or twice, obviously unable to read his own writing by the way he had to focus on them, but he was funny, cheeky and charming, delivering a brilliant best man's speech.

'See, I told you you'd be brilliant,' Nell said.

'I'm so glad that's over. I feel like I can finally relax and enjoy myself.'

'I know what you mean. As soon as the DJ's set up and the first dance is done, I can clock off. Everyone's been brilliant though. I think I could definitely do more weddings here.'

'Definitely.' Tom topped up her glass of wine. 'Everyone's really enjoying themselves. I think we should toast to the future of Holly Lodge as Swallowtail Bay's latest and best wedding venue.'

'Cheers.' They clinked glasses and Nell couldn't wait for the final part of her duties to be over so she could tell this wonderful, caring man exactly how she felt.

Once the DJ had set up, Cat and Kieran took to the floor for the first dance. They were soon swaying and laughing to 'It's the Most Wonderful Time of the Year' and they couldn't have picked a more perfect song for their Christmas wedding. Tom asked Nell to dance and as they moved together, Nell couldn't believe her luck. All those great big romantic gestures she'd imagined in her head were nothing compared to how she felt right now doing nothing more than dancing with Tom in her small hotel. His hand wrapped around hers like a glove. If she'd had the nerve to do so, her head would have nestled on his shoulder, but she wasn't brave enough for that yet. As soon as the first dance was over, she'd take Tom into the garden, to the quiet bench in front of the holly hedges and tell him that she loved him.

Finally, the DJ switched to lively disco classics and Nell had her chance. They separated from each other but instead of letting go of his hand, she held it tightly. He looked confused as she led him out of the hubbub and down the stairs of the conservatory into the dark evening light. They went through the garden, lit with sparkling fairy lights that matched the stars above, and little tea lights in jars lined the path until they came to the holly bench. The squeals of delight from the reception faded into the background.

In the quiet of the garden, it was only her and Tom, and she took a deep breath as they sat together on the bench, his hand still in hers.

'What's going on?'

'Tom, there's something I want to tell you.'

He swallowed nervously. 'There's something I need to tell you too.'

'Really?' Her heart fluttered so violently she could barely breathe. Was he finally going to tell her that he loved her, and that he had done for years? Then she could say that she loved him too but had been too stupid to realise it until now. He spoke quickly as if his life depended on it.

'I've been meaning to tell you for a while, but I just couldn't bring myself to do it. I've been too scared.' Nell felt a breath escape from her lungs and linger in her throat. 'But I have to tell you now,' he said, nodding to himself. Nell nodded along too. His eyes were misting with tears and Nell bit back the urge to blurt out her feelings. Instead of love, Tom's face was filled with sadness and Nell's hopes vanished. 'My eyesight's failing, and I might be going blind.'

It was like someone had thrown a bucket of cold water over her. Even her clothes felt damp, sticking to her and making her skin clammy. Tom linked his fingers with hers, his voice quivering.

'I've got a condition that means my eyesight will fail over time. First the peripheral vision, then possibly the central vision too, and if that happens, I could go completely blind.'

The fear and pain in Tom's face stabbed straight into her heart and she had to look away, staring at the twinkling tea lights that seemed so hopeful lighting up the dark. When she figured out what to say her voice shook with emotion. 'All the accidents recently—'

'Yes. Due to the sight I'm already losing in my peripheral vision.'

'Oh, Tom.' She turned back to him and he went to pull his hand away, but she wouldn't let him. She held it firm. It was a shock, but it didn't make any difference to the way she felt about him. The future they'd have together might be different to the one she'd imagined, but it was a future she wanted – *he* was what she wanted – and she was going to grab hold of it all with both hands.

'I'm sorry I didn't tell you before.'

'How long have you known?'

'That there's definitely something wrong? Only a couple of weeks. I saw a consultant – it's been a lot to get my head around. But I've been worried for a while – the headaches – they were quite scary. In a way, I'm relieved it's not something worse.' The implication hit Nell and she squeezed his hand. It didn't even bear thinking about. 'But there's something else too. I have to tell you now, Nell that …' He took a breath and Nell's heart fluttered once more. 'I love you. I've loved you for years and years. You're the most amazing person I've ever met. And if there's any chance we can be together – if I can see your face smiling at me first thing in the morning – imprint it on my mind before I can't see it anymore – I—'

A few tears escaped from his eyes and Nell reached up, watching the tips of her fingers shake with emotion as she wiped them gently away. Her whole body fizzed as she moved her head nearer and finally kissed his trembling lips.

From the moment her mouth met his it was like every daydream she'd ever had rolled into one magical moment. Her ears tingled and she could have sworn there was music, but whether it was that choir of angels she always imagined or the sound of her soul singing with joy she didn't know. Her body filled with liquid love like it had been poured into her veins. The Christmas wish she never knew she'd made was coming true.

'It's not – it's not pity, is it?' asked Tom, when they separated. 'I couldn't bear that.'

'Don't be such a tit,' Nell scolded. 'If I hadn't wanted to do that, I wouldn't have. When have you ever been able to make me do something I didn't want to do?'

'True,' he replied, grinning.

'Besides, it's what I brought you out here to tell you.'

'It is?' His face registered shock and then happiness.

Nell smiled and the warmth of his love flattened the goose bumps on her skin. 'When we were at the Christmas market, Kieran let slip that you – you know – love me,' she said with a laugh. It still didn't feel real.

'But what about Harry? At the mayor's party you seemed really … close.'

'Oh, Harry's nice enough but … no.'

'But Nell, you do realise that our life together won't be the same as everyone else's. It won't be a perfect movie-type ending. If I do go blind—'

Nell jumped in to finish his sentence. 'It'll be *our* perfect ending and if that means we make some adjustments, we do. As long as I'm with you, it'll be better than any romcom movie ever could be.' She kissed him again and the kiss they shared contained nothing but tenderness and pure love.

On the holly bench, as the music from the wedding reception carried on the still night air, Nell snuggled into Tom and praised herself on, for once, being absolutely right: her head did nestle perfectly on his shoulder.

Chapter 25

Christmas Day arrived in a fuzz of joy, and Nell and Tom snuggled on the sofa in the lounge, next to the fire. The Christmas tree stood proudly beside them, glittering in the pale white light that penetrated the window. The hotel was deserted as all the guests had gone off early to visit family. Mrs Meggett had left, her breakfast duties complete and an envelope containing a Christmas bonus tucked into her handbag. Cat and Kieran were on their honeymoon in Tenerife and had sent a picture of them both in bathing suits and Santa hats, sunning themselves on a sandy beach.

Tom and Nell had already called in to see Grandad Nigel and given him his Christmas present, a whole set of audiobooks from his favourite writer. It meant he didn't have to miss out even though he couldn't read anymore. Nell had made a note to do this for Tom when his sight failed. And for Tracey, for all her support and the love and care she showed to each and every one of her residents, they'd clubbed together and bought her a voucher for a luxury spa day. She worked so hard taking care of everyone else, she deserved some looking after herself.

With Christmas music playing, a blanket decorated in reindeers tucked over their knees, they sipped mulled wine and ate mince pies. Nell had gone a little overboard and bought Tom more presents than she realised. Luckily, even though Tom had been worried by his health, Mr Christmas had still got his shopping done and they were busy exchanging gifts.

'Oh, Tom, you got me that scarf I wanted. Thank you.'

'You're welcome and thank you for my new winter gloves.' He put them on, and Nell giggled because every year without fail, Tom would put on every item of clothing she'd bought him. He was currently sat in two jumpers, hat, scarf, gloves, a musical Christmas tie and enormous slippers that looked like cooked turkeys. When she'd calmed down and opened her next present from Tom – a set of expensive bath soap – she paused before handing over her next gift.

'So, I've been thinking about your shop and the changes we need to make so you can carry on working for as long as possible.'

He moved to the floor, rifling around in the giant stocking he'd brought over for her. 'And?'

'And, I was thinking there are a gazillion ways you can keep your business and keep working. I know you don't want to give it up.'

'Do we have to talk about this now, Nell? It's Christmas Day.'

Nell frowned at him. 'Okay, I'll say it quick then we can put on your favourite song and eat some truffles.'

'Okay then.' He sat back against the front of an armchair, the orange flames roaring next to him.

'So, what if we hire a delivery driver for a few hours a day until Janie passes her test? And I was thinking you could start training Janie up to take over some more of the managerial stuff? She's amazing and so, so clever. She's just like Tallulah. And I've found these amazing magnifiers that fix to your tabletop so you can keep working. And I've been looking at how to change your computer settings to make everything bigger.'

'Okay.' Tom laughed, holding up his hands to slow her down. 'Sounds good. How's Tallulah finding Niall?'

'She loves working for him but I'm going to poach her for some extra hours.'

'Does Niall mind?'

She shook her head. 'Nah, she's going to work weddings with me. I've already had some bookings. Two for next year, and one for the year after. And she'll be a brilliant wedding coordinator. I'm going to ask her after Christmas. And she emailed HotelRater coming clean about the reviews and they've taken them down. I've even had some bookings for early next year for Valentine's Day.'

'Did the Langdon Mansion get told off?' Tom asked, turning his musical Christmas tie on to play once more. The tiny lights studded in it flashed on and off in time with the music.

'It hit the industry press and the chain issued a statement to say this behaviour wasn't typical of their staff and apologised to me. It mentioned something about internal disciplinary action but nothing more. I don't want anyone to lose their jobs over it, not at Christmas. I just hope they get a telling-off. Tallulah told me that she'd heard Find the Sun weren't happy at how shifty they'd been and slammed them too.'

Tom shook his head. 'You're very kind, you know.'

'Thanks.' Nell pushed herself off the edge of the sofa and sat on the floor opposite Tom. The fire warmed her face and she pulled her gigantic Christmas jumper over her knees, thinking that there was nowhere else she'd rather be. Mr Scrooge snuggled in a ball on the hearth, and she stroked his soft fur. Normally, when the exchanging of gifts was over, Nell felt some of the Christmas magic ebb away, but this year she was savouring the day. From the corner of her eye, she saw Tom rifling in the bottom of the stocking he'd brought her.

'What are you doing?'

'You left something in your stocking.'

'Did I?' She was pretty sure she hadn't.

Tom handed over a small box, giftwrapped in gold paper with

288

a tiny silver bow on top. Tom knew she loved tiny wooden decorations to put on the tree and she hoped he'd bought her one from the Christmas market. As Nell opened the box, her fingers shook, and the tremble sprang through every nerve in her body. When she glanced up, Tom was on one knee, wrapping his own shaking fingers around hers and the engagement ring: a beautiful gold band with a small circular diamond in the centre. The exact ring she'd described to him the day they decorated the care home.

'Nell,' Tom began tentatively, his face searching hers for a sign that he was on the right path. If her silly grin didn't tell him so, then he knew nothing about women. 'Will you marry me?'

The squeal that erupted from her mouth made Mr Scrooge jump into the air. When he landed on all fours, hair on end, he looked at Nell indignantly. She threw herself into Tom's arms, knocking him over so they both fell onto the floor. 'Yes! Yes! Yes! Yes!' No other answer would ever have crossed her mind. No matter what the future held for them both, however full of adversity it might be, she wanted to be there with Tom every step of the way. 'Yes, yes, yes, yes!'

Tom pulled Nell up to standing. He wrapped his arms around her waist then brushed her hair back, tucking it behind her ear. He was studying her face, imprinting it on his memory as he'd talked about. His eyes flitted over her features then he took her in his arms and kissed her. Nell knew they were both the happiest they had ever been and a proposal on Christmas Day topped any fantasy she had ever come up with or wish she had ever made. And what topped it off more than anything else was the thought that this time next year, the special Christmas wedding held at Holly Lodge would be their own.

Epilogue

Christmas Eve, One year later

A year later, Grandad Nigel sat in a wheelchair close to the fire, a blanket over his knees and a smart tie at his neck, holding Edith's hand. Next to Edith, Tracey cried even before the ceremony had begun, and Mr Scrooge curled under the Christmas tree. From her spot in the dining-room doorway, Nell sneaked a look around the corner and saw Tom next to the celebrant and Kieran, his best man.

'Ready?' asked Cat, adjusting Nell's long, sweeping veil that fell behind her in a waterfall.

Without a second's hesitation, Nell replied. 'Yes. I can't wait to become Mrs Barton. Well, Barton-Jones. We've decided to keep my name too.'

Tallulah, who was managing the wedding, started playing the music they'd chosen, and Cat fiddled with her own dress. 'Unforgettable' by Nat King Cole rang out from the speakers and Nell ensured the long sweeping gown of simple ivory satin water-falled behind her. 'Okay soon-to-be Mrs Barton-Jones, that's my cue. See you at the end.'

Nell hugged her. 'Love you.'

'Love you too. Now let's go get 'em.' Cat grinned. 'My feet are killing me, and I need a sit-down. This baby is sitting right under my ribs.'

Cat went down the aisle first, her giant baby bump leading the way. Nell continued to sneak a peek from around the dining-room door and when Cat got to the front, she stood to one side and turned to welcome the bride. With a smile at her dad, Nell hooked her arm through his and walked down the aisle. Her parents had come back for the wedding and were staying at the hotel, taking over management duties so Nell could relax and enjoy her wedding and honeymoon. They'd been so pleased when they arrived and couldn't believe what an amazing job Nell was doing.

Hotel and wedding bookings were coming in thick and fast, including Stella and Miles's, which Nell was very excited about, and enquiries were through the roof. She'd received so many they were having a whole new brochure put together to send out with pictures from the weddings she'd organised so far. The dining room was open two evenings midweek, and on Friday and Saturday with different local chefs deciding the menu. They'd loved the challenge and chance to be a bit more experimental and her guests and the town were loving it too.

Careful not to step on the skirt of her wedding dress, Nell took each step with mounting excitement. Tom turned to watch Nell, adjusting his head so he could see her properly and drink her in. His sight wasn't deteriorating as quickly as they had at first feared and his eyes glistened at his wife-to-be. He was having regular check-ups and so far, his central vision was still intact. As he'd lost so much of his peripheral vision, he couldn't drive anymore but they'd hired a delivery driver and things were working out well.

Nell's long dress floated around her feet, and the bodice showed off her shoulders. As with Cat, there was no torturous underwear, no enormous pants to hold everything in. In front of her, Nell carried a small bunch of ranunculuses and winter roses studied with greenery. Janie had done all the wedding flowers and now she was sitting next to Brenda, even more cheerful than usual. She had begun to take on more and more of the duties at the florist's and was enjoying every minute of it. She was shaping up into a great manager. When the time came, Tom would be happy to step back further, knowing that she was in charge and that his business would go on.

At the top of the aisle, in the lounge, next to the twinkling Christmas tree decorated with traditional wooden decorations, Nell stopped in front of the celebrant and the music faded. She let go of her dad's arm and he, Cat and Kieran went to sit down. Tom gently took her hand and she turned to face him. This time, it was she who imprinted his face in her memory, wanting to remember this moment forever. The photographer snapped a picture then moved back. They'd talked honestly with him and been clear about particular shots they wanted so that Nell and Tom could look at them for as long as his sight remained.

'Welcome everyone,' the celebrant began, 'to the wedding of Nell and Tom.'

As they held hands and the ceremony began, their eyes never wavered from each other. When it came to reciting their vows, they both took a deep breath before Tom began. After writing their own in secret, it was with a mixture of excitement and nerves that Nell listened.

'Nell, I've always loved you and that love has grown with each year that has passed. You're my best friend, my soul mate and my true love.' Grandad Nigel gave a loud sniff and they both glanced over to see the old man pull out a handkerchief and wipe a tear from his eye. 'Last Christmas, when you agreed to marry me, you made me the happiest man in the world and I know that no matter what the future holds we'll face it together and that I'll get to see your face every morning. When my sight fails—' At this Tom's voice cracked and Nell didn't know if she'd be able to breathe again, her body was so full of emotion. 'When my sight fails, I'll be able to feel you with me every morning because you're the other half to my whole. I vow to love you, cherish you, protect you and always be faithful to you. I love you.'

Now, it was Nell's turn, and for a second, she looked down at his hand holding hers, summoning her strength to get the words that meant so much to her out of her mouth. 'Tom, you've been my friend for so long, it took me a while to realise how much I love you because it was a love so deep and so strong I hadn't realised it was already a part of me. I can't wait to spend the rest of my life with you as your wife. I vow to …' Trying to keep her eyes on his face she willed back the tears obscuring her vision. 'I vow to be your heart when yours is heavy, your shoulders when troubles become weighty and – and …' She took another deep breath as the tears began to fall. 'Your eyes when you can't see. I love you.'

Without a dry eye in the house, they were declared husband and wife, ready to start the next chapter of their lives. They exited the lounge into a flurry of fake snow from a snow machine Tom had organised without her knowing. As the snow drops danced around her, she couldn't believe how lucky she was to have a man who cared for her as much as Tom did, even trying to give her the white Christmas wedding she'd dreamed of.

Tom offered her a glass of champagne but when Nell refused, he frowned in confusion. Before he could ask what was wrong, she took his hand and began leading him to the holly bench once more. She couldn't wait to tell him her news – the best Christmas present she could give – and giggled at the fact he hadn't noticed anything yet. Her enormous Christmas jumpers had come in handy this time around and with any luck, he'd get to see the face of their baby before his sight failed any more. If he didn't, she'd describe their baby to him and guide his fingers over a tiny nose, tiny cheeks and soft skin. She'd already pictured it in her mind, careful not to go too far this time. No problems were insurmountable when they were together, there were only different ways of doing things. And as Tom liked to point out, she'd always been just a little bit different.

THE END

If you loved spending time with Nell, don't miss out on Katie's brand-new novel *The Secrets of Meadowbank Farmhouse* which you can order now!

Acknowledgements

So that's it! The final instalment of my Swallowtail Bay series. I feel quite sad saying goodbye to this lovely place but I'm very excited for the location of my next series and I hope you'll visit too.

I always find writing the acknowledgements quite hard because there are so many people who go into making a book and I worry about missing people out. Of course, I need to thank my friends and family for bearing with me while I'm beavering away at my little desk in the corner. They're so understanding and I'm really grateful for their support.

There are also all the lovely folk at HQ Digital. My fabulous editor, Sarah Goodey, always does an amazing job in figuring out what I want to do but aren't quite pulling off yet. Thank you, Sarah! It's such a pleasure to work with you and I can't wait till we can actually meet properly! But I'd really like to thank everyone at HQ Digital from the cover designers and marketing team, the sales guys who have worked hard to get me promotions, and everyone else for everything they do. All your work behind the scenes is really, really appreciated. Thank you also to Lisa Milton

Executive Publisher of HQ. You did a fabulous job of keeping us all going during a very difficult and unsettling year and it was always helpful and reassuring to receive your emails.

I normally like to give a shout out to all the book bloggers who spend their time reading and shouting about our books because I wouldn't be anywhere if it wasn't for you guys. Thank you!! This time, I'd also like to say a massive thank you to Rachel's Random Resources for her amazing blog tour skills! Thank you, Rachel! We love you!

Turn the page for a sneak peek at
the glorious new novel from Katie Ginger,
The Secrets of Meadowbank Farmhouse.

Coming March 2021

Chapter 1

Paris

The sights and smells of the Paris flea market were almost too much for Amelia's hungover senses to bear. Only her excitement at living in the city she adored and a need to be out of her apartment, led her forwards.

Though the baking emanating from the nearby shops smelled delicious, the aromas changed with every step causing her stomach to roil and calm in equal measure. One minute the strong scents of garlic and onion were overtaken by that of sweet pastries and butter. The crowds wove around her, all heading for the farmer's market at the bottom of the tiny street or carrying bags laden with fresh produce as they made their way back up the hill. In between, shopkeepers cast open their windows displaying the eclectic range of goods they had to offer. Her eye fell on numerous chandeliers that hung from the ceilings of one store, onto antique vases stood side by side on a small side table. Traditional French furniture lined up outside alongside paintings all stacked together. On the other side of the street, smaller objects like perfume bottles, vintage jewellery and trinkets glittered as the sun hit the windows.

All around, the sound of chatter penetrated her ears, resonating through her sluggish brain. Fluent in French, Amelia could make out most of what was said, but when so many voices merged and the locals spoke so quickly, she struggled to keep up. Amelia pushed her large round sunglasses further up her nose to shield her eyes from the sun's strong glare and as her stomach rumbled loudly decided a stop at the nearest café was a good idea.

Spring in Paris was a magical affair as flowers bloomed around the city giving an overwhelming floral scent. She'd been there for six years now, but the capital never failed to impress her. Each season affected the city differently, but whereas summer could be searing and the streets hazy with heat, spring gave all the golden glow but with a much more temperate feel.

Pausing at a small café with an eclectic mix of folding metal and wicker chairs and tightly packed circular tables, she took a seat and ordered a café crème and a buttery, flaky croissant. The perfect thing to soak up the rest of the wine lingering in her system and wake her up while she waited for Océane to join her. She'd want to know all about her date with Bastien last night. By the time Amelia had something to eat and chatted to Océane, she'd look again for the perfect items to finish off the job she was working on. As an interior designer, Paris, with its chic fashions and varied shops was the perfect place for her business, and so far, Amelia had never regretted leaving the tiny English village she'd grown up in the second she was able to. She hadn't left much behind.

Twenty minutes later, Océane arrived and ordered the same as Amelia. Amelia asked for another café crème before the waiter disappeared, knowing the questioning was soon to begin and a second caffeine hit would help her endure it. Her friend didn't exactly mince her words.

'So?' Océane asked in her heavy French accent. 'How was your date last night? Was Bastien attentive? Did he buy you champagne?'

'No, he brought me wine. And lots of it,' Amelia said, adjusting her sunglasses once more as the sun moved across the sky, climbing higher. The coffee was helping her headache, but she still felt a little fragile. This morning she had hastily scraped her black hair into a chignon and swiped her lips with bold red lipstick knowing it would give her pale cheeks some colour. Over the years she had absorbed the Parisian style of dressing: classic, expensive pieces, simple lines, graceful, but if she didn't make the effort, it only took a moment with a real Parisian to make her feel sloppy and slobbish. Océane was just the sort of stylish friend Amelia had always pictured herself with. She had a natural elegance as well as innate confidence and style. Amelia made a mental note of her outfit today; grey ankle length jeans, plain black ballet pumps and a camel coloured crew neck jumper just visible under the black jacket and large grey scarf keeping her warm. It made her own all black ensemble of cigarette pants and short sleeved jumper seem dull.

Océane swiped her blonde hair over her shoulder. 'You do look a little how do you say ...'

'Under the weather?'

'Pasty.'

'Thanks.' Amelia giggled.

'Did you not have a good time? He is very handsome, non?'

'We had a very good time.' For once, Amelia was grateful that she wasn't prone to blushing as thoughts of his intense and passionate kisses rang through her head. 'And yes, he is very handsome. He took me to an expensive restaurant, wined and dined me, paid me compliments, made me laugh, but I've left him to make his way home while I'm out.'

'You are avoiding him?' Her tone was incredulous.

Bastien was almost perfect and she liked him well enough, but Amelia couldn't stand that boring small talk made the morning after the night before. It served no purpose as far as she was concerned and more often than not it led to those men she'd brought home wanting more than she was prepared to give.

'But you will see him again?' Océane asked. 'You know that he wants you to be together. He is in love with you, I think.'

'Well, I'm afraid he's going to be disappointed because I don't love him.' Amelia paused while the waiter delivered their drinks. As she said it, she realised how callous it sounded. She took a sip of coffee and saw the imprint of her red lipstick on the rim of the cup. For a second, she wondered about the imprint she was leaving on the world. Not much of one, it seemed. She put her mood down to feeling maudlin because of her hangover. 'You know I'm not really in the market for that sort of thing.'

Océane took a moment to understand the phrase, but realisation quickly dawned. 'You are mad and will break his poor heart.'

'I don't think so. I'm sure he'll have left the apartment by now and won't even think of me again. Even if he does like me, he'll find someone else pretty quickly.'

'You know that is not true. You are a cold woman.'

Amelia raised her head at this remark. Was she cold? She didn't think so. She had friends, had been through some decent relationships. She was just focussed on her life and living it to the full. She'd worked hard to get where she was. She was one of the foremost interior designers in Paris and wasn't prepared to just invite a man into her life for the sake of it. She'd always done fine on her own and didn't see the need to change now. She wasn't really the type to get lonely either. She was far too busy. Océane continued.

'I do not know how you can be so immune to his charms. Our men – French men – Parisian men – know how to win a woman's heart.'

'Your French men are pretty charming, but I'm perfectly happy keeping my heart to myself.' Amelia sat back in her chair. 'Besides, I'm far too busy with work to be worried about men.'

'Don't your parent's want you to get married? Mine do. They say that I should marry Émile and have children before they are too old to enjoy being with them. They say my eggs will die.'

'Your eggs?'

'Eggs,' Océane said again, motioning to her lap. 'Your parents do not worry about your eggs?'

A sharp pain shot into Amelia's chest and a pain she thought she'd dealt with stabbed her anew. 'My parents are dead. They died when I was a child.'

Océane's hand paused as she tore off a piece of croissant. 'You have never told me that. We have been friends for a year and yet you make no mention of this. Why not?'

Amelia shrugged one shoulder. 'It's never come up before.' She knew this was a lie and quickly changed the subject unsure why she had suddenly admitted it. Perhaps she was more tired than she realised. She'd been out with friends every night this week. Maybe a decent dinner cooked by herself – something easy with fresh ingredients from the market at the end of the street – and a quiet night in were in order. 'Once we're done here, I'd like to take another look around. I'm after some special pieces for an apartment I'm working on in Montmartre.'

'You will have to do that alone; I have to meet Émile, but you must think about Bastien. There are many women who would like to take your place in his bed.'

'He was in my bed.'

'You know what I mean.' Océane raised one perfectly shaped eyebrow. 'You can be too hard, Amélie. Too independent. One day, you will push a man too far away and he will not bother coming back.'

It always amused Amelia that Océane called her by the French version of her name when she was being serious, but whatever her thoughts on her relationship with men, she'd face that day when it came. 'I have everything I need.'

'You have a great business, yes. You have a great apartment, yes. But you are never alone. Always you are with friends. A person cannot exist on their own. Without love.'

Pulling her compact from her large handbag Amelia topped up her red lipstick seeing as so much of it had been left on the cup. It was a romantic notion, but not one she believed in. 'I've done fine so far.'

After they had finished their coffees and talked about their plans for the rest of the weekend, Océane left and Amelia took another walk around the flea market. Temptation sat on her shoulder and whispered into ear as her eyes fell on different objects that would look good in her already overflowing apartment. Some of her clients liked a minimalist style, but when Amelia saw something she wanted, it was almost impossible to resist. As a result, her small flat was now packed with possessions and her wardrobe overflowing with clothes.

Amelia haggled with a vendor to buy an ornate perfume bottle – a finishing touch for the Montmartre apartment she was decorating – and a copper milk jug for her own place. She'd find somewhere for it to go later. Maybe the bathroom? And made her way back to the metro.

As she climbed the steps from the metro station, the cold, fresh air blew through the elaborate dark green metal bars and under the glass ceiling. The station design was so iconic she had a picture of one in the living room of her apartment. She'd brought it shortly after moving in all those years ago, and though it had been fairly inexpensive, it was still one of her most prized possessions.

Her apartment in Saint Germain was in a typical eighteenth-century block with white shutters either side of the windows and decorative ironwork across them. On hot summer days she would cast open the windows and let the light flood her apartment. As she stepped inside, she gathered her post and made her way upstairs. She pressed the key into the lock, hoping once more that Bastien had left by now. She really didn't fancy talking to him. He'd try and convince her to spend the rest of the day with him and all she wanted was to nap on the sofa as the soft breeze blew over her.

With a gentle push, the door opened and all was quiet inside. No sounds of snoring, no sounds of movement and, sighing with relief, Amelia walked down the hall and into the open plan living room and kitchen, anchoring the milk jug under her arm so she could scan through the post. It was mostly bills as usual.

Glancing up her eyes fell on Bastien, lying naked on her kitchen counter. The copper milk jug fell from underneath her arm, landing on the floor with a deafening clatter, making him wobble precariously and almost fall to the floor. His hand shot out, gripping the edge of the counter as he steadied himself. Amelia nearly dropped the pretty perfume bottle as well but somehow managed to keep hold. She looked around as if it might help her understand why he'd chosen the kitchen to begin his seduction in.

'Bastien. What are you still doing here?'

'I am waiting for you,' he replied, regaining his balance, his voice nothing more than a low seductive grumble. In the current circumstances, it didn't really work. Now he'd pinned her with his eyes, his gaze never shifted from hers and though uninhibited last night, Amelia wasn't quite prepared for a naked man to be spread-eagled in her kitchen and found herself momentarily lost for words.

She placed the perfume bottle on the counter. 'I'm a bit busy today, Bastien. Sorry.'

'Too busy for love?'

The sound of the L word twice in one day caused her to stiffen. He gave her puppy dog eyes and Amelia found her headache intensifying. 'Bastien, can you please put your pants on and get your bits off my worktop?'

He didn't move. 'How can I tempt you?'

'You can't.'

'Come now.' He held out his hand to her.

305

'Bastian, pants on please?'

'Let us spend the day together.'

Amelia sighed. 'Bastien, you're a very nice man and I had a great time last night, but I really can't see you today.'

Sheepishly, Bastien did as he was told. She guessed the kitchen counter had been too cold because his pants were on the floor by her feet. He must have decided to forgo them at the last moment for full on seduction. At least he was committed. Amelia picked them up using the tips of her fingers and handed them to him. His skin made a horrible squeaking sound as he pushed himself down from the counter. Though his six-pack abs were enticing, all she could think was that she'd now have to disinfect the kitchen before she cooked and that meant even less time to chill out on the sofa. Seeing as his pants had been on the floor too, she would have to wash that as well. 'You really want me to go?'

'Yes, please. I'm sorry, but I have work to do.'

'But it is Saturday.'

She looked at him over the edge of the letters in her hand but dropped her gaze when she saw the envelope postmarked from England with a company name, she didn't recognise. Even worse, the town was dangerously close to Meadowbank; the tiny village she'd grown up in with Great Aunt Vera who had begrudgingly taken her in after her parents had died. Curiosity nearly forced her to open it there and then, but she valued her privacy more. Bastien had to go. Frowning as she placed the letters on the counter, she turned away from Bastien and went to get a glass of water from the fridge, hoping he'd get the hint that it was time to leave. Without turning, she was aware of him heading off into the bedroom and a few moments later, he placed a gentle kiss on her cheek and said goodbye.

The cold water slid down her throat and anticipation sent goosebumps over her skin. Or maybe it was concern. She didn't normally get letters from England and the company name sounded unnervingly formal. After wiping down the counter, she sat on a stool and opened the post starting with the bright white envelope postmarked from England.

As soon as she pulled out the thick white paper, her eyes began scanning the words. An unexpected wave of emotion hit her, and her body began to shake in response. For a moment, even breathing became hard and erratic and she willed herself to calm down. Great-aunt Vera was dead and had left her Meadowbank Farm, the draughty old farmhouse they'd co-existed in for ten unsentimental and lonely years. You couldn't even really call it living together. Shaking her head at the memory, Amelia was glad she'd left for university and never returned. Vera hadn't wanted her and if it hadn't been for Adam, the only friend she had in the village, she'd have runaway.

She couldn't even count the times he had talked her out of it when Vera had told her off for doing nothing more than be a child. A moment's respite from such intense emotions came as she thought of him again. He'd been her first love and she regretted that she'd hurt him by leaving but she'd had too. He'd have got over it by now, she reminded herself. Swallowing down her feelings, Amelia re-read the letter. Shock subsided to be replaced by grief and guilt. She hadn't even known Vera was sick. Apart from exchanging Christmas and birthday cards, they didn't speak at all and her most recent Christmas card hadn't mentioned anything about declining health. Had it been sudden? The solicitor's letter didn't mention the cause of death.

Amelia knew her thoughts sounded callous and cold, but she wasn't a horrible person. Unless you knew Vera – knew how cold and hard she was, how unloving – you didn't understand. It was typical of her. Some people were naturally private. It was a behaviour Amelia herself had learned, but Vera took it to a whole new level, hating everyone. Amelia buried the pain threatening to rise and overtake her. She took a breath in, counted to eight and let it out slowly, counting again as she did so. And yet, despite everything, Vera had left her Meadowbank Farm. According to the letter, she'd made Amelia the sole heir. Vera knew how much Amelia had always disliked the village. It was too tight knit. More like claustrophobic with everyone knowing everyone else's business. Had she done this just to spite her or had it been because there really wasn't anyone else?

Amelia hated being forced to do anything and yet, now she had to return to England.

Now, she had no choice but to go home.

Hi, lovely readers,

I can't believe that was our final visit to Swallowtail Bay! How has this year (and this series) gone so quickly? It's been a weird one, hasn't it, but I hope you've enjoyed your time at Swallowtail Bay.

How did you enjoy Winter Wishes? Are you a romcom fan like Nell (and me!)? What did you think of Tom?

Thank you for taking the time to read this book! When time to relax is short, I really do appreciate that you chose my story to spend some time with. That really is the greatest gift anyone could give me. If you enjoyed the story, it would be amazing if you'd consider leaving a review because they really help us find new readers and show our publishers that people like our work!

If you'd like to keep up to date with what I'm up to, you can sign up to my mailing list here: https://bit.ly/3gbqMS0. I send out a newsletter once a month but I won't bother you all the time!

And, if like me, you enjoy wasting time on socials my website is: www.keginger.com. I'm on Facebook at: www.Facebook.com/KatieGAuthor, and Twitter at @KatieGAuthor.

Hopefully I'll see you again soon, but until then, happy reading, everyone!

Best wishes,

Katie

xxx

Dear Reader,

We hope you enjoyed reading this book. If you did, we'd be so appreciative if you left a review. It really helps us and the author to bring more books like this to you.

Here at HQ Digital we are dedicated to publishing fiction that will keep you turning the pages into the early hours. Don't want to miss a thing? To find out more about our books, promotions, discover exclusive content and enter competitions you can keep in touch in the following ways:

JOIN OUR COMMUNITY:
Sign up to our new email newsletter: hyperurl.co/hqnewsletter
Read our new blog www.hqstories.co.uk
🐦 : https://twitter.com/HQStories
📘 : www.facebook.com/HQStories

BUDDING WRITER?
We're also looking for authors to join the HQ Digital family!
Find out more here:
https://www.hqstories.co.uk/want-to-write-for-us/
Thanks for reading, from the HQ Digital team

ONE PLACE. MANY STORIES

**If you enjoyed *Winter Wishes at Swallowtail Bay*,
then why not try another delightfully uplifting romance
from HQ Digital?**